KT-140-549

04632961

# ANATOMY OF MURDER

*Also by Imogen Robertson*

Instruments of Darkness

# ANATOMY
# OF
# MURDER

# IMOGEN
# ROBERTSON

headline
review

Copyright © 2010 Imogen Robertson

The right of Imogen Robertson to be identified as the Author of
the Work has been asserted by her in accordance with the
Copyright, Designs and Patents Act 1988.

First published in Great Britain in 2010
by HEADLINE REVIEW
An imprint of HEADLINE PUBLISHING GROUP

1

Apart from any use permitted under UK copyright law, this publication may only
be reproduced, stored, or transmitted, in any form, or by any means, with prior permission
in writing of the publishers or, in the case of reprographic production, in accordance
with the terms of licences issued by the Copyright Licensing Agency.

All characters – other than the obvious historical figures – in this publication are fictitious
and any resemblance to real persons, living or dead, is purely coincidental.

Cataloguing in Publication Data is available from the British Library

ISBN 978 0 7553 4842 8 (Hardback)
ISBN 978 0 7553 4843 5 (Trade paperback)

Typeset in Poliphilus and Blado by Ellipsis Books Limited, Glasgow

Printed and bound in Great Britain by
Clays Ltd, St Ives plc

Headline's policy is to use papers that are natural, renewable and recyclable products
and made from wood grown in sustainable forests. The logging and manufacturing processes
are expected to conform to the environmental regulations of the country of origin.

HEADLINE PUBLISHING GROUP
An Hachette UK Company
338 Euston Road
London NW1 3BH

www.headline.co.uk
www.hachettelivre.co.uk

For Ned

# ACKNOWLEDGEMENTS

Thanks are due to a great many people. For particular help and advice I am grateful to the composer Gwyn Pritchard, who first mentioned to me the use of the castrati in eighteenth-century opera, and the implications of their position in society; to Maya Magub, Sebastian Comberti, Alex Anderson-Hall and James McOran-Campbell for speaking to me about the lives of professional musicians and singers; to the counter-tenor Iestyn Davies for our discussions of the castrati repertoire and history; to Gerald Stern for speaking to me about the possible and plausible effects of brain injury; to Richard Woodman and the excellent staff of the National Maritime Museum on matters naval; to the staff of the British Library for their help with much other research and to Christine Woodman for a particular moment of inspiration.

My friends and family have continued, very kindly, to provide the essential patience, care and enthusiasm which makes writing possible; I'd also like to thank Richard Foreman and the writers I have met through working with him and David Headley at Goldsboro Books for their support, also my wonderful agent Annette Green and of course Jane Morpeth, Flora Rees and the rest of the Headline team for welcoming me so warmly into the fold. Every day of writing this book I have been cared for, indulged, supported and occasionally scolded by Ned. It helped.

# Prologue

*Thursday, 3 May 1781, sixth year of the American Rebellion; third year of the Franco-American Treaty of Amity and Commerce*

*HMS* Splendour *of the North American Fleet, under command of Captain James Westerman, off the coast of Newfoundland*

*Six Bells of the Morning Watch (7 a.m.)*

CAPTAIN WESTERMAN WAS in his cabin reading the letter from his wife for the fourth time when he heard the officer of the morning watch ring Six Bells. At the last double clang the door opened and his servant, Heathcote, came in with the coffee. Westerman did not need to go on deck to know they were having a good run on a fine day. The creaking of the planks and sound of the water hissing at the stern told him that. The air of happy expectation in the ship had curled into her timbers; even the bell sounded tuneful.

Heathcote tried, none too subtly, to read over James's shoulder as he delivered the coffee. James twitched the papers to his chest.

'Any news from home, Captain?'

'Yes, Heathcote. *Your* wife has run off with the innkeeper and *my* wife is forced to cook her own dinner.'

His servant drew his brows together and pursed his lips.

'Always thought yourself amusing, haven't you, sir? Mrs Heathcote

1

might have the sense to run from me, but she'd never leave Caveley or Mrs Westerman, so there's no good funning.'

James took his coffee and drank. 'Fairly said, Heathcote. Your wife is well and comfortable, as is mine. Harriet says the new Lord Thornleigh has returned to London with his sister and guardian – oh, and the baby uncle – while the rebuilding works at the Hall are carried on. Also, the Squire has sent them a ham.'

'Is it recent news, sir?'

'No – two months old.'

'Well, you do keep running about, sir. Makes it hard to keep track of you.'

James smiled. Other than his First Lieutenant, his current officers on the *Splendour* were a relatively young lot, so inclined to be respectful of their Captain. Heathcote, however, had sailed with him for years, and had got in the habit of treating Westerman like a slightly wayward nephew.

The *Splendour*, a neat frigate of forty-four guns, had been hailed the previous night by the sloop *Athena*. The latter had been dodging American and French sails for a week to reach them, bringing letters from home and orders from the Fleet. The letters were very welcome, and the orders to join and help protect a convoy of merchant ships bound for England equally so. The crew of the *Splendour* had not thought they'd have a chance to kiss their wives for another year, but the merchant fleet was valuable and Admiral Rodney wanted good men to guard it, so had ordered James and his men back to England.

However, it was the titbit from the *Athena*'s Captain that had caused the general state of excitement. His crew had spotted what seemed to be a French frigate the previous day sitting low in the water and apparently alone, heading up the coast. The *Athena*'s Captain had recognised, he regretfully informed Westerman over dinner, that the French ship outgunned him, but reckoned the more heavily armed *Splendour* could take her.

The crew were desperate for a decent prize. By the time they had arrived in the Leeward Isles early the previous year, the place had been picked clean by the Admirals, and though James and his crew had taken some merchantmen and privateers, these had not been sufficient to make their fortunes. If they managed to take a frigate with her holds bulging with powder and ordnance for American rebels, every Able Seaman would receive enough gold to go home a respectable man, and James would be able to buy another estate if he had the mind. It felt as if the ship herself were straining at the leash to reach it.

Heathcote normally left James alone to drink his coffee in the morning, yet today he was slow to leave the cabin. James looked up at his servant's long face therefore with his eyebrows raised.

The man reached into his pocket and produced a pamphlet. Even before he could read the title, James sighed.

'Who had that then, Heathcote?'

'One of the young gentlemen, sir. His mother enclosed it with her own letter. I caught him showing it to the other boys and boxed his ears for reading trash.'

'Thank you.' James picked it up. A rather unpleasant woodcut on the front of the pamphlet depicted a man's body lying prone on a patch of grass. Beside him, a woman stood in a bad actor's stance of horror. There was a castle in the background. The woman looked nothing like Harriet, and Thornleigh Hall, unlike this castle, was an elegant residence fitting for an ancient and wealthy family, but without a turret in sight. The title claimed that the pamphlet was a complete, accurate and astonishing account of the late terrible murders in Sussex and London and the investigations of Mrs Harriet Westerman and Mr Gabriel Crowther. James flicked through it and curled his lip.

'What nonsense this is! Half stolen out of the *Advertiser*, and half the perverted imaginings of the writer.' He held it up and tapped the female figure on the front. 'Does this look like my wife to you, Heathcote?'

Heathcote considered. 'Looks more like the Master Gunner in a dress, sir.'

James did not laugh. A career in the Navy was as much about politics as prizes, and it did him no good to have a wife that drew such attentions to herself. He loved Harriet unashamedly, but such things were, at best, awkward.

There was a knock at the door and one of the youngsters, a bright lad of about fourteen and James's favourite among the Midshipmen, put his head in, his face shining with excitement. 'Mr Cooper's compliments, sir, but he thought you might like to know we've spotted a sail.'

'Did he, indeed, Mr Meredith?' James replied, downing the last of his coffee and clambering into the coat Heathcote was already holding out for him. 'Tell him I shall join him directly.'

Mr Cooper found his Captain beside him on the quarter-deck in moments, already twisting his telescope open as he spoke.

'Good morning, Lieutenant.'

'Good morning, sir. Fine on the starboard bow and a fair way off still, sir.'

James lifted his glass and pointed it where Cooper had indicated. There it was, a little smudge of sail on the horizon. This could indeed be a piece of luck. If they had had no sight of the potential prize today or tomorrow, James would have been forced to abandon the chase to meet the convoy, but there she was, as early as could be expected.

Mr Mansel, the Major in the command of the ship's company of marines, joined them. He had been up in the rigging straining for a better view.

'Lord, I hope she's a fat one,' he said. 'The Americans and those damned French have seemed to know where we are more often than the Admiralty, and keep sneaking round our backs like rats. I met a fella in Kingston says every ship has a soothsayer on it who kills chickens and reads where our ships are in their guts.'

James ignored him. 'Very good, Mr Cooper,' he said, slowly lowering his glass again. 'Feed the men, then beat to quarters and clear the decks for action, please.'

Mr Cooper began to give his orders, Mr Mansel went to tend to his marines, and James rested his hand on the gunwale, a vague smile on his lips. It was possible the ship they were chasing was one of their own, or a prize already taken, but James felt a familiar stirring in his blood. He was sure this was a Frenchman and a prize – her course, her position, the report of the *Athena*'s Captain all suggested it. The *Splendour* herself seemed to agree; she was surging towards that tiny speck between the grey sea, and the grey skies, gaining steadily. The Midshipmen noticed the glitter in their Captain's blue eyes and punched each other's shoulders as they scrambled down the rigging.

*Two Bells of the Afternoon Watch (1 p.m.)*

The mood of excitement had changed to one of wariness. The *Splendour* was ready and warlike. The panels had been stripped from James's cabin, the hammocks rolled up and strung along the bulwarks to stop splinters, and the guns run out with a thunderous roar. Now everything was still again. The surgeon's station was set up in the cockpit on the lower decks, and he and his Mate sat in silence, saws, tourniquets and bandages lying neatly beside them. Ready.

Behind each of the cannon its crew waited, powder, shot and sand buckets standing by. Mr Meredith stood behind the hulking iron back of the 18-pounder under his command on the top deck, trying not to watch the Captain on the quarter-deck out of the corner of his eye. It had seemed at first that the ship in front of them would try to outrun them. When it became clear she could not, her pace had slackened considerably. An hour ago it had become possible to read the name on her side – the *Marquis de La Fayette*; it was also possible to see her flags. A British flag flew above the French, the sign that the ship had already been taken as a prize by some other, luckier, crew.

Another of the Midshipmen, Hobbes, commanding a neighbouring gun, leaned over to Meredith and hissed, 'Doesn't smell right. What would a taken prize be doing on this course?'

Meredith did not respond but kept looking at the *Marquis* as she grew large in their vision. Her gun doors were closed. A figure became visible on the stern, a tall thickset man in shirtsleeves. He watched them approach, then when they were close enough to draw his portrait, the man suddenly shrugged on his coat and shouted something.

'*French!*' Meredith bawled, and threw himself to the deck as the black mouths of two cannon emerged at the stern of the *Marquis* and belched smoke.

He heard the shot tear into the rigging and looked up to see the fore-topsail yard smashed and then the shouts of the Captain as wood and rope clattered to the deck around him.

'Fire bow chasers! Wear away, Mr Mackensie. Master Gunner, ready port guns and fire as they bear!'

The *Splendour*'s forward guns gave a great cough and spat fire. Her gun crews cheered; one had caught the *Marquis*'s stern and left a ragged hole in her. Meredith balled his fists and scrambled to his feet. The French ship had made all sail and was trying to run for it again, but Captain Westerman was having none of that. Even without the fore-topsail, the *Splendour* still had pace enough. Already there were men up in the yards splicing cut ropes.

The ships were horribly close. The marines in the *Splendour*'s rigging were firing down onto the decks of the French ship and doing horrible slaughter, but the *Marquis* had her own men armed with muskets. When Meredith heard a shout and horrible thwack behind him, he glanced over his shoulder to see the Major of the marines on his back on the deck behind him, groaning, a red wound blossoming on his thigh. The Master's wife got her arms around him and began dragging him back towards the hatch to the lower decks and the surgeon, leaving a thick red trail behind them.

Spinning back round, Meredith saw the flanks of the *Marquis* just coming into sight; her guns were run out now. He could see men moving behind them, distorted mirrors of his own crew. The *Splendour* began to rake the stern quarter of the *Marquis*. The guns on all three decks thundered as one, hitting her low and hard.

Meredith waited for his moment, then gave his order. His gunner touched fire to the cannon and the beast roared, throwing herself back on the ropes. Scrambling forward, Meredith peered over the bulwark. Their shot had been as accurate as the guns forward of them. Three of the gun-ports on the *Marquis*'s starboard side had been torn into one great hole. Meredith could see one of the French lying in the opening screaming, his leg crushed and half torn away. Only the stern chasers of the *Marquis* could do them real damage here. The roar and whistle of ordnance passed above him. There was a scream and another man fell from the tops. His body never hit the deck, but was rather swung in the festoon of half-cut rigging like a child in a giant's cradle.

'They must yield!' shouted Hobbes. 'We've shot her to hell!'

Meredith found he was murmuring prayers between gritted teeth, his hands trembling. Then came a yell of victory from the bow. The *Marquis* had struck her colours. It was done. Unclenching his fists, the young man began to stand, the heat of the battle replaced by a flow of relief. The men around him were doing the same. The marines began to sling their muskets over their shoulders and descend from the ropes; Hobbes was all but dancing and his gun crew were smiling at him like proud parents.

Then the Frenchman let fly her sails, suddenly slowing her to allow her guns to bear on the *Splendour*. The broadside struck them hard and Meredith stumbled and felt the ship shudder under the impact. He looked to see Hobbes, his mouth wide and tears in his eyes.

'But she struck her colours! She surrendered! Dear God, how can they?'

Meredith felt an anger slick up his throat like a sickness.

'Reload, you bastards!' he yelled, his voice breaking with rage. His men were already on it, their faces as dark and bloody as his own. A ball from the cannon on the top deck of the *Marquis* burst through the bulwark no more than four feet from him, sending a blast of splinters up around it like a firework. Meredith clutched his leg and closed his fingers round a little dagger of wood. He pulled it out, hissing between his teeth. The cannon ball spun crazily across the deck before tumbling out of a port on the starboard side. It was like a child's marble game. Meredith laughed. James Westerman, his face white, was striding up the deck and clapped his shoulder as he passed.

The *Splendour* would not permit the French to get behind her but let the wind spill from her sails till she was once again in the rear. The *Marquis* let her stern-chasers fire at them on the upward roll of the sea, trying again to savage their rigging. Meredith looked up, but could hardly tell what damage had been done, the rigging was so wreathed in gunsmoke from the marines' muskets. All around him, the balls flew with a sharp crack. The mood was vicious.

The *Splendour*'s forward guns gave another great bark and there was a cheer as the English crew saw that the *Marquis* was hulled at the waterline; the sea was pouring in. Meredith could see men in the hole, nails in their mouths and batons in their hands, trying to keep out the ocean. 'Drown, you bastards,' he murmured. He could feel tears on his own cheeks. He dared not think what damage the broadside had done on the lower decks, but would swear it was the smoke from the guns.

'Prepare to board!' The *Splendour* began to inch back alongside the *Marquis*.

Meredith watched in horrid fascination as a French gunner put a slowmatch to his cannon. The world disappeared in smoke for a moment and Meredith heard the air split with a scream. Hobbes had been caught and thrown to his knees on the deck. His arm was shattered and already his blood was making the boards under Meredith's feet slippery and treacherous. 'Get below, Hobbes!' he yelled, and the boy began to drag himself towards the hatch with his good arm. Then: 'Fire!'

The *Splendour*'s broadside at this distance was devastating. Metal ripped through the French ship like a holy fire. Meredith aimed for the base of the Frenchman's main mast. There was a thunderous crack and it fell towards them, catching on the *Splendour*'s spars and holding the two ships together in a bloody embrace – yet still the French did not cease firing.

The Captain was striding back down the length of his ship, his face set and his sword already in his hand. Behind him, men were lifting pikes from their racks under the mainmast, and the little boys who fetched the powder from the magazine were pressing fresh cartridges into the hands of the marines. Meredith felt for his sword.

'Boarding party!' he roared, and his men dropped their business at the gun and ran for pikes of their own. As he swung his legs over the bulwark, preparing to leap onto the deck of the Frenchman, below him he could see others of the crew clambering from their portholes over their dead and their guns to swing themselves into the *Marquis* through the gaping holes torn in her sides. Meredith leaped and caught onto the Frenchman and hauled himself up. A light wind touched his cheek and in front of him the smoke parted enough for him to see a couple of French officers in fierce argument even as the English surged towards them across their bloody, shattered decks. He looked behind him and noticed a marine, his musket loaded and raised back on the *Splendour*.

'There!' he shouted, pointing at the two men with his sword. The marine nodded and Meredith dropped to the deck as the musket fizzed and cracked behind him, his arms over his head and his whole body trembling. One of the officers fell, the other at once dropped to his knees and began to fumble under the corpse's coat, pulling his sword free with such force the body rolled on its back, gaping up sightlessly at the fallen mast.

The officer remained kneeling and lifted his Captain's sword above his head, shouting as loudly as he could above the yells and gun-shots: '*On se rend! On se rend!*'

Captain Westerman emerged from amidst the smoke: 'Cease firing!' The English cheered and the gunfire came raggedly to a halt. Meredith lifted himself to his feet and looked around him. Dotted about the decks, his fellows from the *Splendour* stood over their French captives looking bloody and wild. The Captain looked more ferocious than Meredith had ever seen him; his sword was red and wet.

The living officer remained on his knees, still offering up the sword. Westerman grabbed it from him, spun on his heel and smashed the flat of the blade against the fallen trunk of the mainmast. The blade flew away from the hilt and skittered on the deck.

The French officer flinched.

'*Rendez vos armes!*' Westerman shouted, and as the pikes, guns and knives of the remaining French crew clattered to the deck, he threw down the hilt of the Captain's sword by his corpse and turned back towards the *Splendour*.

*Eight Bells of the Afternoon Watch (4 p.m.)*

James's cabin was restored to order while he visited the surgeon and sick-bay to find out what men he had lost. When he finally returned to his cabin, there was already more coffee on his table, his wife's letter had been returned to the place where he had left it, and his First Lieutenant was waiting for him.

'How bad is it, Captain?' Mr Cooper asked.

'Forty dead. One of the young gentlemen, Hobbes, has lost an arm, but he took the operation bravely and will live. Major Mansel is dead.'

Around them, the ship echoed with the sound of hammering and the shouts of the carpenter. Mr Cooper shifted on his boots and put his hands together behind his back. His Captain's mouth was set in a thin line. He was like a being formed from the ship's mind. The rage each member of the crew felt at the false surrender soaked through the timbers and into James Westerman's flesh.

Cooper cleared his throat. 'I've been talking to the officer – the one who gave up his Captain's sword.' James looked up sharply and Cooper wet his lips before continuing. 'His English is as good as mine. They had a run-in with one of ours a week ago, but managed to get away. Half the crew was in the sick-bay being treated for their wounds before we came near them. Good thing too, or that broadside would have ripped us to shreds. They wanted their Captain to find a safe harbour for repairs, but he insisted on pressing on. I think they were near enough shooting him themselves.'

James sighed and passed a hand over his forehead. 'Any notion as to why he wouldn't stop?'

Cooper straightened, but continued in a firmer voice, 'She's stuffed with supplies for the rebels, including a vast amount of powder. It's a miracle she didn't blow, given the pounding she received at our hands, so you have made us all rich if we can get her into home waters.'

'What says our carpenter to that?'

'That we can make her sail, though he'd like to tan Meredith for taking out the mainmast.'

'Good. You'll command her, Cooper. Pick your crew as soon as repairs are sufficient to make us both seaworthy.'

'Thank you, sir. But there's something else. It seems their Captain had a guest – a civilian, Frenchman – and the officer reckoned it was on his account that their Captain made them fight so hard.'

'Indeed?'

'Yes. He told them the passenger could not fall into English hands.'

James frowned. 'Is he alive?'

'He is, though he has a nasty splinter-wound in the belly. Seems he owes his life to Meredith. When the French Captain was shot, he had just given his Lieutenant the order to cut the man's throat.'

James began to put his coat on once more. 'Where is he?'

11

'Just being brought over to our surgeon now, sir. Theirs is dead, so our boys are seeing what they can do for the prisoners. What will you do, sir?'

James looked at him, his expression hard. 'There are too many men dead, Cooper. That Frenchman is not going to die without telling me what he knows.'

The surgeon was sent away from his post to rest an hour, and Heathcote placed to give the Captain and his guest some privacy. Heathcote never looked round, though he heard the sounds and could think what they meant. For a moment in the midst of all the French talk spoke low behind him, the Captain's voice harsh and strong, the man from the other ship whispering and gurgling, he thought he heard a thin voice singing. Then there was another rattling gasp, a whimper like a dog struck, and the sounds ceased.

*Thursday, 15 November 1781, Highgate, North London*

Mrs Harriet Westerman was watching her hands. They were shaking slightly. The door to the parlour opened suddenly and she looked up. The owner of the house had entered the room; he started on seeing her then said softly in his light Scots voice, 'My apologies, Mrs Westerman. I had thought you still with your husband. Is everything as it should be?'

Harriet tried to smile at him, but found she could not and looked back at her hands, which trembled still on the stiff purple silk of her skirts like nervous children forced to recite in front of the dining-room draperies. She did not know why she had let herself be persuaded into buying this dress. It was uncomfortable and James had never liked this colour.

'My visit this evening was not particularly successful, Dr Trevelyan,' she said. She heard him take up a chair, positioning it close to her with the sort of sigh that precedes bad news calmly spoken, and she added in a rush, 'Please do not take away my hope, sir.' Even in her own ear her voice sounded rather desperate.

The doctor caught his breath and waited a moment before speaking.

'There is always hope, madam,' he said finally. He stood again and moved across to the fireplace, picking up the poker to stir the logs a little. The flames chattered and shrugged; there was a pale-coloured thread hanging loose from the high collar of his bottle-green coat. 'Your husband's mind is struggling to repair itself. His injury was grave. Because you see his limbs are whole, you expect him to be himself. Do not. He is changed.' Trevelyan turned back towards her, frowning. 'Madam, you push him too much. Your love and energy in your care of him are commendable, but you cannot *will* him into health.'

A wave of frustration knitted her fingers together and made her joints whiten. As the wife of a Naval Commander in time of war she had feared shot, the vicious killing splinters of wood that flew deadly from the impact of a cannon ball, fierce winds and high seas. She had met widows enough, or women whose husbands returned to them with a sleeve pinned up, or swinging on crutches, but she never thought to fear something like this, this invisible maiming. 'It was such a stupid accident.'

'A blow to the head that left him unconscious two weeks, madam.' Trevelyan ceased frowning at her and said more gently, 'But, my dear Mrs Westerman, let me give you hope – I will *not* take it away. I believe parts of his memory are returning. I believe he will, in the coming months, better learn to govern his emotions and behave more fittingly towards his family, but you must allow time to do its work. He has improved since he arrived here, and he will continue to do so.'

She was silent a few moments.

'You said when we first met, sir, there was a man in your home town who recovered from a similar injury . . .'

Trevelyan turned away from her again and let his eyes rest on the painting of a stag at bay that decorated the wall over his mantelpiece. The beast was injured, but its great pronged horns were still lowered, ready to joust with the dogs that had cornered it, its sides torn and bleeding. The morbid little scene was surrounded by a landscape of purple heather which was beautiful and felt nothing. 'I did,' he said, as his eyes travelled over those distant hills. 'John Clifford lived with his family again and earned his bread. But he was changed. Commander Westerman will never again be the man you married, madam. You must both find the courage to accept that.'

Harriet bit her lip and listened to the fire before speaking in a small and rather helpless voice. 'What must I do?'

'Do not come here—' he raised his hand as she started to protest. '*No*, madam, I speak in all seriousness. Promise me you will not visit here for a few days, and when you do, bring your son.'

Harriet thought of her little boy, his face pale and afraid, his terrible confusion. 'Stephen has become frightened of his father.'

Trevelyan nodded slowly. 'Perhaps a little. But he has not seen the Captain in some time. Stay away only for a few days, madam. The Captain will certainly miss you and make efforts to manage himself better when you return, and greater efforts still in the presence of your son.'

Harriet managed to unclasp her hands. 'Perhaps if I no longer tried to force him to recall events . . .'

'A few days, Mrs Westerman. Occupy yourself in other ways.'

# PART I

## I.1

*Friday, 16 November 1781, London, near Black Lyon Stairs*

'COME ON! *PULL*, damn your eyes!'
'No use breaking your lungs at me! He's tied or stuck or something.'

The two red-coated men hunched in the wherry looked down into the dirty waters of the Thames and considered.

It was already full light, or as near to full light as it could be on a London day in November, and up and down the river the city was awake and hustling. Carts and cattle fought for space across Westminster Bridge and the people walked fast with their heads down through the clatter and stink. Among the jostling crowds the hawkers shouted and swore and rattled their pails. Mud spattered up from the horses' hooves and the fat wooden wheels of wagons. The air was heavy with city scents: woodsmoke, horse manure, fried meat; and tanged with frost. In any place within a half-mile of the river bank you'd hear hammering and the crash of stone on stone. Someone was always building, someone else knocking something down. Smoke poured from the chimneys along the south bank into the damp air and blackened it. London's skyline was smudged in blood and soot.

There was no peace on the water either. The Thames, the fat brown God of London, its flowing heart, was belching and grumbling with boats from dawn. It offered to the city its food and

15

trade; all its riches and influence were borne on its broad twisted back one way or the other. Sometimes the mudlarks who swarmed over the shingle at low tide found little fetishes, some ancient sword or offering to the river from times past, to show them they were nothing but the latest of its acolytes. Sometimes the river spat up what it was offered more speedily.

The current pulled at the wherry. The two men it held made an odd sort of couple. One of them was skinny and young; the other had a chest like a rum barrel and a thick beard that stood out angrily from his chin. Proctor and Jackson. Uncle and nephew, now partners of a sort and servants of the river in their way. The passage across the waters put bread on their table. The nephew's ready smile got them trade, and the uncle's strong shoulders got them a reputation for a swift and easy crossing through the currents and their rivals.

Proctor was working hard enough now at the oars to make his face red just keeping his place in the water. With a fierce pull on his right arm he inched the boat far enough upriver so he could see better what they had noticed from the bank. It was certainly a man, or at least it had been. The back of his green jacket was hissing bubbles under the swell, and his wig was still attached to his head; the wisps of horsehair swam about him in searching tendrils. The body's arms were outstretched and the head hung forward like the Christ on the Cross in St Martin's Church, as if the man was looking for something lost in the muddy waters below.

Proctor spat into the river on the opposite side on the boat. Of course the body was tethered somehow. If he hadn't been, the river would have given itself a laugh flying him halfway to Woolwich by now. Nothing stayed in this part of the river that wasn't stuck.

'Well, get a rope round him, cut him loose from what binds him and get him in then.'

Jackson shot him an angry look, before tying a lasso from a length of rope in the bow then slinging it round the body's chest, working it under the arms with an unhappy frown. Drawing the noose tight,

16

he checked the knot on the samson post before stripping off his coat and shirt. His pale skin turned goosish at once. He slipped off his shoes and pulled a knife from his waistband.

'Why'd you never learn to swim then, Proctor?' he grumbled. 'Twenty years on ships and boats and not a stroke. I'd be ashamed.'

The older man scowled back. 'Fate might see it as an invitation to throw me in, boy. Now get to it, will you!'

The younger man drew a deep breath, put the blade between his teeth and hauled himself over the side, gasping as the chill of the waters held him; then, he duck-dived. Proctor held the boat steady, watching as his nephew used the body as ladder and anchor in the muck of the river. Strong tides. He saw the activity in the water, then felt a sudden yank as the weight of the body shifted from its anchor to the samson post in his own boat and the river tried to carry the corpse off over its shoulder.

The boy rolled himself back in – then, settling solidly on the floor of the boat, he pulled on the rope. The wet lengths slapped onto the wood as he hauled on it, then as the dead man's spine knocked against the gunwales, the boy reached back into the water, got his arms round the corpse's chest and with a shout of effort dragged it in over the side. He toppled backwards and the body followed. With a shove and shiver he got out from under it.

'Christ!' He backed his way into the bow to catch his breath and began to rub himself dry with his shirt.

'Least he's fresh,' Proctor said. The boy did not reply but took his place and clambered back into his red coat. They began to pull out for the Black Lyon Stairs. 'Though we could have towed it.'

His nephew looked black. There'd be a crowd there already, ready to tut at the corpse and bless themselves for having survived another day. Damn, his hands were cold! The noise of London was full-throated now. Whistles and shouts rang from the boats making their way up and down the river. Smoke poured out of every chimney and the banks were alive with hammerings and thumps as the warehouses were filled and emptied with sugar and timber, cloth and spices, fancy goods and dried fruits. Off downstream on the far side of London Bridge where the Tower stared down into the waters, the merchant ships would be pulling at their anchors like dogs eager to be off and running again, yapping over the oceans for fresh trade.

The body's head lolled to one side and the mouth drained the dirty water of the Thames onto the floor of the scull.

In other parts of London one could breathe sweeter air. On Bruton Street in Mayfair, a lady paused as her maid plied the door-knocker of one of the graceful buildings at the Berkeley Square end of the street, and touching her high and powdered hair, which so bore down on her neck she was rarely free of a mild headache, she noticed a man on the opposite side of the street. He was consulting a pocket-watch and frowning a little. She marked the cut of his plum-coloured coat and thought it gentleman-like, if rather plain; and saw the man who wore it was not unpleasing, though the dustings of youth had been mostly knocked off him. He had a slightly Roman look to his face, long-nosed and rather serious, but nothing in his dress or bearing marked him out as anything remarkable.

Turning away, she began to think of the gossip she was about to trade with the lady of the house outside which she waited, what she would be willing to reveal, and what keep secret. It might have surprised her to learn that the gentleman whom she had been observing was thinking also of the trading and flow of information, the commerce and management of knowledge. The gentleman was a spy, and a controller of spies. He had ears and eyes in every court in Europe and he collected their whisperings and spun it into the gold of intelligence – at least, that was his intent. Her friend's footman opened the door to her, and the lady never thought of the idle gentleman again.

Mr Palmer, the gentleman who had been under observation, glanced over his shoulder as he heard one of the street-doors open and close again behind him, then returned to contemplation of his pocket-watch. It still wanted a few minutes to eleven o'clock. That was the hour he had suggested in his note that he would call on Mrs Westerman and Mr Crowther, that strange pair of companions recently celebrated for their role in bringing justice to some unfortunates in Sussex, and now, due to the indisposition of Mrs Westerman's husband, resident in London. He did not wish to be early and so looked about him.

Berkeley Square. Some of the richest families in the country made their homes here in the Season, it being near enough the business and pleasure of the town but removed enough to offer some respite from the stink and the squalor. The air was certainly cleaner here than in the city, and the streets quieter than around his offices at the Admiralty in Whitehall. The houses were the work of various architects of the century, but though a number of hands had been employed there was among the buildings a slightly smug sense of agreement as to the fundamentals of tasteful design. Tall narrow windows peered with a certain disdain over the central gardens; the stone steps to their cellars were sheltered with black iron railings which flowered into iron brackets. The lamps they held aloft were all extinguished now, but when the gloom of a November evening stole up again from the river tonight, slippered footmen in powder and livery would emerge to light them till they decorated the square like marsh-lights, each catching the glitter of gold-braid in their little defensive pools against the dark. Mr Palmer thought of those things he had lately learned, and saw himself suddenly as a lost traveller on hostile ground, chasing glimmers, and unable to say if they would lead him to greater security – or into danger.

From his position on the pavement, Palmer could see a group of children at play in the central gardens. Two boys, of about seven he would guess, were neatly tacking up one of the lawns under the leafless trees towards a young girl and a nursemaid with a small child in her arms. They were a well-made-looking group. The boys both appeared sturdy and healthy, their coats streaks of blue and brown against the grass. The girl, still not at her full height, though older than the boys, wore a black silk mantle over a gown of blue. She picked at its edges as she walked briskly by her nurse.

'Thornleigh, engage the enemy!' shouted the boy in the lead, the darker of the two.

'Yes, sir, Captain Westerman, sir,' his blond companion replied.

Mr Palmer watched their manoeuvres for a moment with a smile. So this was Captain Westerman's son and the young Earl of Sussex, with whom the Westerman family were staying in London. He wondered what adventures they were undertaking. Perhaps they were replaying Captain Westerman's capture of the French warship, the *Marquis de La Fayette* in the spring. It had been a valuable prize, since the ship was laden with goods bound for the rebels of the American Colonies from their continental allies, and worth not less than three hundred thousand pounds. It was also the last such victory the Captain would enjoy in his remarkable career. An accident at sea during the repairs to his ship had left James Westerman badly injured. It had been the most appalling piece of luck, and now Westerman had returned home with his brains so shaken up, it was found after some weeks that he was not fit to live with his family but instead must reside under the care of a mad-doctor in Highgate. He was a great loss. The threat to England's supremacy on the seas had never been so great, and the Navy felt the lack of such a competent Commander most keenly.

'Stephen!' the young lady called. 'If you launch a broadside at baby Anne and myself *just* when she is sleeping, I shall have you flogged at the Capstan and – oh, what is the phrase . . .'

The fairer boy paused, then shouted, 'Keelhauled!'

Lady Susan grinned happily. 'Indeed. Keelhauled!'

The darker boy appeared to subtly alter his course, as if the shrubberies to the north of the gardens had always been his intent, remarking only, 'It's just the Dutch do that, actually,' and kicking up the damp late-autumn leaves with his heels.

Palmer smiled at the young lady's management of the boys before letting his thoughts drift back to the mother of the prudent warrior. He had met the Captain's red-headed wife in the past, and on the first occasion, some years ago, he had found her a good-humoured and intelligent woman, and loyal consort. He had seen her again after her husband's return to England, and on official business. Palmer had received information that a man taken captive on Westerman's ship, who had later died from his wounds, might have been possessed of certain knowledge Mr Palmer wished very much to have. He had found Mrs Westerman as helpful as the grief and confusion caused by her husband's injury would allow. James Westerman himself seemed drunk, childlike, petulant, but Palmer had left their orderly and apparently thriving estate in Sussex thinking well of the Captain's wife and family, and grieving for them.

Mr Palmer's most recent meeting with Mrs Harriet Westerman had been in London, and extremely unpleasant. She had appeared at the Admiralty without an appointment and had taken him to task, in vehement tones and in public. She had accused him of harassing her sick husband. It had been an uncomfortable situation and Mr Palmer had his profession's hatred of scenes. Yet now he sought her out.

Examining his pocket-watch again, he watched the minute hand finally creep to the head of the hour. Of her companion, Mr Crowther, he had no personal knowledge, so knew only what the world knew: that the man was known for his expertise on the marks left on a body by violence; known for his wealth and eccentricity; known for having a father murdered and brother hung for the killing, for having refused his rightful title and seat in the Lords to instead sell his estate and study the science of anatomy in obscurity, till Mrs Westerman plucked him free and made him help her save the lives and fortunes of young Lord Thornleigh and his sister. Mr Palmer had read the pamphlets and listened to the gossip and drawn his own conclusions.

He stepped forward.

## I.2

JOCASTA BLIGH PUMPED the handle and filled her pail in the centre of Arnold's Yard. Her arms were strong and she took some pleasure in the work, even on a morning as grey as this, twitching with the winter to come. As the water reached the brim of her bucket she became aware of a presence over her shoulder, a hopeful shadow. Without turning, she spoke.

'Give us it here, Hopps.' Then, putting her own bucket to one side, she took another from the old man who had arrived behind her. He was a shrunken, wasted-looking thing, his teeth all memory and wearing hardly more than rags. 'Why don't you get a girl in to do for you mornings, Hopps?' she said, working the pump again. 'I'd swear you have the blunt to do it, what with the rent we pays you, and I know you ain't spending it all on your fancy clothes.'

Hopps looked down at his ragged linen and laughed a laugh that sounded like rocks dragged over gravel. His breath hit the back of her neck with the smell of rotted onions. 'Oh, Mrs Bligh! Why waste the money on some young thing, when *you* have strong arms still. Gives a man pleasure, it do, to see you working that thing!'

She turned and passed over the bucket a little quick so he panted a bit as he took the weight.

'Most obliged, madam,' he said, looking a little sorry. 'But are you not singing today? It is how I know that the day has begun when I hear the pump going and you crooning some tune from the north. I should have thought a stranger in the yard till I looked through the window and saw your skirts.'

Jocasta was famous round the yard for many things, among them her patchwork skirts, voluminous, multi-coloured, constantly reworked and visible a dozen yards off. No one could say if she had many or few; they changed little by little like the foliage on the pear tree that hung over the pump. You could hardly say they changed one day to the next, till a moment came and you looked and saw gold where all had been green before.

Crossing her broad arms over her chest, the woman looked down at her dried-up wisp of a landlord.

'Here I am though, and as for the singing, we all have dreams from time to time that leave us quiet in the morning.'

'Every day I have them, Mrs Bligh. And always worse to come when I wake.'

Jocasta made no reply, but took up her own pail and hauled it back to her own door, shoving it open with her thigh and growling at the little rust-coloured terrier that yapped about her. Every morning she fetched water from the pump in Arnold's Yard for boiling or washing, and every morning it was the same. Boyo thought it was a game and jumped at the swing bucket and bounced around her ankles and skirts till the water splashed and her stockings were soaked. There, now the step into the hallway was wet and she could hear Hopps's laugh from the courtyard, enjoying the show.

'Dog, will you settle?'

She kicked the door to, got the pail to its place and dipped in a jug to fill the kettle. Her thick knees clicked like knitting needles and as the enamel tapped the wooden side of the bucket she sat back her bulk on her heels. Time flowed round her like water; some more years would pass and then she too would struggle to fetch her water. The dream she'd dreamed in the night whispered through her head and away; she tilted her head as if to pour it out of her mind and into the light. It was The Chariot, or at least something like it – it had run past her or run her over, or had she been swung up inside it to ride alongside a demon in a mask?

Boyo barked, and the sound swept the dream pictures from her.

'All right, all right, I know! The tea's not ready and neither of us fed and there will be a dozen people to tell the future to before we can be just ourselves again.'

She got the kettle on the fire, then twisted round with a grunt to where her pack of picture cards sat on her table. She spread them flat, let her fingers hover over them a moment and drew one out. The Chariot it was. The prince driving it, spear in one hand and the other on his hip, the golden horses surging on below.

'Trials coming then, are they, Boyo?' Jocasta said and rubbed her chin, then clambered heavily to her feet. The dog cocked its head on one side. 'Same as every day in a dirty town then.' She looked round her room. Her walls felt thin of a sudden, and the fire small. If The Chariot did come, how much of its turmoil turning would she stand before her sanctuary was all crumpled to nothing and she herself was back out in the gutter? Well, so turns the wheel. Let The Chariot come, for now she was warm again and the kettle was beginning to sing. 'So let's see what business we can make of living today, shall we?'

The cards waited on the rough little table for their first visitors. Mrs Jocasta Bligh earned her bread plucking truth out of them with a patient hand, and a frown on her heavy face.

## I.3

'LET ME UNDERSTAND you correctly, Mr Palmer. You wish us to go and examine a corpse?'

'Yes, madam.' Mr Palmer had decided that a character such as Mrs Westerman was best approached with a mix of respect and hesitation. He had allowed himself to stumble over his words a little as he arrived. The important consideration was that Mrs Westerman should feel she was being humbly asked for help; that he was a supplicant, not that she was all but being given an order by a servant of her King. He should be careful to avoid waking her temper again. To Mr Crowther he hoped to offer a puzzle and see if flattery might draw him into usefulness.

Placing his teacup on the side-table, Mr Palmer cleared his throat.

The clock on the mantel of the drawing room in 24 Berkeley Square seemed very loud. The space was lit by three high windows looking out on to the Square, and could have easily contained a party of thirty. Small groups of gilded chairs and settees were scattered around it at discreet distances, the walls were decorated with classical, pastoral scenes and moulded garlands, of flowers and bows; large porcelain jars, richly patterned, stood sentinel in every available nook like fat footmen. There was a great deal of gilt in the scheme. Mr Palmer conjectured that Mr Owen Graves, a young gentleman plucked from obscurity by the convulsions of the House of Thornleigh, and thrust from scribbler to guardian of one of the great fortunes of the nation, had probably bought the house furnished, and possibly in haste.

In dress and demeanour Mr Palmer's hosts formed a distinct contrast to the room in which they sat. Mr Crowther's thin figure was dressed in black and he could have passed for a parson. There were some stains, possibly chemical, around his cuffs, though otherwise his person was neat and gentleman-like, though his manner was dry enough to be offputting. Mrs Westerman was dressed like a countrywoman – a rich and certainly handsome countrywoman, no doubt – but she was not polished and powdered to the degree usually seen in Town. She looked a great deal older than when Mr Palmer had first seen her; in her face and manner there was a weariness, a brittle quality. The peculiar sickness of her husband had no doubt caused a strain. She could not be above five and thirty, much his own age, and he knew he was still regarded by some in the Admiralty as a young man. Mr Palmer saw the morning's newspaper folded on the settee, a pile of correspondence on the writing table at the far end of the room. The pair had been camping-out in a distant corner of all this grandeur, waiting for him.

'Perhaps it would be better if I explained matters from the beginning.'

Mrs Westerman tilted her head to one side, examining him as if he were an optical illusion to be squinted at. 'That might be best, sir.' Her tone was somewhat clipped.

Mr Palmer began. 'I have already spoken to you, madam, something of these matters. I shall repeat the story for Mr Crowther's benefit and so bring myself to the reason for my visit and my request for your assistance. *If* that is acceptable.' He turned his head towards Mr Crowther's narrow profile. The man did not look up from his contemplation of his fingernails. 'We heard this spring that certain gentlemen of importance in the French Court were apparently crowing over some new master of intelligence they had recruited and expected to have in place in London shortly. Though we had no particulars.' He paused. 'The war with the American Rebels does not go well.'

Mr Crowther glanced up at that, with a slight tilt to his eyebrows as if to say, 'I did not need a Mr Palmer to tell me that.'

Palmer glanced at the newspaper on the gilded couch and cleared his throat again. The government, the Admiralty were being criticised at every point, for either being too slow, or too foolhardy – both with equal vigour. The brief patriotic fervour that had flared when France made treaty with the Americans had died away. The country was sick with a war fought on the other side of the world and with people she believed to be her kin. The Navy struggled to protect trade, Spanish flags were flaunted in the Channel, and every piece of information that Palmer could not prevent slipping to the French was like a musket shot against his King. He was still young enough to feel those blows, and drive himself to greater efforts, more ingenious methods, stranger allies in his attempts to stem the flow. If the French received the intelligence they hoped from this new servant in London, it would be worth more to them than a dozen ships of the line. He thought of England as a body bleeding vital knowledge of her strategies, struggles and capacities into the waters round her coast. Better organisation of that flow could make the wounds gout blood. He must do what he could to put pressure on the injury, sew up the tear. He watched Crowther's long fingers.

'I believe the Captain found out something of that . . .' Palmer lifted his hand to try and conjure a term from the air '. . . *spy-master* our European enemies wish to install as he interrogated the individual from the French vessel he captured in June.'

Crowther looked at him down his long nose and said simply, 'Why?'

Any question was an indication of interest, surely? Palmer seized on it and turned to Crowther, speaking quickly. 'You know, perhaps, sir, that the ship was laden with supplies for the American Rebels, and this man was not one of the naval officers. I believe his work was intelligence. Captain Westerman indicated as much to his officers after his interrogation of this individual and before his accident. He also made some expression of anger about what he referred to as "traitorous scum in every corner imaginable". That they stained every beauty. Though what he meant by that, we cannot know.'

Mrs Westerman stood suddenly and began to walk up and down behind her chair, her skirts sweeping over the carpet in regular clicking sighs. The contrast between her activity and Mr Crowther's stillness was unnerving. 'Yes, yes, Mr Palmer,' she said agitatedly. 'You told me as much months ago – but as *I* told *you* James remembers nothing of his last cruise as yet. There is no reason to believe he ever will. You have questioned his officers and I even gave you sight of his private letters home to me. That did not prevent you from harassing my husband under Dr Trevelyan's roof ten days ago.'

'Madam, I did *not* harass him! The information is so crucial that if there were any chance—' Palmer stopped himself. 'I did receive two weeks ago a name from a connection I trust in Paris. That name was Fitzraven. I wondered if it might be familiar to your husband. It did not seem to be. I could discover no more.' He drew breath, but could not resist adding in a rush, 'I would have explained as much to you at the Admiralty last week, if you had given me a chance to speak in my defence.' He thought he saw the corner of Mr Crowther's mouth twitch at that, and Mrs Westerman scowled briefly.

Palmer continued more calmly. 'The role of this Fitzraven, his status, his importance in the schemes that move against us – nothing of that could be discovered. Only the name, and with that I was unfamiliar. However, I have made it my business to keep a close watch for him.'

Mrs Westerman had come to a stop and they were both observing him now, with something like curiosity. The thin November light caught the red lights in her hair.

'There are some individuals in the city I employ to listen for items of interest,' Palmer went on. 'Any whisper of that name, anywhere in the city, was to come to me – and this morning I hear that a body was pulled from the Thames at first light, and the body was named by a member of the crowd that watched him dragged up the Black Lyon Stairs as Fitzraven.'

He looked up at Mrs Westerman. Her expression was neutral; Mr Crowther was sitting with his fingers tented and very still. 'I have arranged for one of the Westminster Magistrates, a Mr Pither, to request your assistance,' Palmer ploughed on. 'It is not unnatural that he would think to do so, given your investigation of events in Sussex last year. He would like to add a little lustre to his name by a connection with yourselves.' At this, Mrs Westerman's lip curled. Drawing himself straight in his chair, Mr Palmer made his final appeal with a certain solemnity. 'I have come to you to urge you to supply that assistance and find out what you can of the circumstances of Fitzraven's death. He then added with a half-smile as the thought occurred to him, 'Perhaps a little show of resistance to doing so might be of use. If Pither can tell the story of how he persuaded you, it will cloud the matter in a way advantageous to our greater cause.'

'You seem to have a great ability to find things out yourself, Mr Palmer,' Crowther said with a faint drawl, 'and arrange all manner of complicated affairs in a short space of time.' He drew a neat enamelled pocket-watch from his waistcoat and examined it. Then met Palmer's eye. Mr Palmer noticed that though Mr Gabriel Crowther might be a gentleman the wrong side of fifty, his blue eyes seemed icy and exceptionally clear. 'Why do you not look into the matter yourself? Or use one of these gentlemen you trust. Why such unconnected amateurs as ourselves? Why trust a recluse and a known harridan with the secrets of your King?'

Palmer looked up swiftly at Mrs Westerman to see how she took this description of herself. She did not flinch but continued to examine the wall to his right. He took a moment to select his words.

'Three reasons, sir. The first you should be able to supply, if modesty did not forbid. I have not your expertise in seeing the stories a dead body can tell of itself. Very few men do. For the second let me speak to the matter of trust. I know something of you, Mr Crowther, and all that I have heard suggests to me a man who is unlikely to go gossiping in society of such matters.' Crowther gave a wintry little smile. 'Mrs Westerman has served on her husband's commands. I believe in her loyalty and her principles. Your temper I have felt the heat of, madam, but I see no sign of foolishness in you.' Mrs Westerman still did not look at him, but he was sure he was attended to, and carefully. 'The third is related to the confidential and delicate nature of intelligence in time of war. I must know, for the sake of our country's interests and those that serve them, what is afoot here. Is there a conspiracy to betray this nation to the French? Who is involved in the matter and what damage might they already have done? Who was this master sent to lead? What was the nature of this man Fitzraven?'

Harriet turned towards him suddenly. 'Are there not continually such plots?' she asked.

Mr Palmer nodded. 'I find myself much engaged, but let me complete my argument. The agents of the French are not foolish. If Fitzraven was in some way involved, my appearance asking questions as to his life, activities and death will no doubt send the conspirators into hiding, and what I can learn will be severely curtailed.'

'Whereas Crowther and I can blunder about asking whatever we like, and people will assume we have simply discovered murder to be an enlivening pastime?' Harriet's voice was softer than it had been hitherto, and was laced now with amusement. Mr Palmer smiled.

'Exactly, Mrs Westerman. It will be thought you and Mr Crowther seek only to increase or consolidate your renown and so cannot resist the opportunity to examine a man who died in apparently mysterious circumstances. I wish to know of this man's connections, his habits and nature. I must discover if he was the man my contact learned of, and if, by his death, we may find out what networks of intelligence the French have in this country and where and how deeply they reach.'

'How mysterious *were* the circumstances of his death?' Crowther said. 'Bodies are pulled from the Thames every day.'

'I hope you will let the matter speak for itself. The reports I have are suggestive, but at second hand. Let me not cloud your enquiry with imprecise information at this stage.'

It seemed to Mr Palmer at this moment that his proposal was still under consideration.

Crowther picked at his cuff and said, very softly, 'To whom do you answer, Mr Palmer?' There was a cold steel in the words.

'My remit in these matters is wide,' Mr Palmer told him. 'I have some money and staff at my disposal, and the liberty to act as I see fit in most matters. Lord Sandwich is the First Lord of the Admiralty – beyond that I am answerable to my King, and the law. As are we all.'

The little clock on the mantelpiece marked the half-hour with an elaborate chime that made Mrs Westerman start. But neither she nor Crowther made him any reply.

'We are at war,' Mr Palmer said after some moments of silence. 'Information can be as vital, or as deadly, as ordnance. If news – accurate news – of the preparedness of our ships, stores, or troops regularly reaches the French naval command, men will die. I come in all humility to ask for your assistance.'

Crowther tented his fingers again and said, 'Then, Mr Palmer, you shall have it.'

## I.4

SOME MINUTES AFTER Mr Palmer left Berkeley Square, the promised invitation from Justice Pither arrived. Its tone suggested that the idea of consulting them was all his own. Mr Gabriel Crowther watched Mrs Westerman read the note in her turn. She was pulling on a red ringlet that framed her face, and seemed in danger of straightening it. She was not looking well, and she had told him enough of her last visit to Dr Trevelyan's establishment to know it had not given her any comfort. Her husband's illness had overtaken her like a damp fog. Her lively eyes had become dull, fading from emerald to pondwater in a little more than three months, and her hair, shot through with a fire that seemed to burn when she was angry or afraid, had begun to look rusty and brittle. She was thin. If she were a horse, he would have had her shot. He resisted the temptation to tell her so.

'Do stop glowering at me like that, Crowther,' Harriet said, setting the note down and resting her head in her hands for a moment. 'I am afraid you are conjecturing what my lungs would look like in a jar.'

Crowther had picked up the newspaper again and was reading a report of fears for brave Cornwallis and his gallant little army at Yorktown.

'I do not think, Mrs Westerman, the preparation of a human lung I own could be improved upon at this time,' he remarked mildly. 'So you may rest easy. I have, in fact, been regretting that the excitement of our success last week when I spoke to the Royal Society seems to have dissipated so quickly. I expected you still to be pleased. But you do not seem it.'

'*Your* success, I think. And being told my company is injurious to my husband's health has not cheered me.'

'I gave your insights and investigative abilities their due. The gentlemen were properly impressed by our success in finding out the mysteries of "a certain great house in Suffolk".'

Harriet raised her eyebrows. 'Yes, I got the impression afterwards that you must have been quite generous, since a remarkable number of men in bad wigs and stained coats took the opportunity to be introduced to me and patronise me a little while we drank tea. Their wives approached me as if they feared I would stink still of the dissecting room.' She fidgeted in her chair like a child confined to a schoolroom on a hot day. 'And it seems ridiculous that on these occasions we cannot refer to Thornleigh Hall by its name. Everyone knows the story. Rachel is constantly having to hide the more hysterical pamphlets detailing the circumstances from the children.'

'Such are the conventions. And I must say you are most *un*generous in your description of my colleagues. There were mavericks and thinkers there enough to excite even your admiration, I believe.'

Harriet made no reply, and looking again at Mr Pither's note had to admit to a certain grudging admiration of the way Mr Palmer had engineered the invitation to examine the body. But she put the letter down with a sigh.

'What could I possibly contribute to this matter that you could not manage better and much more properly alone, Crowther?'

Crowther realised where her thoughts had led her and gave the question some consideration. Mrs Westerman was certainly right. It was neither her profession, nor her proper sphere to enquire into the deaths of strangers, nor to bring murderers to justice, although as the pamphlets she mentioned had recorded in great detail, she had done so in the past. He considered briefly the possibility of going alone to Justice Pither's house, but it occurred to him – and it was not pleasant to consider it – that he would not, in fact, be of very much use to the Magistrate or to Mr Palmer without Mrs Westerman. He had spent many years in the study of the human body, and had a particular interest in the marks and traces violence leaves on its victims, but he lacked Mrs Westerman's ability to power forward into other people's lives, asking questions, conjecturing as to their motives. He had tried in his early adulthood to remove passion from his soul with study, scalpel and syringe. It had been only a partial success, but he had winnowed himself to the extent that he still needed to borrow her warmth – if she had any left to spare him. The idea that she might desert him entirely made him uneasy. He was rich, an acknowledged expert in his field, but he needed her – a woman designed by society only to run a household and amuse herself – to turn his expertise into something of practical use. It was somewhat humbling. He examined his cuffs.

'In the initial examination of the body, perhaps not a great deal, madam. But you have a certain animal intelligence that I occasionally lack. Further to that, you do not look well. You are a creature used to activity, and simply writing letters about your husband's health is not activity enough.'

She glanced at him, and something of her old self glinted in her green eyes.

'London does not improve your manners, Crowther.'

'I do not wish them improved.'

'That is lucky.' Harriet stood and paced across the hearthrug like a dog testing the limits of its chain. 'Do you think Dr Trevelyan is in Mr Palmer's pay? That he forces me into an idleness I cannot bear . . . Perhaps I should repair my reputation in the world and stay here still and grieving till I am summoned to Highgate again.'

Crowther considered the threateningly ornate chandelier above them. 'I believe the Captain would wish you to do all in your power to help his friends. And I think, Mrs Westerman, if your husband had wished to marry a woman who would sit by his bedside weeping for *more* than three months at a time, he would not have married you. Or if he did wish some sort of paragon of patience, ready to play martyr, he was already an idiot *before* he received that blow to his head.'

Harriet was surprised into a shocked gasp. He met her gaze with an innocent smile and the gasp became a choking sort of laugh.

'Your complimentary mood continues, I see.' She folded her arms and rapped her fingers against the dull green sleeve of her dress. 'And why do you wish to serve your King?'

'Mr Palmer has flattered me; and besides, I have finished reading my paper.'

'Then let us order the carriage.'

## I.5

ANYONE ELSE WHO had a choice – that is to say those with money enough to make a choice – had moved west of here. The ways round Covent Garden had been bad for twenty years, but Jocasta was happy to stick with what she knew, even when there was gold enough in her bag to crawl towards the cleaner air. The press of people suited her, and the house in which she lived showed no sign of falling down as yet. More than that, people knew where to find her while she bided here. From early in the day till lighting up when the boys went round with their tapers sparking up the oil-lamps on St Martin's Lane she sat at her table and turned cards. She told the fortunes of drunks and whores, pickpockets and thief-takers, of serving girls and journeymen, weavers and sailors. There was no class of person, no matter their desperation or their fear, that did not tend hopes for better times under their greasy clothes. Sometimes even Quality found their way to her and left coins fat and gold as the sun reflected in a puddle. She would tell them what she could see, and tell it gently, and hoped they'd leave a little lighter, because for all her scowls her heart was kindly at its core.

Mostly the fortunes she told were simple enough to unpack. Some young girl would come knocking on her door with a coin warm in her hand and stutter out a question about her lover, or her chances of honest work, and even before Jocasta had let her shuffle and choose her cards she'd know what they were to say, and was forming in her mind some way to say it without it stinging too hard. It led to calm

34

days and regular habits, and times where she'd feel comfortable, almost content, and find herself singing songs from her youth as she pumped her water in the morning. From the moment she'd recalled the dream though, realised its heaviness had shut her lips over her song that morning, she'd known that her latest period of ease was done, and that sometime in the day a man or woman would come in and turn the cards, and they'd be hurtful and snarling, and as ready to burn her own hand as the person she read for.

And so it was. Right now she saw all sorts of pictures swirling about on the table in front of her and none of them tasted good on her tongue. Jocasta Bligh stared at the cards before her and sucked in air noisily through her teeth.

The woman seated opposite her had knocked on the door ten minutes ago as Jocasta was stirring the fire to drive out the cold London damp. She was now shifting in her seat a little restlessly, trying hard not to ask what Jocasta could see. She was a neat and pretty young woman who dressed well, but not so well she looked far out of place in the alleyway outside. A shop girl, Jocasta reckoned. Her hands looked too fine to think her a maid or a cook, and her manner was too quiet to think she would sell gin to maintain herself; she had a bloom on her still and no one who traded for men's affections kept that more than a month. Kate Mitchell, she'd named herself. She'd got herself decent, it seemed, to pay her visit, though Jocasta did not see it as a compliment to herself. The girl had brushed her blonde hair and neatened it to face what knowledge was coming, to try and aid her courage. Her eyes were darting, and she held her hands together on her lap quite tight. When she spoke, her voice placed her as a native of the city, and not educated further than the charity schools, but by the look of her she'd done well after that.

Jocasta looked at the cards again; they seemed to bob and skip lightly in front of her, back and forth. She was tasting salt, and gunpowder.

'You have any sailors in the family?'

Mrs Mitchell frowned and put her head to one side. 'My dad was a sailor, though I can't say I knew him. Him and Mum got married in the Fleet and he was off again before I was born. She said he had a pigtail though, so she's sure he wasn't lying about that. Can't see why he'd show his face in the cards.' She bit her lip and looked down at her hands. 'Though my husband, Mr Frederick Mitchell, he clerks for the Admiralty. That might be what you're seeing.' She craned her neck, trying to spot in the cards in front of her whatever Jocasta was catching sight of, then sighed and sat back. 'I come to you full of concerns regarding him, Mrs Bligh. And in need of some words from a lady of sense and sight like yourself.'

'I smell gunpowder,' Jocasta replied.

Kate's fingers worked at the folds of her dress. 'I cannot say why you would. Fred's business is all ink and papers. But still, his business is war in a way. Making sure the orders are made for the Fleet, and they are firing on the French and Americans every day now. Perhaps . . .'

Jocasta let her attention fall on the picture of The Moon in front of her. It glowed and whispered. She couldn't catch the words, but she didn't like their tone.

'What's he up to, this husband of yours?' she murmured, as if to herself. 'And who's the old woman who doesn't like you?'

Mrs Mitchell looked as if her eyes were suddenly stinging her. She started to speak low and quick. 'We share rooms with his mother. I don't think she is fond of me. She runs a coffee-house on Whitehall and goes to serve the gentry with refreshments at their entertainments in the season too. I think she does a pretty trade, though Freddy and I both turn our wages over to her then she hands out shillings as if we were bleeding *her* dry.'

'Married long?'

'Three months now.' Kate looked very sad. 'I offered to give up my place at Mr Broodigan's perfumes where I serve and help her, and

I thought at first she had a liking for the plan, but now she just tells me to stop where I am.'

'And what does Fred say?'

The young woman smiled suddenly. 'Oh, we used to laugh at her ways at first, but these last couple of weeks . . . I've seen him and his mother talking quiet, and they stop when I walk into the room. I came home last week and there was a man just leaving I've never seen before, and neither of them would say who he was. I'm sure he was leaving our rooms. Freddy says now there's money coming if I'm patient. He bought this pretty table and a brooch for me, though a month ago he was baying at me for buying new gloves, and not fancy ones either! And he's short with me now, won't laugh so.'

Jocasta rubbed her nose. 'We'll pick through this, dearie. But you'll need to talk it out with your boy, somehow. There'll be no laughing again till you do.'

Kate suddenly stooped to pick up her reticule. Pulling a handful of papers from it, she thrust them towards Jocasta. 'And I found these . . .'

The older woman looked up in surprise. 'Sorry, dearie. I read cards, not writing. Never got the trick of it.'

Kate gathered them back to herself, doubtfully. 'They are letters, but not to Freddy or from him, but from—' She stopped herself. 'There now – I'm running on. Mr Broodigan in the shop, he says I always do – but the customers like to have a chat and a gossip while they are trying their scents.' She closed her bag and gave her head a little shake. 'Thank you, Mrs Bligh. You've told me I need to go and speak clear with my husband and stop dancing round it. That's good advice and I thank you for it.' She got to her feet. 'I'll be on my way.'

Jocasta frowned at the shimmering cards. 'I've told you no such thing. I've hardly tasted air. There's some stuff here I need to step through with you. I don't like the look. Sit now.'

Mrs Mitchell lifted her chin and held out a coin, which trembled slightly. Jocasta drew her shawl tighter round her and would not take it, so Kate set it down neatly in the centre of the cards.

'Jenny at the shop was right when she said you were worth speaking with, Mrs Bligh. But I have what I need now, so I'll be away. Don't be offended, I mean nothing against you.'

'Not a case of offended. You're looking all brave and clear now, but this is something fiercer than a little lack of confidence man to wife, isn't it, my dear?' She looked up into the young woman's face. 'Let us pick through before you go charging off!'

Kate opened her mouth to speak, but no words came to her, so she turned on her heel and almost stumbled, such was her hurry to get out of the room. The door clapped to behind her. Jocasta sucked in the air through her teeth again and looked back down in the cards. Their whispering was growing clearer, more insistent. A trickle of coldness started to slick in Jocasta's belly; it grew and spread as if it were embers on dry matter.

Boyo got onto his feet and jumped up beside her. Jocasta put out her hand and rubbed behind his ears, but he could tell he hadn't caught her attention and whined. She didn't hear him, she was still watching the cards in front of her. The Moon, cards of the Suite of Swords several and warlike; and worst of all, though that was serious business enough, in the middle of the spread of cards where Kate had laid her shilling, was the picture of a Tower cracked and burning that filled the air with sparks and injury and people falling from it hard.

# I.6

THE OUTHOUSE INTO which Justice Pither showed Crowther and Harriet was low, and too dark for its size to be properly judged. However, it seemed to be made up mostly of unlikely angles. It was as if a once reasonable-sized space had been gradually encroached upon by the surrounding buildings; as if its neighbours had shuffled inwards at various times and from various directions, so the space had been forced to fold in on itself, jutting out a limb, or fragment of wall wherever it could find a space in the press. The floor was earth and the air smelled damp and brown. Both Harriet and Crowther had to stoop a little as they stepped down through the doorway. The only light came from an oil-lamp hanging from a central beam. Below it, on a trestle table, was a human form shrouded in a white linen sheet. The place bred silence.

The sheet used for a covering had soaked up the damp from the corpse, making it limp and heavy, as if a solid slice of river fog had stolen over the man in his sleep and smothered him. Harriet was reminded of the deepest places in a ship after a long voyage. The air here was a little foul, but she could not say if that was the breath from the body or the river water that clung to it. Either way there was an air of contagion about the place. It was a room for things to rot in, forgotten and brooding.

The atmosphere could not still Justice Pither, however. He had done nothing but apologise since their arrival. He continued to do so now, caught between pride at their coming and embarrassment at the cellar-like outhouse into which he had shown them. He was also disposed to treat both Harriet and Crowther with a deference that the former at least found a little grating.

'I do not wish for miracles, sir, madam,' he said, rubbing his hands together. 'But my wife, she is an energetic woman, saw your names in the paper, the Royal Society . . . and of course we had read about last summer . . . and so when this poor fellow was brought along, she suggested we might call on you for your assistance . . . and she was right. We must do what we can, and we would be so glad of your acquaintance.'

Crowther looked down at him. 'Have you been a Justice long, Mr Pither?'

'No, no, sir. That is to say, not so long – three months now. My wife suggested I put myself forward for it – she says London has a great need of righteous men. And I have been reading of what other men in the metropolis have managed in their areas, so I made some modest proposals . . . The Sheriff seemed most willing – then when this . . . and I thought, perhaps if you were at liberty . . . The manner, the supply of Magistrates in this Borough is uneven . . .'

Harriet looked at his rather pinched and narrow face. She guessed he was a man who, no matter the skills of his tailor, would always look rather swamped by his own clothes, but he seemed to her in many ways a cut above the usual Justices in London. The city was not known for the quality of its officers of the law. Only that spring, Mr Burke had, in the House of Commons itself, called the Middlesex Justices who were supposed to administer the law in the city 'the scum of the earth'.

In the countryside, a Justice was expected to be a gentleman, and a figure of some standing in his community. He had powers, and those powers were traded for influence and respect in the rural body of England, but here, in London, the choking and congested heart of an empire, the Justices took another currency. The populace ignored them when they could, and paid them off when they could not. There were exceptions, of course. Since the Fielding brothers had shown what a Magistrate might be in London from their house in Bow Street, the situation had improved, but it was said that barely half the Magistrates of London could write their own name, and the fragile peace of the city still rested on the ancient and ignored Officers of the Watch, the Constables unable to pay their way out of their obligations to the parish, the prosecutions of thief-takers, the rough justice of the crowds, and the occasional intervention of the troops. It seemed that Mr Pither was trying to follow more in the footsteps of the Fieldings than suck up his living in the wake of the other sort of Justice. Harriet might be a little sceptical about his chances of success, but the little man should be encouraged, surely.

'Sir,' she said, with a graceful nod of her head. The man hurrumphed into his cravat and looked pleased. 'You have mentioned the manner in which this body was found, but no specifics. What was unusual?'

A young male voice spoke from the shadows at the back of the little room. 'He was tied.'

Harriet, startled, found herself looking for a moment at the corpse itself. Then from the gloom behind the body two men wearing the red jackets of the Thames Watermen came forward into the little ring of light. The shadows of the room went back a long way.

The man who had spoken looked almost a child, lithe and slender with high cheekbones, and smooth-skinned enough for Harriet to wonder if he was yet out of his teens. Shuffling out of the dark beside him was an older man, bearded and a little stooped though his chest was broad and his hands, held clenched at his sides, looked fearsome enough. Justice Pither waved towards them.

'These are the fellows who brought him in. They run a wherry from the Black Lyon Stairs. This is Proctor, and this his nephew Jackson. I thought perhaps you might wish to speak to them.'

The older man grumbled under his breath, 'Aye, though it keeps us from our trade half the day and there's rent to be earned. Regular passengers of ours crossing the river in our rivals' boats.'

Harriet looked directly at him, her eyes frowning. 'I know you, Proctor.'

He smiled and kept looking at his boots, saying, 'Why, you're as good as your husband for a face, Mrs Westerman. I would not have spoken, but I served with the Captain when he was nothing but a scrap of a lad, and he touched his hat to me a few times in Gibraltar when you were there and on his arm, and looking as pretty a thing as ever man got hold of.'

Harriet's eyes brightened. 'Of course! James told me you stood between him and a whipping once.'

Proctor laughed, a great throaty rumble from his belly. 'I did, I did. Told you that, did he? He returned the favour in time.' He cleared his throat and examined the earth floor with great concentration.

41

'Sorry to hear he's gone a bit . . .' He touched his hand to his forehead. 'We've been grieving for you and the little ones up and down the river. Us that know him.'

Harriet found she could not speak, but she nodded.

'So tell us then,' Crowther asked. 'How was this man tied?'

The younger man stepped forward and flicked the bottom end of the sheet up the body a little brutally, letting them see a pair of sodden white stockings and the start of the pale breeches above them. The ankles were bound together with rope the thickness of a thumb. Its long end had been neatly curled across the dead man's shins when he had been laid on the table, rather than cut free or left trailing on the earth floor. Harriet's mind flickered with images of ropes coiled on the decks of her husband's commands. She believed a sailor would stop to neaten any piece of loose stuff like that, even if he saw it in a burning house. The stockings dripped onto the floor.

'See for yourself,' Jackson said. 'The other end of the rope was tied to something heavy enough to hold him against the tide. Meant to hold him under, I reckon, though if it was meant to hide him too, it did a poor job in the end. We spotted him from the bank just after dawn. You could see wig and coat enough to guess it was a man.'

Proctor put his head on one side and pulled at his beard. 'Another three, maybe four yards out towards the middle of the river and we'd never have seen him till the fish were done feasting. Tide is a monster on the Thames. Where he was stuck, he would have been covered by ten feet at high water. Funny rope too.' Crowther lifted his eyebrows and Proctor pulled harder on his beard. 'It's braided. Not laid.' Harriet nodded, and Proctor met her eye, satisfied to see she had understood. 'I've not seen it used much on the river, that's all I'm saying.'

'Thank you, Proctor,' Crowther said. 'May I ask if you found anything on this man's body? And how did you know his name?'

The two men in front of him looked rather uncomfortable. It was Proctor who replied.

'His pockets were empty, and there was no fancy stuff on him. As

42

to his name, some woman in the crowd spoke it, but she was gone before she said any more. I don't know this fella. Can't have much business across the river, or far along it, or we'd have seen the face, I'd reckon.'

Crowther nodded. 'Very well, and thank you.' Then, turning to his host he added, 'And thank you, Mr Pither. You may all leave us with the body.'

The three men shuffled out, but as he passed her, Proctor put his hand out and Harriet felt it close with gentle pressure on her arm. She looked up into his face and saw her own history of foreign waters and winds behind his eyes. It was only a moment, and he was gone, ushered back out into the yard by Mr Pither, who looked, beside him, like a pilot fish trying to shepherd a whale.

## I.7

IN JOCASTA BLIGH'S early days in Town, when she worked in the Rose and Grape tavern in the thick of the city, she'd lived in rooms shared with ten others where the banisters were stolen to feed the feeble fires of the residents. A hard place to keep yourself to yourself if that was what you wished, though Jocasta had managed it. Then the cards had arrived, whistling and chattering into her life.

They had come to her by accident or chance, as most things do. She'd discovered them, a little greasy and torn, wrapped in a newspaper, in a dingy corner of the dingy bar where she earned enough pennies to keep from starving. She kept them about her, thinking their owner might come back and ask for them, but a month later no one had done so, and she had grown to like looking through the pictures of strange people, the designs that looked like playing cards, but weren't. Cups and swords, coins and clubs; men, women, stars and angels. Then a seed-merchant, a Frenchman, had spotted her dealing them to herself in a quiet moment when the publican wasn't hovering, and had some talk with her. The cards were known in his country, he said, people used them to tell fortunes, and for a week he found her out every night and told her more; the meanings he gave to the pictures, and how to lay down the cards so their messages bled into each other to make new stories. It was like mixing wines, he told her. One card lay next to another, and some new thing emerged that tasted like neither, only existing where they joined.

The regulars thought for a while that the 'Northern Fortress', – what they called her in those days – might have been breached. But there was nothing in that. Jocasta learned; the seed-merchant completed his business in London and left; and she was there with her picture cards and a little hope.

The drinkers heard and asked, so she started telling fortunes for the people who drifted through the bar, getting them to lay down the cards and turn them over. People began to seek her out, scraping up pennies and the occasional shilling to have her tell them what she heard in the pictures till she found herself with enough chink in her pockets to take this room and leave off working for others. Twenty years ago now that was. Twenty years of pretty comfortable with a candle. Men she avoided, but for the last ten years she'd had Boyo. She was grateful, and when she had walked her feet off to arrive in London, having abandoned her home of mountains and lakes, she had never expected to feel like that again.

Not happy though. Every now and again, just when you were feeling a little too at ease, the cards had a habit of tapping you sharp-like on the shoulder and reminding you there was a price to be paid still. She did not like having to know some of the things they insisted on telling her. There had been a knock or two at the door since Kate Mitchell went off, but Jocasta hadn't moved from her place or shifted the lay she had made for the young woman.

Jocasta looked hard at the cards till her head began to ache. All Swords. A dark woman. The Magician with his sticks and balls laid out before him, upside down. The Moon all sick and fading, The

Hermit with his lantern and stick like the watchman up in Seven Dials – it was so like the man you'd have said they'd used him as a model. Then The Tower. Most of the cards could be kind or vicious with their predictions, depending on how they fell and what conversations they had with their place or the other cards near them. The Tower she'd never seen as anything but angry, though.

She smelled the sea again. She'd only seen it the once, but she remembered the stink. Then she got again that smoky smell, and these lies. Not the normal man∕woman lies, not the kind ones or the cruel, or the words you just let slip that might be true when you say them but are lies as soon as sunlight hits them. Those lies she saw in the cards all the time, but these were others. She put her head on one side and screwed up her eyes. Had the thing been done? Was there still any stopping of it? That the cards would not tell her.

Once, when she was just beginning to turn the cards for other people in the tavern and winter was making the roads more dirty and foul than ever, a man had asked to have his fortune read as a lark with his friends. She'd laid them out and looked up into his square red face, and blurted out that he would be dead before the year's end. He'd stopped laughing, but asked her how, all the time acting like he was paying no mind to it. Again, without a thought she told him he'd be hung, and he pushed his way out of the bar and onto the streets in a rage. His friends had thought it all fine entertainment and given her more than she usually asked for in coins, then followed him out. The next day the whole street was alive with the story, and Jocasta felt ashamed. The day after, news reached them that the man had been taken up by one of the thief∕takers, was a known highwayman and was likely to be at Tyburn before the end of the month.

Jocasta immediately became famous in the parish and found herself dealing cards a dozen times a day. She'd been to the execution, saw the cart bringing the man from Newgate with the priest beside him and the crowd cheering. She was sure he'd noticed her in the mass of people, and nodded to her. The crowd loved him. He went bravely with his head up. Jocasta spent two pennies on a pamphlet of his last confession and got a boy who'd been to the charity school to read it to her. The wood-cut didn't look much like him, and the words, though entertaining in their account of his terrible crimes, didn't sound as if they came from his mouth. Jocasta couldn't watch the drop; just heard it, the clap of the opening trapdoor in that moment of stillness, then the roar of the crowd. She had felt sick and wouldn't read cards for a week. Then she got hungry.

With a growl she swept the cards up again and sat them in their box. Another knock came at the door, and this time she answered it.

When Harriet folded back the damp sheet from the corpse, she found herself being oddly precise about her movements. She was aware that Crowther was, for the time being, still more engaged in watching her than looking at the body.

'Crowther, I am quite well. I have heard more hurtful words about my husband's current condition than those Proctor just used, and with less care and respect in them.'

Her companion did no more than nod, but it seemed the reassurance was sufficient. He continued to lay his knives and hooks on the bench in front of him.

'I must be a little more subtle in my arts here, than we were in Thornleigh,' he said. 'The cut throat on the body you used then as an introduction to myself was a more obvious cause of death than drowning.'

Harriet smiled a little at his characterisation of their meeting. She had bullied her way into his house, she had forced him to place himself in danger, she had caused his most private griefs to become public, yet they had developed between them a friendship that was as valuable to her as the love of her own family.

Since the events of the previous summer he had become a regular companion in her house in Caveley. He would arrive unannounced when the mood took him – or, if he had taken delivery of some

46

exciting preparation or curiosity, they would not see him for a week. She missed him greatly at these times, though she would never admit it, or tease him for ignoring them when he returned. To Harriet's younger, orphaned sister Rachel, he took the role of an uncle, encouraging her, tolerating her, or ignoring her depending on his mood and Rachel's choice of conversation. To her children he also stood something like an uncle. He did not join in their games, but would answer any question her son could think of to ask, until, when he grew tired of the circling logic of a seven year old, he would declare himself hungry and in need of a child to eat, whereupon Stephen would scream with delight and run from the room . . .

Crowther's dry voice broke in on her thoughts. 'So, Mrs Westerman, what do we see at first?'

Shaking herself, Harriet turned towards the body and looked into the dead eyes for the first time.

He was an elderly gentleman, she thought, something older than Crowther. The slight stubble on his face was white, and the flesh of his face was loose and lined. His eyes were grey and his jaw hung open as a man who has been suddenly, unpleasantly, surprised in the midst of a laugh. His limbs were thin, though not malnourished, the nails of his hands neatly and close clipped to the pads of the fingers. She felt their texture. His throat was hidden by a sodden cravat, but there was a red mark high under his jaw on his left side. It did not seem a bruise or tearing of the skin.

As Harriet tilted the man's chin towards her to better examine it, she realised there was something not quite right about the shape of his mouth. Gently retracting the man's upper lip, she saw that his teeth were false, but not made of the usual animal bone or carved and stinking wood. Easing them loose, she passed them to Crowther without comment and he lifted them to examine them more closely under the light of the oil-lamp.

'How very strange,' he said.

'He is of an age, Crowther.'

Crowther did not reply at once, but turned the dentures over in the light, then flicked them with his fingernail. They gave a dull chime like a teacup awkwardly placed on its saucer.

'No, Mrs Westerman. I am not surprised that he required false teeth at his age, or was vain enough to wear them, but these are most unusual. They have been cast of porcelain. I have never seen such things before. A really most ingenious idea. And a rarity. We must make enquiries.' He smiled contentedly and Harriet shook her head a little. Crowther's enthusiasm was not often provoked, but when it was, it tended to be by the most unusual things.

Their examination of the body was methodical. The rope and knot were first scrutinised, then the man's ankles were unbound, his clothing removed and each piece passed between them before being folded and placed on the bench beside the teeth. The man could afford to dress like a gentleman, but all his pockets were empty.

His skin was marked, discoloured in several places, but removing his cravat and exposing the throat had exposed a pattern of bruising that made Harriet draw in her breath. Moving forward, she put her hands, thumbs crossed, on the cold flesh over the Adam's apple, trying to stretch her fingers to reach the marks, then had a sudden sharp vision of it living under her, struggling to breathe, a wet rattling gasp. She sprang away from it and shivered. Thoughts of her husband reared in her mind like agitated mud at the bottom of a pond, then fell back.

'That certainly seems consistent with the bruising', Crowther said. 'If he were throttled, we are likely to find damage to the hyoid bone.'

Harriet remained with her face in shadow. 'Could a woman do that, Crowther?' she asked.

'Mrs Westerman, I am quite convinced that some women can do anything.' He paused, and added in a more measured way, 'Many women would have the strength to kill a man in this manner. Certainly.'

At last Crowther turned towards his knives, and looked enquiringly at his companion. She did not return his gaze at once, but stood with her shoulders tilted and her head on one side, gazing at the poor naked being in front of her. He looked so frail and waxen on the table in the spill of the lamp that she felt a sadness flow up from the cold ground under her feet.

There were times when she hated the brutal honesty of flesh. The body was marked and bruised in places other than the face and neck; odd red, angry patches that seemed to glow out against the general pallor of the skin.

Harriet let her mind clear and her eyes rest on that strange red mark under his chin. It sparked some memory, some trace of thought in her, but the idea would not form itself into a notion she could put into words.

'Shall I make the first cut, madam?'

Since their first meeting, Harriet had only once seen Crowther perform a full autopsy, and that had been on the corpse of a cat. It was known to the members of the reading public, and now to the fellows of the Royal Society, that she had attended Crowther in his examinations of other unfortunates, but they did not perhaps realise how limited, in some ways, those examinations had been. The business of pulling open a corpse was a brutal art; slippery and foul-smelling. It required a scientist to become a butcher, and a gentleman to redden his cuffs with gore and bile.

By way of answer she sat down on the bench a little removed into the shadows, crossed her hands in her lap and settled herself, to show she meant to remain where she was as Crowther went to work with his knives. He adjusted the lamp and lifted his scalpel, which caught a gleam.

'Crowther? Did you examine your father's body after his murder?'

Crowther went still.

'I did not, Mrs Westerman. The Baron had already been buried before I could return from London. And my brother was in custody. The local Justice greeted me with a record of his confession. He later retracted it, of course. But I saw only fear of the noose in that action.'

'Your brother was tried in the House of Lords.'

'He was. The execution was public. I attended both.'

Harriet looked at his profile. His words had been fluent, but he seemed frozen now in his place. She thought it was likely the man on the trestle was of an age of Crowther's father when he was killed. Leaning forward, she placed her forehead in her palm.

'I am sorry I asked you such a thing, Crowther. Whatever tact I had, I seem to have lost in these last months.'

Silently acknowledging her words, and placing the sharpened steel on the dead flesh, Crowther made his first cut.

Justice Pither had had an uncomfortable afternoon's watch. Twice he stepped into his backyard and raised his fist at the door of the old stable to offer assistance or refreshment; and twice he lost his nerve and retreated without knocking to take up his position in his study again, rereading the familiar passages of his handbook for the duties and dues of a Justice of the Peace. Despite his vigilance, however, when the door to his study finally opened and Mrs Westerman stepped into the room, he was surprised enough to drop his glasses, and thought himself for a moment in danger of stepping on them. But Mrs Westerman did not come with enlightenment. She merely requested ink and paper and the use of one of his servants as message boy. Her note written and put into his servant's hands, she turned to leave the room again.

'Do you,' Mr Pither enquired, leaning with one hand on the inconveniently low desk, and in a tone which he hoped both invited confidence and inspired trust, 'require anything . . . er . . . further?'

Harriet considered, her head on one side.

'No. Thank you.' Then she was gone.

Another half-hour or so passed, and Mr Pither heard his street door opening and closing again before a rather young man was shown in by the servant who had taken the message. He was a good-looking sort of fellow, rather thin and tall, and his dress was elegant even if his movements seemed a little uncertain, and his cravat rather sloppily tied. In the few moments he was in Pither's presence he was in danger of dropping his hat twice. Pither offered the gentleman a seat. The offer was declined.

'I am Owen Graves,' he said. 'Mr Crowther and Mrs Westerman sent for me. Where might I find them?'

Mr Pither recognised the name, of course. This young man was guardian to the great estates of the Earl of Sussex, and also of the young Earl himself. He struggled for a moment to think of a phrase that would fix him in this important gentleman's mind as a coming man of intelligence and wit, but failed, and could do no more than show his new guest out through the back door of the house and indicate the old stable. As Mr Graves bowed and stepped forward, Mr Pither retreated and began to wonder if there was food in the house sufficient to feed all these people.

He did not have long to count up his stores, for within ten minutes of the arrival of this Mr Graves, all three of his guests had presented themselves in his study once more. Mr Crowther had something of a glint in his eye, Mr Graves looked merely serious and Mrs Westerman calm, though there was something in her movements as she entered the room that suggested rather more vigour in her person than there had been on her arrival. Mr Pither thought her rather handsome and wondered how it would feel to walk through Hyde Park on a Sunday with her on his arm, telling her of the wrongs he had righted during his week and receiving her respectful praise.

'Well, Crowther, do not keep poor Mr Pither in suspense any longer,' she said.

Crowther looked up at the Justice from under his heavy lids and nodded. 'Very well. Mr Pither, the man presently in your outhouse was strangled, not drowned. Probably some time yesterday. He is indeed called Fitzraven – Nathaniel Fitzraven, in fact – and our friend Mr Graves here informs us he had been a professional violin player. Of late years, the arthritis building in his hands had forced him to become more of an assistant to the management of His Majesty's Theatre in Hay Market, also known as His Majesty's Opera House.'

'Really? A violinist? The Opera House? Oh, I see.' Mr Pither was at a loss.

'Also,' Harriet added with a smile, 'after he was throttled, Mr Fitzraven was left on his back for some hours before being thrown into the river.'

Justice Pither's jaw worked uncomfortably for a few moments. 'But how can you possibly know such things?'

Crowther settled back into his seat to explain, but was cut off by a wave from Mrs Westerman.

'No, sir, please allow me. You shall say everything in Latin and in detail that would stop a decent man from enjoying his dinner.' Mr Crowther blinked but did not protest. Mrs Westerman continued, counting her points on her fingertips and sounding for all the world as if she were rattling off an order to her grocer: 'He has bruises to his throat, and the hyoid bone is broken, thus, strangulation. As to the movement of the body – when a person dies their blood does not freeze, but like water tries to find the lowest level it can and congeals there.'

Mr Pither looked a little nauseous, but nodded bravely. Harriet smiled at him encouragingly and went on, 'Mr Crowther has been instructing me in the matter this afternoon. I now pass on the knowledge to you, sir. Mr Fitzraven has patches on his back that suggest he was lying flat for some hours before he was thrown in the river. Some blood also gathered in his feet, as the process was not complete when he went into the water. He was wearing a rather fine coat. The air trapped in it held him upright from his tether. As to his full name and profession, we noticed a mark on his neck I remember seeing on friends of Mr Graves here, who are violinists by trade, then it was a simple matter to ask him to come here as he knows every fiddle player in London.' She gave him a bright smile and folded her hands again in her lap.

After a moment's pause, while Justice Pither attempted to absorb the information so cheerfully flung down before him, he asked hopefully, 'And who killed him?'

'That we cannot know,' Crowther said dryly. 'Mr Graves here can furnish you with his address.' The party began to stand. Justice Pither scrambled to his feet.

'But please . . . I . . . Mr Crowther, Mrs Westerman. Do not desert me! Please tell me you intend to look further into this matter. My duties . . . I cannot investigate this poor man's death in any satisfactory way myself.' At that moment, in the street, and with a deplorable lack of respect for the solemnity of the moment, a rather harsh-voiced person started yelling that they had mackerel for sale. Harriet and Crowther were looking at each other. 'Surely, you have a duty . . .' the Justice said pitiably. 'Mr Graves, please help me to persuade them.'

Graves looked between the Justice and Mrs Westerman. 'I believe that, in doing what they have already done, my friends have more than fulfilled their duty,' he said. 'Beyond this point, their chances of success are no greater than yours.'

Justice Pither looked distressed. 'I beg you, sir, madam!' His shoulders slumped and he looked at the table in front of him, at his little leather volumes, and said more quietly, 'But I have nothing to offer you. I have no influence, no connections to compare with those which you already enjoy in your own rights. I know most people in this city think me a fool for trying to see the laws enforced, the guilty punished and so on.' He sighed. 'You are right, Mr Graves.' He drew himself straight, trying to be brave. 'Thank you, Mr Crowther, Mrs Westerman, for your valued assistance. I shall do my best – place the proper advertisements and so on. I am most grateful to you both for telling me so much about this unhappy wretch.'

There was a long pause. Mr Pither could hear Mrs Westerman's gloved fingers beating a tattoo on the cloth of her dress, and some part of him began to hope.

'Oh dear,' said Harriet at last. 'Now you have made us your allies in a way all the influence in the world could not. Do you not fear it to be so, Mr Crowther?'

'I do, Mrs Westerman,' that gentleman replied.

Pither almost shook with relief. Harriet offered him her hand and he snatched it up in both of his own, his total confidence in their abilities shining out from him.

'Thank you.'

Harriet patted his hand and released herself with a slight wince. 'We shall regret it, I imagine. I hope you shall not, sir. We are at your service.' She glanced at the clock on Mr Pither's mantel. 'Or at least we shall be so in the morning. The dinner-hour approaches and Mr Graves's house keeps careful hours.'

Graves took advantage of the carriage trip returning them to Berkeley Square to tell them what he could of Nathaniel Fitzraven, musician. It became clear at once that he had not liked the man, and as Graves seemed to like and value most people to a degree Harriet found frustrating, she had pushed him for his reasons and impressions. He had spoken haltingly at first, watching the damp, darkening streets pass by through the carriage window. He shivered.

'He liked to pretend intimate knowledge of his betters. He played in the band of His Majesty's Theatre for some years and the association with the singers and patrons there was a tonic to him. To hear him speak, you would have thought him the confidant of every music-lover of note in the city. Then his talents began to desert him; his fingers stiffened to the point he could no longer perform what was required.'

'The swelling of the joints was not extreme,' Crowther said, his eyebrows raised.

Graves looked down at his own young hands for a moment, then hid them in his pockets. 'It does not need to be extreme to lose a musician his livelihood. He managed to wheedle himself back into the employ of the Opera House, however. Perhaps the manager there,

Mr Harwood, pitied him. This year and last he was running errands for them, and acting as if he was Harwood's right-hand man. He bought last season's selections to be made up into songbooks.' Graves, among his other responsibilities, also managed a small music shop in Tichfield Street, a much less fashionable part of Town. He continued: 'I did not like the way he treated the children. As soon as their true lineage and worth was acknowledged, he became ingratiating. My heart sank if they were keeping me company in the shop and he entered on some pretext or other. I am sure he told everyone he stood like an uncle to them.'

Harriet smiled gently at him as she pulled her cloak more tightly round her throat. 'Lord Thornleigh and Lady Susan know who their friends are, Graves.'

The young man shrugged his shoulders. 'Susan does, I think. But Jonathan is still very young. However, whatever my doubts about Fitzraven, Harwood placed great trust in him this summer. He sent Fitzraven to the continent to recruit singers for the current season. Fitzraven came back bristling with pride, and looking rather sleek. He had engaged Isabella Marin in Milan and, indeed, this new castrato of whom such praises are spoken – Manzerotti. They say he is the greatest singer to come to London since Gasparo Pacchierotti's debut of seventy-seven. One of my customers heard him at a party in Devonshire House some days ago and was all but overcome.'

Harriet and Crowther must have looked a little blank at the names. The noise of London was crashing in on them through the windows of the carriage as it bullied its way along Cockspur through horses, carts and bobbing sedan chairs in the gathering dark. The carriage wheels spat mud up the doors as they jostled between ruts, the light had bled out of the day and already the shadows were deepening and the colours folding in on themselves. A pieman, his tray almost empty, chucked the last of his wares to a group of dirty-looking boys who had been following him down the road. After a brief struggle the strongest of them emerged in victory and held his prize high above the heads of the others. He tore pieces of the misshapen pastry off and stuffed them into his mouth, while keeping the rest out of the reach of his mewling, begging band and their long skinny fingers. Hawkers and song-sellers walked by them shouting out their produce and prices, occasionally running a casual, assessing eye over the carriage, which here at least moved scarcely faster than they did, and over its occupants. A girl, no more than fourteen, but already pox-marked and old in her expression, peered in and whistled at Graves, then noticing Harriet winked at her, and with a swing of her hips was gone. Graves was too busy marvelling at his companions' expressions to notice her.

'Really, Crowther, Mrs Westerman,' he said, 'you are educated people but your ignorance of music is astonishing.'

Harriet looked very serious. 'Forgive us, Graves! We are new to the capital, and I was in the East Indies in seventy-seven and Crowther was in—?'

Crowther looked up from his fingernails. 'Oh, I was in London. And I went to a concert or two, but my occupations were in general less polite.' And when Graves looked enquiringly at him, Crowther met his gaze and said very evenly, 'I was cutting up dead people.'

Graves cleared his throat and crossed his legs.

'Then, Graves, my dear boy, you must educate us.' Harriet smiled and folded her arms. 'Who is this Manzerotti? And who is Isabella Marin?'

Graves leaned forward with a sudden enthusiasm that reminded Harriet that, for all his cares and responsibilities, he was still not yet twenty-five.

'Manzerotti is said to be the greatest soprano castrato living. He is much spoken of. It is a marvellous thing to have him in London! They say that with both him and Marin in the company, the serious opera or "opera seria" could equal the success of *Creso* in seventy-seven, and there were *sixteen* performances that season.' He sat back again with the air of having delivered a startling revelation.

Crowther exchanged a glance with Harriet, and lifted his eyebrows, murmuring, 'Is that good?'

Graves gave an exasperated sigh 'It is remarkable! An opera is judged a great success if it manages a dozen performances. And Isabella Marin! Her name is pure gold on the continent, and it is her first appearance on the English stage. It is a sensation.'

Harriet pulled absent-mindedly on one of her red curls of hair, saying, 'Are there no English singers who can hold a tune? Why did Harwood need to send Fitzraven to the continent to recruit? Are we not at war with most of our neighbours over there?'

'Art knows no boundaries and borders,' Graves said a little stiffly, then, throwing his body back into the corner of the coach and smiling, 'but it is partly fashion. We English love to see something new at the opera. I think bringing in singers from hundreds of miles away to serenade us makes us feel more important. What is nearby is necessarily unexceptional.'

He looked up and to his right into the dark of the carriage. Harriet could tell he was imagining the sound of this Manzerotti's voice in the private auditorium of his mind. Then, coming to himself and noticing the streets outside, he said, 'We are nearly arrived. I hope you dine with us this evening, Mr Crowther.'

Mr Crowther bowed and the carriage came to a halt.

Mr Crowther was not a regular guest at dinner in Berkeley Square, however he thought it might be politic not to return to his own rented house as yet. He had been late at work the previous night; indeed, dawn had already begun to cough at the windows when he ceased his examination of small lesions on the brain of a young man who had died of a seizure. It had been a fascinating study, but he was not entirely confident that he had tidied away all his samples before retiring at last to bed. If he had been remiss it was likely the maid would have been thrown into hysterics by the discovery of part of a brain in a jar and left her post. He had lost two maids in this way since coming to London, and his housekeeper, Hannah, though loyal, had limits to her patience. He hoped to avoid the punishment of a bad dinner by taking a seat at Graves's table. However although the food was excellent, the table was so crowded with good-humour he feared his digestion might still suffer.

Mr Gabriel Crowther was not known for his sociability. Indeed, when the Royal Society invited him to address them it had been more out of respect, than in expectation that he would accept. But he *had* accepted. It was Mr Crowther who had, in September of this year and after careful correspondence, found and recommended Dr Trevelyan's establishment as a suitable place for James Westerman to be confined. It was Mr Crowther who had written to Graves to advise him of the matter, and his letter that had prompted the family's warm invitation to Harriet and her family to treat their establishment as their home while James was resident in Highgate. Mr Crowther had rarely done so much for any other human being. The reward for his unusual activity was to discover in a distressingly short time that he missed the society of the ladies of Caveley, so when the invitation from the Royal Society at Somerset House arrived he drew up a list of reasons why it would be advantageous to spend time in London, and ordered his housekeeper to make the necessary preparations.

His welcome in Berkeley Square had been warm, and he was forced to admit he had been glad to see them all. However, he had not lost his habits of silence and isolation completely. A noisy table of young people could still feel something of a trial. Lady Susan was giving her guardian an account of her day which included a cruelly accurate impersonation of her Italian master. Miss Rachel Trench, Harriet's younger sister, was trying hard to interest her sibling with an account of some wallpapers she had seen, and which she thought might be suitable for the salon in their country house of Caveley. Graves was torn between listening to Susan and preventing his jugged hare from escaping over the edge of his plate. The candles blazed and the footmen went to and fro setting down dishes or taking them away, and Stephen and Lord Thornleigh were competing to entertain the table with their story of a dead rat in the cellar and their plans for the corpse in various schemes to terrify the maids.

At the head of the table, the personification of calm good grace, sat Mrs Beatrice Service. Her dress was modest and neat, and her grey curls were pinned up neatly under a white cap. Her eyes suggested she found the world an amusing and pleasant place in general. When Owen Graves had taken on the task of constructing a proper household in which these two ennobled orphans, Lord Thornleigh and Lady Susan, might grow, he naturally turned to those who had already shown themselves to be their friends in their time of poverty and obscurity. Mrs Service was such a one. She had lived in the street where the children were born, and had known both their parents. A poor widow, albeit a gentleman's daughter, she had passed her days quietly starving and trying not to cause any difficulty for anyone in the process. Now she lived with Jonathan, Susan and their guardian as friend and companion in Berkeley Square. She had a box at the opera, good food when she wanted it, and thought herself a very lucky woman.

There was an element of the governess about Mrs Service's role, though Susan had masters who visited the house to instruct her in music and, despite her early reluctance, French and Italian, but there was never any question among the household as to her status. Mrs Service was counsellor to Graves; she held the keys to the store cupboards; the housekeeper came to her for directions, and she acted as a sort of honorary grandmother to the children. She was by nature retiring, but her principles were sound and held with conviction, so if she ever had cause to speak to Susan about the propriety of her behaviour, her words carried great force, and were attended to. Just now, she gave the Earl of Sussex a mild look and the speeches about the rat came to an abrupt halt. In the little silvered moment of silence that followed she asked Mr Crowther how he had occupied his day.

'Mrs Westerman and myself have been recruited to investigate a murder, Mrs Service,' he replied.

The silver silence became something harder, and the room seemed to still. Graves put his fork down and said, 'Susan, Jonathan. I am afraid Mr Fitzraven, the gentleman from the His Majesty's Theatre, has been killed.'

The children were silent a moment, till Jonathan, looking up at Crowther under his pale lashes, asked in a small voice, 'Was he stabbed, sir?'

Crowther watched him carefully as he replied, 'No, Lord Thornleigh. He was strangled and thrown into the river.'

Lord Thornleigh nodded. He had, Crowther surmised, been thinking of his own father's death; it seemed his sister's thoughts followed a similar trajectory.

Susan looked up at her guardian. 'Graves, did he have any children? He never mentioned any.'

Graves reached out his hand to touch her hair. 'No, my love. He was alone in the world. That is why Mr Crowther and Mrs Westerman must try to give him some justice.'

The argument, Crowther thought, sounded a little weak. He and Harriet had already agreed that Mr Palmer's role in the case should not be known to anyone else in the household. It would seem to involve unnecessary risk to all concerned. However, noticing as he did now the tightening of the muscles round Miss Rachel Trench's jaw, he wished his conscience would let him be more frank. He then became aware that Lady Thornleigh was looking at him with wide and thoughtful eyes.

'You are going to find out who killed Mr Fitzraven, then? I am glad.' Her glance returning to the plate in front of her; the little girl chased some morsel of meat through its gravy with her fork like a god idly steering ships onto rocks or towards treasure. 'Though he was never very nice to me till I became rich. Then he smiled much too much. Before then he used to just ignore us and try and impress Father with talk of the opera. Isn't it foolish to like someone just because someone else has died and left them money and things?'

He nodded. 'Yes, my dear. Very foolish.'

Rachel stood up rather suddenly. 'I had thought you in better spirits this evening, Harriet. I hope this new adventure is not the reason for that. Forgive me, Mrs Service, I have a sudden headache. I fear you must excuse me.'

Mrs Service nodded to her pleasantly. Harriet rested her forehead on her fingertips and closed her eyes. Graves merely looked serious.

'Mr Crowther, I think you have not tried the salmon,' Mrs Service said. 'Let me help you to some.'

As she was so employed she continued, 'Mr Graves, Susan and I were planning on attending the opening night of the season at the Italian Opera. It is tomorrow, you know. I hope Miss Trench will join us. Will you come with us also, as part of your . . . investigations?'

Mr Crowther looked at the pink flesh of the fish in front of him, the buttered pastry flaking around it, and found his appetite, always light, was gone.

'I believe we will be at His Majesty's rather before that, Mrs Service. And of course, Mrs Westerman and I would not wish to expose you or the children to any scenes that might be awkward, or unpleasant.'

'Of course not,' Harriet echoed rather wearily.

Mrs Service smiled and beckoned the footman behind her to remove her plate.

# PART II

## II.1

*Saturday, 17 November 1781, London*

JOCASTA SNIFFED AND adjusted her shawl around her shoulders. The fire was going well enough now to drive out any shred of the London fog from the room; her breakfast had been eaten and tidied away and Boyo had had the fat of the chop. She should have been happy as a cat in a blanket, but there was an itching at the back of her neck. She looked down at Boyo. He scratched behind his ears and then licked his mouth with a smack.

'Don't you be looking at me like that, Boyo.' Jocasta sniffed again and put up her chin. 'There's some as can't be told and that's all of it.'

Boyo sneezed.

'I know, I know. There's trouble there and it's a big thick sort of trouble, and that sort of trouble spills. But why should we go looking for it? Best way to avoid getting caught in it is to step away, not step towards. Just because every time you see a big pile of muck you go jumping into it doesn't mean I have to do the same.'

The fire cracked in the grate. Boyo whined a little. Jocasta narrowed her eyes.

'Boyo! You are as foolish a dog as I ever knew. A good dog should look after his mistress, not encourage her into all sorts of worry. The cards are saying one thing's done, and another is following sure as

63

Tuesday follows after Monday night, so what would you have me do!'

She was looking fierce at the little dog now, though it didn't seem to bother him greatly. He sat down smartly and scratched behind his ears again.

'Yes, I could talk to her again. See if she'll listen, but she won't. No woman with a mouth that shape or an eye that blue ever listened to anyone other than the man she's tied to. You know it. Only three months married. No, she won't listen till she's run through six.'

Boyo made no answer. 'And in November. Who knows how much of the day we might have to wait in the cold? And it'll be dark early. And you'll be keening to be back indoors again within the hour. I know it sure as I know Mrs Peterson waters the milk and Granger sells meat that could walk out of the shop itself.' She paused, then stood suddenly and raised a finger at the terrier. He jumped up and began to dance in little circles on the hearthrug.

'Well, on your own head be it, lad. Trouble and more trouble and we must go ferreting it out as if it's all fun and skittles. I give you a fire and fat, but will you stay still and like it? Not a chance, not a hope of it this side of Judgement.'

She tied the shawl fiercely in a great knot and put her hand to the latch. Boyo tilted his head to one side and waited. With a sigh she pulled it open.

'Well. Awez then!'

'What is it, Mrs Westerman?'

'I don't believe I spoke, Crowther.'

'Sometimes your silences are speaking.'

The carriage was carrying them briskly along Piccadilly and Harriet had been admiring the passing mansions with her chin in her hand. It was possible that she might have sighed.

'I still do not feel we can share Mr Palmer's secrets with anyone at Berkeley Square,' she said.

'I quite agree.'

'Yet I cannot help thinking, did you not sense there was something of a mood of unhappiness at the table when you spoke about Fitzraven and our agreement to help Justice Pither?'

He smiled at seeing the spark in her eye. 'Perhaps a little. One could characterise it as an affectionate concern, perhaps.'

Harriet arched her eyebrows. 'Yes, I suppose one might, Crowther. But that is not what troubles my conscience the most. I feel I must confess it is likely that had Mr Palmer not called, had the note arrived from Mr Pither without introduction, I should probably have found myself in that outhouse and driving with you to His Majesty's this morning in any case.'

'I see, madam. You feel you are become the monstrous and unfeminine ghoul some have already made you out to be, and you feel Miss Trench does not approve?'

'My sister made it perfectly plain to the whole house that she does not approve, yet I feel neither monstrous nor less a woman than I was two years ago.' She turned towards him and folded her arms. 'I will do what seems right to me, but I have to allow that Rachel has a better sense of social niceties than I do, just as her sense of music is superior to mine. I make myself appear foolish at times, and that reflects on my family.'

'Miss Trench has wished you to have something other to think of than your husband's illness, madam.'

Harriet smiled a little unhappily. 'Yes, Crowther, but I think she would rather I was diverted by her plans for redecorating the salon at Caveley than by whatever corpses we find strewn in our way.'

'She must accept the sister she has, Mrs Westerman. I can only hope she does not raise your temper by suggesting you should behave in any other fashion. I have noticed you are at your most sharp when you suspect you are in the wrong.'

'I shall put it down to your influence, and you shall shoulder her disapproval for me.'

'I would if I were able, madam, but I fear Miss Trench will not be diverted. She is quite as stubborn as yourself in her way.'

This time Harriet certainly did sigh.

When at last they exited the carriage in the middle of Hay Market, Harriet looked up at the simple frontage of His Majesty's Theatre with curiosity. She was no great admirer of the opera herself, though she had found it pleasant enough the few times she had attended such performances on the continent. She knew, however, that many of the most fashionable and most influential men and women in England proclaimed the opera a marvel and cast themselves into this place like the devotees of some new religion scrambling for a seat near an altar. The King and his family were indeed often entertained here, as were many hundreds of his subjects in the course of a season. On Saturdays and Wednesdays from November until Easter they would tumble in from their carriages with high expectations and strong opinions. They paid their twenty guieneas for a box for the season, then came to look at each other and admire the diversions the management gave them in dance and song. Indeed, as well as confirming one's idea of oneself as a creature of elegant tastes, the operas often provided great spectacle. One might see gods and ancient warriors here, beasts and men flying through the air, armies of chariots crossing the stage, storms and summer days recreated on its grand platform. It was as if all places in the world and all history were gathered roughly up, set to music and squeezed into the theatre behind this simple frontage to be poured down the throats of the crowd like the pap fed to infants.

When Harriet woke from her thoughts, she saw that Crowther was reading a notice pinned neatly to the wall by the closed theatre gates. He felt her attention on him, and read aloud: "'The owners of His Majesty's Theatre are pleased to announce the first performance of a new opera with music by several eminent composers, under the direction of Mr Bywater. *Julius Rex* will be performed tonight, seventeenth

November 1781. Primo Umo, Sengor Manzerotti, Prima Donna Mademoiselle Marin". There are also several other names.'

He stooped forward a little to better read the printing. 'Ah, they will be providing three ballets between the acts, also. And the scenery is new painted.' Looking up at the theatre, he went on, 'What a costly business we make of entertaining ourselves. Well, Mrs Westerman, shall we go in and deliver the sad news of the demise of Fitzraven to the management here? Though from what Graves has said, I'd be surprised to notice much genuine grief.'

His eyes scanned the frontage, the firmly bolted outer doors through which the pleasure-seekers of London would pour during the evening. 'The front door does not look very likely an entrance. Let us find another way into this Temple of Art, madam. One often learns so much more by approaching a place from an unexpected direction.'

## II.2

HARRIET AND CROWTHER were lucky in the moment and direction they chose. Final preparations for the evening's performance meant that the stage doors had been propped open to allow the traffic of various servants of the place to fetch and carry from the little yard. It was a pleasingly busy scene. Men and women came and went full of the whistles and calls of their professions. A woman in plain wool with her hands on her hips seemed to be in heated negotiations with a boy carrying a string of unplucked pheasants. Harriet and Crowther had to step back smartly to avoid collision with a man who carried what seemed to be the head of some antique Colossus through the outer gates at breakneck speed, then in the next moment their eyes were caught by a woman so engulfed by the quantity of flowers she was carrying, they seemed to be watching the progress of an ornamental border with legs. They followed her as she ducked into the building itself, scattering rose petals and scraps of foliage as she went, and found themselves in a high, wide corridor that seemed too long and deep to be accommodated behind that ordinary-looking frontage. There were a number of doors open along its length, and their attention was caught by a shout behind the one nearest to them. The voice was deep, angry and powerful.

'No! Not at all! Fool! Have you never seen a tree! Do you never step back from your work and consider? The panel must be done again. I will not be disgraced by you tonight, and if we get wet paint on the costumes, Bartholomew will scream to the heavens. Get a fire in here.'

Crowther pushed the door wide with the flat of his hand, and Harriet moved into the doorway beside him. The room was very large, and light even on such a dull day. The smell of paint was almost overpowering. Crowther's eyes smarted a little from the fumes as he looked upwards.

The room was double the height he expected. The most exacting hostess would have been pleased to hold a ball for fifty people in such a space, but the place was almost bare of furniture, and the walls only rough plaster. It was not empty, however. A number of large painted canvas panels were strung from the high ceiling by a combination of ropes anchored on capstan, pully and cleats. Crowther's eyes skipped through them, catching at their overlapping edges shreds of various views and interiors. A flower garden, some part of a city street, some grey stonework on canvas that suggested a temple of antiquity, a forest, ruins of some castle. They hung at various heights, and were in various states of repair. It was like looking into the memories of an old and romantic traveller, flashes of time and place and mood, layered and confused.

On the long wall opposite them, Harriet saw panels of sky and sea, and leaned up against them a ship, its prow standing some eight feet above the stone floor. No, not a ship, rather the flat ghost of a ship, rudely, roughly cut off twenty feet along its length; and not wood, but the simulation of wood on a canvas frame. Along its edge were painted wavelets so delicately done, she could almost hear the sounds of the ocean, and thought she could taste the familiar tang of salt on her lips.

In the centre of the space available stood a high stool. On it sat, or rather crouched, the figure of an extremely tall man dressed uniformly in deep brown. His hair was the same shade of chestnut as his clothes, and unpowdered. He sat with his black shoes hooked over the bar halfway up the height of his seat. It seemed to almost fold his body in two, like a pen-knife blade, just open. Poised with his hands on his knees, all his attention was focused on the far end of the room.

Where he looked, stood two other men. The elder of them, his coat off and his shirtsleeves rolled up, was towering over a boyish figure in an apron who seemed near to tears. The younger man held a painter's palette in his left hand. He was biting his lip and looking down at the floor. Behind him was a painted scene of trees. It looked to Harriet extremely well done. Without noticing the new arrivals in the doorway, the older man crossed the room towards the gentleman sitting on the stool, looking sorry and concerned. When he spoke, they recognised the voice they had heard from the corridor, although its volume was now low, and its tone suddenly respectful and apologetic.

'I am sorry, Mr Johannes. You are quite right. Boyle here has made an error. I am sorry I did not take note of it before, though some might call it only a small thing . . .' The man on the stool looked up sharply at this, and Boyle's tormentor hurried on nervously, 'But of course, no error is unimportant, and there is time to correct it before evening.' When the man on the stool did not move, the other realised that more was asked of him. He cleared his throat and carried on. 'I am most terribly sorry not to have taken note of it before. It is the last piece, and the . . .' he paused, 'the *ingenious* nature of your designs have put us a little behind. My apologies.'

The man on the stool nodded, then with a gesture indicated that the shirtsleeved man should approach him more closely. He did, and the man in brown seemed to whisper something in his ear. Shirtsleeves straightened again and turned his attention back towards the boy with the paint palette.

'Well, there it is, Boyle. You know what must be done.' The man paused, then added, 'And Mr Johannes wishes me to tell you, this lapse aside, he is pleased with your work.'

The boy flushed. 'Of course, Mr Gooch. Thank you. And thank *you*, Mr Johannes.'

Mr Johannes gave no indication Harriet could see of acknowledging these thanks, but instead, as if just becoming aware of observation, turned his head slowly towards the door and looked at her. Harriet blinked. The man's face was very pale; his eyes seemed unnaturally large and were both a violent green and a little bulbous. His skin looked very fine; it had a thin glow about it that she noticed sometimes on the skin of her little son's face. It was smooth as rosewood. She was reminded of the blank, but somewhat inhuman, faces of angels she had seen in mosaic on the walls of the churches in Constantinople. The other men, Mr Gooch and the boy painter, had also now seen them. It was Gooch who spoke, rather gruffly and with a frown.

'May we be of assistance, sir, madam?'

Crowther smiled at him benignly and replied, 'We are looking for the manager – a Mr Harwood, I understand?'

'He'll be in his office at present,' Gooch said with a snap, and turned back towards the canvases around him. 'Now set to, Boyle, and I'll call up the boys. Every other panel will need to be placed yet, and if that piece isn't perfect by the time the doors open, I'll cut you up and stuff the bits into sandbags myself.'

Johannes continued to look steadily at Harriet and Crowther, and lifted one hand to point upwards, indicating, Harriet supposed, where those offices might be. His limbs seemed unnaturally long and his fingers were as thin and as pale as his face. The pose made her think of those attending angels again, pointing the attention of the penitent to their Judge and Saviour above. Harriet nodded her thanks and, with Crowther, retreated into the corridor, not sure whether to feel comforted by the picture the strange figure presented, or uneasy.

In the space of the corridor, Crowther looked down at her, saying, 'I think we are in the right place, Mrs Westerman.'

'Why do you say that, Crowther?'

'Did you not notice the ropes in that room? I would call them the twin of that wrapped round Fitzraven's ankles.'

Jocasta was whistling between her teeth as she walked down St Martin's Lane. There was a vigour in her step that would make any of the pedestrians negotiating the mud think twice about demanding she gave right of way. Jocasta Bligh would move off the pavement for a sedan chair – since no one who wanted to keep body and soul together would do otherwise – but for the rest she yielded no ground. Within three streets of her house in any direction of the compass, it would never be in question. The women nodded to her, the men lifted their hands to their foreheads, a little wary perhaps, for everyone was aware that she had all their secrets under her fingertips and knew their minds and business better than they, for the most part. Twenty years had proved she knew how to keep her knowledge to herself, however. Unless something moved her to drop a harsh word in the ear of some man who was too free with his fists, or a girl too free with her favours.

She came to a firm halt outside the chophouse on the corner of St Martin's Lane and Turner's Court, just where respectable roads crumbled into the hodge-podge hell of the rookeries. There were pockets of such places all over the city – houses with a dozen doors in and out of them, areas of squalor and desperation where no lawman would go without a company of redcoats at his back. Jocasta looked in at the tobacco clouds, steam and clatter within the shop for a second, and whistled. A lad helping with the serving turned away from his customer and, catching her eye, jogged up to her side while the gentleman in yellow wig and stained coat was still halfway through ordering his beer and pie.

'Afternoon, Mrs Bligh. Something for you from the kitchen? Does Boyo here fancy a scrap?'

Jocasta looked down at her dog. He widened his eyes, and she narrowed hers.

'No. He's getting me into trouble again. He'll have to wait.'

Boyo got down on the floor and put his front paw over his nose.

'What I need from you, Ripley, is a place. You know the Mitchells? Young ones. He's a clerk, she sells perfumes somewhere. Married. Room with the mother. I need to know where they stay.'

The boy rubbed his nose for a second.

'Yeah. I know the old woman. And he comes in here for his dinner three days a week. Clerks for the Admiralty, doesn't he? They've got a place in Salisbury Street. He's all right. His mother's a sharp-faced old bitch though. Works their girl into the ground and lives like they've nothing to eat but sawdust, though if she's got enough blunt to front a coffee-house, they can't be hurting that much. Mind you, a month ago he was whining that the landlord's putting up her rent and they might lose it. Guess that's why they still send the girl out to the shop to sell Mr Broodigan's perfumes.' The boy looked a little startled at having said so much. 'She ain't a friend of yours, is she, Mrs Bligh?'

Jocasta winked and pulled her cards from the pocket of her skirt. 'Pick a card, Ripley,' she said, fanning them out.

The boy bit his lip, then with sudden decision, yanked one free from the middle of the pack and passed it to her. From the back of the room, a man, his apron held together by grease and bad memories, his belly so wide he could hardly waddle between his tables, shouted out.

'Oi, Ripley! Why ain't you serving, you whelp?' Jocasta flicked up her eyes from the card Ripley had chosen. The fat man coughed. 'Er, sorry, Mrs Bligh. Didn't see you there for a second. You look after her, boy.' Ripley didn't even bother looking round.

'Well? Anything for me, Mrs Bligh?'

Jocasta scratched her nose. On the floor, Boyo growled. 'Watch yon weasel-faced fellow, middle table, blue coat with a mourning band. He's going to try and pass you false coin for his dinner.'

Ripley turned slowly with his eyes narrowed and spotted the man. He gave a little hiss between his teeth, he then swung back to Jocasta, blinking.

'You got all that from one card?'

'No. He's been going through his coin under the table all the time we been talking and trying it with his thumbnail to find the bad stuff. He'll mix it in. Don't break his arm though. He got took, now he's trying to take. Card just says "watch your back", though if any one of us stopped doing that, we wouldn't be stupid for long.'

'Thanks, Mrs Bligh.'

'Much obliged to you too, youngling.' And with a nod to the fat man, Jocasta turned to go. Boyo sat up, and having given the room his own commentary in the form of a short sharp bark, trotted out on her heel.

## II.3

IT TOOK SOME little time for Harriet and Crowther to make their way through the theatre and find the offices of Mr Harwood. The corridors were crowded with people, each making their own, very determined way in several directions. Harriet spotted a cluster of Roman maidens turning into their path. From a distance they looked as lovely as goddesses, but as they approached they coarsened. Their gold hairpieces turned to painted card, their soft white robes were in fact not entirely clean, nor securely fastened, their faces were vivid with paint. Harriet pondered as they passed the mystery of drama. At forty paces these ladies were beauteous examples of Ancient womanhood, at five they were monsters.

Sounds of a band at rehearsal drifted past the pair – the throb of a cello and the scattered bright tones of a harpsichord. A fat little man barrelled towards them, almost hidden by the load of feathered skirts he carried in his arms. A boy turned a corner too fast, still shouting something over his shoulder, and collided with Crowther. The lad stumbled and let go an armful of manuscript paper with a slithering rustle; music still caught between lines on the stave pooled like water round their feet. He cursed and scrabbled them together again. Harriet bent to help him and he grinned at her boldly before dashing off again with the pages clamped to his chest. And everyone they passed seemed to find it necessary to speak, continually, and at unnecessary volume. Those who were not braying at their companions or to the air, sang. Scales and fragments of tunes fell about them in a constant clatter; a dawn chorus of competing human voices. Crowther had to draw on all his reserves not to cover his ears.

Then, when they managed to find the door to the main theatre lobby and went through it, the scene became unnaturally calm. Harriet, used to being in such establishments with a great crowd, was unnerved. It was as if all the confusion they had just stumbled through had been swallowed in a single gulp. She felt as if she had fallen from a carnival into a cathedral. The place was decorated with devotion. Along the corridors they had just walked, the walls and ceilings were plain and serviceable – all unpainted plaster and the sort of lamp-holders Harriet used in her kitchen or servants' quarters, but here the doorways were slung with plaster garlands picked out in powder blue with little golden cherubs floundering happily among them; the lamps, great torches in clouded glass swirls, were held in the white hands of semi-clad goddesses who seemed to be pulling themselves free of the flat walls behind them. The carpet was crimson, thick, and flowed up the stairs towards the private boxes like a mounting wave. The ceiling showed the Muses of Dance, Song and Epic seated among the clouds, sharing the duty of holding a laurel wreath above the lobby: it circled the glass rotunda through which the weak daylight crawled. Yet, with the lamps unlit, and the hubbub of the building suddenly stilled, the atmosphere was eerie rather than splendid. Harriet thought of the shadows in Justice Pither's outhouse, and shivered. Crowther's voice seemed oddly loud when he spoke.

'I believe this place must have shared a decorator with the former inhabitants of Berkeley Square. Ah, there.' He pointed to a door that led off the landing above them. 'I believe that to be the sort of situation a manager would choose for his office, do you not agree, Mrs Westerman?'

She nodded. 'Indeed – just where he can put his head out of the door to see how the crowd is filling out.' They ascended the stairs, and all was silent but for the swish of Harriet's skirts on the carpeted steps.

Harriet had to admit that the words 'theatrical manager' had conjured a certain image in her mind. Mr Winter Harwood seemed fashioned to destroy it. Where she had expected a character of high colour who bore the signs of a life of fine food and plentiful wine, Mr Harwood was a trim man, long-limbed, but with enough breadth in his shoulders to carry his height, clean-skinned and with pale-blue eyes; where she had expected someone who dressed in the colourful and ornate style of the building he managed, Mr Harwood was simply dressed in a close-fitting dark-blue coat and fawn breeches; his waistcoat was free of fobs or chains, and his wig made none of the slightly hysterical claims to originality that seemed to be the current fashion. He dressed like Graves, in fact, and where she had suspected a manner slightly over-enthused, highly sensible, innately dramatic, Mr Harwood showed himself, on hearing their news, to be a master of understatement and emotional control.

'Fitzraven is dead, you say? Thank you for the information.'

His desk, Harriet noticed, was too tidy. Mr Harwood's writing equipment was laid out in front of him as if it had been placed there with the aid of a set square and ruler. To his right sat a neat pile of letters, unopened. To his left, several sheets smoothed out flat and others folded and ready, it seemed, for the penny post. Having spoken, he took another letter from the pile to his right and broke the seal on it. Then glanced up again at his visitors, as if surprised to find them still there.

'Is there anything further?'

Crowther spoke. 'The rope that bound his legs together came from this house. We intend to seek his murderer here. If you know anything that would expedite that search, it would be good of you to reveal it, and save us both some inconvenience.'

Mr Harwood sighed, and put down his letter very carefully.

'I doubt I can be of much assistance. The rope came from here, did it? You are sure?' Crowther simply nodded. 'How unfortunate.' There was a long pause. Harriet was, she knew, appallingly bad at letting such silences stretch. Her impulse was always to leap into the conversational fray, to charm and chatter those with whom she talked into confidence, but she had learned from Crowther the power of stillness.

Mr Harwood looked at them sharply and eventually continued: 'I am glad murder is still so rare a thing, even in these fallen days, but we have enough experience of it to know that unless the perpetrator is found with the knife in his hand, or makes the mistake of mentioning his guilt in public, it is unlikely he will ever be found. Is that not the case?' Again, neither Harriet nor Crowther replied. Mr Harwood frowned. 'What use then to tell stories, and force people into slandering their neighbours and colleagues with suspicion? Are there not other amusements in Town sufficient for you?'

Harwood got to his feet and moved to look out of his window into the street outside, linking his hands together behind his back. Harriet could hear the scrape of iron wheels on stone, the shouts of the chair-carriers.

'I know your names, of course. Do I assume you are once again – now how did that rather colourful pamphlet last autumn put it? – "taking up the flaming sword of truth on behalf of your King"?'

Harwood turned to look at them over his shoulder, one eyebrow raised. 'Well, I wish you could choose a more noble object for your crusade. Nathaniel Fitzraven was a rather poisonous little man, though he was a good musician in his time. Why make his sordid little life your subject? I doubt he has any hidden heir or suffering children for you to save.' He moved away from the window, and with a gentle nod, continued, 'Do you know, one of my colleagues was offered a one-act interpretation of your adventures last summer for the public stage? Were it not for the fact a rather neat little comedy called *The Coffee-Shop* became available, you would have had a run in Drury Lane.'

His lip curled a little, whether at herself and Crowther, or at the quality of the drama about them, Harriet could not say. She was annoyed to feel herself blush; she would have given a great deal to hide her discomfort. When Crowther spoke, however, his voice showed no sign of embarrassment or awkwardness. His tone was as dry as Mr Harwood's and his words more distinct and glassy. She did not need to look at him to know that his right eyebrow was raised and he was examining the manager along the line of his thin nose.

'Unlike yourself, Mr Harwood, I cannot dictate the manner in which the populace chooses to entertain itself. It is not my concern. Mrs Westerman and I were asked by a Magistrate trying to do his duty, a Mr Pither in Great Suffolk Street, to examine a body. The body, we discover, was that of Mr Fitzraven. He was not the victim of some casual robbery, or public confrontation. He was throttled, then some hours later his body was tied and thrown in the river in an attempt, I believe, to conceal the crime and rob him of a proper burial.' Harriet found her discomfort gone and began to enjoy herself as Crowther spoke on: 'If he had friends capable and willing to search out his killers, I would gladly hand over those duties to them. It seems he did not, and if Mrs Westerman and I can discover a murderer, and prevent him from killing again, then we shall do so. Pamphlets, stage plays, orphans and heirs . . . these are irrelevant.'

Harwood looked at them both with attention as Crowther finished, then having taken his seat again spread his hands wide on the table.

'Very well.' He closed his eyes for a moment then pinched the bridge of his nose with his right hand before going on. 'I will tell you what I can of Fitzraven, though I would request you make no further enquiries in this house today, at least, whatever your suspicions. These people must entertain their Sovereign tonight and nerves are stretched. I do not ask this lightly.' He looked up at them, Harriet met Crowther's eye then turned back to give Harwood a slight nod. The manager spoke through clenched teeth. 'I will speak to everyone after the performance and give them your names. Mrs Service has a box, of course, and her company are normally invited to the Green Room, but . . .'

'Mr Crowther and I have no plans to attend the opera tonight,' Harriet said calmly.

'Good. Fitzraven was an irritant, but useful at times. He was keen to continue his association with the Opera House after we ceased to ask him to play, so I employed him to supervise the copying of parts and run errands. There are two boys we employ during the season who do much the same work, and for much the same pay, but since Fitzraven dressed in a frock-coat and talked like a gentleman, mostly, many assumed his responsibilities were more extensive than they were.'

Harriet lifted her chin and now comfortably meeting his gaze, said, 'Yet this summer we are told that you placed considerable trust in him. Did you not send him to Milan to recruit for the current season? Why, if you were doubtful of him, did you do such a thing?'

Harwood settled back in his chair and seemed to lose himself in contemplation of the far corner of his office. The decoration in this room seemed to find a mean between the plain functionality of the backstage rooms, and the gaudy extravagances of the lobby. The decoration was present, but polite. Three or four portraits in heavy gilt frames formed the main interest of the room. They were all of solid gentlemen, richly dressed – the former Managers of the Opera House, if the little plaques under the frames were to be believed. They looked down on their successor with a weary disdain, and intense self-satisfaction.

'I did. It was a risk, but the prize offered was well worth reaching for. I have been attempting via my agents abroad to persuade Miss Marin to come to London each season since I took over management of His Majesty's. I heard her sing in Paris four years ago and was astonished. I expect all London to be astonished now. However, she was always snatched away from me by another, richer employment elsewhere on the continent, and I fear my voice was only one among many. Then, in the spring, Fitzraven came to me and said he was in private correspondence with the lady, and believed he could persuade her to come for this season if I agreed to let him act as the agent of the theatre in Italy over the summer.'

'And you trusted him?' asked Harriet.

Harwood shook his head. 'No. But he showed me parts of a letter from the lady to himself that seemed warm in its tones and asked him to visit her. I admit I was surprised at his success in eliciting the invitation, but he had managed it and I thought it was worth the risk to send him. I limited his expenses and gave him no great latitude in his negotiations. We have good friends among the bankers of Florence and Milan, and I did not believe they would allow him to damage us with extravagant fees. To this point I have had no reason to regret my decision. Miss Marin is here. I have heard great things spoken of Manzerotti: several influential judges of music told me of his talents, and from what I have heard of his voice, those praises have been justified. Some of the other singers I think may have been selected by Fitzraven more for their ability to put money into his pocket than their skills, but they are . . .' he shrugged '. . . competent.'

'And how did Fitzraven enter into this correspondence?' Crowther asked.

Harwood lifted his palms. 'I cannot tell you, Mr Crowther. I heard a story once that the fair Miss Byrne was so moved by correspondence she received from one music-lover, it was all her friends could do to prevent her from eloping with the gentleman, sight unseen. I believe he turned out to be the son of a button-maker and still in the schoolroom. Perhaps Fitzraven had a similarly convincing epistolary style.'

Crowther frowned. '*Did* Fitzraven have a talent with the pen?'

Harwood shifted in his seat. 'He did, from time to time, send paragraphs to the newspapers in praise of the productions here, or to alert the public of the personages about to appear. Much as your friend Graves did before his sudden change in circumstance.'

'Graves, I believe, was never in the pay of those about whom he wrote,' Harriet said.

'Indeed, Mrs Westerman,' Harwood replied, studying the ceiling. 'To our cost and his own, Graves always insisted on his independence.'

There was a light tap on the door; a servant leaned into the room just far enough to nod at Harwood, then withdrew. 'You must excuse me now, however. I am called to see this wondrous duet that closes Act Two. Everyone who has heard it swears it will get half a dozen encores.' Harwood rose, then said as an afterthought. 'Come with me. It is a public rehearsal and I shall watch from the King's Box. I also hear that Mr Johannes, our master of stage mechanics, has come up with some piece of trickery that will astound me, and you may have sight of the artistes of whom we were just speaking.'

Harriet and Crowther rose with him. As she moved aside to let him lead the way out of the room, Harriet remarked lightly, 'I have always been astonished at the marvels the stage can contain. All those descending angels, mountain ranges a man can climb and so on.'

Harwood bowed a little. 'It is part of the spectacular – though we have had our failures. Some years ago I was convinced into releasing live birds during one scene. The effect was brief, and the inconvenience considerable. The coronation scene that followed did not benefit from one of the chorus getting a sparrow caught up in her headgear.'

## II.4

JOCASTA WOULD NOT have chosen Salisbury Street as a place to live. Not while there was a dry corner anywhere else in London. The mist never cleared from these alleys that bent towards the broad Thames, and the whole street had that air of miserable decay that comes on any creature or place forced to stay damp the majority of the time.

Walking up to the door of the first house, she rapped once and hard. A pinched-looking face appeared at the window. A second later, the door was opened a crack and a frighteningly thin nose appeared. So narrow was the face behind it that Jocasta felt she was talking to a door-wedge.

'Mitchell?' it said in response to Jocasta's question. 'Third house down.' The door snapped shut again and Jocasta thought about spitting bad luck onto the step for bad manners, but decided against. Instead, she had a tap at the door of the third house down, peered into a parlour done up nice enough but empty, and getting no answer or sight of any person, settled herself on the step opposite. Boyo turned twice and burrowed at her feet. Then put his paws over his nose.

Jocasta lifted her head and said with a nod, 'True enough, Boyo. Too much river water in the air here. Still, I'll have no complaints from you. You know sure enough this was all your plan, and I'm just too much of a silly old fool to do anything but listen.'

Then she waited. Through her mind danced a pattern of swords and a clatter of gold.

As they took their places, Harwood called down to a young-looking man at the harpsichord in the pit that he was all attention, then added in a lower tone to his companions, 'As we have not the libretto to hand, I shall act as chorus. Mademoiselle's character is mourning for her lover, played by Mr Manzerotti, whom she believes lost to her for ever. They meet by accident in the rose garden and she sings this aria to him, "*C'è una rosa*". It is the sorrow of a woman deeply in love whose love has now been rejected. Mr Manzerotti tells her it is inevitable and asks for her forgiveness. He continues to do so as she restates her love and incomprehension at his changed heart.' Harwood covered his mouth with a hand and yawned. 'He does love her, of course. They are kept apart by Manzerotti's loyalty to the enemy of Miss Marin's father. Very tragic and noble. This opera is largely a *pasticcio.*' He noticed the confused expression on the faces of his guests. 'That is to say, it is made up from segments of other operas by a variety of composers, and there are certain arias that performers prefer and of which they make a showcase. We agree to include them in any performance. However, I wished to have at least a couple of original songs, and this is one. Our young composer, Mr Richard Bywater, went walking all summer in the Highlands, I understand, to gather his ideas, yet they seemed remarkably thin still when he returned. I only hope inspiration has struck finally with considerable force and the performers have the tune down.'

Harriet began to take in the scene as her eyes became used to the darkness of the auditorium; only the stage and pit where the musicians huddled were afforded any light. There were any number of people moving around the shadows, however, though it was still empty by comparison with the heaving and pushing crowds she was used to seeing in the pits and galleries of an opera house. Some scattered ladies and gentlemen had attended the rehearsal as part of their afternoon's entertainment. She could also see three or four women at work in the boxes, polishing the fittings and neatening the arrangements of chairs. Two men were at the same business of cleaning in the pit, with a lad following them throwing lavender down in loose handfuls on the floor. At the side of the stage another pair of men were at work on one of the hoop chandeliers, filling the little oil-lamps and trimming the wicks.

Two figures sat on chairs placed on the right of the stage. The male figure, the great castrato Manzerotti, was unusually tall and slender. He wore a coat of the most startling scarlet, decorated with a profusion of gold braid, and the high heels of his shoes were an electric blue that so engaged the eye, even from this distance, Harriet thought they must be made of lapis lazuli. They seemed to spark up towards her and sting her eyes. The lady sitting next to him, the writer of the warm letters, Miss Marin, wore many folds of dove grey, gathered at the waist and flowing into a remarkably full skirt. It was balanced by the extravagant size of her hat, whose broad sweeping brim must render, Harriet thought, half the world a mystery to her.

These figures now lazily stood and moved to opposite sides of the stage, exchanged words with unseen watchers in the wings, and waited. Mademoiselle Marin noticed them where they were watching and smiled upwards. It was a pleasant smile – rather shy, almost apologetic. Harriet found herself returning it, and regretting her promise to Harwood not to have conversation with the singers before the morrow. Then the first note was struck on the harpsichord and the fiddlers, still finishing their own conversations in the pit, took up the theme.

The stage did indeed look very like a rose garden, though Harriet could see no blooms. Patterned panels created a vista that seemed to stretch for half a mile into the distant depths of the stage, ending with a folly perched on a hilltop. Nearer to the singers on either side were clumped patches of deep green foliage, and in the centre of the stage a fountain depicted Apollo and Leucothea embracing and pouring over each other's forms water that flowed from the cups they held above their heads.

Then Isabella began to sing.

Her voice was clear as water and produced apparently without effort or any sign of strain. Strange pictures and memories began almost at once to dance behind Harriet's eyes. She thought of her husband. She knew a little Italian, but not enough to understand what was being sung. The music had to bring everything to her and it seemed, as the music continued, as if it was sadly dropping rose petals into her palm. The melody that had begun simply, a lilting lost thought, circled and grew more complex till it took the soprano's voice to heights that seemed to Harriet impossible, inevitable, then fell away again in a rapid waves of triplets that sounded like tears. Then, as Marin's voice faded like a ghost, exhausted and distressed, Manzerotti began to sing. It was a sound unlike any other human voice she had ever heard. Its pitch was as high as Isabella's but so strong it made her think of gold polished white. She thought of bells, hunting horns. It cut its way up and under and between the players in the pit like a scarlet ribbon woven into a cloth of some coarser stuff. The voices joined, waters flowing together, a strange alchemy.

Suddenly Harriet noticed that on stage in front of them, roses were beginning to bloom. Yellow roses, apparently drawn into life by the song, pushed their way silently out of the deep foliage around them. They appeared first severally as buds, then as the song swelled, each one opened a full and heavy bloom till the stage was full of them. As the voices peaked once more, together, one lost in grief, the other tender but inflexible, the water of the fountain was transmuted into gold, and glittering showers ran over the carved muscles of the statues. The band yearned upwards, and as the lovers reached the end of their song, still separated and unresolved, the woodwind called out three high and reaching chords that made Harriet's hands clench together in her lap, such was the force they carried, their bitter, painful sweetness. Mademoiselle Marin turned to the pit, and the young man at the harpsichord, and kissed her fingers to him. He blushed and looked down.

Silence fell. Harriet blinked and looked about her. All activity in the auditorium had ceased. The cleaning women stood mute and unmoving in the boxes, their cloths held unnoticed at their sides. The men and boy sweeping the pit had stopped their work and turned to the stage; the men changing the candles were held, open-mouthed, staring at the singers. All conversation between the ladies and gentlemen had ceased.

Manzerotti smiled and turned towards the King's Box. The moment passed and the listeners began to go about their business again. Harriet saw the musicians in the pit lean back and sigh; the cellist covered his eyes with his hands briefly. Isabella turned and smiled frankly at them again, then without waiting for any sign, exited the stage. Only the young man at the keyboard did not move, but remained head bowed over the keys. Harwood nodded towards the stage, then seemed to slip back into himself, staring up at the painted ceiling of his little world.

'Good,' he said simply.

Harriet heard Crowther cough slightly and turned to look at him. He seemed as surprised as she felt herself. He wetted his lips slightly and said 'Remarkable.'

Jocasta and Boyo had a long cold wait of it, but towards the middle of the afternoon the little terrier sat up and barked, and Jocasta turned to see Kate Mitchell stepping down the lane. She almost stumbled over Jocasta before she saw her, and gasped when she recognised the old woman.

'Mrs Bligh! Are you waiting for me?'

Jocasta spat over her shoulder. 'I am, lass. We are to have words.'

Kate hesitated for a second, then shook her head firmly. 'No, Mrs Bligh. I don't think we shall.'

Some children who had made the mistake of teasing Boyo had felt the surprisingly strong grip of Jocasta Bligh on their arm. Kate felt it now.

'You spoken with your husband?'

'No, not yet.' She shivered a little. 'He was home late last night, and out of sorts. I'll pick my time.'

'Pretty brooch you have there. That the one your boy got you?'

Kate looked down at the little paste flowers on her shoulder. 'Yes, it was a present from Fred, Mrs Bligh. I told you. Do you – do you . . . want it?'

Jocasta flung her arm away from the girl and spat again. 'I don't want to rob you, you daft child. I want to know how a clerk affords such things. Doesn't sound like you get much help from his mother.'

Kate rubbed her arm a little sulkily. 'Well, I don't know. They've been working awful hard. Perhaps they gave him a tip. When the Navy Board is sitting he can be there all night. There's a war on, you know, Mrs Bligh. Or maybe he won it at the cockfight, and he just didn't want to tell me he'd been in such a low place.'

Jocasta rolled her eyes. 'He's doing something, and he's being paid. And you know as well as I do it's not honest work.'

Kate folded her arms. 'I know no such thing, and if I find it so, I shall make him stop. There. Now leave me alone, Mrs Bligh. I thank you for your trouble, but there's no need for it.'

'Look, you daft piece, I know some swift bad is coming to you.' Jocasta jabbed Kate's shoulder with her finger. '*You*, personal. Now you gather your papers and we'll see what we can figure out. But if you stay in this house, St George and the dragon together wouldn't be able to save you.'

Kate hesitated, her hands closed round the reticule. Jocasta wondered if she'd been hanging on to those papers all night and day. Jocasta willed her on in her mind. *See it, girly*, she thought. *See it how it is, then come away.*

'I can keep an eye on you, girly,' she said, a little more softly.

Kate shook her head again. 'No, Mrs Bligh. This is my husband you're talking of. This is my place. I'm not leaving it.'

With that she turned to the house and let herself in. Jocasta watched the door and saw her shape moving round in the room at the front, but her eyes were clouded with The Tower card, the great cascades of sparks.

Mr Harwood made no immediate move to leave the King's Box after the duet was done.

Harriet said quietly, 'I can understand now how Fitzraven valued his connection to the opera. It would be hard to hear such things, be near to them and then give them up.'

Harwood was shaken free of his reverie. 'You do him too much credit, Mrs Westerman. He did have musical ability, but he was not . . . sensitive. It was not the music that attracted him to us, that made this place valuable to him, but something else.'

'What else is there here but music?' Harriet asked.

It was Crowther who answered, though Harwood gave a short, mirthless bark of laughter. 'There is fame, Mrs Westerman. There is renown, and wherever fame and renown are known to be, there is money to be made. Am I correct, Mr Harwood?'

'You are,' that gentleman replied. 'Fitzraven was one of those individuals whose passion is to be close to those the public celebrates. He had a talent to amuse perhaps, with his gossip and a sharp tongue, and he knew how to flatter. It was to that I ascribed his success in recruiting those singers of quality he brought us here. But he was desperate – and I use the word without unnecessary theatricality – desperate to be near those whose names we read in the newspapers, and think himself their friend. He would have done much to feel himself of significance in their lives. It is a sickness that comes over many. By the close of the season I will have another dozen men and women who will need to be watched for at the door, or they will create havoc and distress trying to get close to the objects of their devotion. They become convinced they have a particular bond with some performer they have spotted and made a focus for their admiration.' His eyes flicked up to Crowther. 'I know a woman in Milan, of good family, was killed last year throwing herself under Manzerotti's coach. She carried his portrait snipped from a newspaper in her locket as a lover would. She was not the first, nor will she be the last to die for love of a person she has never met.'

'How . . .' Harriet paused to pluck the right word out of the air '. . . oddly pathetic.'

Harwood tilted back his chair, running his eyes over the gilt and splendour of the King's Box. It was twice the size of the other private boxes, though the Prince's Box at the other side of the stage was also generous, and had a little divan at its rear. All the boxes were ornate, but here everything was just a little more. The velvet draperies had a few more folds, the chairs a little more room for gilded wreaths, the upholstery a little more plush. Harriet found herself thinking that where she sat this afternoon, a King would sit in the evening. It gave her a little cold thrill of connection.

'Indeed,' Harwood went on, 'I know Fitzraven was not here for the music. He obviously made some useful connections in Italy. He told me he had received a letter of introduction from someone – he did not say from whom – to Lord Carmichael's house, for instance, and had been invited back to attend that gentleman more than once. He did not go *there* for love of art. Lord Carmichael has little to recommend him, I believe, other than his wealth.'

'Lord Carmichael?' Crowther said. Harriet was impressed with how much disdain Crowther could invest only two words. She wondered briefly if there might be some sort of mathematical formula for it. Perhaps she should suggest it to her new acquaintances at the Royal Society.

Harwood smiled at the ceiling. 'I see you know Lord Carmichael, Mr Crowther.'

'I knew the *gentleman* in my youth. A man I would go some way to avoid. It seems Mr Fitzraven was not very particular in his choice of friends.' Harriet looked at Crowther with surprise. He seldom spoke with such passion about anything he had not recently dissected.

'I would agree,' Harwood replied evenly. 'However, he is a peer, very rich and since making his acquaintance Fitzraven revelled in the connection.' He let the Queen's chair tip back onto four legs and turned with a slight smile to Harriet. 'I say this so you do not mistake Fitzraven's devotion to this place,' a casual wave of his hand took in performers, music, audience, waves of gilt, 'for a devotion to art or music. He was one of those strange hollow men. I do not think he existed in his own self at all. He was all light reflected. Sometimes from us here, sometimes from a creeping acquaintance with the great and good.'

Harriet rested her chin on the palm of her hand. 'Can you tell us, sir, what were Fitzraven's last duties for this place?'

Harwood considered. 'I should imagine preparing the parts for the duet you have just heard. He readied them on Wednesday for its first rehearsal on Thursday morning.'

Crowther turned towards the manager and said very evenly, 'Mr Harwood, are you sure you have been quite frank with us about the nature of Mr Fitzraven's duties here?'

Winter Harwood met his look, and said with a polite inclination of the head, 'Of course, Mr Crowther.'

Jocasta was almost back at her own door again, and walking so quick that Boyo had a job of it to keep up with her, when she came to a sudden halt. He stubbed his nose on her ankle and yelped.

'I don't want to speak of it now, Boyo,' Jocasta said. 'I'm too ruffled and fretted.' She stayed where she was, though, the people passing on the pavement occasionally turning to give her a quick, sidelong stare, then moving on. She sighed and thrust her hand into another pocket under her skirts, pulling out a handful of dirty coins.

'All right then, Boyo. I will if it'll keep you quiet. Though we must work in the morning if you want meat this week.'

Boyo smacked his lips and Jocasta turned again and made her way back towards the chophouse, jingling her money.

## II.5

THE INVESTMENT IN transporting Isabella and Manzerotti from Italy had, it seemed, been justified. For an evening so early in the season the crowd that night at His Majesty's was remarkable.

The Hay Market was almost completely blocked with carriages from five o'clock. The torches outside the Opera House doors flared and roared, casting folding shadows up the brickwork. The scrum that thundered for entrance into the pit and stalls extended far along the pavements towards Northumberland Palace, and up and down its lengths went a dozen boys and girls selling copies of the libretto for a shilling and nuts for a penny. Two other children with piles of books in their arms like schoolboys late for the bell scurried between the carriages, handing more copies of librettos through the windows. Shillings were pulled from silk purses by long, gloved fingers and dropped into the boys' waiting palms. A couple of street singers, one turning the wheel on the hurdy-gurdy round her neck, sang the crowd songs from the previous season above the general noise and put out their hands for tribute. A man with a brazier had set up shop roasting chestnuts beside them and the air filled with the sweetness of the black papery skins.

Amongst the general noise and excitement the Londoners were getting on with the serious business of looking at each other, till, as the bells of Westminster rang out six o'clock there was a groan from bolts in the locks and the high entrance doors were swung open by liveried footmen. At the same moment the door to the pit was loosed, and the stagehand who opened it was almost crushed by the weight of people rushing in waving papers and arguing for cheap tickets at the tops of their voices, long before they were in earshot of the harried clerk at his booth. Through the smarter entrance to the lobby and private boxes passed brocade and silk, feathers and high head-dresses all bulked up with horsehair and smothered in powder. Fans flicked open and closed, little high-heeled shoes in ivory and red picked their way over the grot of the pavement. Tail-coats flicked up as the men showed their legs and bowed to the ladies. A murmur of spray diamonds and stones glinted their way into the lobby. Those of the crowd who were not fighting their way in kept up a commentary on the dresses and faces passing by. When one lady descended from her carriage in a skirt of particularly daring design, a shout went up from the jostling observers. Mr Harwood heard it from the relative peace of his office and smiled.

The party of Mr Owen Graves, consisting of himself, Mrs Service, Miss Rachel Trench and Lady Susan Thornleigh, were not so extravagantly dressed, but the crowd knew them anyway. Susan heard her name whispered as she stepped through the throng with her guardian's hand on her shoulder, and kept her eyes down till almost at her elbow she heard a voice ask her: 'Off to listen to the music then, my Lady?'

She turned and looked up into the full fat face of a woman with her arms crossed under her breasts. She did not know the woman but the face looked kindly enough so she smiled at it and replied, 'Yes, thank you, ma'am. I like music.'

The fat lady roared with laughter. 'Aww! Ma'am, she says! Bless the little chicken leg!' Then, as Susan felt her guardian's hand steer her firmly forward, she heard the voice continue, 'Oi! Ursula! You'll never guess who just "ma'am-ed" me! Lady Thornleigh! Yeah, all them murders! Little bit that she is!'

Susan lifted her chin and kept her eyes straight ahead.

Crowther was in the library of the house in Berkeley Square, which, despite his having his own establishment, had become acknowledged as his domain. He had covered some pages with a record of his observations of Fitzraven's body when Mrs Westerman entered the room and took a seat in one of the well-stuffed leather armchairs in front of the fire.

'Do you regret refusing the invitation for the opera, madam?'

Harriet shook her head, and Crowther returned to his writing. Despite the pleasure she had taken in the rehearsal this afternoon, an opera was not how she wished to employ the time available to her. From the sights and stories, when they did not put too much of a strain on her good sense, she could take some amusement, but music itself seemed to her a language she understood only partially. When she attended concerts or indeed any gathering where music was more than a stimulus to dancing, she felt as if she were being told fairy tales in Portuguese. Some sense of the drama reached her, some element of the subtle excitement everyone around her seemed to be able to taste, but she could not understand fully what she heard and was unable to work out the proper sense of it.

She remembered listening, one evening the previous spring, to a small group of musicians who came to play in the little assembly hall by the coaching inn in Pulborough. Rachel, her sister, had been very keen to attend, so Harriet had escorted her there. She had been listening to some slower piece the gentlemen were playing, and thinking it quite pleasing when she caught sight of her sister's profile. Rachel had been not merely attentive, but transfixed, and her eyes were, Harriet had been astonished to realise, full of tears. Harriet had looked about her and seen a similar look of divine reverie on the faces of several of her acquaintance in the crowd, recalled it on the face of her husband when he had persuaded her to go to some concert on his arm. She had felt stupid and slow by comparison and judged herself as oddly insensitive, even though she was sure she loved, feared and dreamed as passionately as anyone else in those audiences. Now, since James's continued illness had brought them to London and the home of their friends in Berkeley Square, she was continually surrounded by music. Lady Susan Thornleigh was, at eleven, an accomplished player on the harpsichord. Graves studied and loved music, as well as having it occupy his business life. It was as essential as air to them both.

Harriet remembered questioning Graves earlier in her stay about the effects of music, somewhat petulantly, when she had been a mute witness to an impassioned discussion of the technicalities of one of Mr William Boyce's symphonies, and its relative merits compared with some new score by a Mr Haydn just brought, with great fanfare, by a gentleman who had been travelling in Austria.

'But Graves, what does it all mean?' she had said.

Graves crossed and uncrossed his legs several times before replying, drew in his breath and lifted his hand as if about to begin, then let it fall again, till at last he said with an apologetic shrug of his shoulders: 'Mrs Westerman, music does not *mean* anything at all. You cannot ask it to speak to you in such concrete terms. It can evoke, affect, cajole and persuade, but its language is not that of speech. Indeed, if a composer can *say* in literal terms what his music means, he had much better write prose than notes.' He saw that his answer did not satisfy her, and after a moment tried again. 'Let music, when you hear it, work on you in its own way, Mrs Westerman. Let it flow around you and find its own way to touch you. It is not something you must translate moment by moment. Give it your attention. If it fails to speak to you in its own manner then, well, it is a failure in the music, not in yourself.' Harriet had promised to try his advice, but remained doubtful.

She sighed again and Crowther's pen ceased to scratch.

'Mrs Westerman?'

'I do not understand this city, Crowther,' she told him, 'and that is a concern to me. The noise, the continual bustle of the place, the air. How are we to manage?'

He placed his pen down on the papers in front of him.

'If it is any comfort, I do not believe we understand or know the country either. We will manage as everyone does, Mrs Westerman, as best we can.'


Mr Harwood heard the last chords ring out from the auditorium and waited. The signs during the performance had been promising, but it was now in this moment of silence that the fate of the season would be decided.

Two, three seconds passed – then a roar of noise broke like a tidal wave across the theatre. It lifted and expanded; a storm of applause. The panelling of his room seemed to swell with the force of the muffled 'Bravos!' making the portraits shift on the walls. The little plaques below each were a product of his own imagination. His predecessors had been primarily businessmen like himself, and never bothered to commemorate themselves in oils. He had bought the portraits as a job lot from a man who had lost his fortune one night at the card-table and now used that man's anonymous forebears to suggest an artistic lineage he did not have. Everything within these walls was spectacle.

The audience were still hysterical with pleasure. Harwood smiled. He thought how, on such an occasion, he could have guaranteed that even in this moment Fitzraven would be falling over his threshold to tell him the details of the rapturous reception. He would have noted the encores of each aria, gathered compliments or overheard twenty little fragments of other people's conversations he would be desperate to scatter across Harwood's desk like an explorer throwing down gems before his prince.

Harwood went to the window; he still had a few moments before he needed to play host to his royal guests and shower warmth on his performers. The Withdrawing Rooms this evening would be heady with the scent of glory, a golden sweat, his artists glutted and drunk with their triumph. He doubted if they would register the news of Fitzraven's murder at all.

Looking out across the damp grey and shadowed roads around him, he wondered if the strength of the applause might be audible in Great Suffolk Street, where Justice Pither had his house and Fitzraven rested, wondered if its echo flowed over the man's cold corpse and whispered in his empty ear. Then, smoothing his coat, he turned away from the night, prepared to leave his office with a proper air of modest pleasure. He would appear gratified, and each word of praise he solicited would sound to him like gold knocking on gold.

# PART III

## III.1

*Sunday, 18 November 1781*

LONDON ROLLED OVER in its bed and yawned at the approaching morning, then cursed it. In the churches, old men turned large keys in the doors and shoved them cautiously open, letting the darkness out before the first worshippers found their way in. Those who had got enough pennies together to drink the night before, flinched at the dawn and their empty pockets. In the better houses, young girls, their hands already worn red with work and cold water, cleaned the grates and set the fires, dreaming of the narrow beds they had just left. In the rookeries the day began with angry growls and hands grasping for what comfort they could find in the dark. Another day to live through.

The night had gone and dawn was wearying away at the skin of the November gloom as best it could when there was a low tap at Jocasta's door. She was in her usual place among the patchwork blankets on her little settee, but everything existed in only shades of grey. Her fire had gone out and she had lit no candle. Until she jerked her head up at the knock, the scene could have been one of stone; even Boyo was still and waiting.

'Come in then,' she said, not bothering to raise her voice. The door opened a crack, and a little boy peered round its edge. He looked very young, and mangy. His fingers were black with filth, and his hair so greasy it looked like he'd been dipped into a tar pit by his heels.

95

'Mrs Bligh? Ripley said I should come to you once I'd seen the morning in. Tell you what I been looking at on Salisbury Street.'

'Good lad. Ripley said he'd send Sam. That you?' He nodded. 'You been there all night?'

The lad began to sidle round the door and rubbed his nose on his hand. 'I have, Mrs Bligh.' He paused.

Jocasta waited a moment then looked up at him frowning. 'Out with it, boy.'

'Mrs Bligh, I don't mean no disrespect, but are you a witch, Mrs Bligh?' The words tumbled out of him like a sailor's pay.

Jocasta sucked on her few good teeth. 'Wish that I were. But if I were, you'd see more frogs and toads round here and fewer men. I have my talents. See forward sometimes. Right – I've satisfied your asking, now satisfy mine.'

The boy looked a bit confused and Jocasta thought for a second he wouldn't have the sense to stop with his own questions, but he seemed to take a hold of himself and said, 'Ripley told me at your asking to stay outside the Mitchell place. By the time I got myself there, there was a candle lit, and a lady walking about inside. Young, like.'

'Kate.'

Sam shrugged. 'Can't answer to her name. So she closed the shutter, then evening-timeish came a man, not that old, all yellow-haired and milky-looking . . .'

'That'd be Fred.'

'I guess so. Anyhow, he was in a while then he came out and spotted me, lurking, and he gave me a penny to carry a note to Hay Market. Said it was urgent. Told me to give it to Mrs Mitchell in the coffee rooms there.' He puffed out his chest a bit as he said the last, then his shoulders dropped again. 'I wasn't sure what to do, so I got my mate Clayton to stand watch while I went. Was that right?'

'It was.'

The boy looked relieved.

'So I took it where I was told and she was there flogging oranges and coffee fast as she could take the money. She read the note and looked bitter as dry lemons, and made a face like she's smelled something real bad, and said, "You go back to the man that gave you this, and tell him to come fetch me at midnight and say nothing but sweets till then", and sent me out of the place. She made me repeat it a couple of times first.'

Jocasta nodded slowly. 'Can you read, boy? Did you look at what was writ?'

The boy scratched the back of his neck with sudden energy and force for a moment then replied, 'No, Mrs Bligh. But I brought it with me.' He reached into his waistband and pulled out a crumpled bit of paper. 'She just dropped it after I gave it her, so I picked it up again, pretending to be after touching her manky oranges. Cost me a slap.'

'No use handing it to me, lad.'

'Oh,' he said, and put it a little disappointedly on the table between them.

Jocasta pulled her shawl round her shoulders. 'All right then, boy – then what?'

'I went back to that milky bloke, gave him the message and he gave me the penny.' The boy looked sadly at his feet. 'I gave it to Clay, though I might've kept it because he said no one had been or come since I was gone.' The corner of Jocasta's mouth twitched. 'Then late, real late, Milky Boy heads out again, and about an hour later I see them turn in at the top of the street and stand there a while.'

'Just standing, were they?'

'Fighting, I'd say. The Mitchell woman was all hissy and him cowering like a kicked dog.'

'Did you hear what passed?'

The boy looked suddenly miserable. 'No, Mrs Bligh. I tried, but they kept their voices low. Her maid was following on behind, and I didn't want to be seen. He looked like he was asking something, getting her to say a yes to it. Just guessing, mind.'

'All right then, lad, say on.'

'They went in the house, both looking sour, and there were a few lights about.'

Jocasta rocked herself back and forth a while, sucking on her teeth. Thinking on it, she forgot the boy for a moment, and was almost surprised when she came to herself and saw him still standing in front of her.

'All right, Sam. You can earn back that penny, if you like. Get that fire going and cook up the bacon in the crock under the window and you can warm up and have your breakfast here. My dog Boyo will whine at you for a share, but don't you be fooled by his blandishments. But stroke him if you care to.'

Sam beamed and got to work with a vigour, although till the fire was bright and the bacon starting to sing, Jocasta could see his thin shoulders were still shivering from the cold of his watch. Out all night in nothing but rags, enough to make you spit.

She looked at the paper Sam had retrieved lying on the table. There were a few words on it. What they were, she had no way of knowing.

## III.2

GABRIEL CROWTHER MAY not have attended the opera the previous evening, but by the time Mrs Westerman made her appearance in the drawing room in Berkeley Square on Sunday morning, he thought that he might as well have done. He was shown into the room just as the other ladies had come back from church and he was pounced upon by Rachel, Harriet's younger sister, and by Susan as a fresh audience for their enthusiasms. As they began to talk to him, Lady Thornleigh skipping round his chair like a puppy in need of exercise, Crowther bowed to Mrs Service, who gave him a friendly nod and took her usual place in the corner, fetching out her work basket.

If there had been some element of appeal in Mr Crowther's glance, she chose to ignore it and did not check her young charge, thinking, as many did, that a little liveliness would do Mr Crowther no harm, but sat by the fire with her sewing and smiled as she listened to the retelling of the opera.

Susan Thornleigh knew enough to realise it had been a great indulgence in her guardian to let her attend the opera with Rachel and Mrs Service and himself, and perhaps suspected she should not let herself be as obviously excited as she was, but the joy of an audience and pleasure in having something to tell was too intoxicating. Her natural abilities as musician and actress made her retelling more interesting than monologues from little girls usually are, and the palpable joy with which she told Crowther the whole argument of the entertainment was so innocent and wholehearted, to hold her back would have been an unnatural cruelty.

'Then Fléance – Signor Manzerotti, you know . . .' She pulled herself up straight, opened her eyes wide and set her shoulders down and at an angle. The effect was so like Manzerotti, Crowther could not help smiling. 'He is convinced he must leave Indomida – that's Miss Marin.' Now she pointed her chin upwards and fluttered her eyelashes, her hands clasped and raised. Again, it was uncanny. Crowther was surprised into a dry bark of laughter which made Susan skip with pleasure before taking up her story. 'Indomida does not know why Fléance is become so cold and is very upset, and it is just after that, they sing the duet! You heard it yesterday – Mrs Westerman told us you did.' He nodded, and Susan began to hum the tune. 'Oh, it is so beautiful, isn't it, Rachel, dear?'

Miss Trench nodded and said dreamily, 'They had to encore it twice, Mr Crowther, and even the composer was given his own "bravo!" The roses on stage! Oh it was heaven, and such noise in the theatre, I thought the ceiling would go flying off! In truth, if the performers had not left the stage, I think that we would be applauding still. I certainly should.'

'Did the composer seem pleased?' Crowther asked.

Susan shrugged and replied, 'Not really. Just a little embarrassed, I think. Some people are shy like that.' Lady Thornleigh put the composer from her mind with a brutal simplicity. 'Then there was another ballet, which was very nice, I thought, except one of the dancers danced like this.' She put her arms out in front of her and performed a few steps with a strange halting diffidence, looking about her as she did as if trying to copy the invisible performers around her. 'However, she was at the back, so didn't spoil it much.'

Crowther did not comment, though he saw Mrs Service look up from her work with an eyebrow raised and caught Susan shrugging an apology while mouthing, 'But it's true!' across the room.

He hid his own smile to ask, 'And how did you enjoy the rest of the opera, Susan?'

'Oh, it was very pleasant, I think. Though mostly in the old style. Graves said Mr Bywater saved all his originality for the duet. That is where he is now – Graves, I mean – supervising the printing of the duet to go on sale in the shop tomorrow. He'll sell thousands! Everyone will want it. Everyone was talking about it at church today, weren't they, Rachel? Even people who weren't there.' Susan shook her head at the madness of the world, then continued, 'Though *I* don't need the music, I can remember it all anyway. And Manzerotti sang, "*Sia fatta la pace*", his favourite aria. He sings it every time he performs, you know, and it was quite wonderful.' She hummed a little, then exclaimed, 'But we must show you what happens in the end! There is a sea battle and a very funny bit where Manzerotti is chased round the stage by the Furies. Rachel, I shall be Manzerotti and you must be Miss Marin because that is not so hard. All you have to do is clasp your hands and blink as if you have dust in your eyes.'

Crowther missed the retelling of the Third Act however, as it was at that moment Mrs Westerman came in to join them.

'You see, Crowther?' she said. 'We are the best entertained household in London.' She looked at Rachel and Susan playing Manzerotti and Marin in front of the proscenium arch of the fireplace. 'All of the luminaries of the theatre and music world come to us here in the shape of Lady Thornleigh.'

That young lady grinned up frankly at Harriet then swept a theatrical bow to her. 'Madam, I thank you.'

Rachel put her arm around Susan's shoulders, her good humour apparently dissipated by the arrival of her sister. 'Come along, dear heart. Let us see what mischief the young gentlemen are about and leave Harriet and Mr Crowther to talk over unpleasant things.'

Mrs Service began to put away her work.

'An excellent plan, Miss Trench,' she agreed. 'Then let us set Susan to work at her keyboard and see how many of last night's arias she can pull out of the air.'

Before Susan could be shepherded from the room, however, Harriet put up a hand.

'Susan, Rachel! One moment, my loves. You said something about being allowed to visit the performers at the end of the evening?'

Susan turned on her heel at once. 'Oh yes! And you told us we must tell Mr Crowther about it too.' She flew back to her stage in front of the fireplace, ignoring the slight frown of Mrs Service. 'Well, everyone was just standing around being awfully polite to each other as people do. The King had left – he seems like a nice man, though he must be terribly worried about America. Then Mr Harwood came in and beckoned Manzerotti and Bywater and Miss Marin over to him.' She took a couple of steps over to her right, then with a frown crooked her finger at some imaginary artists, looking very serious. 'Rachel and I guessed that he was telling them about Mr Fitzraven, didn't we?' Rachel nodded sombrely. 'From where I was standing,' Susan went on, 'I could see Miss Marin best. She did this.'

The little girl actually went pale, and staggered slightly. Crowther found himself on his feet ready to take her arm. She grinned, enchanted at having fooled him.

'Come, Mr Crowther, stand here on my right. You are now Mr Bywater. Miss Marin clutched onto his arm and sort of half-fell on him for a second. Mr Bywater was facing forward still and his lips got all bunched up. He looked a bit like a confused herring.' She dropped Crowther's arm and took a smart step to her left. 'Manzerotti just went very still – like when he got turned into a statue at the end of Act Three – and all the others just started talking. I thought Miss Marin's maid was going to lead her away, but after a few seconds she straightened up again and started talking to Lord Sandwich. I like him. He knows a lot about music for a naval man.'

She smiled round at the adults watching her, expecting more of their praise, but each seemed lost in his or her own thoughts.

'Then Mr Harwood came and made a bow to Rachel and said he hoped Mrs Westerman and Mr Crowther would be successful again in their efforts for justice. And I said I hoped you would be too, for although I was not fond of Mr Fitzraven, no one should be thrown in the river like that.'

Harriet, who was standing with her arms folded, apparently lost in an examination of the carpet at her feet, said, 'And what did Rachel say?'

Susan looked at her with a frank smile. 'Why, nothing. You just curtsied, did you not?'

The young woman nodded.

'And she did so very neatly – you need not be ashamed of her, Mrs Westerman. Three times in ten when I curtsy I still catch my slipper on my petticoat.'

No one offered any remark to that.

'There! Did I help?'

'Yes, Lady Thornleigh,' said Crowther. 'You certainly did.'

'Good,' she said, snatching up Rachel's hand and dragging her towards the doorway where Mrs Service was still waiting for them. 'I like to be of help.'

Harriet took the seat Rachel had just left, and they had the room to themselves.

'It seems,' Harriet said after a few moments, 'that Miss Marin was worth the trouble of her hiring. If the congregation of St James's is anything to measure by, all of London is enraptured. Do you think her reaction to Fitzraven's death is suggestive?'

Crowther tented his fingers. 'You think she too might be a spy? Though of course we have as yet no reason to believe Palmer's suspicions of Fitzraven to be accurate.' He seemed lost in contemplation of his cuffs, though Harriet knew wherever he directed his gaze at such moments, he saw nothing. The strange chemical stains that often appeared round his wrists were testament to that. He continued: 'I pity Fitzraven. From what we have learned of him, this would be the sort of day to make him very happy.' He reached into his pocket and produced a piece of paper. 'I have had an interesting note this morning from our friend Justice Pither. He gives us his full authority, and a great deal of thanks, and would be delighted if we can – and I must quote him here – "perform those duties due to the dead man from which pressure of other business under his jurisdiction keep him".'

He passed the note to Harriet and she read it, wincing. 'That is an ugly phrase, "duties due". Strange man, Justice Pither. I wonder that he cannot hear his own awkwardness. However, I presume he means he would like us to find him a killer if we can.'

'Note also,' with his long fingers Crowther tapped at the significant passage in the paper Harriet held, 'he reminds us that a considerable award is available to those who bring such black-hearted villains to the King's Justice.'

Harriet put the note aside and half-smiled at the floor in front of her. 'Very well then, Crowther. It seems Mr Palmer has managed to arrange authority for us through whatever means. I feel sorry for Mr Pither to be used so, but I suppose we are in the service of a greater good. Let us see what we can do. What do you suggest?'

Crowther returned to his examination of his fingertips, saying, 'Graves said Fitzraven had lodgings in a house in Great Swallow

Street. I suggest we go there and see if there is anything which might suggest that Palmer's suspicions are well-grounded.'

'Crowther,' Harriet said slowly, 'I have been thinking more about Mr Palmer and whether, by engaging us to act in this way, he hopes I will continue to press James for what he learned from the agent aboard the *Marquis*. Might that not be his primary motive?'

'I cannot say, though I believe that when a man like Mr Palmer, however frank his demeanour, says he has three reasons for a course of action, he in all probability has four or five,' Crowther replied. Upstairs, the faint song of Susan's harpsichord began. The notes seemed to tumble through the ceiling rose and dance like dust motes in sunlight around them. 'However, I do not think any additional motive he has renders the reasons he stated invalid.'

There was a laugh from above. Harriet recognised the voice of her sister. Her hand lay on the arm of one of the elegant but functional chairs that were dotted about the room. Under her fingers the wood seemed to change from gilt into the smooth timbers of a ship's gunwale, and the scattered brightness of the instrument playing over their heads became the sound of water rippling under the bow on one of those blessed days where the wind is generous, though the sea is calm. It had been on such a day in the East Indies when her husband's ship and the merchantman she shadowed had been attacked by a privateer. The attempt would never have been made against a ship of His Majesty's Navy, had not the crew of the privateer received intelligence of the coming of the ship, and the wealth of the merchantman she accompanied. It had allowed them to take advantage of the play of coast and prevailing wind, and the engagement had been sharp. Three members of James's crew had never been ashore again. It was one of the crew of the merchantman who had betrayed them. Harriet had seen the man hung and felt no qualm at his death.

'I hate spies, Crowther. The fact that Fitzraven seems to have been a prying, sneaking little man makes me suspect him strongly.'

'We should bear in mind that the most successful of their breed are more likely to wear a charming and honest face.'

That was the last moment when it occurred to Harriet that she still had time to withdraw. She could picture the scene upstairs – Lady Susan entertaining the younger children with Rachel, and Mrs Service at their side – and wondered to herself if she might join them, might be free and easy, and foul neither her mind nor her reputation with further association with violent death. Then she thought of her husband and felt, with a sensation like sand running through her hands, that her days of ease were perhaps in any case over. She might join the party upstairs, but at present she would only bring darkness with her.

Let Palmer make use of her, then.

## III.3

JOCASTA, SAM AND Boyo made a breakfast from the strips of bacon the boy found in the crock, and it did Jocasta some good to watch him cooking the meat with such a tender care, humming to himself over the fire. When the first knock at the door came and a thin man in a tatty overcoat arrived to have his cards read, Sam skipped out to clean their cuttles at the pump, and when there was a gap in the flow of people coming to be told what they already knew and bite their thumbnails over it, he set the kettle to boil over the fire and brewed a dish of tea for her. She sat back in her seat to drink it, and nodded to him to get some into himself too. It had been an ordinary morning. Three girls coming to ask if they should marry, an older woman wanting to know if her husband was getting too friendly with their neighbour's wife, and the thin man who'd been told if he handed ten pounds to a friend of his to hold he'd have fifteen before the end of the year. The girls would marry, though two were tying themselves to lazy fools if the cards were right, the woman was unjust, and the man would have less trouble if he just threw his money into the Thames today and have done. But while the cards had told stories to each of them in their usual way, they had not ceased teasing at Jocasta. At the centre of every spread she laid out, she saw that house in Salisbury Street. Now she set down her tea and sniffed, pulling the box towards her. Sam sat up with interest and watched her lay out the cards cross-fashion.

'All right, all right,' she said under her tongue as she slapped them down. 'Have your way and talk if you will. Stop you interrupting stories other people have paid for, at any rate.'

Here it all was again. This time with The Tower high and present. She could almost hear the little people diving from it, screeching as they fell. She thought of Kate's heart-shaped face, and weak little chin.

Sam leaned over and tapped it all careful, careful.

'I do not like this card,' he said. Jocasta glanced across at him, all serious but with the sweets of childhood about him still. He looked to her like a box unopened, a roll of fabric still wound tight, a pack uncut, dice rattling across a playing board before they are still and the number is fixed for counting and paying.

'Where are your people, Sam?'

He did not look at her. 'I haven't got any people. Ripley, maybe. He used to let me sleep round the back of the chophouse and drop me ends and leavings when he could, but the bastard who runs the place found out and threatened us both with a stealing charge if I came back.'

There were so many homeless children in London, and so few made it even as far into the game as this little scrap.

'And previous to that?'

'Workhouse, with my dad. Southwark. Drink killed him a while back and I ran.'

Jocasta swept up the cards, straightened and shuffled them and offered the pack to him. He cut it and lifted his half to show the picture at the bottom. Page of Cups.

Jocasta considered it, then shifted on her seat and rubbed her nose. 'Do me a job now and fast, and I'll let you have the chair here tonight.'

Sam was all attention. 'What's to be done, Mrs Bligh?'

'Go to Salisbury Street again. See what that family are about, then go get Ripley to read that note. Then come back here. That fair?'

'Thanks, Mrs Bligh. I'll be right back here.' He stood up and almost fell over his feet in his eagerness to be of help. Then he turned back with a wide grin. 'Bye, Boyo!' The terrier got to his feet and wagged his tail hard.

'Dog, you are a tramping thing,' Jocasta muttered as the door closed. 'It was my bacon you breakfasted on.' Boyo snuffled and tucked his nose under Jocasta's hand, his tail still going like the clapper in a fire bell.

Great Swallow Street was respectable enough, and many of the houses there would begin to fill as the season progressed with people of middling gentility. Some of the buildings, however, had been split and resplit into ever-smaller apartments, and though the lodgings there were palatial in comparison with the piled-up, patched-up hovels and garrets into which most of London's populace were crammed, they suggested nevertheless struggle and compromise. The road itself was a thoroughfare to the farms that fed the great city, and as Harriet and Crowther walked along the pavement, the road was jammed with families making their way out into the fresh air in Sunday clothes and bad temper.

They found the house where Mr Fitzraven had been lodging without great difficulty, and summoned his landlady to the door. Behind them, the laughter and calls of the crowd mingled with the sound of horses and cartwheels churning the mud and mess of the city. One cart had become lodged in a rut, and the owner was trying, red-faced and sweating, to force his horse into movement under the heavy stare of his passenger – a large woman in a drooping bonnet and skirts of ferocious rigidity. She held one child in her lap while two others, who had the alarmed look of the recently scrubbed, hopped about in the cart behind her, more fully driving the wheel into its wedged position. A rather pale-looking young man with a good-looking wife on his arm walked by. The girl seemed gay enough, her blonde curls bouncing out from under her neat little bonnet, but her husband looked tense and unhappy. Behind them, a woman of middle-age followed, her mouth a thin line and her spine straight as steel. She had her eyes on the back of the young woman's head and there was no fondness in them.

Fitzraven's landlady gave her name as Mrs Girdle when she finally made her appearance at the street door, then led them into her own parlour, a narrow room at the front of the house where the business of the street and the comings and going in her own home could be easily observed. The room suited her, being somewhat pinched, cramped and pretentious without elegance. The furniture was too large and dark for the space, and gave the impression of a room filled with fat and uncongenial relatives forced into a joint vigil round a miser's deathbed. She herself was a narrow woman, thin and straight, with iron-grey curls showing under her cap and a strangely high collar. It seemed when she spoke that her chin was constantly lifting and worrying from side to side, as if it feared it was about to be drowned by the starched lace below it. Harriet suspected that trying to maintain her gaze would lead to sea-sickness.

When they told her of Fitzraven, Mrs Girdle at once burst into tears, collapsing back into her armchair like a snapped plank and lifting her apron to her face. Then, after a few moments of sobbing, her back straightened and her words came forth in a torrent. Her voice had a high-pitched whine to it as if the words were being forced out of her pursed mouth under considerable pressure. Much of what she said at first neither of them entirely understood, but it seemed Fitzraven had been a man of talents and civility without parallel, a man who would lay down his life for the right, and shared every opinion of hers she had ever thought to form, displaying a judgement so sound even her father, a man of rigour in these matters, would have been happy to praise, and his loss would never be appreciated by anyone as keenly as herself. She had, it seemed, been on the point of an introduction to Manzerotti himself, who was Mr Fitzraven's great friend, she assured them, and she had sent her particular compliments to that gentleman through Mr Fitzraven, and been told they were received most graciously. And now who was to pay the rent on his rooms? He'd taken them through the season and she'd turned down a dozen other gentlemen. Not that she blamed Mr Fitzraven himself, of course.

She was beginning to plot through her tears a series of letters both to the opera house itself and all the newspapers, when Harriet felt compelled to stop her, partly to save her own sanity, and partly because she could see Crowther was starting to enjoy the display of a certain sort of feminine stupidity, and she found his amusement intensely irritating.

'Mrs Girdle, may we see Mr Fitzraven's rooms?' The torrent of words stopped abruptly and Mrs Girdle examined her suspiciously with red-rimmed eyes.

'If there is anything of value there, it is mine by rights. If I can't get another lodger into those rooms straight away, I'll have troubles.'

'We wish to find who killed him, madam,' said Crowther mildly. 'We have no interest in robbing his estate.'

'Some jealous musician! I know it! Oh, he was modest, and a circumspect man, but I could tell he'd been betrayed and disappointed in his trusts.' She blinked at Harriet. 'I could tell, madam, having been so often myself disappointed by my fellow creatures. Oh, the stories he could tell of that place, of His Majesty's! The rivalries! The intrigues!' Her voice had taken on a conspiratorial hush.

'What manner of stories, Mrs Girdle?' Crowther adopted a slightly sceptical smile. 'You would be acting as an agent of justice, you know, if you were to tell us them now.'

The landlady flushed a little and lifted her chin so high it seemed it might escape being swallowed in her collar, after all.

'Oh, dear Mr Fitzraven was far too discreet a gentleman to say anything very *specific*, even to me, sir. But it was the tone in which he spoke of the opera, Harwood and Manzerotti and the pretty French girl and them all. The disgraceful behaviour he saw there, again and again! I am sure there came a point when he could take no more, made his stand and was cut down for it. I said to him once – he was sitting just where you are now, madam – "You know things, don't you, dear Fitz" – that was my name for him – and he nodded and said, "Dear Mrs G., things that would turn your hair *white!*"

'However,' the lady continued, drawing herself upright and cocking her head to see the effect her revelations were having on her guests, 'if you wish to see the room I have no objection. I hold the key to every door. It is a condition of tenancy. This is a respectable house.' Standing up, she went to a bureau squeezed awkwardly into a corner next to the wall and opened a drawer. She moved like a bad actress playing Queen Elizabeth; she was too self-conscious to manage the rather grand effect she attempted. Her guests also stood and she passed them a small sparkling brass key with studied condescension. It appeared that having experimented with horror, and found no echo, she would now attempt dignity. 'There. First door on the top of the second flight. You can find your own way.'

Crowther bowed, and was rewarded with a faint wave of her hand.

Harriet had paused on the first landing to glance at the length of the passageway and count the doors that led off it, then moved aside for a flat-faced serving girl to pass her on the stairs, so Crowther had already opened the door to Fitzraven's room before she joined him at the top of the second flight. He had pushed the door ajar to give a full view of the apartment, but not yet entered it. She was about to pass by him when he stopped her.

'Wait, Mrs Westerman.' She frowned, then, following the direction of his eyes, gave the room her full attention from their current vantage point.

The room was orderly enough and had little in it that was not plain, functional or both. It seemed the apartment was made up of two chambers. In the original conception of the architect it had been designed as a single space, but wooden shutters now divided it into this parlour room and, presumably, a bedchamber beyond. The ceiling was low, but there was a window looking out to the back of the house that provided some light, and under it sat a writing desk that seemed rather messier than the rest of the room. It did not take Harriet long to see why Crowther had stopped her. The chair that served the writing table had been overturned and lay on its side, a number of newspaper pages scattered around it.

'A sign of an altercation, you think, Crowther?' she said.

'It appears so.'

'May we conclude that Mr Fitzraven was murdered here?'

'Conclusions of any sort are a little previous at this point,' he replied, 'but possibly. Is there not something unusual about the way the armchairs are arranged?'

Harriet walked into the room, the full skirts of her dress washing over the bare floorboards. If she had had the business of arranging the furniture, the chairs would have been further forward, and closer, so that two people taking their ease there could enjoy each other and the fire. Here, however, the armchairs stood either side of the fireplace, facing out into the room like the porcelain spaniels that framed the mantelpiece of Lady Thornleigh's modest bedroom in Berkeley Square. Behind the legs of the armchair nearest to the writing desk, a sheet of the *Daily Advertiser* had been curled and crumpled.

'They have been moved backwards, I think,' Harriet said, then turned towards the prints on the mantelpiece above the fire.

Crowther went to the writing desk. A large leather volume sat open at its centre, and whatever disturbance had turned the chair on its back and scattered the newsprint to the floor, it had been insufficient to move it. Crowther peered down. It was a book of cuttings. He noticed a little pair of scissors lying next to it, the sort most commonly found in a woman's sewing basket, and a glue pot. The open page was filled with an advertisement similar to that which Crowther had seen outside His Majesty's Theatre for the performance of the previous night, neatly glued and placed squarely in the middle of the sheet. He picked up the book in his arms and turned over the pages.

Most of the sections of newsprint Fitzraven had decided to preserve were of a similar nature; advertisements and reviews of the offerings of the opera house from winter 1778 to the current day. Crowther imagined that Fitzraven himself must have been the author of several of them, and having read a few words thought his literary style had little to recommend it but enthusiasm. Other paragraphs had been judged worthy for inclusion. Crowther found himself reading an announcement that Razini had arrived with his companions in the city on 25 October 1779, and that his performance in the *opera seria Demofoonte* was awaited with much delight. There was also a portrait of Miss Marin. It was perhaps a little idealised, but still very like her. Under it, a neat hand had written *December 3rd 1780*, and added an exclamation point.

Flicking over another page, Crowther found a series of letters from the pages of the *Mercury Post* which debated the arrangement of private boxes in the theatre and the relative merits and demerits of the old and new systems. Crowther turned again to the last few pages that Fitzraven had reached. There was a paragraph on a private concert Manzerotti had given at the Duke of Cumberland's house the previous week, and on the page before, an article detailing some entertainment of the upper classes in St James's. Crowther could see no obvious connection to the opera until he noticed Miss Marin's name as an attendee in the final line. He noted with a sneer that Lord Carmichael's name was also mentioned.

He looked up from his study and out into Mrs Girdle's yard, thinking of the man who had stared out of this window only two days before. It took him a moment to realise, as he saw the body and the marks made on it again in his mind's eye, that he was in truth staring up and across the yard into the windows of the house opposite and into the moon-face of a young woman. Seeing that she had been noticed in her observation of him, she started and disappeared into the depths of the house again. Crowther frowned. How could the citizens of London murder one another without being seen? This house itself was full of people, and when one enjoyed the daylight available from the windows, one must also expose oneself and one's business to the citizenry. He thought of his collection of anatomical specimens in his house in Hartswood, each body part delicately prepared for public display so strangers such as himself could peer through the glass and conjecture on the form and play of muscles, on the variety, invention and cruelty of nature. Crowther himself was a private man, and the idea of being so constantly under the eyes of strangers made him shiver.

'Lord, Crowther! This place tells us as much as his poor corpse did. You must prepare another paper for the Royal Society.'

Crowther turned to her. 'I'm sorry, Mrs Westerman. Yes, perhaps. Though unless the French Navy have a passionate interest in the Italian Opera in London, I cannot see how the information Mr Fitzraven has gathered might be of use to them.' Harriet shrugged, and Crowther found himself smiling at the gesture.

'Do you see there is no candle on the desk there, but there is one in the fireplace?' she said.

'I see that. So what do you conclude, Mrs Westerman?'

'I observe – I make no conclusions. You have warned me against them, repeatedly. Someone lit a candle and placed that candle unusually in the room. Now what shall we say to the chairs, Crowther? They were moved after the fight took place, the newspaper behind the chair leg shows us that.'

'I do not know. Fitzraven was probably killed here and left lying for some time, until darkness came and the body could be hidden. The patterns of pooling blood in his tissues tell us that much. But why create this space for a man to lie in the middle of the room, rather than leave him where he fell?'

He imagined the vigil of the killer. A figure seated in one of the armchairs, panting with the effort of having killed another man, waiting for darkness and keeping company with the cooling corpse, while all around them London continued to live as it liked best, in ignorance and noise.

'Thieves!'

Harriet and Crowther turned to the open door to find Mrs Girdle standing there, one hand covering her mouth, the other pointing at the floorboards. Her grey curls quivered with indignation. 'I have been robbed! Where is my hearthrug?'

There was a moment of silence before Harriet smiled, showing her neat white teeth. 'I rather believe, Mrs Girdle, that Fitzraven's body was wrapped in it before being removed from your house.'

Mrs Girdle paddled her hands around her face. 'Oh, the horror!' She beat a swift retreat from the doorway.

Crowther raised his eyebrow at his companion. She folded her arms across her bodice. 'Yes, perhaps that was a little cruel. But the woman is very wearing.' She crossed to the door to the bedchamber. 'Now, shall we see what else we can learn?'

# III.4

SAM WAS BACK quick, and his visage was red with running. Jocasta wondered how such a wisp of a thing could survive friendless in London. Indeed, not many did, but here was a miracle catching its breath by the fire. Put a bit of bacon in him and a scrap of warmth and he was already looking a bit brighter and dashing about. A week of half-decent food and he'd look like a lad who'd grown up chasing round Brasslethwaite and drinking real milk.

'They've gone on a jaunt, Mrs Bligh. That's what their maid said, anyway. Gone out walking. Left straight after church.'

Jocasta frowned and rubbed her nose. That didn't sound so bad. Perhaps Kate had pulled her boy back from the edge and The Tower would stay whole and all would be well and healthy.

Sam still hunched over with his hands on his breeches, panting hard.

'And I took the note to Ripley. He sends his respects to you, ma'am, and says the words say "I think Kate knows".'

The faint warmth of hope in her belly twisted into something sharp and black. Jocasta got that cold feeling again, as if she'd swallowed an ice house. She was up on her feet before Sam could shut his lips together again. 'What is it, Mrs Bligh? I haven't done wrong, have I?'

Jocasta put her hand hard on his shoulder.

'Which way did they go?'

The bedchamber was small, but between the chest and bureau that shared the space with the bedstead, more informative in the practical truths of Fitzraven's day to day than the bare parlour. Crowther watched Harriet's lip curl in distaste as she opened the drawers of the man's chest.

'It must be done, Mrs Westerman. The dead have no privacy, I am afraid.'

Harriet nodded, then turned away from him. Some little time passed and having found nothing but clean linen, a few trinkets and another full book of newspaper cuttings about His Majesty's, she slammed home the last drawer and sat on the bed with a sigh.

'Anything, Crowther?'

That gentleman looked up from his examination of a neat little bureau tucked into the corner of the room.

'Perhaps. Mr Fitzraven seemed to take great pleasure in reckoning his expenses.' He passed a little green journal to her, and she leafed through it. 'It was tucked away at the back of his bureau.' As Harriet looked at the pages her attention became focused. The numbers were neatly penned and each page tallied. They had a story to tell, certainly.

'Indeed, Crowther. The start of this year he is buying only the bare necessities, yet this month he has been buying fobs and snuff

and new cravats as if he were a rich man. Is that his snuffbox there?'
Crowther looked where she was pointing and handed it to her. It was
a rather flashy object. She spun it in her fingers as she continued to
read. She paused and snorted, then in reply to Crowther's look of
enquiry said: 'Oh, only he spent almost two pounds on a pair of
breeches. He was a fool as well as vain. Do you think his trip to the
continent gave him such riches to idle away like this? I see no note
here of his incomings.'

'It is possible he did very well from his trip, especially if, as Harwood
suggests, he was bribed to engage some of the singers. But there are
some considerable sums here. And the rent for these rooms is far in
excess of what he was paying earlier in the year, so he must have taken
them in expectations that his income would continue high. Yet I have
found no ready money in his bureau – though there are some empty
pigeon-holes here. He may have been robbed as well as murdered.
Also, if you observe, while he was more generous to himself after his
trip, it was only some three weeks ago that he began to spend with
real extravagance.'

'I wonder what happened three weeks ago?' Harriet said, squinting
at the journal.

'I think that is when the company engaged for this season arrived
in London.'

'Now that *is* an interesting coincidence.' Harriet passed the little
book back to him, and Crowther slipped it into his coat, then her
eye was caught by the violin case that lay open on the bed beside her.

'Poor orphan,' Harriet said, and let her fingers rest on the honey-
coloured wood. It was her thought that if Fitzraven had no relatives
to claim the estate of newspaper cuttings, some printed music and
clothes, it would in all likelihood be sold by Mrs Girdle to cover the
rent he had agreed to pay. She wondered about buying the violin
herself as a present for her son. Graves could tell her who was best
to teach the boy. James would have loved his son to develop an
affection for music like his own. *Would have.* She had squeezed her

eyes shut, trying to close the thought away and on opening them again lifted the instrument from its case. She was turning it in her hands to catch the light creeping apologetically in from the street outside, when Crowther picked up the case and turned it upside down, shaking it vigorously.

'Good Lord, Crowther, what on earth are you . . . ?' Then Harriet found herself interrupted by the sound of the case's inner lining giving way and a little tumble of letters fell onto the bed between them. She picked one up and had just unfolded it, hoping for state secrets but catching only a flowing feminine hand, when she heard footsteps in the outer room. Turning towards the door in expectation of seeing Mrs Girdle, she was surprised to find herself looking into the shocked face of Isabella Marin. From behind her, as if appearing out of the folds of the soprano's skirts, a short, bullet-headed woman stepped forward, saw what Harriet held, and whistling put her hands on her hip.

'Well, that's torn it, Issy. I told you we should have started out earlier, but no you have to go and show off at church, and then show off to Lady Georgiana, yabbering away about millinery as if it's something you either knew or cared a damn about.'

Miss Marin remained still and silent throughout this little speech. She blinked and parted her lips, but no sounds issued forth.

Her maid, or so she appeared by her dress, if not her manner, nodded to Harriet and Crowther. 'I'm guessing you are Mrs Westerman and Mr Crowther that Harwood mentioned to us last night. I'm Morgan, and this chatty little piece is Isabella Marin. Though I suppose you know that.'

On hearing that the famous French soprano Miss Isabella Marin was in her house, Mrs Girdle was only too ready to put her parlour at their disposal and provide tea for her guests. She seemed reluctant to leave them to themselves, but she soon quailed under the eye of Miss Marin's formidable maid. Harriet was amused. She would never have

117

thought it possible at a time when French maids were regarded as essential to any woman of fashion in London, that a Frenchwoman would hire a Londoner to see to her needs; particularly one with such unusual manners. Morgan spoke like the urchins and street-sellers that rolled along in the London muck. It seemed she had managed to get her position without troubling herself to learn the more refined accents used by most upper servants.

Harriet watched Morgan bustling Mrs Girdle out of her own living room with some admiration. She reminded her of the wife of a master shipwright in Gibraltar. A woman born in the back streets of Plymouth, she had dealt with the social niceties of the naval community by cheerfully ignoring them. She would treat an Admiral in the same way she would a Midshipman or her own servant, and had ended up with friends in every rank of the Service.

Miss Marin herself had hardly said a word since they met her and now she turned towards the fire and fell into a study of the flames. She seemed only a ghost of the woman Harriet had heard singing the previous day, and she wondered what toll the rigours of performance took on women like this slight French girl.

Having secured the room, her maid took a seat a little way behind her. The fire cracked and Harriet was beginning to cast about in her head for some words that could wake the young lady into conversation again, when the maid, without shifting her head from the study of Mrs Girdle's mantelpiece, said, 'Well, Issy love, if you are to tell, then do so. They have seen the letters, and I don't think they'll hand them over till they know what's in them from us, or read them on their own – not now that bastard is dead. You must confess, so do so and have done.'

Harriet was startled. Whatever the relationship was between the two women, it was very different from the one she had with her own maid.

'I reckon you can trust 'em, dearie.'

Isabella gave herself a little shake. 'Yes, I suppose I shall have to,

Morgan. Lord, but how to begin! You were right – I should never have replied to his bloody letters.'

At this, Crowther and Harriet had to struggle to keep their jaws closed. Isabella spoke with the same accent of the London slums as Morgan. She looked up at them and smiled ruefully at their expressions.

'Yes. I am more a native of this place than you, or Mr Crowther I think, Mrs Westerman. I was born and raised in London and I'm sorry to say it, but there it is: Nathaniel Fitzraven was my father.'

Crowther and Harriet continued to look at her in astonishment. Morgan peered round at them both carefully.

'Well, they weren't expecting *that*, Issy.'

Sam bobbed along behind Jocasta looking scared and getting tangled up with Boyo at her heels.

'Is it because of the note, Mrs Bligh? It meant something bad, didn't it? I knew it soon as Ripley said, that's why I ran back so fast.'

Jocasta powered on. 'Yes, lad, you did well. Out along Oxford Street?'

'Yes—' Sam said, and almost got a crack round the ear for knocking into a man with a pie halfway down his throat. 'Maid said that puckered-faced woman had been asking for a quiet place to walk.' He had no idea that Mrs Bligh could have any more speed left in her, but her pace picked up again and Sam danced among the mess and mass of people to keep up with her.

Isabella shrugged, then looked back towards the fire and began to speak. 'I was born and raised in London. Not this part of town, though – never made it out of Southwark till I was seven years old. My mother died about then, and she asked Morgan here to take care of me. She was always a good friend to Mother – helped her out when she could and showed me how to make enough money to feed myself by the time I could walk. Tell them, Morgan.'

Crowther looked at Morgan as if for the first time. She was perhaps

119

in her sixties, small and rounded in her figure. Her eyes were uncannily blue. Crowther did not think himself a snob, despite his ignored title and his still considerable wealth, but he was aware that the woman in front of him was changing in his eyes from an addendum to Miss Marin to an individual herself.

'I used to sing ballads in the bars and streets for pennies. That was my trade and that's when I met Issy's mum, Tessa. She used to hang about to hear me sing for hours, when she was just big with this little bird.' She frowned at the floor between them, and scratched her chin. 'Issy's mum was a good girl, but she was never going to get to old age in this town. Too feeble to do the hard work, and too much an easy mark for bad men. Oh I'd tell her, time and time again, I'd tell her. I learned to spot a wrong 'un young, but she'd never listen. She'd defend them, not speak to me for a month then come round to my room dragging Issy behind her with fresh bruises and nothing to cover herself with but her stays and a skirt too raggedy for even them to steal off her. Some people learn. Some people just roll about in the mess they've made and complain about the stink.'

Isabella twisted in her chair as if about to complain, but Morgan held up a hand. 'Oh, don't fret, Issy! Your mother was a good kind girl and I miss her still, but she wasn't fit or fighting enough to be poor. You know it. Bless me! By the time you were five, if someone cheeked you on the street you'd let fly and they'd be crawling off with the crowd laughing at them before the minute was out.' Morgan put a hand to Isabella's face, pulling back a strand of her black hair. Isabella squirmed in her seat, but allowed it, and Harriet and Crowther saw a jagged little scar on that otherwise velvet skin. Morgan let her fingers brush it, and the hair fall back. 'One of the last did that when Issy took against him for knocking poor Tess about. At seven she tried to fight a grown man, daft little bird.'

'So you taught her to sing, Mrs Morgan?' Crowther asked.

The woman nodded. 'Just Morgan, sir. No need to pretty it up. Yes, I taught her. She used to come along to keep her clear of Tessa's beaus, and learned by listening. By the time she was waist-high she was earning more than her mother and feeding them both – *and* whatever man was about. Though even then I started holding on to her money for her, so they couldn't get their fat paws on the lot.' She paused and sniffed. 'Too late for poor Tessa, though. She was already worn down and the first chill she got in the winter of sixty-seven killed her in a week, no matter how many oranges and red meat that little girl brought her.'

Harriet looked at Mademoiselle Marin, who was staring into the flames as if she could see all her history there, burning and tumbling. Harriet thought of the little girl trying to ward off all the evils of the world with the most expensive fruit she could find. It was never a fair fight.

'Still,' Isabella said now with a sigh, 'no reason you should have any interest in that. You want to know about Fitzraven, don't you, and who killed him. My mother's dying had nothing to do with those things. Fitzraven charmed her in a house where she worked and he taught fiddle to the eldest son. He promised her roses and marriage then ran for it and would have nothing to do with her when she was cast off. Then came some bad times and they are best forgotten.'

'Miss Marin,' Crowther said, 'did you never see your father when you were a child? Did your mother make no attempt to speak to his conscience?'

Isabella nodded slowly. 'Once, only once. It was on London Bridge. I was with Mother and she spotted him on the other side of the road. It was before they knocked the houses down, and the way was so crammed I thought we'd be crushed under the wheels of the carts. I was about five, I think. There was this gentleman, or at least he looked a gentleman to me, picking his way along the pavement, and my mother ran up to him and shouted at him, pushed me under his nose. It was the only time I ever saw her stand up for herself like that.' She shifted in her chair. 'He pretended not to know her at first, then he said he didn't think I was his flesh at all. She wouldn't let him get away, not till he had to push her over. I think a couple in the crowd would have had him for that, but he was too quick for them. I remember him disappearing among the people, and my mum on her back in the mud crying like a lost thing. She told me his name, but I never thought to look for him after that, though.'

She fell quiet and put out her hand towards Morgan without turning her face from the fire. The woman took it and held it between her palms.

Harriet began to feel that if she ever met Fitzraven's murderer, she would be forced to congratulate him. 'So then, how came you by your name, your training?' she asked gently.

Morgan patted the hand in her lap and replied for her. 'Well, Mrs Westerman, after Tess passed in sixty-seven, me and the little bit carried on as we were for a year or two, then a musical gentleman took up residence just round from one of our favourite corners for a song up on the far side of London Bridge.'

Harriet thought of the street singers they would pass from time to time in the busier thoroughfares, pinched and dirty faces glimpsed only for a moment as the carriage rolled by, the horses high-stepping as though they were too fine to set their hooves in the muck. She had seen children enough at the same work, their hands outstretched and their voices pale and forced through the cold and soot-soaked air. She realised she had never thought much about their lives before, nor paid attention to their songs.

Morgan's voice was low. 'He heard Isabella and told us he was a teacher of singing and would give her lessons every week without payment. I thought at first he might be one of those gentlemen who like ladies very young, if you take my meaning, but I have to give it to him, there was never a sniff of that sort of nonsense about him. We'd go there every week and I'd sit in the corner and he began to teach her. Me too, I suppose. He'd tell us stories from the opera, and the business of the thing, and show us all the new music and teach it to her, just for the pleasure of it.'

Isabella looked up. Her eyelashes were very long, and her features seemed too delicate for a creature reared in the stink of the city. 'I loved those stories,' she said. 'All those gods and heroes. He had a way with his telling.'

Morgan nodded. 'And I saw on his card at his door one week that he normally charged two shillings an hour for that sort of work, but he'd never take a penny from us. "Morgan," he used to say, "I spend all my days hammering tunes into the heads of the silliest girls in this town. It's a pleasure for me to teach what I know to a true musician".' The old woman wagged her finger at them. '"A true musician" – that's what he called her. Well, once a week turned into twice, and then three till it got to the point we were there every day during the season, and her voice bloomed with the care of it.'

Isabella said: 'He paid for me and Morgan to get into the gallery at His Majesty's and I fell in love with it. The idea that I might be on the stage myself one day was more than I could dream of. All those beautiful women, those costumes. It was as if my heart would burst just at the thought of it.' She was lost for a second in her memories, then said with a quick grin, 'I have never told this story. It feels like a pleasure to tell it – isn't that strange? I always thought it'd be a secret I kept to the grave. Yet here it comes, tripping off my tongue like an old tune.'

Crowther folded together his long fingers over his knee and wondered if every person in the world had some such story, one that could release the teller in the telling. He had his own story, but he had never found it easy to speak of it, even when the confession was forced into the open as Marin's was now. When he told his story it did not come cloaked in this nostalgia; he told it with no charm. He stated the facts and was stared at like a grotesque.

Morgan picked up Isabella's thread. 'The next time we saw him was the last. He had been a little queer in his ways from time to time, sometimes shutting his door and not crawling out of it for a week, and here was another moment of it. We have the lesson as usual then he closes the lid on the harpsichord and says, "Isabella, I have taught you all I can. I have made you a fine singer, but I know another teacher who can make you great. There is a man in Paris called called Le Clerc – all the great singers of Europe go to him. So must you." Well, we just laughed at him straight out. Here we were earning pennies on the street corner, and he wants us to go to France. "No," he says. "I mean it," and he hands us a letter addressed to Le Clerc, lots of bits of paper with official stamps on them and a little bag holding more gold in it than I had ever seen in my life. Turned out he'd been planning and saving for us for a year.'

'I was thirteen,' Isabella said, 'and never been out of the city. I was so scared I thought my head would fly off.'

The image made Harriet laugh, and Isabella looked up as if she was afraid of being mocked, but seeing nothing to alarm her in the other woman's green eyes, she simply gave the same shy smile Harriet had seen on the stage of the theatre.

'So off we went,' Morgan continued, crossing her ankles. 'Issy learned at Le Clerc's school for four years, we could earn enough to pay our way in the usual fashion, and she picked up the lingo till she could jabber away like a Frenchie born. Then when Le Clerc wanted her to start singing at little concerts and that, he told her to change her name. He said no opera singer would ever succeed keeping the name Baker – that was Tessa's name. So we settled on Marin and there we go. She did good, then better, and everyone just thought she must be French, even the Parisians, and we never bothered correcting them.'

'I sang at the opera house in Paris in seventy-seven – it was only a small part, but then their prima donna fell ill, and I was asked to sing in her place. I think Mr Harwood saw me there.'

'He told us he was transfixed by your performance,' Crowther said. Isabella made no reply, but simply nodded.

'We visited Milan one time and liked it there so stayed,' Morgan said. 'Everyone knows the best women singers come from Paris, so wherever we went it suited us that they believed Issy was Frenchborn. I took charge of the money, and where she would be going and when, and we started trotting along very nicely. Sang to more Kings and Bishops than I thought the world had room for, in opera houses and palaces all over the continent. Not London though. Not till now.'

'I got my first letter from Fitzraven this spring when I was singing again in Milan,' Isabella said. 'There was a picture of me in a newspaper in Paris, and it got sold in London too, as I've been talked about here a bit. Morgan almost cried when she saw it, said it was so like my mother she couldn't credit it. He saw it too, worked out his dates, and wrote care of the opera house, knowing they'd find me.'

Crowther thought of the exclamation point under the portrait in Fitzraven's notebook. He must have thought the gods were dropping honey on him when he saw it.

'Morgan advised me not to answer, not to admit I was his daughter. She told me to remember he'd got my mother into trouble then left her with nothing but a nod, but I couldn't help myself. Especially when he said he worked for the opera house. I thought, Oh, so that's why it felt like home, that's where all the music has come from. He talked about me coming here, and I remembered that night I first saw an opera was at His Majesty's.' She turned towards Harriet and Crowther. The glow on her face was no trick of the firelight in the gathering dusk. The woman was shining from within. 'So you see what last night meant to me? How many people get to have a dream become real in such a way? It frightens me a little. And it was just as I hoped it might be, and with that duet. The rest of the opera is pleasant enough, but the "Yellow Rose Duet" . . .' She looked back into the flames. 'When I first heard the tune it was as if someone had found the gold in me and made it really shine. Can you understand me? I felt it was written for me alone.'

Harriet struggled for a phrase. She felt she could discuss many subjects with authority, but not music. 'Mademoiselle, your talent is remarkable and the tune very beautiful,' she said, and Isabella seemed satisfied.

'And to sing it with Manzerotti! Whatever I have been through, what *he* has had to suffer for the sake of music, what heights *he* has reached . . . I may spend the rest of my life trying to find such a moment again. Yet I have had it. A Golden Hour. I shall always have that.'

'So Fitzraven came to see you in Milan, to hire you for His Majesty's. Did you like him?' Harriet said. 'We have heard . . . differing reports.'

Isabella looked a little pained and it was Morgan who, once again, answered for her.

'We did not like him. Issy tried to. For all the fight in her, she still had her sentimental ideas of what a father is. Gave him money too.' She frowned. 'Mr Harwood has been a far straighter man to deal with. And Fitzraven knew he had a hold on us. If it came out in the papers now that the beautiful Parisian songbird Mademoiselle Isabella Marin was just plain old Issy Baker from Southwark, we'd be laughed at all round town. He never did anything about it. Just, you know, suggested we should all keep the secret together. I could tell his game. I'm glad he's dead. Bet there are others that feel the same.' Morgan looked at them fiercely.

Harriet though was observing Isabella, who was pulling on the folds of her dress. The stuff of it was so soft it seemed to flow over her hands like liquid, like mercury.

'Do you feel the same, Miss Marin?' Harriet asked.

'It's a bitter thing to say, Mrs Westerman, but perhaps I do. I wanted to love him, I wanted to show him I was his daughter and he had wronged my mother. I had an idea he'd beg forgiveness, that we'd visit Dead Man's Place together and think of her. But he didn't care about my mother. I don't think he even cared about music. When he started talking about the opera to me, I could see he didn't feel about it as I did. To him, it was all about the fuss and gossip. I wanted to be unhappy when Morgan told me he was dead, but I wasn't, in truth.'

'Morgan told you he had died?' Crowther said, looking up from his hands and with an eyebrow raised. 'I thought it was Mr Harwood who informed you after the performance.'

The old lady crossed her arms and sniffed. 'I was about yesterday morning. Watching a body brought in from the river is not the opera perhaps, but it's always of interest.'

Crowther's mouth twitched into a smile. 'It was you that named him on the street.'

'Just sort of blurted it out like bad wind when his head lolled back as they carried him up the steps. Told Issy. My first thinking was, Good, he can't go blabbing tales about my Issy now.'

Harriet looked between Morgan and Isabella. 'But it was not just Fitzraven who knew the secret of your origins. What of your music teacher? You must have written from France, and visited him since you returned to London, this man who did so much for you.'

The two women were silent for a moment before Isabella replied, 'We cannot find him. He began to answer our letters less and less. Nothing would come for months then twenty pages all written very close – strange rambling things they were, deeply earnest one page then light and airy and gossip filled on another.' She swallowed. 'Then they stopped all at once. I would love to sing to him again, show him what he made me. Remember, I was a thing of the gutter when he first found me. Morgan tried to see his old landlady as soon as we arrived. She said he had been taken off to a madhouse by his family over a year ago, but we have no further information. We have struggled . . . I have asked Mr Bywater to look for him on my behalf.' Crowther thought he detected the beginnings of a faint blush as she mentioned the composer's name. 'I would not trust Fitzraven to do so, but Mr Bywater has had no success as yet and we have all been greatly occupied.'

Harriet cleared her throat. Even before she began to speak she could feel the colour spreading up her neck and across her cheeks. 'Mademoiselle, my husband was recently injured. An accident on the ship he commanded. He is in health now, physically, but his understanding has been impaired. He is currently in a private asylum on the outskirts of London. I tell you this because, if your teacher had been prone to worsening fits of melancholia, perhaps he too could have ended up in such a place. I am sure Dr Trevelyan knows most of them. May I make enquiries on your behalf?'

Isabella's voice was soft in reply. 'I am sorry your husband is unwell, Mrs Westerman, and I would appreciate anything you could do on my behalf in this matter.'

Harriet managed a small smile. 'Just give me his name, Mademoiselle. I will make what enquiries I can.'

'His name is Leacroft. Mr Theophilius Leacroft.'

## III.5

BEFORE THEY LEFT Upper Brook Street Harriet and Crowther had also taken the time to knock up the other lodgers present and found that even with the thin walls and close quarters of the building, no one had heard or seen anything out of the ordinary on Thursday. Various people had heard footsteps on the stairs, but no one had noticed any altercation, nor had seen someone leaving with a body wrapped in a hearthrug over their shoulder in the early hours. Crowther was not surprised, saying simply that if they had done, it was likely they would have mentioned it before now. The lodger they had most wished to speak to, however, had not answered their knock. This was the gentleman who had his lodgings at the rear of the first floor, directly under those of Fitzraven. He was away from home, though Mrs Girdle was sure he had been present on Thursday afternoon. The young man was apparently living on an allowance from his parents, and attempting to find some position in London from his base in Great Swallow Street. His name was given to them as Tobias Tompkins, so Crowther and Harriet wrote a note asking him to call on them in Berkeley Square in the evening, and hoped that the impressive address might tempt him into making their acquaintance.

They did not return immediately to Graves's home, however. Crowther, when he hailed a cab in Brook Street, instead asked the driver to take them to Somerset House. When he settled back in his seat he realised Harriet was looking at him with her eyebrows raised.

'I have an acquaintance, Mrs Westerman, who I know will be making use of the Royal Society's library today. He is an expert in matters dental.' He reached into the pocket of his coat and produced a small silk bag. He pulled the string loose and shook out Fitzraven's false teeth into his palm.

'Good God, Crowther! Have you been carrying those things with you all day?'

He looked at her with mild innocence. 'Does this concern you, Mrs Westerman?'

Harriet folded her arms as the coach rattled through the muck of the street. 'I am only glad I did not know you had them earlier. I do not think I could have listened to poor Miss Marin's account of her struggles with an easy mind, had I known you were sitting there with her father's teeth in your pocket!'

Crowther did not seem discomfited, but lifted the teeth to the level of his eyes and clacked them together. 'Indeed, it was an affecting tale.'

Harriet raised her eyebrows. 'You do not believe it?'

'It is not that, Mrs Westerman,' he said with some hesitation. 'Only I am surprised she was so eager to know Mr Fitzraven. I heard her reasons, of course, but she had a powerful motive for revenge. The man mistreated her mother quite horribly, for one thing, and for another he knew that her official biography is a lie. He could have turned her from the fêted star of the season into a laughing stock.'

'I liked her.'

'That is charming, Mrs Westerman, and so did I, but it is not evidence. Fitzraven's accounts indicate that he was receiving money from someone recently arrived in London. She would seem a likely candidate. We may well find that he died because of some treachery more minor than Mr Palmer thinks.'

'You may have your suspicions, but I cannot think Isabella likely to throttle a man, then hurl him in the river. Now, please do put those horrible teeth away.'

Crowther slipped the teeth back into the bag without protest. 'Yes, I believe that women, when they turn murderess, more often use poison. And seldom tidy up.'

Harriet settled into her corner and turned her head to look out of the window as they turned off Brook Street. There was some sort of commotion on the road beside them – an open cart with a man and older woman sat up in the back. The woman had her arm around the man's shoulders, which were shaking with sobs. Harriet recognised them as two members of the little walking party they had seen passing earlier in the day.

She looked down into the back of the cart as they passed. There was the third, the blonde pretty woman. Her husband was holding her in his lap and rocking her back and forth. Her arm hung loose by her side. As their coachman waited to negotiate a way through, a man in a dirty coat emerged from the barber-surgeon's where the cart was stopped. He climbed up in the back in a rush and felt for the woman's pulse.

Harriet craned round as the coach worked itself free and held the picture in sight long enough to see the man shake his head and pat the younger man awkwardly on the shoulder. The cart driver crossed himself. Then they turned the corner and the sight was lost.

Harriet leaned out of the window and shouted up to the driver 'Slater! What was all that?'

The man sucked his teeth and half-twisted to shout back without taking his eyes from the traffic in front of them.

'Accident, ma'am. Young woman slipped and fell, up by the brick kilns. Stove her head in.'

Harriet retreated into the carriage again and met Crowther's enquiring eye.

'What is it, Mrs Westerman?'

'Nothing of significance, Crowther. Some other little tragedy.'

# III.6

A S JOCASTA CAME to the main road towards Brook Street, her view of the way was blocked by a carriage with a phoenix on the door. It was working into a free space on the road, so the wheels came very close to her, almost snagging her skirts. It brought back her dream of The Chariot with a sort of sick lurch, and she stopped dead, so as it pulled away and she saw the cart and Kate's limp body supported by her husband and mother-in-law, it was like being at a theatre and watching the curtain swept back.

The sight of it almost knocked her down. She had to put her hand out palm flat to the wall of some fancy goods shop behind her to keep from falling. Kate's face was dirty and there was red on Fred's breeches.

She stumbled forward to the edge of the crowd where she could hear the voices talking.

'Slipped and her husband tried to catch her . . .'

'Such a pretty girl too . . .'

'Dead before he could pick her up again . . .'

'Constable's writing it up now. His mother was there – saw the whole thing . . .'

'He's taking it hard . . .'

The crowd shifted and Jocasta saw Mrs Mitchell reach down, unclasp the little brooch from Kate's shawl and slip it into her pocket.

Jocasta pushed her way through and started to shout.

'Oh no, not Milan Mr Crowther, not Milan!'

Harriet did not think she would ever become very fond of Mr George Gillis. He had a face that reminded her of a self-satisfied raisin pudding, and his eyes looked like dubious oysters. That, if unappetising, she could forgive, but his voice, drawling and nasal, seemed to find its way to some sensitive spot in the middle of her forehead and attack it with a brass pin.

He was sitting back in his chair in the reading room with his legs crossed and toying with a lorgnette tied to his waistcoat with purple ribbon. His tone from their arrival had been one of conceited disdain. Having made lengthy remarks on how honoured he was to be asked for advice by the *great* Mr Crowther, he had been of no assistance whatsoever, answering only in negatives and evincing very little interest in Crowther's curiosity, despite his avowed expertise in matters of the kind. The lorgnette continued to twirl and wink between his fingers. Crowther did not reply but simply watched the man with level attention. Harriet looked about her. The reading room of the Royal Society was a place of some beauty. This north wing of Somerset House had been only recently completed, and the high ceilings, comfortable armchairs scattered in groups, and conveniently lit reading desks all gave an air of elegant confidence. It was a place built by and for men who believed absolutely in their work, and in their capacity to unfold the various mysteries of the universe. Men like Crowther, but also it seemed men like Gillis. She could not believe that such a being would contribute much to the knowledge of his countrymen, yet Crowther had referred to him without irony as an expert, and stood waiting for him now.

Gillis gave a dramatic sigh. 'There may be . . . I suspect there was a reference in a letter I had from a correspondent on the continent some weeks ago . . .'

He paused. Crowther raised his eyebrow and Harriet clenched her hands together in her muff.

Gillis unfolded himself and with a slowness Harriet thought could only be deliberate, reached into his pocket for a notebook and began turning the pages. It seemed necessary that he read each page complete before moving onto the next, and all the while he wore the same amused self-indulgent smile that certain people reserve for their own work.

After a pause of some minutes he gave a little nod and tapped the page with his forefinger.

'Ah, yes. Here it is. My friend has been travelling on the continent and made the acquaintance of an apothecary called Alexis Duchâteau. He has been experimenting with porcelain for false teeth rather than ivory or wood. His experiments have not become particularly commercial as yet, though my friend says he had supplied some people with sets by way of experiment. Apparently he tries to give them to the great and good, or their friends, to try and build their popularity.' Gillis looked up at them and blinked.

'And where is Mr Alexis Duchâteau's shop? Is he resident in Italy?' Crowther asked, a little impatient.

Gillis smothered a yawn. 'Dear Lord, no. Why would you think that? The French are the experts in this area. These teeth came from St. Germain-en-Laye, near Paris. Nowhere else.'

## III.7

MR PALMER FOUND that his thoughts turned over better in his head when he could move rather than stare at the walls of his office at the Admiralty. He knew the ways well enough to walk without paying much attention to his immediate surroundings, instead thinking over his various stratagems and those he suspected might be in play against himself and his masters. He was just returning to the building and deciding how best to arrange a private meeting with Mrs Westerman and Mr Crowther when he realised he was about to trip over a small and very pale-faced lad who was looking fearfully up at the building's imposing frontage.

'Can I help you, boy?'

The boy started. 'I'm looking for the Admiralty Board. The Head Clerk.' He reached into the waistband of his breeches and pulled out a piece of paper, only slightly crumpled. 'I've got a note.' He then noticed the paper was bent and began to try and smooth it against his thin chest. Mr Palmer thought this treatment might do it more harm than good and put out his hand.

'That's Mr Jacobs, I shall give it to him.' Once he had hold of the paper he flicked it open. The wife of one of the clerks had died suddenly and the man was requesting a half-day to bury her on the morrow. 'Very well. Tell Mr Mitchell he has the permission.' He reached into his purse and pulled out a shilling and put it into the boy's hand. His fingers shut over it smartly and he turned to hurry out into the road again. Mr Palmer frowned.

'Boy!' The lad turned again and came back with great reluctance. When he had got close enough he opened his palm and offered the coin up again.

'I knew you didn't mean to give me a whole shilling.' His face was so sorry Mr Palmer couldn't fully conceal a smile.

'No, boy. You may keep the coin. I just wanted to ask how his wife died. Was she with child?'

'Broke her skull,' the boy said rather miserably. 'So *he* says, anyway.'

Mr Palmer, his head full of Fitzraven, simply nodded. 'Indeed. Convey our regrets and sympathies.' And when the boy looked entirely blank: 'I mean tell him the gentlemen here say they are sorry for his loss.'

The clouds on the boy's face cleared and he trotted out into the road.

## III.8

MRS WESTERMAN HAD been oddly subdued on their journey back to Berkeley Square, and had retired to her room as soon as the household had dined, complaining of a headache. Crowther shut himself in the library in an ill-humour and wondered briefly if she had been thinking of her husband again.

Mrs Westerman was very rarely ill, but since her husband had returned she had suffered headaches with greater frequency. It irritated Crowther that she was now unavailable at times when he wished for her company, and he hoped that as her husband's health improved, her own would do the same. Her indisposition was not the only reason for his souring mood, however. The discovery that Fitzraven had been strangled rather than drowned had been a professional disappointment. It would have been of interest to add to the literature on the state of a body after drowning, to see if the pink foam in the throat he had observed in some animal experiments was present, for example, but a throttling was ordinary. Equally, an active investigation into a death ran counter to his habits of solitary study. It put him out among people far more than he liked, or was used to. However, he had agreed to help Mr Palmer and serve his King, so with a slight growl in his own throat he went to work composing and sending a large number of notes, then awaiting their replies in the comfort of the library. Thus he avoided at least the perils of conversation for some hours. If he realised the inconvenience he caused in Graves's household by sending off its staff to several corners of the city bearing his requests, he gave no sign of it. He had enough left of those habits of command that he had developed in his youth to ignore completely what it did not suit him to see, and his rather brittle mood made him even less likely to consider the convenience of others than usual.

His activities caused enough upset in the house for the housekeeper, Mrs Martin, to be more than a little shocked when she came back from her half-day and found her domain downstairs to be in nothing like its usual order.

'It's no good frowning at me, Mrs Martin,' said the cook over her shoulder as she tried to assemble a nursery tea in a battlefield of unwashed crockery and the wreckage from the preparation and serving of dinner. 'Mr Crowther's been sending 'em out one after the other since we cleared table, and you know what they're like. They're all, "Ooh, we're helping solve a murder, Cook!" as if they are heroes and heroines in a storybook. Alice and Cecily sent themselves into hysterics imagining they might be carrying a letter of accusation to the killer himself, but when I told them they should wait till Philip or Gregory got back and let *them* do the carrying of notes, if they were that nervous, they looked daggers at me and rushed out of the place so fast they hardly had time to fasten their cloaks.'

She pulled open the bread drawer and began to attack the loaf she found there with a sharp knife. She was an experienced cutter, but Crowther might have questioned the delicacy of her movements. 'I'm sorry this Mr Fitzraven fellow is dead, but I wish he had just got stupid drunk and fallen in the river like a decent man. I have no idea what I am feeding those little kiddies with this evening, and if Mr Graves and Mrs Service want to give supper to their guests tonight, we'll have to send to the chophouse. There's not a clean pan left to roast in anywhere in the kitchen, and Mary should have been mending this evening, not setting fires.'

Mrs Martin did not reply, but put on her apron. The vigour with which she began to scrub the half-empty dishes was eloquent enough. She had been very pleased to gain her position at Berkeley Square, since she was still rather young to have such responsibility, and most would have thought her a little delicate in her appearance for such a role. However, Graves had liked her, Mrs Service was pleased with her references, and her generous pay meant her only child could be comfortably boarded in Putney. Yet things had changed. The household she presided over was now twice the size it had been, and up and down the streets around Berkeley Square the talk was all Mrs Westerman and Crowther and murder. Biting her lip, she picked up another dish which, albeit very elegant, seemed designed only to catch brown scraps of gravy in its corners and nurse them.

The young people's tea was a great success, fortunately, and Lord Thornleigh, his sister and their friends spent much of it in debate trying to think what good deed they had done to deserve their bread and butter being cut so thick.

Crowther had been lucky in Graves's choice of servants. Each one of his messengers returned with communications, written and verbal, for which he thanked them sincerely. They then resumed their duties with a certain energy – enough to make Mrs Service remark when she put her head round the door, that Crowther had managed to do them all a power of good. He had looked at her with surprise. She did not try to explain, but withdrew to go about her own business and that of the children with a smile of her own.

When Harriet found him out as the evening deepened and the candles settled coins of light around them, he was seated behind Graves's desk with a number of pieces of paper arrayed about him, a frown of concentration on his face.

'I forgot to tell you,' she said. 'I heard from Daniel Clode yesterday. Things seem to go well without us in Sussex. I left Graves with his head bent over the new plans for the works at Thornleigh, I have seen the accounts after the harvest at Caveley, and Michaels sends us his regards.'

Crowther nodded but did not reply. She walked up to the desk and peered at the sheets in front of him, trying to read his thin high script upside down. 'But what have you been about this afternoon, Crowther? You seem to have spilled a quantity of ink. To what purpose?'

Her tone rankled, but he punished her for it by making her wait while he gathered his papers and tapped them straight before he replied.

'It has been spilled usefully, I think. We shall call on Mr Manzerotti tomorrow morning. It appears he is in residence at Lord Carmichael's.'

'Is he, indeed? How interesting! I wonder how that came to pass.'

Crowther answered with a drawl. 'Lord Carmichael has travelled extensively on the continent and has a reputation as a music-lover. I would not be surprised if he made Manzerotti's acquaintance there. Whoever gave Fitzraven an introduction to Carmichael was probably also someone he knew from his time there.' Harriet looked as if she were about to ask something further, but Crowther continued: 'And later in the day I have an appointment to meet Mr Bywater at the British Museum.'

Harriet raised her eyebrows. 'Why there?'

'Apparently Bywater has tickets for admittance and hopes I might enjoy looking at old pots.'

She sighed and took a seat in front of the fire, settling deeply into the armchair like a child. 'I cannot imagine he phrased it so.'

'He did not, but his own rather florid rhetoric drives me towards the demotic'

'And how am I to spend my time, pray, while you are admiring the antiquities?'

Crowther did not look at her when he replied, 'If your health allows it, madam, Lord Carmichael will be at the Foundling Hospital between the middle of the day and when he returns home to dine. He would be happy to have some conversation with you then.' She was silent and he knew she would be looking at him now, concerned and seeking.

'I have never seen you scared of meeting another man, Crowther.'

'It is not fear, Mrs Westerman,' he said, with a slight snap of annoyance. He could hear the tap of her fingers against the cloth of her satin sleeves; it was a sound like rain on canvas.

'Did that man have some involvement in your father's murder?' she asked finally.

He was conscious of relief that he had not needed to be more direct with her, and gratitude that she knew him well enough to reach this conclusion so swiftly, but more than anything he was aware of the regularity with which the past kept reaching forward across a passage of thirty years and placing its cold wet palms on his throat.

'The motive for my father's murder by my brother was financial, Mrs Westerman. He was not well-disciplined; had run through his allowance and collected a large number of debts. My father was not the sort of man to be forgiving in such situations.'

Harriet did not respond. He knew she was allowing him to speak in his own time, and could not decide in the strange mist of emotion his memories dragged through him, if he was pleased or a little humiliated by her unusual tact.

'Lord Carmichael was a friend of my brother's – or so my brother thought,' he continued. 'The man was poor then himself, but used my brother's money to fund his own debauches and then led him into a way of life that destroyed him. I would say that, more than any other man, *he* is responsible for the deaths in my family. He since married money. That is the source of his current wealth though his wife died some years ago.'

He ran his fingers down the edges of his papers, though they were already straight. 'He also at one time caused my sister to fall in love with him. His attentions ceased when it became clear that my father would not give her a penny if she persisted with the match.'

There was a rustle of fabric on leather as Mrs Westerman drew herself straight.

'You have a sister, Crowther? Is she living?'

He looked up to see her staring at him, her lips slightly parted and a blush of surprise on her face.

'I do. She is. She married a gentleman from Austria and has lived abroad since my father's death.'

'Crowther,' Harriet sighed, 'you never fail to astonish. You, who know so much of all of my household, announce that you have a sister – and seem to think it strange I am amazed by the revelation.' She paused, and the firelight caught the red in her hair. 'Though why I should be surprised, I do not know. After all, you have never even told me your brother's name.'

Crowther dropped his gaze back to the table-top. 'It was Adair. Lucius Adair, more formally, but my mother only ever called him

Addie. My sister has a son, but lives apart from her husband. I have never had a wife or children. Is that biography sufficient to you?'

'Adair. Is that not an Irish name?'

'It is. My mother was Irish.'

She was quiet again, and Crowther looked sideways at her profile, trying to see if she were angry with him. She seemed only calm and thoughtful, however.

'I can understand why you might think it more politic for me to meet with Carmichael alone, but do you not fear encountering him when we see Manzerotti?'

'My Lord expects to be at cards all night, and will not rise till he must to travel to the Foundling Hospital.'

Harriet slumped again in her chair, and with the appearance of brisk good humour, said, 'You have our itinerary for the day mapped out. I thank you. Any other information gained?'

Crowther felt some muscle round his throat relax and began to speak more easily. The memory of the lightness Miss Marin had achieved with her narrative passed like a breeze through his mind.

'The main points are these,' he said. 'Mr Fitzraven's last employment at His Majesty's Theatre was supervising the copying of parts for the band for the new duet on Wednesday afternoon, as we know. He was seen about the opera house on Thursday morning. Mrs Girdle was visiting her sister in Clapham on Thursday, so when he returned to his lodgings, and for what purpose, we cannot say.'

'Anything further?'

Crowther cleared his throat. 'I have the correct and relevant information as to the movement of the tides on the Thames. It is likely the body was weighted and thrown into the river at high tide, and that would be roughly halfway between midnight and dawn on Saturday, according to the boatmen at Westminster.'

Harriet leaned forward and put her chin in her hands. 'So where are we at, Crowther? Here is Fitzraven, a deeply unpleasant character, possibly a traitor, who abandoned his daughter then found her again

140

when there was profit in it; who has managed, we know not how, to continue his employment at His Majesty's Theatre despite being disliked there, and insinuate his way into the graces of a peer.' She glanced up at Crowther, then back to the fire with a smile. 'You must resist the temptation to sneer whenever Lord Carmichael is mentioned, Crowther. It does not become you. We also believe that he spent some time in Paris, collecting teeth and Lord knows what else, when he was supposed to be only in Milan, that he loved the opera for all the wrong reasons, and suggested to people he knew its secrets. We know too that he had more money in his pocket since the performers arrived in London, though Miss Marin says she did not give him that, and someone has recently found it convenient to throttle him. Have I everything clear so far?'

Crowther leaned back in his own chair. 'You do, madam. Though I have one more fact and one more conjecture to offer you.'

'You proffer them like sweetmeats to a baby. Say on, sir.'

'The main performers of the serious opera arrived three weeks ago; the players of the comic opera and the ballet-master arrived only earlier this week, so it seems unlikely that any of them paid Fitzraven, though he may in that time have given them reason to throttle him . . .'

Harriet nodded. 'And your conjecture?'

'I was thinking again of the papers in Fitzraven's bedchamber. The letters from Isabella were well-concealed: we would not have thought to examine the case but for your moment of musical whimsy, but there were no others. He must have had other correspondence, yet no sign of it remained, nor were there any records of his income, which given that he was so careful to note his expenses, seems unusual.'

Harriet frowned. 'You are suggesting, I think, that someone other than Fitzraven . . .'

'I am wondering, Mrs Westerman, if we were not the first to search Fitzraven's room, and what those missing letters might have contained.'

As Harriet sprang to her feet again, Crowther wondered vaguely if she had ever managed to keep her seat for more than ten minutes at a time.

'It would certainly explain the lack of ready money, or any note of where Fitzraven's newfound wealth came from,' she said. 'And it would seem to suggest that my liking of Miss Marin is well-founded. She would not have left her own letters there and removed his pocketbook, only to return for them later. Perhaps Mr Tompkins from the rooms below will be better able to tell us of the comings and goings in the house.'

She turned to him and smiled. He thought perhaps her looks were beginning to improve a little.

'But I must visit the children. I hear the day has been full of spectacular military victories and Anne has learned to say "cake". I am the mother of prodigies.'

Crowther expected her to leave at once, but instead she paused and with an unusual hesitation in her manner turned back to him. He placed his papers flat on the desk and gave her his full attention.

'Crowther, Dr Trevelyan has suggested I take the children to see James, and I am afraid.'

He folded his fingers together. 'Your son is a thinking child, Mrs Westerman. Be open with him.'

'But if James . . .' Harriet halted and drew breath before continuing '. . . if James does not recover, will not Stephen then always remember his father as he is now?'

Crowther considered before he spoke. 'Dr Trevelyan is a good man. Follow his recommendation. As for Stephen, he will grow up with the portrait of the Captain at Caveley and the testimony of your household and yourself to temper whatever impressions he gains now. He must know it is a thing that can be spoken of.'

Harriet thanked him and left the room with her brow furrowed. Crowther drew out his pocket-watch and tapped the glass gently. Now he would have to sup here and wait for Mr Tompkins to appear. He thought of the desk in his study in Hartswood where the maids were not so flighty and the air clearer, and with a spasm of irritation cursed his King and the Navy and most especially Mr Nathaniel Fitzraven.

The door to the round house opened and Sam started up from the shadows like a pointer-bitch spotting game. Jocasta shuffled out with Boyo in her arms. The Constable had some words with those left inside and pushed the door to again, making it fast with a flick of his wrist. Sam watched as Jocasta put something in the man's hands and heard the clink of coin. He waited till the Constable had turned his back again and picked up his pipe before he slipped into step beside her.

'Youse all right, Mrs Bligh?'

She jumped at the sound of his voice. 'You here, are you? Yes, lad. I'm all right.' She bent down and set Boyo on the ground beside them, stretching her back like an old woman as she stood again.

'They're not sending you up before the Justice, then?'

'No, Sam. I came to an arrangement with the Constable.' She spat the last word out and set off again. The little boy bobbed at her side.

'Was it true, what you said?'

'It was.'

'That Milky Boy and that sour mother of his killed that pretty lady?'

'I've just said so, haven't I?'

'They got awful angry with you.'

Jocasta didn't see any need to reply, so after a moment Sam tried again.

'What are you going to do, Mrs Bligh? No one believes you, do they? I mean, no one that matters anyway.'

Jocasta straightened her back, and her pace became more assured. Sam had to scurry a little to keep up.

'Neither they do, boy. But then they think my cards are nothing but fairytales, and I've got nothing but a scrap of paper with four words on it otherwise.'

'You ain't going to let it lie though, are you?'

'No, boy, I ain't. Did that once before and it ruined my peace a while.'

Sam hopped along beside her a few more moments, then said in a rush, 'May I stay with you again tonight? It's cold.' Jocasta stopped and turned to look at him. He blushed then held out his hand. He had a shilling in it. 'You can have this.'

Her eyes narrowed. 'Where'd you get that, Sam?'

'Honest!' he said. 'After the Constable pulled you away I watched them take the lady home again. Milky Boy gave me a note to take to his offices and the man there gave me this.'

'So you know where the Admiralty Office is then?'

Sam nodded so hard, Jocasta thought his ears must be ringing.

'All right then. Come on. I need bread and bed. There's much to think on.'

'What will you do though, Mrs Bligh? People never listen to us.'

'Papers and facts and times and things seen in the real – that's what those people like. We'll find 'em and we'll make them listen, Sam. We'll make them.'

Harriet was greeted in the nursery with great affection. Her little daughter Anne, with Susan's promptings, displayed the full range of her talents at pointing out objects around the room or fetching them on the other children's instructions. She did not, it seemed, resent being ordered about by her fellows, but fetched ball, and hoop and soldiers with a firm waddling gate and great pride, laughing and clapping her hands at the praise she received. Harriet's son, Stephen, was a little more withdrawn than usual when the initial rush of excitement at his mother's presence had worked itself out, so when Susan had Eustache, Jonathan and Anne curled in a corner looking at the pictures in *Little Goody Two-Shoes*, Harriet took him on her lap, and as he pulled on her copper-coloured curls and played with the rings on her left hand, she asked him if anything had upset him that day.

'No,' he said carefully and exactly. He had taken off her promise ring and was examining its opals now in the last light of the fire. He had the dark hair and blue eyes of her husband. Love for them both fell over her in a sudden rush, and she pulled him close to her. It was a terrible thing to love. It made the whole world dangerous. Her son submitted a moment, then wriggled his shoulders. She bit her lip and released the pressure of her embrace. Stephen leaned against her and continued to twist the ring to make the milky stone in its centre catch colours. After a few moments he said. 'Mama, do you remember when I was very little and Hartley got hurt?'

Harriet struggled for a second then nodded. He was speaking of one of the many cats their housekeeper in Caveley had owned during the years they had been in residence. Hartley had been an adventurous beast, and having made his way out of a window on one of the upper storeys of the house, had slipped on the damp roof-slates and fallen to the yard. Stephen had found him while walking the grounds with his nurse. The cat had still been breathing, but was badly hurt and in pain. It had tried to bite Stephen when he attempted to comfort it, and Harriet had asked her coachman, David, to break its neck.

She stroked her son's hair. 'I remember Stephen. It was very sad. Why did you think of that today?'

He fidgeted against her and tilted his head towards his chin. 'Nothing,' he mumbled, 'only there is a cat who lives in the Square reminded me.' He said nothing further.

Harriet drew in her breath. Stephen, you know your papa is very ill at the moment.'

'Yes, Mama, that is why we must live here. So that he can be looked after by people who are almost as clever as Mr Crowther.'

'That's right, young man,' she said very carefully. 'But you know, don't you, Stephen, that Papa loves us still very much, and we love him. He is just not able to show it at the moment. Just like Hartley loved you and would come and sit on your bed in the mornings, but he could not show it when he was hurt.'

The little boy was silent. Harriet lifted his chin so she could look into his eyes. He was so like his father, yet there was at times a softness in him that did not come from herself, or her husband. He had plucked it from the sea winds when she sailed, big with him, feeling his kicks under her belly as the ship rocked, and bound it into his character.

'Your papa loves you,' she said. 'And you liked Dr Trevelyan, didn't you? He is going to make Papa well again.'

He looked at her. 'Then may we all go home?'

Harriet's voice was steady as she replied, 'Yes, my love. Then we may all go home.'

There was a light rap at the door and the housekeeper peeped into the room. 'Excuse me, madam, but a gentleman has called for you and Mr Crowther. He asked that you should be told. I'll help get these off to bed, and there's some supper laid out.'

'Thank you, Mrs Martin.' Harriet kissed her son's hair once more and lifted him off her knee.

She paused briefly at the pier-glass in the hallway and touched her hair into some sort of order. For the first time since August she recognised herself in the mirror.

Catching hold of the banister, she ran down the stairs to meet Mr Tompkins.

## III.9

'SAM,' JOCASTA SAID, when they had something inside them and Boyo was chasing rabbits in his dreams in front of the fire, 'you made any friends since you left the workhouse? Other boys who might be keen to earn a penny or two is my meaning.'

Sam wrapped his arms around his knees. 'Couple, I suppose.'

'Will you fetch them along in the morning, bright and early times?'

He nodded, then reached out his hand towards the coverlet that spent its days draped over Jocasta's settee. 'It's pretty,' he said. 'Did you patch it yourself, Mrs Bligh?'

'I did, boy.'

'Like your skirt.'

'Like the skirt.'

'It's so many colours . . .' He shifted and settled on the floor with his hands under his head. Jocasta watched him. No one had ever waited for her before. She'd never, it seemed to her, in all the years she tramped through, been looked for and expected by another being. She sniffed.

'It's patchwork. I've read cards enough for every draper's girl in the Strand and they know my likings. However small an offcut, if it's jewel-bright or patterned they'll save it for me, and bring it along next time they need to know if their fella likes them. Then there's the tailors and maids, and often-times if you know where to go, you'll find some old thing a lady's worn dancing about in the candlelight that's worth paying for, for the bits in the folds that have not faded.' Sam's eyes were open, and she saw that, as she spoke, his eyes were dancing across the patterns and colours of the coverlet. The bits of silk caught the firelight from the air and shivered with it, and the poplin and cotton seemed to glow with a pulse.

'Times I sit here,' Jocasta murmured, 'and I think to mesel, What things have you seen? to one square or other. Were you a dancing dress in a fine house, bunched up in a fat wardrobe with a dozen others, or were you stretched by the back of some sour red-faced old Justice drooling after the next bribe to find, and spitting on the floor?' His eyes were closing. 'Times I'm sitting here, Sam, I feel like a dragon in her lair sat on a great pile of jewels and stories . . .'

His breathing was a sleeping pace now, and she turned and picked up a plain blanket from the end of her bed and dropped it over him. She sat a while longer in the dying firelight though. It seemed that when she had seen that pert little girl in the back of the wagon, her head all bloodied and her eyes closed, the world had cursed and roared at her. It reminded her of when, as a child, she had seen a man dead and watched another walking away from the body. She had told then, and been cursed as a storyteller. She'd been stubborn, but not stubborn enough. She earned a reputation as a liar that followed her round the valley, and never got a man or child to hear and believe her. She could still see the man in the green coat disappearing into the woods. It hadn't helped that she'd been so scared she'd run up the fell and shivered an hour before heading back to her aunt's house where she bided. The story of the Baron's death was being chanted outside every door in the village by then, and they thought she was just trying to draw eyes to herself. Not for all her weepings would they listen, and they hadn't today neither, though she'd felt like a child again, crying against the storm, shouting and baying as if she could stop the world from turning. She was not a child now, however. There'd be a way, a way to watch and gather and patch it all together and make the seams strong. She'd make a noose of it all for Mother Mitchell and Milky Boy's necks, and for all it was strung together with her sewing, it'd throttle them. Then she'd pluck that brooch from Mother Mitchell's corpse and bury it in Kate's grave with her.

# PART IV

## IV.1

HARRIET HAD DREAMED of her husband, of battles at sea, and of Manzerotti and Marin singing the 'Yellow Rose Duet' on the deck of the *Marquis de La Fayette*, and woke sombre and wondering in her mind, but with a dark energy curling through her veins that felt more like herself. It was unfortunate that Mr Tobias Tompkins had spent the crucial hours of Thursday afternoon asleep over his books, and his visit had therefore been no more than annoyance, but nevertheless Harriet felt a sense of purpose in her blood this morning and was grateful for it.

When Crowther looked up from his newspaper at the breakfast-table, he was glad to see her approach with a firm step, if a little concerned for his continued peace. Graves had the good sense not to speak during the breakfast hour. It was a habit Mrs Westerman refused to learn. This morning, before she had even set down her coffee-cup on the table she had declared her intention of quizzing them both about the race of the castrati. At this, Mrs Service declared it was time Susan began her Italian practice, and Miss Trench, with a speaking look which her sister ignored, found it an excellent moment to go and consult with Mrs Martin about a receipt for a burns salve she had recently been sent. Crowther could see the wisdom of Mrs Westerman informing herself before their proposed meeting with

149

Manzerotti, but he was not, as a rule, at his most brilliant at this hour of the morning, while when she was in health Mrs Westerman always seemed to have an unnatural store of energy on waking. He wished it was as easy here as it was in Caveley for her to walk it off before they met in the mornings.

Harriet freely admitted she shared the suspicion of many of her countrymen regarding castrati. She appealed to the gentlemen for better information and Graves began by telling her of the remarkable musical training the castrati received from childhood.

'It gives their voices a power unparalleled,' he said. 'They were used instead of women when the fairer sex giving voice on stage or in church was regarded as an offence against God, and they have been at the heart of Italian opera ever since.'

Harriet was impatient with the explanation and snapped her toast into indignant crumbs.

'But how could God be *less* offended by the practice of maiming His creatures in childhood?' she demanded. 'Graves, you cannot approve of the fact that these children are operated on in such a way. It must be the ruin of their lives, whatever the success that some achieve. Though you may envy their training I doubt you would change places with them. And they become so . . . strange as a result.'

Graves shifted in his seat rather uncomfortably at the mention of the operation.

'I believe, Mrs Westerman,' he said, adjusting his coat, 'that there is a polite fiction that these boys were damaged in their . . . lower parts . . . and that disease or accident rendered it necessary to . . .'

On seeing Harriet roll her eyes and attack the preserves, Crowther put down his newspaper and took over.

'It is of interest what the removal of the testicles before puberty does to a child, though I agree that morally, it seems indefensible.' He had Harriet's attention, but apparently she had also noticed Graves twist in discomfort again, and was amused. Crowther continued, 'The voice does still alter as the subject ages, but retains its high register.'

'I have never heard a castrato speak, rather than sing,' she said. 'Describe it.' Then bit down on her breakfast.

Crowther watched the movement of the muscles of her jaw for a moment before replying; 'The speaking voice of a castrato is rather pleasant, if a little strange. It is rounder than a woman's and not shrill, but rather has a sort of cooing. It recalls the pigeons in the Square outside here.'

Crowther had thought this information would suffice, but Mrs Westerman did not seem to agree. Apparently she would shake all the facts out of him, as a terrier shakes the life out of a rabbit when it has it by the neck. Dabbing at her lips, she returned to her coffee, giving him a slight wave.

'Say on, Crowther. I have my prejudices, I know, and come to you for enlightenment. You cannot refuse a pupil.' It was an encouraging indication that having something more to occupy her mind than her husband's recovery was improving her health and spirits already. However a man is generous indeed who can take delight in such things so early in the day.

Crowther knitted his fingers together as he gathered his thoughts. 'Physically, the operation has several effects that are not yet fully comprehended,' he began. 'Development is hampered and altered as the child becomes adult in ways other than those that affect the vocal cords.' He coughed slightly. 'I had the privilege of attending the autopsy of a renowned castrato in Milan some years ago. He serves as my example.'

Harriet interrupted: 'How came you ghouls – sorry, gentlemen of science – by such a body? I thought any known castrato must have money enough for a lead-lined coffin and a man or two to stand guard by his grave while he rotted in peace.'

Crowther was not disposed this morning to find Mrs Westerman entertaining. He snapped, 'The gentleman in question was a man of means, indeed, and a great friend of one of the Professors of Anatomy at the University. He suggested that his friend would like to examine

151

his corpse long before he died, and repeated the offer on his deathbed in front of other witnesses. He was glad to be of use to his friends at a time when mortality has normally robbed us of the pleasure of doing service.'

Harriet wrinkled her nose. 'Very well. Though I cannot imagine making a similar offer myself – even to you, Crowther.'

'No matter, Mrs Westerman. I doubt the examination would produce any scientifically significant results.' Harriet, in spite of herself, looked a little put out at that. He continued smoothly on. 'Many of the castrati grow unusually tall – why, we cannot say. The bones of the gentleman I examined were sound, however, so their height does not seem to weaken them physically. Their thyroid cartilage does not grow as pronounced as in ordinary men . . .' He paused on seeing her raise an eyebrow. 'Their Adam's apple is small, madam.' Again she gestured him to carry on, then renewed her attack on Mrs Martin's jam. 'And of course they have a tendency to collect soft matter in a manner unusual for their sex, and somewhat more like a woman. The gentleman I examined was unusually fleshy around his chest and hips, though that of course is not guaranteed by the operation. Manzerotti is, as we have seen, rather slender, for instance. In summation, the effect can be highly unusual. I remember walking into a drawing room· where a castrato was present among the fashionable crowd. To see this mountain of a man, some six feet tall perhaps and covered in soft fat under his finery, holding forth in that strange fluting tone was . . .' he paused and looked up at Graves's ceiling rose for inspiration '. . . odd.'

Harriet considered the picture he had drawn for a moment. 'I have heard questions as to their temperament,' she said, making Crowther consider his fingernails.

'It would be a foolish man who would venture a concrete opinion on the results the procedure has on the character of a growing boy. We are formed, I think, by a mixture of many factors, though such a violent operation and its after-effects are likely to have complex consequences.'

At that moment, Graves stood and began to prepare to leave for the shop in Tichfield Street, gathering up the sheaf of papers that had been his study over breakfast.

'I have met a number of castrati in my time in music,' he told them, 'and have found them as mixed in character, I think, as any group of men. Some have been all that is good and generous; others have been like violent children and thoroughly unpleasant to deal with, vain and demanding and very tiresome.' He shrugged. 'But whether that is because of some physical effect of the operation, or because their fame and talents tend to mean they are so thoroughly indulged . . .'

Crowther was still watching his fingertips as he replied, 'I suppose these beings are kept by the operation in a sort of half-childhood, never allowed to mature physically along the path nature intended for them, never forced into adulthood by having children of their own – though they can still enjoy intimate relations. Perhaps it is to be expected they can remind us of infants at times.'

Harriet shuddered. 'It is a monstrous practice.'

Graves was still juggling his pile of papers. Some slipped onto the floor, as many objects that Graves tried to carry tended to do. He bent to pick them up then became very still and looked up at his companions.

'I would agree. But those voices, Mrs Westerman – the voices of the best of them, at any rate. They are a blend of boy, man and woman. I do not think there has ever been a sound on earth quite like it. When I heard Manzerotti sing on Saturday evening, I was sure that such is the voice an angel might have.'

Harriet watched him quizzically, his young face still lit by the memory. It was an expression she associated normally with those of a religious bent. 'It is strange you mention angels, Graves. The only time I thought of angels in the opera house was when we glanced in at the scene room and saw that strange gentleman dressed in brown.'

Graves at last had control of his belongings and stood again with a jerk. 'You mean Johannes? The new genius of the stage machinery!

The man who makes yellow roses bloom, water turn to gold dust and the Furies to fly. He is a castrato too, you know, and a particular companion of Manzerotti: they always travel together. Every production where Manzerotti has been *primo umo*, Johannes has been in charge of the scenery.'

Harriet's toast paused halfway to her mouth. 'But he does not sing,' she said.

Graves shrugged. 'Not every boy who has the operation develops a voice like Manzerotti's, Mrs Westerman. Many become shrill and unpleasant. It is a horror, I think. To make that sacrifice, or have it forced upon them, then to discover it was for nothing.' He rubbed his chin. 'They are often given other musical training; in Johannes's case, he simply turned his hand to the trade of theatrical illusion. It is making him almost as famous as a voice might have done. He does not like to speak, however; he communicates in whispers where possible, so the oddity of his voice is less noticeable.'

His papers assembled, Graves began to look for his gloves. Worried that the search might dislodge his load again, Harriet picked them up from the side-table and handed them to him.

'Thank you,' he said. Then: 'Who can say? I think there is a growing fashion against the use of castrati in the current age. We are beginning to prefer it when our romantic heroes look and sound a little more like real men. Perhaps in time Johannes will be the most gainfully employed of the two.'

# IV.2

IT WAS A little early to call on a gentleman. Harriet and Crowther were forced to wait in Lord Carmichael's drawing room for almost half an hour before Manzerotti made his appearance. If the home that Graves had leased for the children in Berkeley Square was rather more opulent than he might have wished, it still looked no more than quietly genteel in comparison with Lord Carmichael's home.

This was designed as a place to entertain and impress. No surface was without a display of elegant china, no niche without some antique head or fragment of some ancient Colossus. There was a profusion of moulding. Above each door hung golden festoons of plaster fruits and above them, oils of Gods and Monsters. Each room therefore had its crowds of the celebrated and worshipped sneering at each other before any living beings entered. Harriet peered at the marble head of a young woman caught, her lips slightly open and now shyly turning her face away from Lord Carmichael's guests for as many years as he chose.

'Our host appears to be a collector,' she said, straightening again. 'Do you think that is why he invited Manzerotti to reside here?'

'Undoubtedly,' Crowther replied. He was standing in the middle of the room and looking down at the top of his cane. It was as if, Harriet thought, he would refuse Lord Carmichael the compliment of even seeing his collection of treasures.

She tried to think clearly about the room in which she found herself. Many of the pieces were very good, even beautiful. There was a sense of harmony and balance in the decoration of the room, yet the overall effect was subtly disturbing. She made a swift inventory of the artworks in front of her. There was a small sculpture of a Spartan, lying dead on his shield; above the door was an image of Paris choosing to whom of the three Goddesses he would hand his apple. In the alcove that twinned the one with the girl with her lips parted and face turned away, was a larger piece. A young God held a woman in his arms: tears were visible on her face, and her hands were in the process of transforming into leaves. With a shock, Harriet realised that the large oil opposite the fireplace, which at first glance she had taken to be a standard rendering of a great crowd jostling in the middle of some scene of classical antiquity, was in fact a depiction of the Rape of the Sabine Women. She shivered, and found she had no desire to examine the elegant paintings on the various amphora which the room offered up for her inspection.

There was a movement in the corridor outside. Harriet expected him to fling open the door, one foot forward and his free hand raised, but Manzerotti entered quietly and bowed to them both with grace, but without great show. She looked up at him from under her lashes as she made her curtsy. He was beautiful. He had looked so on the stage of His Majesty's but, having been tricked by other performers, Harriet had assumed the effect was one of lighting and paint. However, Manzerotti was more lovely in person than she could have imagined. He looked like a great romantic's conception of what a human being *should* be – the pattern, rather than the faulty and various copies that stumbled about the earth calling themselves the children of God. His face was, like Johannes', entirely smooth, softly rounded and perfectly white. His lips were full and dark, though the mouth through which the miracle of his voice was gifted to the world was small. It was a bud at first light in the rose garden. His eyes, though, were large, and a deep brown that blurred into darkness. They seemed to pull the light of the room into their depths and give nothing back, oddly passive like black, polished marble.

Harriet felt she must fight the impulse to stare at him as she would a creature set up for display at Smithfield's Fair. There was something unsettling in his physical proximity. He seemed in the drawing room – and, she imagined, in any company of ordinary men and women – a beautiful but alien bloom. It was as if in her walks round her estate in Sussex she had found an orchid from the West Indies planted among the flowering grasses at the edge of the lawn, or in the shade of her oak tree. His presence had something of the fever dream about it.

'Forgive me for keeping you, madam, sir. We performers are not the earliest of risers. I hope that Lord Carmichael's collection has been entertainment enough in my absence.'

His voice was unnerving. A falsetto almost, high but gentle, and without the shrillness of a child. His English was perfection, nothing but a trace of an Italian accent.

Harriet said, 'The room is full of many treasures, though their subject-matter seems uniformly dark.'

Manzerotti smiled. 'Do you not think, madam, that the greatest art is inspired by tragedy? The most beautiful songs I sing are of loss and grief. Joy leaves no lasting impression on the world.'

'That seems a rather depressing philosophy.'

He was watching her as she spoke and Harriet found the completeness of his attention settled on her like sable, and made her long for luxury. 'I do not mean to suggest there is no place for joy in life, Mrs Westerman. Only that as life reveals its true self only in death, and that as love shows itself most fully in its loss, it is perhaps no surprise that the glories of great art often treat with subjects of suffering.'

Crowther spoke: 'Our apologies, sir, for calling on you so early. You know the reason for our visit.'

Manzerotti with a gesture invited them to take their seats and nodded, suddenly practical.

'You wish to know of my dealings with Fitzraven. It is simply stated. I was pleased and flattered to be offered the opportunity of singing here. I know I have been spoken of in London, and I wished very much to give substance to the kind words of praise that have been carried across the Channel to this place. A successful season in London is an important thing.'

Harriet looked directly at him. 'Did Fitzraven expect you to pay him for the opportunity?'

Manzerotti smiled at her again and she thought briefly of the woman who had thrown herself in front of his coach.

'He did, madam. I found on my arrival here that it had been an unnecessary expense. Mr Harwood told me he had expressly instructed Fitzraven to secure my services, and those of Johannes, if he could.'

Crowther examined his cuffs. 'That must have been an annoyance, sir.'

'It was. I was angry. But not enough to kill him, if that is your implication, Mr Crowther.'

The two men looked at each other for several silent moments. Harriet's eyes rested on a small painting of a slave market that hung to the left of the doorway.

'Bribery seems common practice in opera,' she remarked.

Manzerotti stood and crossed to the fire and held his hands out towards the flames.

'I am glad to be singing in London, but I miss the warmer weather of my own city,' he remarked. There was a strange muscled grace apparent even in his most ordinary movements. 'It is perhaps more common than one would like, Mrs Westerman. But the arts require the patronage of the rich and influential. A recommendation here, an introduction there, the chance to sing for an Emperor or some lady of taste and influence – on such things we poor servants of music must build the fragile structure of a career. Where such things matter, you will always find people looking to make a little profit of their own. I myself am ready to tip the gate-keepers to gain an audience.' He looked back into the flames. 'Sometimes I make an introduction or recommendation of my own. Sometimes it becomes necessary to use more blunt forms of payment.'

Manzerotti had a trick of colouring the pitch and timbre of his speaking voice so that each phrase left the outline of music in the air. Harriet had the impression of being rocked to and fro as he spoke in oily waters.

Crowther looked at him and said with a slow blink, 'But surely your talent speaks for itself, Mr Manzerotti?'

The castrato nodded in return, as if acknowledging a compliment, though the slight twist of his lips suggested he recognised the satirical edge to Crowther's question. 'Thank you, Mr Crowther. But a man may be talented indeed, and gain no foothold in these arts. We must also be fashionable to receive our opportunity to perform. To be a romantic artist, slave only to the music, might sound very fine, but it is uncomfortable and does the music no service if it is heard only by its singer. I flatter, I practise, I perform. This is my trade, just as Dr Gregson's trade is his secret recipe for pills against gout. He takes an inch or two in the *London Advertiser*, I make influential friends and celebrate their taste.'

'Such as Lord Carmichael,' Crowther said.

'Indeed. My Lord is a gracious host and I met him first many years ago in Milan, so he invited me to make his home my residence during the season. Though I must sing for my supper here also. I am part of the collection, albeit on a – let me remember the phrase – a *temporary* footing. Lord Carmichael is entertaining the better people in Town at a reception here tomorrow evening. Miss Marin will sing also. I hope you shall attend?'

'Was Fitzraven also to be part of the collection here? He seems to have been made of less fine stuff than yourself, yet we know he boasted of being admitted here after his return from the continent.'

Manzerotti lifted his shoulders. 'There are many people in Milan through whom he might have gained that introduction. I did not put their hands together, nor was I here when he visited Lord Carmichael.' He shrugged again and the silk of his coat rippled up and down his back. 'Perhaps my Lord found him amusing.' He continued in a brisker tone 'But I am not being very helpful to you – perhaps I can be more so. When I first met Fitzraven I was pleased to be his friend for the opportunities he offered. But since I arrived in London to take up my appointment at your opera house, that liking for him has diminished. I believe I observed him following me not less than three times since I arrived, and I think he did the same to others in the employ of the opera house.'

'Indeed?' Harriet said with calm interest, pleased to note her voice did not flutter when she spoke to him. 'And why should he do such a thing, do you think?'

Manzerotti picked a scrap of lint from his left sleeve. 'I think he had long made it his business to know a great deal about the people of distinction with whom he came in contact. He liked to come up to me in the opera and say, "Did you dine well at such and such a place? Did such and such a tailor please you? If not, I can recommend for you another place, another tailor". I believe that in doing such things, he hoped he was gaining my friendship.'

Crowther placed his long hands in his lap and felt the glow from the fire on his grey skin. 'It seemed he failed,' he observed.

'He did. And if his aim was to find out something to embarrass me into further gifts of money, he failed in that also. My life here is . . .' he lifted his hands, his palms raised and open '. . . blameless.'

'And, of course, you no longer require his friendship?' Harriet said.

Manzerotti turned his eyes on her again. 'Dear Mrs Westerman, you make me sound very brutal . . .' Harriet opened her mouth to apologise and say she meant nothing of the sort, but Manzerotti spoke on. 'Remember, I had cause to cut him. Had he been honest in his friendship with me, I would have been loyal to him. But he stole from me more than was polite.'

'Has your work taken you to Paris of late, Mr Manzerotti?' Crowther asked the question in a rather bored tone and examined his fingertips.

Manzerotti frowned. It was the first time Harriet had seen that perfect brow furrowed in any way and she felt a sudden impulse to smooth it clear again with the tip of her glove. 'Not of late, Mr Crowther. Why do you ask?'

Crowther did not take his eyes from his cuffs. 'I am fascinated by the glamour of a life so much unlike my own, perhaps. No matter. But what is more germane, who else in the company do you think found themselves with Fitzraven playing their shadow?'

Manzerotti continued to watch the older man carefully. 'I observed him following Bywater. Perhaps he found more than matters of tailoring and dining on those expeditions.'

'You suspect Mr Bywater of something, sir?' Crowther's voice by comparison with the avian coo of Manzerotti seemed like wheels on gravel.

'Of nothing – but he is very much in love with Mademoiselle Marin, Mr Crowther. And the duet . . .'

'What of the duet, Signor?' Harriet asked. She was sorry to note that her voice did sound a little breathy, even if it did not flutter, as if she were in the presence of a holy relic. This man seemed to make any space he occupied like a church or a theatre.

Manzerotti shrugged again and said with a smile, 'It is too good, Signora. Bywater is a man of at best moderate talent, but the duet is the work of a master.'

# IV.3

JOCASTA DIDN'T GO to see Kate buried, guessing that if Fred and Mrs Mitchell caught sight of her, she'd be up in front of the Magistrate before the grave was full and that he'd impose more 'fines' on her than the Constable had. She sent Sam and the two boys he'd fetched along with him though to keep an eye on them, and gave him some scraps of copper and a few words before he went. He'd taken Boyo with him too. The terrier liked him, and she knew he'd get fretful, shut in with her all morning.

Her time between readings she spent in contemplation, thinking over the years of her childhood between the death of the Baron and her coming away. There had been a fuss about his death, and much was left to lie, that even as a child she thought should have been dug up and shook about in the air. The bad feelings, the bitterness at being ignored had rotted and poisoned a place she loved. She'd escaped as far as Kendal by means of an early hopeless marriage, then abandoned that as no way near far enough, and made her way to London. It had taken four weeks of walking, and when she set her bundle down in Charing Cross, she'd sworn never to go back up north, and never to marry again either. Marriage seemed to her just a way to find someone to lie to every day.

Sam came trotting in eventually with a pair of pies and plenty of news.

'Don't think they noticed me at all, Mrs Bligh.' He wiped the crumbs off his face. 'Milky Boy's twice given me money now to run about with his messages, and he still wouldn't know me if I kicked him. For all his reading and writing, I think the fellow is daft.'

'He doesn't see you, Sam. He just sees a child and doesn't think to mind you.'

Sam shrugged. 'Anyway, it was just the two of them and the priest, and they made quick work of it. I did as you asked. Clayton is keeping an eye on Milky Boy, and Finn's going to follow *her* about. What are we going to do?'

Jocasta looked at the boy. 'What age have you, Sam?'

He fed the last of his pie to Boyo and scratched the terrier's ears. The dog licked his lips with a smack and leaned into Sam's hand. 'Don't know, Mrs Bligh. I went into the workhouse in Camberwell two winters past when my mum died of fever. I think I was about eight when we went in, so ten now, I suppose.'

'Know your birthday?'

He shook his head. 'No. Once when Dad was red with the gin he gave me a belt round the ear and told me it was a birthday gift. That was in the spring.'

They sat in silence for a while till their food was settled. Then Jocasta got up with a grunt. Sam scrambled to his feet.

'Where we going, Mrs Bligh? Are we going to visit the grave?'

Jocasta frowned. 'What use would that be? Think she'll leap out and tell us how it was and how to prove it?' Then, relenting: 'Maybe later, lad. First we are going up to the kiln. I want to see where she fell.'

Having concluded their conversations with Manzerotti, Crowther and Harriet made their way to visit Graves at the music shop, it lying, as it did, on both their ways. They found a notice in the window informing them that all copies available of the 'Yellow Rose Duet' from the opera *Julius Rex* had been sold, but that more would be available the following morning. Smiling to see it, Harriet pushed open the door. She found not only Graves and his assistant Jane in the little shop, but also her sister Rachel, and Lady Thornleigh. Susan was playing the harpsichord, her first instrument, in the centre of the shop while the adults around her were occupied in setting the room straight. Graves was counting the large amount of money he found in the cash-box in front of him.

'Dear heavens!' Harriet exclaimed, looking around her. 'Have the musicians of London been rioting?'

Lady Susan looked up from the keyboard and grinned. 'Mrs Westerman! Can you believe it? There was such a crowd here, Graves had to send to the house for Alice and Cecily to help. So Rachel asked Mrs Service if we might come along and see, and she said yes, so we came here and I played, then you wouldn't believe it but Miss Marin *herself* came in and we sang together and everyone was very nice!'

'You play and sing beautifully, my dear – I am not surprised they were nice,' Harriet said.

Rachel sighed. 'It was remarkable, Harriet. Miss Marin sang some selections from the Ranglegh songbook too, and I do not think there is another copy left of that here either.' She turned to curtsy to Crowther. 'I think my sister might have enjoyed the sight, had she not been out chasing murderers while we enjoy these lesser excitements, but I think Mr Crowther would have disliked the crush.'

Crowther failed to repress a shudder.

'How interesting that Mademoiselle Marin happened past,' Harriet said, choosing to ignore Rachel's other remark, and wandered over to the counter to at the few remaining songbooks on display.

Graves's lips thinned a little as he commented, 'I do not think it was an accident. I am sure she planned the whole thing very neatly, and there was a man I recognised here from the *London Advertiser.* He was not buying music. I should not be at all surprised if we read of this in the paper tomorrow morning. I am sure there will be mention that Susan was playing here. I should not have let her perform.'

Lady Susan had abandoned her place at the keyboard and come over to join them. Mrs Westerman put her arm around the young girl's shoulders.

'I did not ask you first, Graves,' the girl said kindly. 'And you were too busy to stop me.' Her guardian continued to look guilty. 'They will call me "tragic Lady Susan" again, won't they? And talk about how Papa died here.' She looked at the space in the middle of the room where she had cradled her father as he bled to death. Her look was sad, but not horrified. Harriet remembered a Midshipman who had lost his arm under her husband's command. He had been up in the rigging again within a month: the capacity of the young to heal was remarkable. She did not reply, merely stooped and kissed the top of her head. Susan looked back up. 'But I wanted to play, and I had many happy times here with Papa, too. And all the concerts he used to have here.' The memory brightened her.

Graves continued his attempts to reckon up his money. 'It is not really fitting, Susan.'

'Pah! Papa often had me play to his customers.'

'You were not Lady Susan Thornleigh then, my love,' Graves reminded her.

'Pah again! I was. It was just we didn't know it, is all.' She sighed very deeply. 'I wish Miss Chase had been here to hear it.'

At this remark, Graves seemed to lose his place in his numbers for a moment.

'Do stop saying "pah", Susan,' he said stiffly. 'If we cannot make you behave in a manner fitting to your rank, at least make some effort to speak like a lady!'

Having said this, he turned his back and Harriet found the little girl looking up at her dismayed. She gave a half-shrug and a small smile and Susan looked down at the ground ashamed.

The music shop sold a variety of scores and songbooks, most of which were engraved in the workshop which took up most of the yard behind the house. There, Lord and Lady Thornleigh's father had worked with copper-plates, hammers, scrapers, punches and press to record and disseminate the music of London's composers and players, having chosen independence over fortune and rank. Now the room was the kingdom of a Mr Oxford Crumley; a taciturn gentleman without wife or family who had arrived in response to Graves's advertisement for an engraver of music. He took up residence above the shop, nodded over the tools provided, had Graves arrange an apprentice for him, and settled down to work without further comment. Graves had as yet learned little of him other than he was more than proficient at his work, sober in his habits and showed his much younger master a friendly respect for which Graves was very grateful.

When Harriet had been introduced to Mr Crumley, soon after her arrival in London, she had remarked to Crowther: 'He is rather like you, I think. He sits all day in a single room surrounded by strange metal tools, so fixed on his art that the place could burn down around him before he even noticed the heat. However, his trade has its advantages. He ends his day covered only in ink.'

Crowther had not replied, but only continued to read his newspaper.

Mr Oxford Crumley now hovered in the doorway to the parlour and back rooms of the shop. He nodded to Harriet and Crowther then made his way to the counter and Graves, and without a word pushed a song-sheet towards that gentleman. Graves glanced at it, then smiled broadly.

'Susan, Mrs Westerman, Mr Crowther, do come and see this.' Graves turned the sheet towards them, and Susan clapped her hands together with a little shriek. Mr Crumley's work was worthy of her applause. It was the music for the 'Yellow Rose Duet', but rather than a plain statement of the notes such as the shop had been selling that morning, this had a frontispiece of a full-blown rose curled as it might be on a coat-of-arms, and framed by the profiles of Isabella and Manzerotti. The work was finely done. Mr Crumley saw they were properly impressed and almost smiled into his cravat.

'I was at work at it last night, and in the day, but have only just had the time to finish it, Mr Graves. Might it do?'

Graves reached out a hand and rested it on the older man's shoulder, still admiring the paper in his hand.

'Very well, Mr Crumley. I had been wondering how many more copies we could possibly sell, especially as every back room in Town will be trying to copy and produce their own versions as we speak, but this will draw them in. You have caught Miss Marin's likeness very well. I did not know you saw her before today, or Manzerotti for that matter.'

Mr Crumley shrugged his shoulders. 'Neither I had, but the boy was in the pit on Saturday night and I got him to describe them both as I drew.' He jerked his thumb over his shoulder to where his apprentice skulked, inky and shy in the doorway. Susan waved at him cheerily. He blushed to his ears and withdrew. 'It's a little like riding blind, but once you get the idea of which questions to ask, it's no great thing. Though I was glad when I glanced in earlier to see that Miss Marin at least was a match.'

Harriet beamed at the paper in front of her. 'You have Manzerotti to the life as well.'

Crowther spoke for the first time since entering the shop. 'I must leave you to the admiration of Mr Crumley's artistry. I have an appointment at the British Museum.'

Harriet handed the song-sheet back to Graves. 'And I am to go to the Foundling Hospital and meet Mr Fitzraven's most recent patron. I hope for the sake of his soul I shall find one being in London who will speak well of him.'

166

Graves placed the sheet on the counter-top. 'As do I, though the hope is not strong, Mrs Westerman.'

# IV.4

'HOW DO THE pictures work then, Mrs Bligh?'
Jocasta and Sam had been directed up this path by a young woman sweeping the steps outside one of the better houses on Tiburn Lane. For the chance of getting her cards read she had been chatty enough, and was glad to tell them about the older woman coming running down the lane yelling for help till Old Beattie had hauled his cart over, and then the younger man following with the lady in his arms all broken. She had watched them go up this way too, and reckoned by her memory of the pattern of her duties done that there had been no more than half an hour between Kate turning up this way looking happy and bright, and her sad return.

The way was muddy, and Jocasta thought it an odd walk to take on a Sunday with the clean paths of Hyde Park so close, but it had been chosen for its quietness. London was pushing out west like a growing baby stretches and pulls out its mother's belly for new space. Here they were near its edge and limit. On one side of the way sat the high brick wall of one of the fancier houses, on the left as they walked was hedgerow and a view of the fields. As they cleared the backs of the gardens, she sniffed the air and it tasted of green things hiding away for the winter, and woodsmoke. The quiet settled on her. It was a way that led up to the Marylebone Burying Grounds, now becoming over-run with new rich life and buildings, if you followed it, but Jocasta reckoned the little party could never have got that far and back in half an hour. It took her a few moments to hear Sam's question, and a few more to answer him.

'Hard to say it outright, stripling.'

'The cards tell you things though?'

'That's how it seems to me. The different pictures have different thoughts attached to them. When they are laid out, those thoughts come together. The Frenchman I met called them Tarot.'

Sam had picked up a stick from the way and began fighting the earth with it as they went along. Boyo snatched at the other end and they tugged against each other. Jocasta sniffed and rubbed her nose. It reminded her of her younger brother when they used to go walking along the old Corpse Roads behind Brumstone Bridge. He'd be near forty now, probably with children of his own if he'd lived. She had no way of saying if he had.

Sam stopped a moment and looked up at her. 'I was watching when you were laying them out yesterday. And for that girl just now. They look pretty. Most of them.' Boyo, seeing the game was paused, dropped his end of the stick and headed into the hedgerow.

'I'll show you their manner of speech sometime,' Jocasta said slowly. 'If you want.'

His face shone, and he ran ahead along the path with a skip. The young can shed things. Not that she had, not entirely, but Sam's face was bright again for now. He was not thinking himself orphan and poor, nor of the girl with her head stove in. He only knew he was rested and fed and had power over his limbs – and that was sufficient.

Jocasta walked on, looking over the ground right and left with no clear idea what she was searching for in the scrappy grass. She could hear Boyo yapping at Sam's heels up ahead. The image of Kate in the back of the cart kept coming in on her, though. Her little face had been unmarked, and she had looked more of a child than ever, just her hair all disarranged and her bonnet hanging back from a ribbon round her neck. Such a little face for all its pride. Jocasta could have covered it with the palm of her hand. She imagined doing so and lifting her hand away to find the woman breathing again, as if she'd just forgotten the trick of it for a moment and needed reminding. Her husband had been looking down on her, whiter than ever and wondering, with tears in his eyes.

There had been a boy in Jocasta's village who used to love to catch rabbits in the woodland on the flanks of the hills round Derwentwater. He came back past the water-pump dark-eyed one day and Jocasta was told he'd found one living and suffering in the traps, and had had to break its neck. Terrible sound an injured rabbit makes, like a baby stuck with something sharp. He grew accustomed in the end, of course, and six months later had been one of the ringleaders of a badger-baiting out the back of the Black Dog. Still, she had remembered that look, and it came back to her now, thinking of Fred bent over his wife's corpse with his mother like a crow behind him.

Jocasta's eyes flicked up. They were roughly abreast of the brick kiln now. It smoked into the air, tall above the trees and hedgerows, a great upturned funnel firing the building blocks for all the spreading habitations of London. Up ahead of her, where the path reared up to cross the hedgerow through the trees into the next field, she could see Boyo worrying at something on the ground, and Sam standing over him. Boyo was yapping. Jocasta walked on a little quicker.

Within moments of the carriage turning into the grounds of the famous Foundling Hospital, it became clear to Harriet that her visit here was likely to be an expensive one. First she saw the extensive gardens laid to turf, the modest solidity of the building itself, but then she saw the children. Young girls in high caps and white aprons over their brown skirts; small boys in red flannel waistcoats – all, she thought, out of infancy, but younger than Susan. They stood or walked about in twos or threes, and all turned towards her as she passed. There were so many of them, and these were such a tiny proportion of those born into dreadful want. Neither building nor gardens suggested great softness or comfort, but here was something like a paradise in comparison with the squalor of the city. This is what other beings with money or talent had brought to their city. Mr Coram had built this refuge, Mr Hogarth had filled its walls with paintings, and Mr Handel had crowded it with music. Harriet looked at her hands and wondered if there might be better use for them than turning over the secrets of the dead.

The kindly-looking matron who showed her in and escorted her towards the parts of the building where the committees met and the records were kept, spent the time of their walk telling her something of the place, and with each story she told, Harriet could feel guineas bleeding from her purse into the charitable trust.

'I've been here forty years now, madam, and it's a blessing to see how many have lived and thrived that would have starved in the workhouse otherwise, or been smothered by their poor mothers. Though many of them come too late or too sick. Time was, we used to bury more than half before they were six years old. The newborns go to wetnurses in the country that answer to us, then we look after them here and they are apprenticed out as soon as they are of an age.'

Harriet said she admired the gardens, and commented that the children must be glad of a place to play.

'Yes, the boys do the work of it. And well-trained they are too. The head-gardener at Hampton was brought here, starving, as an infant and now he is as sleek as any Lord and twice as hearty. And, of course, lots of the boys go to the ships.'

Harriet let her pace slacken a little, remembering the young boys who had served on the *Splendour*. Some had been raised within these walls. 'Does Lord Carmichael do much work for the hospital?'

She thought she sensed her companion stiffen a little. 'He organises some of the musical activities of this place, and likes to attend the service here on a Sunday. Once in my memory, someone put £100 in the collection plate! I do not think that was Lord Carmichael, however.'

'Others have been more generous?'

'Indeed, madam. Mr Hogarth designed their little uniforms, and Mr Handel all but built the chapel with the performances he gave here.' She sniffed. 'They were truly charitable gentlemen.'

'Is it wrong of me to guess you do not like Lord Carmichael?'

'There's no liking or not. In my opinion he spends time here because other rich gentlemen do, and it's a stage to strut about on. The King himself is our patron, and on the Sunday when the children sing, the chapel is as full of titles and fine furs as the House of Lords. Though people might say I have a prejudice. One occasion, Lord Carmichael wished a young girl sent out to a friend of his as servant. I did not like the friend and told the committee so. He tried to have me removed from my position.'

'I'm glad to see he was unsuccessful.'

The lady put her hands together lightly in front of her. 'My roots here are deep, but it was an uneasy time.'

'What became of the girl?'

'She ended up working for a butcher in Holborn. Married the son of the establishment last year and I held her flowers for her at the back of the church. But here we are, madam. If you would like to take a seat here, I shall tell Lord Carmichael you are waiting for him.'

Detaining her a moment, Harriet reached for her purse and handed over the money meant for new papers for the salon to the little Matron.

She did not have to wait long; before many minutes had passed, there were footsteps on the stairs behind her and two gentlemen approached. The elder she took for Lord Carmichael, and a straighter back she had never seen. Crowther's words had conjured in her mind a being weasly and small, slicked with ill-deeds and ill-humour. This man was not such a one. He was wigged and powdered, dressed with a perfection that made Harriet feel slovenly, and he had the figure and proportions to bring the best valet into tears of gratitude. His face was long and his nose aquiline; it seemed when he turned towards her and smiled as if a bust of a classical Caesar had become animated. The intricate embroidery on his waistcoat was in gold thread, the patterns of leaves and tendrils swirling across his stomach glowing. Each item of his dress fitted as if it had been sculpted on to him by some follower of Michelangelo. He was taller than Crowther and his face less lined. Harriet wondered if he dressed himself to take a place amongst his collection; he would be his own centrepiece in that drawing room, making even Manzerotti seem cheap by the comparison.

My Lord's companion was a much younger man who wore his own hair tied darkly at the nape, and Harriet would have called it a handsome face, as handsome as any young man of her acquaintance, were it not for the fact that the gentleman seemed to be carrying some great distress. His eyes were rather red and he was holding so hard onto his hat in front of him that his knuckles were whitening.

'Mrs Westerman.' Carmichael came forward and bowed and looked her carefully up and down. 'I am glad to make your acquaintance. I am Carmichael. This young man is my stepson, Mr Longley, and I fear because of him I shall not be able to have the conversation with you that was promised.'

'Indeed, sir? I am sorry to hear that. It is a matter of some urgency.'

Carmichael raised a perfect eyebrow and Harriet wished she had dressed with better care. 'Is it, madam? I fear Mr Fitzraven will remain a corpse no matter what you do. But perhaps I should leave it to Mr Longley to explain why his affairs carry me away from you.'

Mr Longley swallowed and wet his lips. Harriet put up her hand. 'No, really, Mr Longley. You have no need to explain your affairs to me.'

Carmichael was watching them both with a smile. 'Come now. It is my duty to my late wife that he should learn better manners, and my pleasure that he should explain to you how his behaviour has led to this state of affairs. I must insist.'

Mr Longley was on the verge of weeping. Harriet turned a little sharply to Carmichael and said, 'Yet *I* insist on not hearing it. You may force Mr Longley to speak, sir, but you cannot force me to listen. Very well. I shall bid you good day and hope to speak to you another time.'

'No – please don't go!' Mr Longley held up his hand, and rushed on in a whisper, 'He will be more angry with me if you do.'

Harriet hesitated, then turned back to them with a nod.

Mr Longley stared at the ground. He could not be more than eighteen. Carmichael continued to watch him, his expression one of indulgent amusement.

'I have been very foolish and find myself unable to pay a debt of honour. I can get no more from the Jews in Whitechapel, and rather than leave the country unprofitably, my father wishes me to pay my debts in another way. I must travel to Harwich.'

'Leave nothing out, Julian,' Lord Carmichael said, caressingly, but watching Harriet.

'The debt is due today. My father takes me to speak to the gentleman to whom I owe money.'

'And?'

'I am a disgrace to my family and my name, sir.'

'You are not addressing me at this time, Julian.'

The boy turned towards Harriet's shocked and angry face. 'I am a disgrace to my family and my name, madam.'

Harriet stepped forward, and ignoring Carmichael put a hand on the young man's arm.

'I am sure you are no such thing, Mr Longley.' The latter choked a little. 'Every man makes mistakes. It is how we learn! Do not think yourself worthless so young. You have a whole life in which to redeem yourself.'

'Do *you* learn from *your* mistakes, Mrs Westerman?' Carmichael said. Harriet ignored him.

Longley looked into her face, his eyes red and lips trembling. He seemed to her very far away, like a man drowning who sees his ship carried further from him by the waves and knows it is beyond his strength to reach it.

Lord Carmichael touched his arm, and he flinched and withdrew a step or two from Harriet. Carmichael turned towards her with a bow. 'Forgive me, madam. As you see, we must do a little tour of my stepson's debtors. I hope I shall see you at my house tomorrow evening.'

Harriet found she could do no more than nod, but as Lord Carmichael led the boy away, holding him firmly under the elbow, she called out: 'You will be in my thoughts, Mr Longley.'

The young man looked back and tried to smile bravely at her as Carmichael pushed him forward out on to the gravel forecourt where his carriage waited.

The guardians of the British Museum were still basking in the acquisition of Sir William's remarkable collection of Greek pottery and very ready to show them to anyone who made an appointment. It seemed, from the nods Mr Bywater received and the information he imparted, that he was a regular visitor there. He spoke in hushed tones with knowledge and affection of the shards in the display cases as their little group was encouraged from exhibit to exhibit.

Crowther could not see the appeal. The Greeks had been of use to the sciences, but he saw nothing remarkable about that which was in front of him other than its age. In the end, he thought, we all become old. Instead, he watched his companion. He seemed rather young, Crowther thought, to hold so high a position in the opera house, but he recalled that such a position often involved hack-work and wondered if Harwood had paid for his expensive performers by employing a cut-rate composer. His face was blandly handsome, and occasionally attractive when he spoke with animation. His manner was nervous, however, and his gaze flicked on and off Crowther's face as if it was afraid of settling there. His eyes were darkly shadowed and their were ink-stains around his cuffs.

'Do you tend to work at night, Mr Bywater?' Crowther said.

'I do. Though it is foolish during the season when there is so much work to be done in the day. I should not exhaust myself.' Bywater looked surprised. 'How could you tell?'

'I am familiar with the signs.'

As the main group moved forward, Crowther lingered and took the chance offered by their relative seclusion to say, 'Did you kill

Fitzraven, Mr Bywater? We have been told he was following you around the town and the annoyance may have provoked you to murder.'

It was said in the same light conversational tone they had been using for the last half-hour and Crowther did not look up from the display case in front of him as he spoke. He glanced up as he finished however.

Bywater had gone white. He opened and closed his mouth once or twice, then went red.

'I most certainly . . . Of course not – how could you think . . . ?'

'You're quite sure? It would so enhance the reputations of Mrs Westerman and myself if we could offer up a felon to Justice Pither with such expediency.'

Bywater stifled a gasp. 'Of course I'm sure. Look, I am most sorry, of course, to do damage to your reputations, but I cannot help you. It is not by my hand that Mr Fitzraven found himself in the Thames.'

'You did not know he was following you then?'

'No, I did not. Was he, indeed?'

Crowther had apparently become more interested in the pottery than his wandering gaze had hitherto suggested.

'Strange. He seemed to flaunt the knowledge he got rather than conceal it.'

'I have known Fitzraven three years. It was my experience that he liked to pretend he knew a great deal, but tended to say very little specifically – perhaps to Harwood, but not to the principals involved. Really, Mr Crowther – why would *I* put Fitzraven in the river? This is not a reasonable suggestion, sir.' He attempted a laugh, not with any great success.

'Murder is seldom reasonable, I think. The motivations of men are mysterious. What is valuable to one, may mean nothing to another.'

'All that is valuable to me, is my art.' Bywater crossed to a display case on the other side of the room and tapped on the glass. Crowther joined him. In the adjacent room a group of three ladies were standing by a display case of burial ornaments. Two were only girls, perhaps a year or two older than Lady Susan. They stared around the ceilings with wide vacant eyes, only looking at the case to admire their own reflections in it. The other lady, Crowther thought their governess perhaps, was keeping up a steady commentary on what was before them, though without, it seemed to Crowther, any genuine hope or expectation of capturing their interest. Education for the ladies and gentlemen of the growing empire. Crowther wondered if they would learn anything more than the appearance of sophisticated taste, but perhaps, in this instance that was the aim of the lesson; those not able to achieve real learning would study how to give the impression of it, and grow the wealth of the nation by consuming what they were taught was good and never have to trouble with forming an opinion of their own.

Bywater wished him to look at another piece of pot. 'Do you see what this says, Mr Crowther?'

Crowther peered through the glass and examined the Greek lettering. '*Androkidias made me.*'

'Think of that, sir. To have created something that can last through the centuries in this way. A man made this, but through his art, through his talent and craft, he has become an immortal.'

Crowther smiled a little. 'And luck, of course. Better pots, better painted, might have been crushed under the heels of careless Greek housewives.'

Bywater flushed. 'No. Look at the beauty here. Art of this quality, art of great quality *must* survive and carry the name of its creator forward.'

'Do you mean the shape of the vessel or the designs drawn on it? One man might shape, another paint – and who of us can say whose name it is that we read here? It may be the man who owned the house where the craftsmen worked.'

The effect of this speech of Crowther's was rather more extreme than he expected. He had spoken only to dampen the fire in Bywater's upturned eyes, but somehow his words seemed to have extinguished it entirely. His shoulders drooped and he turned away as if to hide symptoms of distress. If Crowther had, with the force of a man twenty years his junior, struck the composer in his belly, he could not have produced a reaction any more marked. He looked at the younger man with naked surprise. Noticing this, Bywater made an effort to straighten his back.

'I choose to believe this object was made by the man who put his name to it, and that because of this thing of beauty his name shall live', he said a little hoarsely.

'You must believe what you wish, of course. I do not deny you that right.' Crowther worked his thumb over the silver head of his cane. 'You expect immortality because of your duet?'

Bywater waved his hand as if troubled by a moth. 'No, no. That is nothing. I am surprised by its success. I have written much better pieces, and will write greater works in the future. Though its popularity might be of use.'

'In what manner?'

'I need time to give voice to the music of which I know I am capable.' His words were suddenly passionate, coming out in an angry hiss. 'That means I require commissions, patronage. If some rich music-lover is seduced enough by the "Yellow Rose Duet" to provide me with that, it will have served its purpose.' He seemed alarmed at his own vehemence and said, more lightly, 'Perhaps, sir, you would like to have a Mass I have been in the process of composing the last three years dedicated to you. It wants only a little work before it is ready for performance.'

'I am no expert judge of music,' said Crowther, ignoring this last, 'any more than of pottery, but I have been told by people who are, that "*C'è una rosa*" is a far greater piece of work than anything you have accomplished hitherto.'

Bywater clenched his fists. 'Nonsense,' he ground out.

Crowther sighed, and wary of another request for his patronage, said, 'Tell me, Mr Bywater, how far have your investigations into the fate of Mr Theophilius Leacroft progressed?'

Again the young man started. Crowther was almost sorry to rain down so many blows on his thin shoulders.

'Mademoiselle Marin told you? Of course, why should she not. She was seeking an old friend of her singing teacher in Paris at his request. But how could that be part of your investigation into the death of Fitzraven?' Crowther did not trouble himself to reply. 'Very well. I have made no progress. I wrote a number of letters and visited some physicians who had rooms in the area of Mr Leacroft's last address.' Bywater halted suddenly. 'Is Mademoiselle Marin displeased with me in some way? I did not think she attached great importance to this man . . .'

Crowther lifted his cane to his eye-level and blew from it some piece of dust only visible to himself before replying.

'No great importance? Indeed. Perhaps Mrs Westerman and I will have greater success. We are recruited now to hunt out mad singers as well as murderers.' He made as if to leave, then turned back to the young man, who was looking very pale. Crowther wondered if the extreme emotions Mr Bywater appeared to be labouring under were an example of the workings of an artistic temperament. If so, he was happy not to share it, since it seemed to be exhausting. 'I am glad, Mr Bywater, that you showed me this piece. It reminds me that what is perceived as a single creation might sometimes be the work of several hands. We have assumed that the person who put Fitzraven in the water was the same being who killed him. Perhaps that was not so, and yet another owns the enterprise that conspired to remove the man.'

Bywater looked at his feet and said sulkily, 'I have heard of you as a man of science, yet you display a fertile imagination.'

Crowther rolled the head of his cane between his fingers. 'Natural philosophy demands both the rigour of detailed, dull work, and the occasional flight of fancy. It is not unlike music in that way, I believe. At times your work is to stitch together the achievements of other men and lay down chords for the likes of Manzerotti to leap off and fly from, and at times you show signs of great inspiration yourself, such as in the already famous duet. It would be a depressing sort of hack-work, would it not, without those moments of blessed guidance?'

Bywater did not reply, and after observing him a few moments Crowther turned to leave Montagu House once more. The composer remained with his palm pressed to the glass of the cabinet that contained the Androkidias vase; it seemed he was trying to draw something from that ancient object into himself. Crowther would have said he had no use for talismans of that kind, but as the thought glanced over his mind he caught sight of his hand on the silver ball of his father's cane, and was forced to smile.

Harriet had time before Crowther returned from the British Museum to write to Dr Trevelyan with an enquiry after Theophilius Leacroft. She sent her affection to her husband at the same time and managed to write some civil replies to a number of James's friends. Their regrets and good wishes came from all over the globe as the ripple of news – Captain Westerman's great success, then grievous injury – unfurled through letter and word of mouth through the Service and striking at the edges of empire and exploration, began to flow back to Caveley and on to London in the form of these letters, travel-stained and smelling of salt and wood. They made the room in which she found herself seem very small.

There was a knock at the door and Rachel slipped into the room.

'Harriet? I am not disturbing you?'

Harriet shook her head and pointed to the bed, where Rachel seated herself while the last line of the latest letter was formed.

'What can I do for you, my love?' she said a little absently as she blotted her sheet and began to fold it.

'Harry, I have seen Miss Chase.'

Harriet swung round to face her sister. 'What? Verity has been here? Why was she not announced? I have not seen her since we came to London.'

'She came in the back way – we talked in the kitchen.'

'Lord, I hope her father does not know. He thinks his daughter a princess. If he thought she were paying visits through the kitchen he would blow out the windows of his house with his huffing.'

'Harriet!' Rachel said very sharply. 'Why must you always make fun?' Mrs Westerman was startled into silence and looked at her sister, who was twisting her hands together in her lap, an angry flush of red on her cheeks. 'Do you think of nothing but yourself? You do realise, I hope, that the living have their problems and puzzles and difficulties to deal with, as much as the dead.'

Confused, and a little cold in her stomach, Harriet began to say, 'Dear girl, has Mr Clode—'

'There – you see? You must always think yourself one step in front of us. It is not a puzzle and I have nothing to say of Mr Clode. You are *not* my pattern in that way!'

'Rachel, I . . .' Harriet rocked back in her chair, letting her hand fall to her side.

'Miss Chase came to talk to me because she feared Graves no longer thought of her as he once did. There seemed to be an understanding between them, but with the sudden elevation in his fortunes, his hatred of living on Lord Thornleigh's money . . . I came for your opinion on a matter she wanted to ask about.'

'I am sorry, Rachel.'

'It is so like you to assume! You are unfair! Mr Clode is a man I much admire, but there is no understanding between *us*. Honestly, Harry, do you think he is the kind of man who would approach me, behind your back and with James in such a way?'

'Rachel . . .'

'Though he will most likely never wish to be in company with me again now, when he hears of . . . He is a country lawyer, his reputation must be his fortune. How could he be respected with a sister-in-law who likes nothing better than chasing corpses into the gutters of London and offending every person of rank she approaches? All the time while her husband is sick and she chases after cheap scandal in a borrowed carriage!'

Harriet's movements became very precise, and while her sister found her handkerchief and wiped it angrily across her eyes, sealed up the letter she had been writing with infinite care.

'I am sorry if my behaviour offends you, Rachel, or Mr Clode,' she said very quietly. 'But I shall not alter it.'

Rachel's voice had grown more steady, but her tone was still insistent. 'He has said nothing, how could he know? But if he did! Oh Harriet, if not for me, will you not think of your daughter? What of baby Anne? James is no longer able to grant you respectability and force people to think well of you.'

'Graves, I think, accepts what I must do.'

'Graves is an oddity in society, Harriet. He is tolerated because he controls the patronage of the Earl of Sussex's estate. And he is a man.' Harriet flinched. Rachel closed her eyes for a long moment, then opened them again to look at her sister. Her green irises were ringed in gold: Harriet had forgotten that. Her tone when she spoke again was bitter and loaded with sorrow. Harriet had never heard it in her sister's voice before. 'Tell me, who will marry the sister or daughter of the notorious Mrs Westerman?'

Harriet felt a cold white rage begin to build under her skin.

'Any man that wants her twenty thousand pounds will take Anne, Rachel. Just as Clode will swallow my behaviour for your ten! The papers were drawn up before my husband became an imbecile. Your money is quite safe.'

Rachel went very white as if she had been struck, then drew a shuddering breath. Harriet found herself thinking of Marin's appeal to Manzerotti in the 'Yellow Rose'.

'You married for love, a respectable man. Yet you say you will give your daughter to some man who cares nothing for her reputation but wants only her money? How could any woman be happy with a man who took her on such terms? Listen to yourself, Harriet! Last summer your enemies threatened to make you an outcast and they failed. Yet in investigating another killing now you seem intent on doing their work for them. James has made his family rich, but we are not Earls or Barons. What is allowed to them, will be marked against us. Already people talk. Are your children to be blighted before they come out of the schoolroom?'

'Blighted?' Harriet raised an eyebrow and looked into her sister's face. She was still so young. Her face was all velvet. Her lips trembled and she held her handkerchief clasped at her chest, a pattern of feminine distress. Harriet turned back to her desk and took up her pen again. 'Thank you, Rachel. I think you can have nothing further to say at the moment. I shall see you at dinner.'

Rachel stood and held out her hand. 'Harry, I only say these things because I love—'

Harriet held up her hand sharply, keeping her eyes fixed and unseeing on the new page in front of her.

'Do not say it, Rachel. Leave.'

She heard the tap of her sister's slippers on the Earl of Sussex's floorboards and the click as his finely fitted door closed behind her. Mrs Westerman lowered her hand, but made no further movement for some time.

# IV.5

JOCASTA ARRIVED AT the hedgerow at a smart pace, picked up Boyo by the scruff of his neck and dropped him into Sam's arms. 'Did he find something, Mrs B?' And when Jocasta frowned at him: 'Mrs Bligh, I mean to say . . . ma'am.'

She looked back into the grass without replying. The way was scattered with odds from the kiln behind them. The fires must have been burning there for fifty years, and it had had the time needed to throw its offcuts around. When the man who owned this field now turned them up with his plough, or the boy walking in front to guard his blades found any, they were picked up and chucked to the edges – thickened and twisted slices of unglazed slate, half-bricks. She took a step or two from the path and reached down to where Boyo had been snuffling. There was a little pile of stones here; not so raggedy and fallen-about-looking as the others, and whereas between all the other little heaps and falls, grasses had stuck their heads up and fallen back, no living thing had been given time to crawl up among these.

Jocasta lifted the topmost piece and put it aside, then pushed away one or two from the edge. The bitter and sick taste crawled into her mouth.

'What is it, Mrs Bligh?' She felt the lad come up and look over her shoulder. 'Oh. I see it.' His shadow slunk away again.

Under the top slate sat a half-brick, with a jam of red on it and a little swirl of hair. The ends not caught up in the blackening slick gleamed guinea gold in the last of the daylight. Jocasta carefully placed the slate back on the pile, and looking about her added a couple more, then sat down on the stile and stared back the way they'd come.

Sam tucked Boyo through the hedgerow beside her, so he could gad about without snuffling at the little stone tent she'd made.

'Fools,' Jocasta said at last. 'If they'd left that rock lying in the path, I might have said, "Jocasta, old girl, the cards are taking you scrambling".' She patted the stile beside her. 'Might have thought, the girl could have stepped up here and fallen off and knocked her head on one of these stones. Easy enough to do. Might have thought all those lies in the cards were just chatter and they were no more than mocking me with an accident to come. But no. Those two hid the stone – and that means they are as guilty as the serpent himself.'

Sam put his head on one side. 'But you've got them now, haven't you? I mean, if you bring the Constable out here or take him the brick . . .'

'It's the placing that tells the story, lad. They can say I did that if we don't know the whys as well as the ways. Let it bide there. If we have a fuller story, then they'll see it with our eyes. We've time.'

Sam kicked at a bit of stone on the other side of the path. 'But why are you looking so sudden sad now, Mrs Bligh? You knew they did her in yesterday. You called them murderers to their faces, I heard you do it.'

Jocasta leaned back, watched the sun turning the clouds purple and pink and sighed. 'Don't let anyone ever tell you, lad, that being right leads to being content. Most of the time in my experience it leads just the other way.'

It was some time later that there was another knock at her door and Harriet jumped. She half-expected to see Rachel come back into the room, but it was Lady Thornleigh who stepped in.

'You and Rachel had a fight,' she said without preamble, and hopped up onto the bed.

'Yes, we did, my Lady. Did she send you to plead for her?'

Lady Thornleigh dropped back onto Harriet's blankets and plucked at her skirts. 'Pah! Of course not. There was shouting, then she ran out of here crying. Was she telling you you should be more lady-like?'

Harriet twisted round in her chair to find Lady Thornleigh's clear blue eyes peering at her from the heap of cushions. 'She was, in her way. How did you guess such a thing?'

'When Graves or Mrs Service are angry with me, that is usually the cause.'

Harriet smiled. 'They are right, Susan. Do not follow my way.'

Lady Susan turned onto her front and sighed loudly. 'But if you had been ladylike last year I might be dead now. And Jonathan. And Graves too, most likely. Isn't that so?'

It was a fair remark, and Harriet paused before answering. 'Perhaps. But Rachel tells me I must think of baby Anne now.'

Lady Thornleigh crossed her ankles and scratched at her side, complicated manoeuvres that dislodged her slippers from her stockinged feet.

'Well. When Anne is nineteen, I shall be . . . twenty-eight, so very old and respectable and married, and rich and with plenty of *rank*. So I will find her a nice husband if you are too busy finding murderers and saving people like me.'

Harriet was surprised to feel her throat tightening. 'Thank you, Susan.'

The little girl sprang off the bed and kissed her. 'I'd be glad to, you know. Now it is time for you to dine soon, and Cook has been cross and had a great deal of trouble getting oysters today, so remember to be especially nice about them.' Then she pulled her slippers back on and was out of the room before Harriet could say another word.

## IV.6

CROWTHER HAD A sense of some danger as he mentioned to Harriet that he had asked Mr Harwood to call on them after dinner, and then murmured his reasons for doing so. Mrs Westerman's movements were constrained, her only remarks insipid in the extreme and the muscles in her jaw tightened considerably when Rachel joined them. Once the formalities of dining were disposed of, rather more swiftly than usual, and she had spoken at some length of the quality of the oysters and demanded the recipe be brought to her as soon as convenient, Harriet retired to the library. Crowther did not linger long over his wine with Graves, and joined her there after only a few minutes.

'Dear God, Mrs Westerman, what was that?'

She was slumped again in the armchair by the fire – which, Crowther hoped, indicated that her performance was at an end.

'What are you talking about, Crowther?' she said wearily, without looking up.

'I understand you have had some disagreement with your sister, but it seems cruel to subject Graves, Mrs Service and myself to your simpering parody of good manners. I am glad it was not one of the occasions where Lady Susan dined with us.'

Harriet folded her arms. 'Do not lecture me, Crowther.'

'You are a guest in this house.'

Harriet was silent for a while. She had been angry, she still was, but it was that most bitter and uncomfortable anger that came with a sensation of guilt. She did not think it would ever occur to Graves, admiring her as he did, to question her behaviour. For that kindness she had called him a fool in the blackness of her heart. Mrs Service was never anything but reasonable and friendly. Rachel was still in many ways a prim little girl, much more the vicar's daughter than Harriet, but she did not deserve Harriet's scorn, and it had been scorn that was the driver of her performance at dinner. She had been mocking and humiliating Rachel, she had known she was doing it, and now here was Crowther to tell her so. Graves it had left confused, Rachel miserable, Mrs Service slightly exasperated and Crowther angry, and she had got no relief from it.

'Should I apologise to Graves and Mrs Service?'

Crowther took a seat on the opposite side of the fire. 'Personally, I never compound an offence with apologies,' he said. Harriet laughed suddenly and glanced across at him. Some of the gravity had left his expression. She felt a weight shift from her shoulders and let her breath out slowly before speaking.

'Very well. Did Rachel tell you she and I had disagreed?'

'Not as such, but she sought me out to ask my advice about the love affairs of Mr Graves and Verity Chase. I cannot imagine she would have done so unless you had already proved an unwilling audience.'

'We managed to be at each other's throats before she had much chance to tell me a great deal. What was the matter of it?'

'Miss Chase wishes to plan her wedding to Graves, but knows he hates the fact that the food he eats – that we all eat – is paid for

186

by the estate of the Earl of Sussex. He cannot make his own fortune while he is managing another, and is too proud to add a wife and family to the charge he makes on Lord Thornleigh's fortunes. Miss Chase wants him to use her marriage portion to buy the music shop from the estate of the Earl of Sussex, and so provide them with an independent income. However, she fears he no longer wishes to marry her. Perhaps she is dazzled senseless by the enormous quantity of gilt in this house. I think Rachel assured her that he does, but wished to know if I thought it likely Graves would approve of the plan for the shop, or whether his pride would prevent him acquiescing.'

Harriet found herself amused by the idea of Crowther receiving this information from her sister and wondered what his expression had been as he had listened. 'And your reply?'

'I said that in matters of the heart my concerns are more practical than metaphysical. If she wished to bring me Mr Graves's heart in a jar I could tell her if it were healthy or no, but further than that I had no idea and advised her to talk to Mrs Service.'

Harriet sighed. 'Poor Rachel. We have not been of great assistance. I wonder why she did not go to Mrs Service at once, having instructed me on my proper behaviour.'

Crowther put his fingers together and said lightly, 'I imagine because she knew you and I would be having this conversation at some point during the evening and wished you to be informed of the plan for the music shop. Your sister is young, and a little over-cautious of your reputation perhaps, but she is no fool, Mrs Westerman. And my remark about Mr Graves's heart made her smile.'

'I am hasty with her.'

He did not reply but let the silence unfold between them till Harriet said: 'I fear I learned very little from Lord Carmichael other than I do not like him, and his stepson is wholly in his power. He had nothing to say of Fitzraven that did not confirm what we knew of him previously. Tell me of your meeting with Bywater.'

Crowther put his hand to his chin. 'That gentleman is certainly guilty of something.'

'Of love?'

'As we have already said, I am no expert in such areas, but of something more, I believe. However, I do not think him a likely spy for the French. He claims he had no idea that Fitzraven was following him. My impression is he wishes public renown rather than private riches. That would make it unlikely for him to trade secrets for money, though he might for influence, but really, what could a composer with limited connections know that would be of interest to the French?' Harriet assumed the question was rhetorical so did not reply. 'And, Mrs Westerman, we have an appointment tomorrow morning.'

'With Bywater?'

'No, madam. With Mr Palmer. There was a note delivered here this afternoon. We are invited to call on a Mrs Wheeler in Conduit Street, where we shall meet an old friend. I assume that is Mr Palmer.'

'He is most circumspect.'

'He most likely has his reasons. If his suspicions are correct, and Fitzraven's having spent time in France this summer, when Mr Harwood thought him only in Milan, suggest they might well be, then we are on dangerous ground. It is a high-stakes game. Men are hung for murder. They are drawn and quartered for treachery.'

Harriet was still digesting this comment when there was a rap at the door and Mrs Martin stepped in.

'Mr Crowther, Mrs Westerman. A gentleman is here and wishes to speak to you. A Mr Winter Harwood from His Majesty's Theatre.' She paused then held out a piece of paper to Harriet. 'And here is the recipe for the oysters, ma'am.'

It may have been he was only clearing his throat, but to Harriet it sounded suspiciously as if Crowther laughed.

Jocasta, Sam and Boyo had made their way back into the heart of the city through the shadows and were all weary and slow by the time they reached Jocasta's alleyway. There was a stirring in the dark under the pear tree as they approached and two boys emerged from the gloom and exchanged nods with Sam.

He pointed at each of them. 'This is Finn, Mrs Bligh. And this is Clayton.'

They touched their foreheads to her and shuffled their feet. Jocasta led them into her room, where Sam set about making the fire. The shorter of the two, Clayton, sat on his hands to warm them and said Fred had changed his coat in Salisbury Street after the burial, then gone to the Admiralty Office. He'd come out with two other men like him and got settled in at the ale-house in Crag's Court.

'He looked funny though.'

'What do you mean, boy?' Jocasta said.

'He was walking slow and heavy, and the others were sort of holding him up. He was wailing a bit, and the others were looking about them as if they were worried he'd be heard. He looked to me like he didn't want to go anywhere with them, but they wouldn't let him be. He was there a while then went back home on his ownsome. I thought—'

'Tell on . . .'

'I thought he was crying like, as he was walking along. Then I met up with Finn in Salisbury Street, and we thought we'd head back here.'

Finn, the taller, skinnier one who had red hair, had been keeping an eye on Mrs Mitchell.

'She didn't do much. Got to her coffee-shop after the burying and stayed there till supper, then headed back to Salisbury Street. There was a man paid a visit – he was just leaving when Fred came back.'

Jocasta sniffed. 'Her man?'

'Couldn't say, Mrs Bligh,' the boy said, thrusting his hands in his pockets. 'Tall fella. Dressed plain. That Fred was very respectful of him, bowing and scraping as they talked like he was the Emperor of China. Got the feeling the words between them weren't kindly. Tall

Man said something and Fred flinched and wiped his eyes and tried to stand a bit straighter. Then Clayton came and tapped me on the shoulder and by the time we turned back, Tall Man was gone and the door was shut.'

'Fairly said.' Jocasta folded her arms. 'Anything more?'

'I got talking to one of her boys what help out in the shop.'

'What did he say, Finn?' Sam asked, as he set the lighter stuff for the fire, and started to strike up Jocasta's steel.

'That some weeks ago the missus was looking grim, but last Tuesday the landlord was in and she put money in his hands like she was the Queen of Sheba tossing away stones. Oh, and that he likes Wednesday and Saturday best because he gets extra tips selling books to the rich-livers in the coaches.'

'Books and coaches?' Sam asked, then started to blow on the embers.

'Mrs Mitchell has the right to sell coffee and oranges and storybooks. She gets the words from the theatre, then has them printed in Hedge Lane, the liberrrettos,' he trilled, enjoying the word. 'She pays fifty pounds a year for it. Wednesday and Saturday are when they do the singing there, at His Majesty's Opera House in Hay Market.'

Mr Winter Harwood was very poised.

'You asked me to come here, Mr Crowther, and I have. It was not convenient, but I came. Is it too much to hope you have found out who killed Fitzraven and that the matter is concluded?'

Harriet found Mr Harwood a most interesting study. Without appearing impolite he had taken a seat, declined all offers of refreshment and done so with such economy of movement and word, this speech sounded by comparison like an oration. Harriet thought if he were similarly thrifty with his resources at the Opera House, for all its extravagances he was probably amassing a considerable fortune there. Though the question was addressed to Crowther, it was she who replied.

'Mr Crowther has been wondering at your continued employment of Mr Fitzraven after he ceased to play for you.'

A slight frown appeared between Mr Harwood's fine sandy eyebrows. 'I believe I have already explained, Mrs Westerman . . .'

'Indeed,' Crowther interrupted, 'running errands, writing puffs in the newspaper and so forth. But I have been wondering, Mr Harwood, if you did not find it convenient, dealing with the great individuals on and off the stage, to know a little more about them than it was agreeable to ask in person.'

Mr Harwood's face gave no sign of shock or anger. Harriet found she was holding her breath. If Fitzraven had followed the leading players of the opera around the place with Harwood's blessing, it would give them meat indeed for Mr Palmer. Fitzraven was quite possibly trained in the value – the monetary value – of information before he went to France, and had no difficulty with trading in it.

'You are suggesting . . . ?'

'I am suggesting that Fitzraven spied for you, Mr Harwood,' Crowther continued. 'You knew his reputation to be bad, but he was obviously of some use to you, even before his miraculous delivery of Miss Marin and Manzerotti. I think you made use for your own purposes of his love of finding out the details of the lives of those influential or renowned beings with whom he came into contact.'

There was a long pause. Very few men had the courage to remain so calm under Crowther's eye. Mr Harwood would be a remarkable opponent at the card-table.

'You are very blunt, sir.'

Through the closed door to the library the small sounds of the household filtered; a living thing. One of the servants moving through the passageway. A door upstairs opening and closing. Lady Thornleigh was practising at the harpsichord before retiring; its soft voice curled down the main stair and whispered sweetly under the door.

'Mr Harwood,' Harriet said, 'if Fitzraven was bringing you information about the personalities in your establishment, we would like to know. How you manage the Opera is your concern, but if he found something in his wanderings after your employees and patrons and that knowledge led to his death . . .'

Mr Harwood pursed his lips and looked into the fire. Then nodded. 'The arrangement was unofficial and unacknowledged,' he said. Harriet felt her breathing steady. 'I may look to the world like a little king in His Majesty's, but in truth I merely preside over a number of rather independent Baronies. The costumers, the singers, the musicians, the magicians of stage machinery, the house poets . . . all have their areas of responsibility and expertise, and all compete. Fitzraven would come and see me from time to time, with one titbit of information or another. It has helped me avoid some minor problems in the past, and take advantage of some small opportunities at others.'

'I see. For example?' Crowther's voice was dry.

'Aside from making use of the petty jealousies within the theatre, it becomes a great deal easier to renegotiate the arrangements for a singer's benefit if you know he has lost a large sum at cards the previous evening.' Harwood met Crowther's gaze evenly. He neither defied judgement, nor invited it.

'And you paid for this service?'

'It was usual that having delivered his information, Fitzraven would ask me for some small loan. Those loans were never repaid.'

'And have you made many small loans to him this season since he returned from the continent?'

'No, Mr Crowther. I was rather surprised, I admit, to find this the case, but since he came back from the continent I have not made one.'

Jocasta had fed the boys with meal and milk, then Finn and Clayton had headed out into the dark looking warmer and brighter for the feeding. Clayton had a place he was sharing in one of the ruined houses in Whitechapel, and Finn always slept in a couple of barns he knew off the Islington Road. He'd never slept in a proper bed. 'Don't think I'd like it, Mrs Bligh,' he'd said. 'I like to have some space about me, and a clear run at the fields. Being inside makes me jittery.' They told her they'd call by the next day and see if she had work for them, then made their way out into the inky blackness of the alleys. She saw the want in Sam's face though, the little scrap, and gave him a nod. He went out with the others, but ten minutes later was slipping back in through the door like the shadow of a cat, and curled himself up in a corner away from the fire. It was as if he didn't want to be blamed for stealing the heat of it.

Jocasta didn't sleep so soon, and Boyo kept her company on the couch. She pulled at his ears and watched the fire burn out, then stood to fetch Sam's blanket and drop it over him. Strange how already she thought of it as his own. All she could see though was the rock with that blonde wisp jammed to it. It would have been quick anyway.

She must have dozed, because something woke her, and she could tell by the taste of the night air creeping in that it was coming up to dawn again. Boyo had been woken too and was looking at the door. He was rearing up against the coverings of the couch, his ears flat and teeth bared, and a low growl starting in the back of his throat. Jocasta frowned, then stood slowly and crossed the room. The latch lifted odd, strangely reluctant under her thumb. She pulled it open, letting more shadows tumble into the room to pile on the heaps of greys already curled around her bed and spilling out from the cold grate of the fireplace. There were a pair of rats, quite dead with their little white teeth showing, slung on a bit of string and hooked round the latch on the outside of her door. Someone had gone to the trouble of tying a noose round each furry throat and pulling it tight. The hallway was empty, and the only noise in the house was the quiet of its people sleeping.

Jocasta threw the bodies into the stink heap in the yard and looked about her. Nothing but the shake of the pear tree, old man Hopps coughing in his sleep in the front room opposite, a light footstep out on St Martin's Lane. The little corpses were still warm.

# PART V

## V.1

*Tuesday, 20 November 1781*

Rachel knew she had upset her elder sister, and however right she believed herself to be, it was in her nature to feel guilty as a result. At breakfast the following morning she fetched her sister coffee and toast and handed her her letters with careful naturalness. She did not dare smile yet, but neither did she frown. Harriet accepted this as an apology, and by thanking her sister gently, but without meeting her eye, made her own.

Lady Susan and Mrs Service grinned at each other when they thought they were unobserved, and Stephen Westerman and the Earl of Sussex were aware enough of the pleasantly warming atmosphere to start chasing each other round the table until the threat to my Lord's china made Mrs Service speak rather sharply to them.

The first letter Harriet opened made her give a little cry of delight. Graves had just walked into the room and was peering under the covers in hopes of warm eggs. He almost dropped the lid from his hand.

'Some good news, Mrs Westerman?' he asked, juggling the silverware.

'Very,' said Harriet, and looked about the table. All those older than ten looked back. 'This note is from the good Dr Trevelyan. It is not about James, dear heart,' she said to her sister, seeing a frown of concern on Rachel's face. 'It is about Miss Marin's old singing teacher, Theophilius Leacroft.'

'Has he been found, Mrs Westerman?' Mrs Service asked. At the same moment she put out her hand in front of Lord Thornleigh, palm raised. The young peer looked a little glum and handed her the cat's cradle he had been playing with under the table since his races had been stopped. It disappeared into Mrs Service's reticule and he despaired of seeing it again before dinner. Oblivious, Harriet continued reading from her note.

'He has indeed. Dr Trevelyan thought he had heard a colleague of his who runs a private madhouse down Kennington Lane mention a melancholic musician, and sent to him at once. The colleague confirms it. Mr Leacroft is confined for his own safety, but is in no way dangerous and I have his address before me.'

Susan clapped her hands. 'Oh, Mademoiselle will be very happy!' Then she looked confused. 'But why is her singing teacher here? Did she not grow up in Paris?'

Graves coughed. 'I'll explain it to you later, Susan. I promise. But that is good news, indeed. Mrs Westerman. As soon as you have written your note, Philip will take it straight to her rooms in Piccadilly.'

When Crowther arrived to accompany Mrs Westerman to their assignation with Mr Palmer, he walked in on such a scene of domestic harmony and goodwill that he felt as if someone had doused him with a pail full with the milk of human kindness. He did not enjoy the sight of Mrs Westerman and her sister in dispute, but this improving scene of family business and pleasure was almost equally exhausting. He thought of the privacy and quiet of his workroom with a now familiar nostalgia, and steeled himself to be spoken to by several people at once.

It was not long before they were interrupted, however; Alice knocked on the door to tell them Mr Tompkins had returned and was waiting for them in the library, with apologies for his early call. When Harriet opened the door, their visitor shot to his feet as if he feared he had committed some deadly sin by sitting in the first place.

Mr Tompkins was not a very sensible young man. His clothes were all in the current fashion and had, no doubt, cost his father a fair penny, but instead of making him look at home in society, they rather marked him out as a man rather easily seduced by his tailor. Every line of his dress was a little too one thing or the other. He was already rather fleshy for his age, and seemed to be made of softer stuff than other men. In his conversation, when he wished to be manly and authoritative he overtopped it and seemed more a boy than Stephen, and when he tried, as he had done on their previous meeting, to make some elegant compliment, he sounded like a poor actor, over-rehearsed but stumbling nevertheless. The general impression was of a hen who had dressed herself in peacock feathers and was trying to pass them off as her own with a casual shriek on the summer terrace of Thornleigh Hall.

Harriet made a silent promise to be kind. When last this gentleman had visited, he had had nothing of interest to tell them, and had told them that nothing in an uninteresting manner. She had made no effort with him, but before he left the house Graves had opened the door to speak to them, and spent a few minutes in conversation with the man. He had been generous in his attention, perhaps reminded of his own arrival in London and his early difficulties. Because of his kindness, Mr Tobias Tompkins had left the house rather more comfortable and a little less afraid. The incident had made Harriet ashamed. Now she looked at the young man again she thought his coat suspiciously like the one Graves had been wearing on the evening in question.

Tompkins began to speak as soon as the door opened.

'I have had a thought, madam! At least, I had a thought, and I ... and I hope ... I mean – oh, forgive me.' He bowed and the shoulders of his coat strained a little. 'Good morning, Mrs Westerman, Mr Crowther. You are both looking terribly well.'

Harriet managed not to laugh and, ignoring the sigh behind her from Crowther, she stepped forward and offered her hand.

'Thank you, Mr Tompkins. Now do take a seat and tell us about this exciting thought of yours.'

Crowther remained standing, and as Tobias sat down he could not help glancing up at him from time to time like a rabbit who has spotted something unsettling in the undergrowth. His nose was rather flat and his jowls had a pronounced swell. It looked as though his wig, a little elaborate for a morning visit, had forced his cheeks too low on his face.

'Well, that is . . . I mean, after I called and we . . . The thing is . . .'

Crowther had turned his back on them to shuffle some papers on the desk. 'Do take a breath, Mr Tompkins.'

Tobias made a visible effort to collect himself.

'I know I was not of any great assistance to you when we last spoke.' He looked very miserable, as if suddenly deflated. 'I wish I had been reading some other stuff; if I'd had a novel in my hand I'm sure I would have been awake and heard everything. Being a lawyer might be a respectable career to aim at, but one has to read a great many very dull books.'

'You prefer novels?' said Crowther, still with his back turned.

Tobias lifted his chin. 'Some novels can be very improving!'

Harriet tried to remain patient. 'Yes, though those sort can send one to sleep as quickly as law books, I find.' Mr Tompkins considered and was forced to nod fiercely in agreement. 'But please, Mr Tompkins, your idea.'

'Of course. I knew that you had spoken to Mrs G's other residents, but I was thinking surely someone must have seen something. I mean, in London one never really seems to be alone.'

Crowther did not turn away from his papers, but said, 'I have often thought the same thing.'

Tobias visibly brightened at this moment of communion and

continued, 'So I was wracking and wracking my brains to think of someone till they hurt, you know, they really actually hurt! And then I remembered Gladys.'

Harriet realised that Crowther had taken a step towards them. His voice when he spoke had lost its unpleasant edge, and became one of cautious interest. 'Gladys?'

'Yes, Gladys,' Mr Tompkins said, and looked between them with a happy grin.

'And who,' Harriet said, willing patience on herself, 'is she?'

Mr Tompkins slapped his forehead with the heel of his hand. 'I *am* a fool – how should you know who Gladys is?' It was perhaps fortunate that he did not look up at Harriet and Crowther at precisely this point. 'The house we live in shares a back yard with the houses on King Street, you see, and Gladys lives in the one that backs onto ours.' Mr Tompkins rubbed his chin. 'She is a daughter of the lady who lives there, a widow, but she is a little simple-minded and likely to turn into a spinster. Never gives anyone any bother though, and nods to us all in the street, but not really with her full wits.'

Crowther took a seat, murmuring, 'Who among us can lay claim to that?'

Tobias gave another deep nod. 'Yes, indeed. Well said, sir! So, to continue, she has a little perch by the back window where her chamber is and watches the birds flying about and the cats and things. Just watches, you know. Spends half her days and nights there.'

Crowther looked at him with new attention. 'I saw her,' he said. 'She seemed to be looking straight into the room as I was at Fitzraven's desk.'

'Mr Tompkins.' Harriet's smile became quite genuine. 'Mr Tompkins, you have had a very fine thought indeed. We shall certainly pay a call on Gladys.'

Mr Tompkins blushed. 'Oh, I have already had a word with her, Mrs Westerman. Didn't want to send you round to see her if she'd been out that afternoon or some such; she goes on her walks, you see. Would have felt even more of a fool! And as I mentioned, she's a little simple. I didn't want her to be frightened, and she knows me slightly, so I popped round there yesterday evening to say hello. I knew her mother would want to hear all about Fitzraven anyway, so there would be no bother about it.' He stopped speaking.

Harriet felt her jaw beginning to clench again. Crowther tented his fingers together and said very slowly, 'And what did she say, Mr Tompkins?'

Mr Tompkins's hand went to his chin again. 'Well, as it turns out, she *was* out most of that day.' Harriet tightened her grip on the arm of her chair. 'But it was a rum old thing. I was asking her about that afternoon, and telling her mama the news, and of your involvement.' He tried a little extra bow from his chair, then recovered himself. 'Fearsome lady that, and Gladys said I shouldn't worry about Mr Fitzraven, because he was a very, very good man and she knew he was in heaven. She's rather religious as well as simple,' he added in an apologetic undertone to Harriet, then continued in his normal voice, 'I didn't know him very well, but I never thought of him as terribly pious, so I said how was she so sure and she said the strangest thing!' Mr Tompkins examined the carpet and shook his head with wonderment at his fellow creatures.

Harriet managed to force her words out between gritted teeth. 'What did she say, Mr Tompkins?'

Tobias looked up again. 'Oh. Yes. Indeed. She said she knew he was in heaven and had been very special, because in the night God sent an angel to come and get him.'

# V.2

JOCASTA PAUSED AND looked about her. So used had she become to Sam's little figure trotting at her side with Boyo, when he was not there she sensed it like a physical thing. He was still hanging round the way into the alley and looking up or down the street.

'They aren't coming, Sam. So have done with looking.'

Sam came towards her smartly enough at that, but he was still looking over his shoulder.

'But they said they'd be here, Mrs Bligh. And they're friends of mine, Finn and Clay. Finn's shared food with me a couple of times, and Clay let me sleep in his doss-down once. But I didn't like the other fellows there. Or the lady.' Jocasta could tell by the tone of his voice there weren't many he could call friend.

She sniffed the air, saying, 'It's not a bad day. Like as not they found easier work to do, and they think you're the daft one for sticking with me.'

The boy rubbed his nose with the back of his hand, smiled a bit and seemed comforted.

'What are we to do then, Mrs Bligh?'

'I've been thinking on that, youngling. You know where Fred works then, do you? This Admiralty Office?'

'That I does, Mrs Bligh. It's that big place down Whitehall from Northumberland House. You want me to go and watch?'

'No, I'll find it. You keep an eye on his mother.' The lad nodded and was about to disappear off again when Jocasta stopped him. 'Sam! Stay low, and stay out the way, eh? Just keep an eye out; no need to make any enquiries or get chatting with the lads or anything.'

He nodded again and headed away from her at a pace. Jocasta felt a prickling up the back of her neck and thought of the little thud the rats' bodies had made when they hit the heap.

Mr Palmer was waiting for Harriet and Crowther in Mrs Wheeler's parlour. He thanked that lady gravely as she showed Harriet and Crowther in, then after she had withdrawn said: 'Mrs Wheeler is an old friend of mine, and of the Service. I ask that you trust her as I do. If anyone has seen you enter, it is enough to say that you are acquainted via your husbands. Now please, tell me what you have learned.'

It was Harriet who took the role of narrator of their investigations and conclusions to date. Crowther merely watched her as she spoke, adding the odd detail or explanation when called upon. Her tone was calm and measured. The seriousness of Mr Palmer made her careful in her choice of words and the weight she placed on them. As Crowther looked at her, he conjectured he had made this woman a voice for part of himself; or rather some part of his intellect had blended with some part of her own, and this voice, calm but warmed with life and curiosity, was how it spoke. She concluded with Mr Tompkins's call.

'I believe, if Mr Tompkins will introduce us to this Gladys,' she said, 'we may have means to find out who this angel is.' Palmer looked at her with interest. 'I thought at first, of course, we could take her to the opera house and see if she could recognise this angel among the people and company there, but I am aware . . .' her voice slowed, 'that persons of her sort may find the unaccustomed noise and confusion of such a place painful to a degree that might make any such recognition unlikely.'

Mr Palmer sighed. 'I believe what you say. What do you propose?'

'Mr Graves has in his employ a gentleman very gifted in taking likenesses, even without seeing the individuals himself in the flesh, only by description.'

'A remarkable skill,' Palmer said with a smile.

'Indeed, and a useful one. I hope we may ask him to make some portraits which we could then show to poor Gladys in her own home, and see if her angel is among them. We intend to employ Lady Thornleigh to instruct him, since she knows the personages well.'

Palmer nodded. Harriet sighed and leaned forward; her voice became her own. 'But are you convinced, Mr Palmer, that Fitzraven is indeed the man mentioned by your agent in France? He was, it seems, a rather lowly creature. What could he know, or discover, that the French would be willing to pay for?'

Palmer was not a man who rushed into speech. He considered before he replied.

'I believe Nathaniel Fitzraven was the man mentioned. The proof that he has been in France would be evidence enough to make me extremely suspicious, but your discovery of his account book, his new wealth, your suspicion that the room was searched before your arrival, convince me of it.' He paused and adjusted his cuff. 'I believe he must have made some contact with an agent of the French in Milan. Someone there must have noted his habits and character and decided to make use of them for the benefit of our enemies. I fear there are spies of every colour in every city across Europe.'

Harriet sighed. 'Indeed, you have your friend who heard of this "spy-master", and of Fitzraven's name.'

A look of pain crossed Palmer's face like a cloud as he said, 'He was likely then sent to France to receive money, or the blessing of my counterparts there, or further instructions, and had time to acquire his remarkable teeth. He has had, it seems, more money since, but if that is a result of spying or some other petty, private blackmail, I cannot say. As to what the French thought he might be able to tell them, it seems he was a man who liked to boast of his knowledge and connections. Of course, the French Navy has no interest in the gossip of His Majesty's Theatre, but that place is attended, throughout the season, by some of the most important men in our land. He could well hear things, follow men about, find others like himself. For whomever is at the core of the French intelligence operations here he might have proved a useful servant.'

Crowther watched these various conjectures move across Palmer's face, like the weather on a deep lake, ruffling its service one way or another.

'You do not think Fitzraven our spy-master then, Mr Palmer?'

Mr Palmer stood and walked to the window. Harriet noticed that when he looked out, he kept his body to the left of the windowframe. From the street he would have appeared only as a shadow. 'The French would not have been proud of so small a man. They had arranged some coup. Fitzraven was a pawn in the game. A little man, and a little death.'

For the first time since she had begun to learn something of Fitzraven's character, Harriet felt some pity for him.

Palmer went on, 'He may have aimed to recruit others. Or he may have acted as a go-between with agents already in place in society. He had much influence with Miss Marin, for instance.'

'She had grown to dislike him,' Harriet said.

'So she told you, madam. But the bonds of blood can prove very strong. A woman may be wronged grievously by a father or lover, then betray herself and all she holds dear to seek still the love of that man.'

Harriet visibly stiffened. 'A man might do the same.'

Palmer gave her a slight nod. 'Indeed. But I am speaking of Miss Marin. She is a very beautiful woman. Many men of rank and influence, in hopes of gaining her admiration, might tell her titbits that the French would be very glad to hear. Those she could pass on to her father in hopes of the reward of his affection.'

Crowther spoke before Harriet had any opportunity to launch into a lengthy defence of Miss Marin. 'What of his sudden association with Lord Carmichael?'

Mr Palmer turned round and looked directly into Crowther's icy eyes. 'He was involved in the case of your brother and father, I believe?'

Crowther's throat went a little dry and he said simply, 'Peripherally.'

Palmer turned back to the street outside. 'I shall not tell you to guard against prejudice. I have my suspicions of Carmichael and would be glad if you could tell me more of him and his connections. I am wondering if he offered accommodation to Manzerotti in order to tempt a number of noble lovers of song into his house. He has a hunting lodge close to the Kent coast and a great many people seem to work for him in some capacity or other. He moves in the political world, yet does not involve himself directly. He is rich indeed, but his habits are expensive. He would be a great asset to the French, and could be the conduit through which information flows to France.'

Harriet frowned and sat back in her chair. 'But he is rich enough to pay for whatever he wishes, *and* pay his stepson Longley's debts. Why risk death to spy?'

Mr Palmer came and took the seat opposite her again.

'There is a darkness in the souls of men, Mrs Westerman. The stimulation of it, perhaps. I know he gambles and has fought duels over trifles. Who can say?'

Crowther's voice seemed unnaturally loud in his own head when he spoke. 'He enjoys manipulating those whom he knows, or suspects, to be weaker characters than himself.'

Harriet folded her arms. 'That I can believe. I found him a deeply unpleasant character, and I fear for his stepson. He was being sent to Harwich,' she added quietly. 'Might Carmichael risk sending Longley to France bearing intelligence?'

'I fear for him also. I can arrange to have him pursued. Quietly,' Palmer replied with a deep sadness in his voice, then he watched Harriet with steady attention as she continued.

'So let us say we believe Fitzraven was a spy, or to some degree involved in espionage. For what reason was he killed?'

'I do not know,' Palmer said, 'and I believe it is important that you find out if you can, madam. He may have thought to betray his conspirators. It may have sprung from other causes. We are putting our faith in you.'

Harriet was looking down at the floor, deep in thought. She did not appear to revel in this statement of his trust. She stroked her brow as if trying to dislodge some irritation in her brain. 'Dear Lord, treachery, bedroom gossip, men of such malignancy as Carmichael and Fitzraven. My husband fought clean battles for his country.'

Mr Palmer's expression lost its softness and became fierce. 'And some of them he won because of information that persons such as myself managed to procure for him and his fellow officers.' Crowther saw the note of rebellion in Harriet's green eyes. Mr Palmer saw it too perhaps, and possibly his memory of being at the sharp end of

Harriet's temper returned to him as he went on in a more conciliatory tone: 'Life becomes more . . . complex, the more closely we consider it. Would you not agree, Mr Crowther?'

'Undoubtedly.'

'Wars, battles, competition for trade, struggles for liberty or control – everything is influence: networks of information, moments of confrontation or compromise. Yes, we like to believe in the grand victory nobly fought, but life delivers very little to us so tidily, no matter what our own abilities or the rightness of our cause. So, Mrs Westerman, you must understand that such business is as much a part of war as brave officers and well-trained men. This matter with Fitzraven is sordid, but we may save the lives of our men by our actions. We are in danger of losing the colonies in America, and more perhaps, our reputation as masters of the sea. This cannot be. Whatever we can do to prevent or lessen our losses will be bringing some happiness, saving our countrymen from treachery, defeat, poverty, shame.' He rubbed his eyes tiredly. 'I have not heard from the agent who supplied Fitzraven's name for some time. I can only hope she is well. She is a brave servant of her King.'

It seemed to Crowther that with that last remark Palmer had won his point with Harriet, for after a moment she asked in more subdued tones: 'Has much damage been done already, Mr Palmer?'

'Perhaps, and our enemies aim to do a great deal more. I wish I had some comfort to offer you. Fitzraven's death is strange. It has drawn our attention and it may be the unravelling of whatever organisation is in place before it has the chance to deal our Navy fatal blows across its back. Let us hope that is the case.'

Mrs Wheeler knocked at the door to tell them Mr Palmer's carriage was waiting, then spent half an hour in calm conversation with Harriet and Mr Crowther on neutral subjects until they thought it safe to summon their own.

## V.3

JOCASTA HAD A long day outside the Admiralty Office watching for Fred, and had little profit on it. She marked the man appear at midday and have some talk with two others. They held their heads low. Then they went their separate ways and in twenty minutes Fred was back inside wiping crumbs from his mouth. The sun had got as high as it could in the sky and fell shamefacedly backwards in the murk. It was then Sam tapped up beside her. The days of food and rest in a warm bed had been doing him some good, but as he appeared at her side he looked pale and shivering again.

'What's with you, lad?' Jocasta asked with a frown. Taking a grip on his chin, she tilted it up towards her. 'Tell me.' She could feel the tremor in his bones.

'Nothing. Just. I haven't seen Finn or Clayton all day, and there's stuff being said.'

'What manner of stuff?'

'A man stopped by me where I was watching and told me all laughing to get indoors because the Bogey-man was about and carrying off boys like me and eating them. Told me to watch for lights in the dark.'

She could feel that cold prickling up her neck again; she let his chin go but held his eyes. 'Was he drunk?'

Sam thrust his hands into the pockets of his trousers. 'Stank of gin and smoke, made me think of my dad, but . . .' He looked down, digging his shoe into the muck at his feet. 'Could you not ask the cards on 'em, Mrs Bligh?' And when Jocasta sighed and folded her arms: 'I mean, there's no proof needed there. Not like Milky Boy and the lady. I just want the knowing. Please, Mrs. Bligh?'

'They don't work neat as that, or I'd just ask them where Old Hopps has hidden his money and then go buy mysel' a carriage, wouldn't I?'

He put his hand out and laid it on her arm and came up close, his face all pleading. 'But do them for me, and if they say I worry overmuch and all is well, then I'll be restful. Promise.'

Jocasta gave a quick nod and pulled out the pack, then settled on the doorstep behind her. She handed the greasy cards over to the boy.

'Shuffle them up and lay down three before me.' He did so. Jocasta watched for a second or two as the cards danced in front of her, then snatched the pack off him, put the laid cards back on top and shoved them back in her pocket.

'What do they say, Mrs Bligh?'

'Nothing. Reckon they don't work right in the open air. But if you're going to fret at me all night then we'll pay a visit to Clayton's doss-down and see for ourselves he's all right. You know where he is, do you?'

Sam got to his feet eagerly. 'Yes, ma'am. In the rookeries behind Chandos Street.' He hesitated again. 'But don't you want to wait and see what Fred's up to?'

Jocasta had already set off. 'He's bad today, he'll be bad tomorrow and the day after too. Now awez, lad.'

It was not until Harriet had entered the coach to travel to Lord Carmichael's evening party that she had become nervous. She had dined in the company of foreign princes, but the top rank of London society was unknown country for her. The Earl of Sussex may have asked for her help in getting his cat's cradle back from Mrs Service that morning, but that would be of no help to her now.

'Crowther,' she said, staring out at the passing streets, 'why on earth have we come?'

Crowther was a little surprised. 'To observe Lord Carmichael I believe was our intention, was it not? And to ask again about his connection to Fitzraven.'

She was silent.

'I should not have asked you to talk to him alone, Mrs Westerman.

Mr Palmer has suspicions of the man so I must meet him. I am happier to do so when surrounded by company. We were invited for this evening, madam, and it may be useful to Mr Palmer to know with whom Lord Carmichael associates. We should not scorn such opportunities.'

Harriet threw herself back in the carriage, threatening to undo all the good Rachel had managed with her hair, and continued to look out of the window rather miserably. Her hand went to the double strand of pearls around her neck, pulling and twisting at them. Crowther watched her for a moment.

'Mrs Westerman, are you nervous of the company?'

Mrs Westerman did not reply.

'My dear woman, parties such as these are unutterably dull and the people who attend them often the same. Not a soul that you see here would not rather be in their own bed, or clubs, or amusements but they come because it is done and they follow like sheep. They may be gilded and bejewelled but they are sheep! Look of the conduct of this ridiculous war and you will see there are hardly enough competent men of rank to govern the country. We would be better off as a nation if we fed the whole pack of them to the mob. Do not be so cotton-headed as to be intimidated by unearned wealth!'

Harriet was touched and a little surprised to watch him become heated. It was as if Crowther had put on a new being with his evening dress.

'Crowther! You are a revolutionary.'

He glanced outside as the carriage jogged along the roadway. The streets in this part of Town were quiet tonight. Those who lived here moved by carriage or chair in the evenings or kept to their beds.

'I will not have you think poorly of yourself in front of such braying puppets as these, or so low a creature as Carmichael,' he said. 'There are dogs in St Giles with better morals and more honour.'

Jocasta set Sam down in the chophouse, making sure she had caught the proprietor's eye so there would be no fuss about it, and marched fast as she might up St Martin's Lane till she came to the alleyway into her own yard.

'All right, Mrs Bligh?'

Her wrinkled old landlord pulled his threadbare coat around him and looked up at her. He was perched on a stool in the entrance to his own place.

'How do, Hopps? Anyone been asking for me today?'

'Couple of your usual girlies turned up and peered through your window, looked mournful and headed off again. You give up working?'

'Never you mind.'

'But I have an inkling you are asking if anyone unusual came a-calling, ain't you, lady?'

Jocasta nodded.

'Tall fella. Didn't like him. He wanted to know if you'd been about and gave me two shillings to keep an eye out and tell him your movements, if any, when he returned in the morning. That more the thing you asking, dear?'

'More like. And what will you say to him when he comes back?'

'That I, nor no one else here, has seen any sight of you. If that's your liking.'

'Thank you, Hopps.'

'Not a matter of thanking or not thanking, dearie. I didn't like the man. Never could abide foreigners.'

He spat on the ground and Jocasta returned to the chophouse, the back of her neck tickling and prickling so bad she thought the devil was teasing at it.

It was certainly a good thing that Crowther had put some steel into Harriet's spine. The level of conversation in the long drawing room of Lord Carmichael's house dropped perceptibly when they were announced, and many of its occupants, gorgeous in silks and shining in the candlelight with more jewels than Harriet had seen on the necks of Maharajahs, turned to stare at them both quite openly. A voice to Harriet's right spoke deliberately clearly, each syllable sounding like a champagne glass being broken with a tiny ivory hammer.

'I thought the eunuch was to be the curiosity of the evening. Lord Carmichael has outdone himself.'

Harriet turned to find herself staring into the cool grey eyes of a handsome woman of her own age. Her hair was dressed very high and heavily powdered. A spray of diamonds over her right ear caught the glare of the chandeliers and danced it back every colour of the rainbow. It was a jewel that could have bought Caveley twice over. Harriet nodded very slightly to her, and received a vicious little twist of a smile in return.

'Mrs Westerman! An absolute pleasure to make your acquaintance!' She looked round to see a gentleman of late middle-age with a long chin and deeply hooded eyes come barrelling towards her and stopping with a bow.

'I am Sandwich, you know.' She made her curtsy and when she raised her head again, John Montagu, Fourth Earl of Sandwich and First Lord of the Admiralty, took her hand and placed it on his arm. He then announced to the room at large: 'This lady's husband is the Captain Westerman who took the *Marquis de La Fayette* in the spring, you know. A remarkable prize.' There was a scattering of applause. Then, turning back to her, 'Now let us find somewhere more comfortable and have a proper conversation about things of significance, such as your husband's improving health – and I wish to know your opinion on a number of matters I have on my desk at the Admiralty. Lady Sybil there,' he nodded towards the woman with the diamond spray, 'has been driving me half-silly with her thoughts on the latest marvels at His Majesty's and everyone in this room knows she can't tell Handel from the wheezings of a hurdy-gurdy.' There was a little light laughter around them and Lady Sybil went rather red under her powder. 'And you are Mr Crowther, of course. We shan't bore you with naval talk, sir, but you will find Sir

William Fontaine in the card room. He has been telling us of your recent paper at the Royal Society and is eager to ask you more.'

The gentlemen made their bows, and Harriet prepared to be carried off by Lord Sandwich.

Off Bedford Street and late in the day. The stink of filth was choking, as they turned into one of the nameless overbuilt yards. Jocasta could hear the grunting of pigs on the offal pile. Every few yards a brazier burned and round it a few wretches gathered. A man wearing hardly rags enough to keep him decent was singing at one desperate-looking fire. One arm was slung over the shoulders of a dirty-faced girl, in the other he held a bottle. They were both glassy-eyed and laughing the way the damned laugh. Jocasta thought of the days before the cards came when she paid tuppence a night for a share of a bed in a room not far from here. She thought she'd never get the hell of it out of her. Strange what you can become accustomed to, what you can forget.

There was no use in trying to mind where they walked. The foulness was everywhere, but she kept her eyes down to check that she wasn't going to break her neck falling down one of the open cellars. Bending over, she picked up Boyo and thrust him into Sam's arms. He took the dog and then pointed to the house just opposite them.

'That where Clayton stays, is it?' she asked, and he nodded. 'Up or down?' He gestured up.

Jocasta stepped into the doorway. The door itself was long gone. There'd be no banister either and her bones were cold and stiff from the day. There was another, leering shout of laughter from the singing drunk and his girl, and Sam darted to Jocasta's side. They started to climb through the dark and stink, Jocasta feeling the wall with her palm to watch they didn't fall into the night below.

## V.4

LORD SANDWICH DID wish to have some conversation with Harriet, but first he wanted to walk her on his arm through the various rooms that were full of company. She was grateful, but it was a great relief to be led, finally, to an empty settee on one side of the drawing room to talk about naval matters for a little while. However, as they sat Sandwich said rather abruptly: 'You are looking into the death of this little man from the opera, are you not?'

Harriet was surprised, and searched his face for any indication that he might know of their dealings with Palmer. She saw none. 'Indeed. That is how we come to be here this evening, for he was acquainted with both Lord Carmichael and Manzerotti. Did you know him, my Lord?'

My Lord scratched his jaw. 'Had no idea of the fellow's name till Carmichael told me of his death, and said that you were coming here. He meant to embarrass you, you know, my dear. I have no doubt Lady Sybil was in collusion with him for that bit of unpleasantness. However, I shan't have the wife of one of my best men treated that way, no matter what strangeness she gets involved with.'

'Thank you, sir,' Harriet said, and thought of Rachel.

'But I remembered him when he was described to me. I love the opera, you know, madam. Not the fuss, just the music – though no one comes close to Old Handel, of course. Yes, I'd seen that fellow sneaking about. I saw him a week or two after my poor Martha was shot outside Covent Garden. Man was practically drooling with excitement. If you find the fellow who killed him, he must be hung – but I'd be happy to shake his hand first. Sure his death has something to do with His Majesty's?'

Harriet looked down at the small glass of champagne a servant had placed between her fingers.

'I'm afraid so, sir.'

The Earl harrumphed into his cravat. 'Very good. No. Sorry, I know no more of him than that. Well, murder and whatever scandal you discover aside, Harwood has a spectacular success on his hands. Mademoiselle Marin and Manzerotti are both here to sing this evening, you know – the only reason a nasty little man like Carmichael has such a crowd in here. Beautiful girl, that Marin. Odd sort of mood this evening, though.'

'Indeed? I had hoped to see her in good spirits tonight.'

Sandwich pulled his waistcoat straight. 'They are funny sorts, these singers. Particularly the women. She has been very prettily behaved towards me since she came to London, but tonight she can hardly look at anyone. Say whatever you like to her, it is clear her attention is elsewhere.'

'And what do you think of Manzerotti, my Lord?'

'Marvel of a voice. Beyond that I have nothing to say on him. But tell me my dear, how is the Captain? Such a tragedy. He is sorely missed in our current trials.'

As Harriet looked at the bubbles glinting in her drink, the pink and white noise of conversation seemed to rattle and echo in the glass. 'He is not well at all still, sir. Dr Trevelyan doubts he will ever be the man he was.' When Sandwich patted her knee like an uncle unused to dealing with small children in distress, Harriet straightened her back and looked him in the eye with a determined smile. 'But I live in hopes of continued improvement. Shreds of his memory are beginning to return. He is recovering something of himself, I hope, though his mind runs a great deal on spies and espionage at the current time.'

'Seeking enemies everywhere? Such things occur, when people's wits are disordered. When my wife was in her decline she thought the coal scuttle was a devil from hell come to claim her, and myself a monster come to torment her.'

Again Harriet was forced to remember that there were people other than herself who had suffered, and did it with a better grace than she often managed. Lord Sandwich had seen his wife descend into madness, and his lover Martha shot by a jealous rival, and had still done his duty as First Lord well enough to be regarded by those active in the Service as 'a good sort'. This was the highest praise possible for any man not currently under sail.

At that moment, Lord Sandwich looked up over her shoulder, and Harriet turned to find that Isabella Marin and Manzerotti were close behind her. Isabella did not look entirely well, and Harriet had to fight the temptation to place a hand on her forehead to check for fever.

'Dear Mrs Westerman!' the young woman said. 'Manzerotti tells me we are to sing very soon, then I think I must . . . but I wished to say thank you. I have seen him.' Harriet made to stand. 'No, do not disturb yourself, please. But thank you.' Isabella turned on her heel and swept out towards the further room again in a blossoming of pink silk. Harriet felt Manzerotti's black eyes travel over her for a moment, as dark and drawing as ever before he bowed to them both and followed her.

'See? Told you. Funny bird,' said Sandwich, with a shake of his large head. 'But no matter. We should go and hear the music, madam.'

Harriet put an arm on his sleeve. 'Will you do me a kindness, sir? I have not seen Lord Carmichael yet. Whatever his motives, I should thank him for his hospitality. Do you know where he might be?'

The twist of her mouth drew a throaty chuckle from the peer.

'Nothing easier. He is on the other side of this room talking to Mr Crowther.'

Harriet glanced up to see the gentlemen exchange bows and separate. Catching her eye, Carmichael bowed, Harriet nodded in response and the gentleman moved on. He was dressed again with great elegance. Harriet took in the tableau around him, the gilded furnishings, the marble fireplace behind him – even the smart goblet held between his fingertips. It shall all outlast him, she thought. His lips were rather red and he was looking after Crowther with a slight sneer. She could see no sign of his stepson in the crowd. Harriet continued to watch him as she addressed Lord Sandwich.

'Why do you come here, sir, when you do not like your host?'

Sandwich gestured towards the company. 'There is as much government business done at events such as these as in Parliament, dear lady. The season is just beginning, and there are, as yet, not too many of these parties. There were people I had to meet tonight. Some of my most successful alliances have been forged over champagne. And here the women may guide us about and whisper in our ear. We think we are statesmen. They remind us we are politicians.'

Harriet began to feel guilty. 'Then I have been keeping you from your duty, my Lord. And you may have to treat for peace with Lady Sybil.'

He patted her knee. 'No matter, my dear, this do will rattle on a while yet. And Lady Sybil and I are old enemies and get great satisfaction from our battles. Now – the music. And give my regards to your husband, if he might have any use for them.'

Harriet thought of James in his room in Highgate, then of him in shirtsleeves in his cabin, looking up at her with a quick smile from his charts and logs. She had had some hopes that when the war with America was concluded he might be persuaded to take up the life of a country gentleman. They had been much separated since Stephen's birth and she had wished to know her husband better – another ambition that put her apart from much of the company in the room. She thought of the open fields surrounding Caveley, the orchard there. She had been told the harvest had been splendid this year. Usually, she and Stephen would walk among the pickers and help serve their midday meal in the yard. This year, she had been in London.

Harriet recalled Justice Pither's low outhouse and Fitzraven's body lying under the oil-lamp. The taste of champagne began to turn a little bitter in her mouth. She remembered seeing the girl selling milk from the pail in Berkeley Square and wondered where she was laying her head tonight; thought of the abandoned children who did not find their way to the Foundling Hospital. A man to her right, his chin receding into the lace of his cravat, gave a braying laugh. She turned to watch him wave his soft white hands in the air. His audience, two young women, their high colour painted on and in nooses of emeralds and silks, laughed back up to him, fluttering their eyes and flirting with their fans. When she noticed her hands again she realised her fingers were white around the glass. That little thrill of sitting in the Royal Box at His Majesty's, the pleasure of taking Sandwich's arm that she had felt, now disgusted her. '*Vanitas vanitatum, omnis vanitas*,' she murmured, then stood and allowed the Earl to guide her forward.

Jocasta reached the top of the stairs and paused a moment to get her breath back. Boyo whined and a voice shouted out from behind the closed door, 'Who's there? One of you vermin brings a dog in here, I'll kill it and eat it in front of you.'

The door was pulled open so hard it rattled against the wall behind, and Jocasta could have sworn she felt the whole house shake. A woman peered out, sniffing the air of the corridor as if there was blood in it. She was a vast mound of a female, a tower and ball of flesh squeezed into the shape of a woman with stays and skirt. Her skin was slick and shiny with grease and her thin and scrappy hair was glued down to it in black wisps; her fingers clutching at the doorframe while she peered round at them on the landing were fat as sausages, the skin pulled tight over them as if they were about to burst.

Jocasta looked straight into her half-swallowed eyes and said, 'You touch my dog, missus, and I'll curse you with boils so mean so you can't sit for a month. Don't think I won't or can't – I can and I will.'

'What do you want?' The woman turned back into the room as she said it, swaying her huge body from side to side as she went, but left the door open. Jocasta took that as invitation enough and walked in. The garret was larger than she had expected, but very dark. There was a window or two, but the glass was long gone and the gaps stuffed with rags or covered with paper. A stove was going in the middle of the room, a vast armchair beside it, black where it had been sat on, and sunk into, and four or five boys slinking into the shadows where the incline of the roof hit the floor. The stench was as bad here as in the hall, and all the worse for the heat in the room. As Jocasta felt the boys watching her from the shadows, the fat lady went up to the pot and sniffed it.

'News of Clayton,' Jocasta said, trying to see further into the shadows.

'What – he stolen from you?'

'No.'

She didn't seem to care much, picked up a spoon to stir whatever was stewing and licked her lips. 'Not that it's my business if he did. Anyway, I ain't got no news of him. He ain't here now. Wasn't here last night.'

'Has that happened before?'

'Do I look as if I had any share in the whelping of him? It's no matter to me who comes and goes. Though he did always seem to be hanging about. That one!' She turned and spat at her feet. 'He'd dare to come home with the hunger on him and not so much as a handkerchief.'

Jocasta stood still a moment. Her head was starting to ache with the smell and the heat. She had begun to turn to go when a voice spoke up from the dark.

'He's always here. Been here every night for a year. But he ain't coming back.'

Jocasta couldn't see the face of the boy who had spoken. He was a shadow among shadows.

'Why do you say that?' she asked.

Another voice, softer and with a foreign lilt to it, sounded up from the other side of the garret. 'Tonton Macoute took him, lady.'

Despite the heat, a new chill began to grow and turn in Jocasta's belly.

'What did you say?' she demanded.

The same soft voice spoke again; it lapped at her ears like the slap of water in a clean brook. 'He's a giant and speaks so sweet and moves like a cat, but his knapsack is full of little bones. He's a devil-man. I never saw him before last night, just heard tell of him and smelled him in the shadows, but I saw him leading Clayton off as I came home.' As he spoke the little boy crept forward into the room. His face was dusky brown like sugar, and he looked up at her with large brown eyes and blinked. 'Tonton Macoute took him.'

The fat lady kept stirring the pot, her face expressionless.

Another boy piped up, 'He takes boys that stay out too late, and girls too if he can find them for the crack of their bones. Everyone knows that. Where else do you think the children go, lady?'

Sam had inched into the room. 'Anyone seen Finn today?' he said, his voice high and full of tears.

The boys shook their heads without speaking and began to shuffle back again into the shadows. Then the dusky-faced child spoke again from the depths under the eaves.

'Tonton Macoute.'

Jocasta turned and walked out, pushing Sam in front of her. The pot on the stove bubbled and belched a little and the fat lady kept stirring, her face shining in the steam.

## V.5

HARRIET FOUND CROWTHER at the very edge of the crowd preparing to enjoy Manzerotti and Isabella's performance. He watched her as she approached. Even at first glance it was clear she was not of a type with the other women in the room. It was not simply the lack of diamonds round her neck, or the relatively casual arrangement of her hair and dress – Crowther had seen some concoctions on the heads of other ladies there that must present some danger to their spines – but there was something in the air around her that seemed a little foreign. The men and women in the room knew it. Some were fascinated by it, perhaps, but most it repelled. Her life at sea, her adventures at his side had perhaps acted like some alchemical fire, and turned her into some other substance than the usual flesh of man and woman. Whatever process had occurred – *was* occurring – it might well, he supposed, lead to estrangement from her sister, even from her own children in time. He believed, however, that even if she had known when her husband bought Caveley, how events might make the raw stuff of her develop, she would have walked the same path with her bright green eyes open.

As Isabella began to sing, he turned his attention to himself. Was it his own otherness, his own separation from the body of men who made up his country, that had perhaps brought them together? Crowther had for many years feared and distrusted being bound to any other being in any way; he had cut those connections with his scalpel, and in all that time successfully defended his isolation even from his own sister, yet he had to confess there was a bond here, something in the complementary way their intellects functioned, though she frustrated or exhausted him at times with her impatience, her leaps of logic, her teasing. However, the more she distanced herself from the norms of the world, from her family and more quotidian commitments, the stronger the bond between them grew. He had thought her arguments with Rachel merely an annoyance, but now, for a moment as he thought of them he felt a touch of selfish pleasure. He looked down at the cane he held in front of him, the fat silver bundle of foliage under his thin fingers, and expected to feel ashamed. He did not.

'Tell me you have forced Carmichael into an admission of murder and espionage and we may leave this place,' Harriet whispered as she reached his side. 'The colour scheme of gold and pink in this room is making me feel as if I had swallowed my own weight in sugar and rosewater.'

'I have elicited no such confession. Have *you* presented Lord Sandwich with the proper naval strategy to turn the tide in America?

I recall a conversation in which you seemed quite certain of your plans, if only they could be followed.'

Harriet narrowed her eyes. 'I had not thought you were listening that morning.'

'Your tone can be insistent.'

Harriet laughed, and a woman in front of them in the crowd turned her whitened face towards them. Harriet did not flinch. Crowther made her a slight bow.

'What of Carmichael then, Crowther? I did see you in conversation. Did you have more success than I?'

'Yes, your tour of the rooms on Sandwich's arm made him more amenable than he was this morning. He claims that Fitzraven came to visit him first some three weeks ago with a letter of introduction from a mutual friend.'

'What friend would that be?'

'He took advantage of the crush to be vague upon that point. Beyond that, he said only that Fitzraven had called once more last week and seemed rather angry. He told Carmichael that Isabella was madly in love with Bywater, and he with her. Apparently he took it as some kind of affront.'

'Interesting. Perhaps Fitzraven was hoping his daughter would marry a Lord and carry him closer to this shining company.' Crowther glanced across at her. Her mouth was set in a thin line. She continued with a clenched jaw, 'For all Sandwich talks about doing business in this room, I cannot see any true or honest thing in this flimflam. I wish I were dining with Michaels in the Bear and Crown, or on the *Splendour*, or even in the nursery. I have never missed the sea wind as much as I do here among all this scent. I used to think you had sacrificed something, renouncing your title and such society as this. Now I see you gave up nothing.'

Crowther raised his eyebrows. 'You appear to have overcome your earlier nerves, Mrs Westerman.'

She grinned at him. Her anger passed as swiftly as it had come, like the shadows of the clouds chased across the hillside he used to watch as a child. 'Indeed. With your help I have found a way to feel greatly superior to anyone else in the room, so now I am having a much better time.'

'I am glad, Mrs Westerman.' The song ended and the room rattled with the applause of gloved hands, the feathering thud of fans struck against brocade dresses and a flurry of polite exclamations. A new chord rang out on the harpsichord. Harriet leaned towards Crowther again.

'What it might have to do with the murder, I cannot say, but I am sure Mr Palmer would be pleased if we managed to discover the identity of this mutual friend that links Carmichael and Fitzraven.'

Crowther nodded. 'I imagine Carmichael's study will be on this floor. Shall we leave the music for a while?'

'Why not. Let me add to my disgrace with a little burglary, if at all possible.'

By the time Jocasta and Sam had reached the end of Chick Lane, Sam was crying hard. He had not put Boyo down again, but was clutching the little dog to his chest as he wept. Boyo did not struggle to get away. It was as if he understood his role as comforter to the frightened lad, and endured his fierce embrace with stoicism.

Jocasta's mind felt white with it. She did not believe in Tonton Macoute or the Bogey-man, but felt sure now that those two rats on her door had been more than a warning. They were a reckoning of things already done. Spotting an alley, she pulled Sam into the shadows with her.

'Mrs Bligh? They're dead, ain't they – Finn and Clayton. Tonton Macoute got 'em. Fred got the devil working for him and now they'll be coming for me.' His voice was rising and gasping and he was trembling hard.

'You got some place to go, Sam? Any other places you can doss down? Don't reckon it's safe being by me.'

He gave a little wail, and still holding Boyo to him with one arm, he flung the other around Jocasta and buried his face in her side. She almost staggered with his small force. 'Nowhere. I don't know no one. Don't send me away, Mrs Bligh. The devil will get me. You knew, didn't you – before we went? You saw it in the cards! What else, Mrs Bligh? Am I going to get got by the devil too?'

Jocasta let her arm drop awkwardly round his shoulders and he clung closer to her.

'Whist, lad! I saw you standing lonely, but I saw you standing. For now anyways.' She looked unseeing into the dark around them and gripped his shoulder. 'It ain't a devil, it's a man, my lad. And men can be trapped and stopped and hung.'

Sam's voice was muffled. 'But how? We spent all day watching and we're no wiser!'

Jocasta went down on her haunches so she could look the boy in the eye and took hold of his shoulders. 'Neither we are. But we will be.'

Sam drew in his breath and tried to stop his weeping. 'Don't send me off alone, Mrs Bligh. Let me stay with you and Boyo. I won't be any bother. Please, you won't send me off alone, Mrs Bligh?'

She was caught by the asking in his eyes, then shook her head. The relief in his face struck her like a fist and she looked down at the ground between them. Sam put Boyo out of his arms and the little dog nosed his mistress.

After a few moments Sam spoke in a whisper: 'Mrs Bligh. It weren't your fault that the devil-man took 'em.'

Jocasta felt her belly clench. She thought of the two young boys sitting in front of her fire, eating meal and milk.

'It was, lad. It was. They're lost over a day's work I paid them a penny for. I was stupid. And I am now for not driving you off. Cards sometimes see a long way, sometimes close. I haven't got any promises that you'll be safe with me.'

The little boy waited till she looked up at him again. When she did he was standing straight as a soldier, and his fists were closed and

223

tight. 'Don't need the cards to tell me that, Mrs Bligh. Or you. I know it for myself.'

She smiled and roughed up the hair on his head. 'Do you now? Well, we ain't going home tonight, but I know a place. Then tomorrow we will see where we are at.'

Crowther was right. There was a study just adjacent to the room where Isabella and Manzerotti were performing. Crowther began to look through the papers on the desk.

'Anything of significance?' Harriet asked him. She was standing near the doorway and rubbing the nape of her neck.

He did not reply but began to open the desk drawers in turn. Harriet looked about her. The walls were high and lined with gold-tooled volumes. Most, it seemed, were in Latin.

'Is Carmichael a scholar?'

'He never was. They are show. Everything here is show. There is nothing here. Or I cannot say rather whether there is or not.'

'Would a spy bring a letter of introduction? "Dear Traitor, the man bearing this letter is another such as yourself and in the pay of the French. Make use of him".'

Crowther scowled. 'It seems unlikely. But there must have been some signal between them. Something that could have been hidden in plain sight, yet which showed they were servants of the same master.'

Harriet came away from the door and began to walk back and forth on the thick Turkish rug in front of the fireplace, avoiding the draught from the open window.

'Something that could be hidden in plain sight . . . That a musician might carry across any number of borders, and do so free from fear of detection.' She came to a sudden halt. 'Do you remember that gentleman who visited Graves with a manuscript from Mr Handel? Music! A code, a language of its own. It was in the music Fitzraven was carrying!'

Crowther nodded and returned quickly to a leather folder on the desk in front of him.

'There are pieces of manuscript in different hands here,' he said. Harriet watched him, her blood thudding under her skin. In the next room, the music was replaced by applause. 'I may have something, Mrs Westerman.'

The door suddenly opened and Lord Carmichael stood in the entrance. He looked between them with curiosity. Harriet took hold of the mantelpiece and staggered a little.

'No, Mr Crowther, do not trouble looking for the salts any more, I swear I am quite recovered.' She stumbled again, forcing Carmichael to come forward and take her arm. She looked up at him from under her long lashes. 'Oh, thank you, my Lord. I am so sorry . . .'

Crowther had to stop himself from staring at her in astonishment. He would at no point in his long career of study, from the ancient wisdom to the best thoughts of the modern day, have believed that the ability to fake a swoon was something he would admire, and that would save him.

'Carmichael. Do you have smelling salts? Failing that, I was looking for paper to burn under Mrs Westerman's nose. It seems to cure a variety of female ills.' Harriet blushed a little. His tone was harsh, impatient.

Lord Carmichael turned his lined and slightly ashy face between them. No man would have thought the pair in front of him friends or allies.

'Really, it is not necessary, sir!' she said sharply in Crowther's direction, then looking at Carmichael said more softly, 'I am so sorry, my Lord. It is simply I found myself overcome. The song is one of my husband's favourites. He sings it still . . .' A single tear ran down her cheek and she blinked her green eyes. 'You know he is very unwell. Hearing it so beautifully performed . . .'

Carmichael looked at her cautiously. 'Oh course, madam. Quite understandable.'

'And Mr Crowther assisted me from the room.'

'How good of him.'

'How is your son, Lord Carmichael – Mr Longley, whom I met yesterday.'

Carmichael's smile was unpleasant. 'He is atoning for his sins.'

Crowther looked sternly at Harriet. 'Recovered then, Mrs Westerman? If so, I think it best if we take you back to Berkeley Square where you may more comfortably indulge your grief.'

Harriet lowered her head as if chastened. Crowther turned to his host.

'Oh, Lord Carmichael. On this sordid little business of the opera house – is Mr Johannes in residence here? I understand he goes everywhere with your house-pet Manzerotti.'

Lord Carmichael led Harriet to a chair and seated her there with a low bow before replying.

'Manzerotti is an artist, not a house-pet. Johannes makes his own arrangements in Town. He would not be comfortable here, I think. He is an artisan, and from time to time a very useful one. But he is not a guest in this house.'

Harriet looked up at Carmichael as if he was a saviour. He touched the bell and said, 'Emotions seem to be running very high this evening. Miss Marin was so overcome by her own performance she had to leave immediately after the duet.'

The carriage was summoned and Carmichael moved to leave the room, adding to Crowther with a bow, 'Ah, women, Keswick. Such delicate ornaments to our society. They should be protected, yet you drag this poor woman through the mud. What an oddity your family has become.' Then he left the room before Crowther could find any answer to give.

Jocasta fell asleep as soon as she had arranged the blankets round her. She and Sam had gone cautiously through the streets till they reached the cellar of a cobbler Jocasta knew. She had read the cards for the man a number of times and he, his wife and children thought her as great a sage as any in London. She had directed the man to a lost brooch of his wife's, and predicted in a cloudy way the coming of a stranger who would do them a good turn the night before a careless maid had begged him to mend a shoe of her mistress she had broken at the heel. Maid and mistress were so pleased with the work he had done, he had found himself with a new steady stream of commissions from that lady and her friends. The new income had allowed the family to take an additional room where they now slept, so they were more than happy to let Jocasta and Sam lay their heads down in the cellar workshop. It had been a struggle not to let them give up their own beds. Now Sam and Jocasta slept with the one entrance to the place shut and fastened, and the family promising them secrecy and peace.

Jocasta dreamed. It felt as if she had woken; sudden. The room seemed quiet enough, Sam and Boyo both snoring away in their corners, though it had a soft, buttery sort of feel to it, as if she were in a painting of the place rather than the flesh of it. Then it seemed to her that Kate was standing right in front of her and beckoning. For all the stories in the cards, Jocasta had never seen anything like a ghost before, so she was puzzled to find there was no sort of fear on her. She was curious, was all, and felt more friendly and trusting of the vision than she was of most living creatures she knew.

She stood up from her bed, and Kate took her hand and turned to lead her off. As she did so, Jocasta caught what seemed like a glowing glimpse of the back of her head. It was red and matted, and the sight of it sent a tremor through her that Kate's ghost seemed to feel. She turned again and shrugged with a twisted smile. Then without waking or sleeping, with no space in time you could slip a card in, it seemed that they were in the front room in Salisbury Street. There was a big ugly dresser in the corner of the room, made of heavy wood and squat on the floor as if it was hunkering and frowning. Then in front of it, a pretty little table in rosewood, oddly placed in the room.

Kate led Jocasta towards it and, taking hold of both of Jocasta's hands in her own, lifted them to the overhanging lip. Kate's hands seemed very cool and dry; there was no clammy deathliness about the touch. She placed Jocasta's fingers on the hidden surface of the wood, and moved them along a bit. Jocasta felt a button, a space in the wood, and pressed. There was a click deep inside the wood, and with a shuffling whisper, a long thin drawer popped out from under. There were papers in it, smoothed very straight and flat, and all covered tight in black writing.

Jocasta looked up at Kate, who didn't move or smile. She gave no nod, she spoke no word, made no plea for justice, gave no news of what waits on the far side of the grave. She simply moved to Jocasta's side. Jocasta felt a light touch in the small of her back, Kate's other hand drifted over Jocasta's eyes and rested on her forehead, and she pushed. Jocasta felt her centre give way.

Then found herself in another place, struggling to get back onto her feet in some version of the rookeries round behind Chandos Street. Strange fires leaped in the braziers, and the drunks lolling round them were interspersed with other figures. She recognised them from the cards. A man in motley with a staff over his shoulder and a sharp little beard was dancing for the drunken Irishman and his girl. When he laughed, you could see his crooked gums, his teeth all black and yellow stumps or gone. The High Priest stumbled past, his red and gold cloak trailing in the muck and his layered hat on backwards; spittle hung from his fat open lips. Jocasta felt her elbow knocked and her hand went to her purse; she found herself looking into the blank eyes of The Magician. He was throwing up a ball in his cup and catching it again. He moved past her, and behind him she saw a figure sitting on the step of a doss-house on the other side of the way. He was winged like a bat, and the thin skin of his wings twitched slowly. On his head were horns that seemed to move and taste the air like the soft stalks of a snail. They reached about him, moving shadows thrown by the flames of the brazier. He lifted his head and looked straight at her. She saw a face made of burned and twisted roots, his skin like charred bark. He had his familiars with him – winged, sharp-eared and naked – the shape of young boys. They turned towards her with terrible slowness. Their faces were those of Finn and Clayton. The Devil hissed.

She sat bolt upright in her bed in the cellar and waited for her heart to slow. Boyo and Sam slept on, just as she had seen them. But there was no ghost in the room and the air felt damp, rotten and familiar. Jocasta lay back down, turned to the wall and wondered.

# PART VI

## VI.1

*Wednesday, 21 November 1781*

STEPHEN WESTERMAN'S DAY had begun well. He had been overjoyed to be woken by his mother and taken out to play a while in the gardens of Berkeley Square before he had even washed his face, and skipped among the shrubberies in front of her, describing the various anchorages and landing places, the haunts of strange tribes which would amaze even Captain Cook that he and Lord Thornleigh had discovered between the rhododendrons. It felt like a sort of miracle to have her complete attention. She had laughed and praised his courage, gasped when he described his battles with the French and Spanish navies and nodded sagely as he described his negotiations with the natives of the newly christened isles of Servicia and Gravesonia.

But then one of the servants had come out of the house with Jonathan and leading Anne by her fat little fist. The woman had spoken to his mother out of his hearing, and she left him at once, only wishing him fair sailing and kissing him distractedly on the top of his tousled head. He watched her go and meet two figures on the far side of the lawns. One was Mr Crowther, the other he could not recognise at this distance.

The little boy hated watching her grow small in his sight, and wondered if he had missed breakfast, and how he could be forgotten so quickly. Would she remember that he still had her ring? It was

231

tucked in his waistcoat now. Part of him hoped that she had forgotten, as that meant she would not ask for it back. Some other part told him that it was bad if she had done so. That the ring, like himself, should not so easily be dismissed.

Just then, Jonathan slapped him between the shoulders and began to dash along the path in front of him. It was a challenge, and could not be ignored. Turning, Stephen began to race after him, ignoring the cry of the nursemaid to mind his step.

'Good morning, Crowther, Dr Trevelyan.'

The good doctor looked worried. Harriet was so used to his demeanour of calm good sense, she hardly knew him with his eyebrows drawn together and his chin low. Her heart fluttered and her mouth became dry.

'Sir, is my husband well?'

Trevelyan placed his hand on her arm and said quickly, 'Indeed he is.' Harriet's world steadied again and the sounds and sights of the Square returned to her.

'He is quite well, I did not mean to alarm you,' the doctor went on. Harriet managed a faint smile and drew in her breath. 'It is on the matter of Mr Leacroft I wish to speak to you, and I am sorry to call so early in the day. I met Mr Crowther as I was hesitating on your doorstep.'

Harriet dismissed his apology with a shake of her head.

'What do you have to tell us?' she demanded, then caught herself, continuing to calm her breathing. 'My apologies, sir. Would you rather come into the house? You have had an early ride.'

'No, madam,' Trevelyan said. 'I must be returning to Highgate as soon as I may. I come because my colleague from Kennington Lane and I met by chance at our club last night, and something of what he said has been troubling me. I found I could not be easy till I had told you of it, though the significance of his words escapes me.'

They turned and began to walk along the pathway that ringed the

232

gardens. It was a broad path, and it was easy for all three to walk abreast. Trevelyan found himself with Crowther on one side and Mrs Westerman on the other, and had a fleeting sympathy with felons accompanied to their places in court.

He went on: 'When I met this gentleman, we of course remarked on having found Mr Leacroft. I do not know why you enquired after him, and on being asked, said as much. My colleague – his name is Gaskin, by the way – told me it was most strange, as after some year or so with no enquiries being made to his well-being, or visitors received, Mr Leacroft had found himself the subject of a flurry of calls very recently, culminating in the arrival yesterday afternoon of Miss Isabella Marin, the soprano.'

'A flurry of calls, you say?' Crowther asked, and came to a halt. He had his cane with him, and began to twist it slowly into the gravel of the pathway.

Trevelyan nodded. 'That was his phrase. He was entranced to meet Miss Marin, of course. She swore him to secrecy about her visit, but having happened to meet me, he could not resist informing me that she had been in his house. I wondered if she were there because of your enquiry.'

If Trevelyan had been hoping that his words might lead to some sort of explanation from Crowther and Mrs Westerman, he was disappointed. Harriet sat down on a bench by the walkway and gestured for him to join her. He did so. Crowther remained standing in front of him, his eyes low and still twisting his cane.

'Can you tell us anything more of his other visitors, Dr Trevelyan?' Crowther asked, without looking up.

The good doctor found that the weight of their attention was making him nervous. 'I asked him,' he replied. 'He said the first was ten days ago, a rather nervous young man whose name Gaskin did not recall. He was apparently closeted with Mr Leacroft for some hours. He returned a day or two later, again for some considerable period, but has not been seen since.'

Harriet put her hand to her face. 'Could that be Bywater? He was making enquiries, after all. So Bywater did find him! Yet he said nothing to Isabella, despite their fondness for one another . . .'

Crowther looked up and met her eyes, which were heavy with thought.

'Remember, Mrs Westerman, that despite that fondness he believed only that Mr Leacroft was some acquaintance of her French singing teacher. He did not know the connection was personal. He may have thought that in concealing his discovery he was doing her no great injury, especially if he found some other greater advantage from his visits.'

Crowther and Harriet turned their attention to Trevelyan again. 'But two visits, and another from Miss Marin yesterday does not constitute a "flurry",' Crowther said. 'What more?'

'The second visitor was on Wednesday, only a week ago, and was a much older man. He too spent some time with Leacroft, and Gaskin was careful this time to remember his name. It was Fitzraven. That is the name of the gentleman whose death you have been investigating, is it not? As Mrs Westerman mentioned in her note.' He looked up at Crowther, who merely nodded. There was a long silence.

Crowther leaned forward on his cane and addressed Mrs Westerman. 'So let us suppose that Fitzraven followed Bywater on one or other of his visits. Might he have been able to enquire what sort of man Bywater was visiting, his profession, the nature of his malady – *without* announcing himself?'

Harriet turned to Trevelyan, who raised his hands. 'Hardly impossible. Gaskin has a number of servants, of course. A man may gossip about his employer for the price of a drink. Such is the way of the world.'

'So,' Crowther said, 'let us suppose that Fitzraven knew Bywater was visiting a mad, secluded musician. Then a week ago he decided to visit the man himself. What encouraged him to make that visit?'

234

'Wednesday last . . .' Harriet said, rapping her fingers against her dress with increasing speed. 'If the *"C' è una rosa"* duet was first rehearsed on Thursday, then the parts would have to be got ready the previous day.'

Crowther ceased to dig his cane into the pathway. 'Which was the responsibility of Mr Fitzraven.'

'Dr Trevelyan,' Harriet said very slowly, 'does Mr Leacroft continue his musical pursuits? Does his condition prevent . . . ?'

The doctor turned to her with his kind grey eyes a little confused, but as frank and honest as ever. 'No, Mrs Westerman. Theophilius Leacroft has a harpsichord in his chamber and spends most of his hours at the keyboard.'

'What does he play?'

'A great quantity of works of the masters, ancient and modern, I understand. And he finds some relief from his melancholia in composition.'


Dr Trevelyan found himself at liberty to return to Highgate very shortly afterwards. The moment Harriet stepped into the hallway of the house in Berkeley Square, she asked for the carriage to be sent round as soon as it could be managed, then began to pace up and down the corridor.

'It must have been Bywater who visited first, Crowther. Surely!'

'But it must be proved.'

'Fitzraven must have followed him on one visit or another, and having seen the music for the "Yellow Rose Duet". . .'

'Concluded that Bywater had not had a sudden inspiration, but had rather stolen the tune for his great triumph. Indeed, Mrs Westerman, I think it likely. But we cannot assume that it is true. Mr Leacroft had many pupils when in health. Some gentleman may have just returned to Town and decided to call. We are building castles in the air.'

Harriet came to a sudden stop. Her skirts eddied round her ankles. 'Crumley has not yet completed his portraits to identify the angel

Gladys spoke of, but perhaps he has done Bywater already. I asked Susan to help him yesterday.'

'Yes, we did Mr Bywater,' said a sleepy voice from the stairs. They turned to see Lady Susan descending the main stairway in search of breakfast. She rubbed her eyes and smiled at them. 'Shall I go and fetch it? I brought it home. It's in my Italian book.'

Harriet clapped her hands together. 'Oh, yes, Susan. Please do.'

The girl spun on her heel and dashed back upstairs again, all the sleep shaken off her.

Crowther frowned. 'Mrs Westerman, we are neither of us great musicians.'

'Truly said, sir,' she replied with a grimace.

'Suppose that Mr Leacroft's compositions *are* the source of the "Yellow Rose Duet" – will we know it for sure?' Crowther fretted. 'If it has been altered in some way, will we be able to swear?'

Harriet shook her head and began to bite the edge of her thumb, still pacing the corridor. When Susan came skittering down the stairs again, a paper in her hands, she asked her, 'Susan, where is Mr Graves this morning?'

'He had to go and see a lawyer. Something to do with investments of Grandpapa's just coming to light, I think.'

Harriet thought for a second, then took the girl by the shoulder, saying, 'My dear, we need you to come with us. Go and fetch your cloak.' Brightening with excitement, Susan turned to ran upstairs again.

Crowther had taken the piece of paper from her before she went and looked approvingly at the profile and full-faced image of Richard Bywater. The picture was accurate. Once again, it seemed as if much of his and Mrs Westerman's luck seemed to depend on the people their friends chose to employ.

Gregory approached. 'The carriage is ready, ma'am.'

'And where is Mrs Service?'

Susan came downstairs again at a pace. 'Oh, she is teaching Uncle Eustache his ABCs. Shall I tell her we are going out?'

Harriet glanced impatiently at the door. 'No need, my dear. Gregory, will you tell Mrs Service that Mr Crowther and I have taken Lady Susan out and will return before dinner?'

The footman nodded and Harriet took Susan's hand and made for the doorway.

## VI.2

'WHAT IS THE day, Sam?'

'Wednesday, Mrs Bligh.' Sam was looking better for a sleeping, though his eyes were still red. He ate the bread he was handed with an appetite but Jocasta could see the thought of his friends pass over his face from time to time.

'An opera night . . . Does the servant from the house work there on opera night?'

He shrugged. 'I should think. She was following on when the Missus and Milky Boy were coming back that night I watched.'

Jocasta looked unseeing at the cobbler's tools around her, hung up and waiting for their master – dead things till a man put his hand to them and gave them purpose.

'Boy, we have business today. Ripley first, another place later. You fed?'

Sam swallowed and nodded.

'Right then. Let's be off.'

Mr Gaskin was much impressed by the carriage, and Harriet's first thought as Slater guided it into the driveway was that she was very glad she had had Crowther's counsel when finding a place for James to recover. It was not that the house in Kennington Lane was particularly unpleasant; Harriet knew enough from accounts published that some institutions where those whose wits were troubled found themselves were hells almost beyond imagining. Mr Gaskin's establishment was a pleasant villa, not unlike Dr Trevelyan's home and place of business, but there was an air of neglect here which made its atmosphere very different to the neatness and calm good order in Highgate. The garden borders were obviously only occasionally tended; the floors in the public areas of the house were swept badly, and the woodwork on the sash-windows at the front of the building had grown rotten and not been replaced. Harriet wondered if the friends and relatives of those confined here visited a great deal. She imagined not. It was a place where people were forgotten, and only thought of, briefly, when the bills for their accommodation and care arrived on some sunny breakfast, then were forgotten for another quarter.

The air of general neglect spread to Mr Gaskin himself. He was a short man, and very broad. His coat was a little dirty, his linen grey, and his wig oddly yellow in places. He resembled nothing so much as a bundle of clothing done up for the laundress to take away and beat back to a civilised appearance. When he smiled, Harriet's eye was drawn to a loose wooden tooth set in the front of his mouth, and looking as unsound as his windowframes. There was nothing to disgust immediately in his manners, but his breath stank.

He bowed low as Crowther presented himself, Harriet and Lady Susan. Harriet watched her young friend steel herself as Gaskin bent over her hand on the weedy gravel of the driveway, and was proud of her.

'Lady Thornleigh! A delight! An honour to have the scion of the noble house of the Earls of Sussex in our establishment.'

Crowther explained calmly to Gaskin that they wished to see Mr Leacroft and ask about his other visitors. He withdrew a folded sheet from his pocket.

'Was this the man who visited first?' he asked.

Mr Gaskin took the paper and squinted at it, holding it at various distances from his slightly yellow eyes and cooing: 'Oh yes indeed! To the life! What a fine hand!' He bent his almost spherical body towards Susan. 'Is this perhaps the work of my Lady? I sense a certain feminine grace in it.'

Susan edged a little closer to Harriet. 'I cannot draw. Jonathan can, but I cannot.'

'Lady Thornleigh is a musician,' Harriet said. 'We should like to introduce her to Mr Leacroft.' It was not until the words were in the air that Harriet wondered about the wisdom of bringing the child to a place such as this, to meet a man of uncertain temperament; to involve the ward of her host in such an investigation as this. Still, it was done now and Mr Gaskin was, with a variety of speeches to which Harriet did not closely attend, leading them towards a room in the back of the house.

The general grime seemed to thicken as they found their way. On the walls of the corridor hung a number of inexpert watercolours. The artist had been productive, but his or her works had been carelessly treated. The frames were cheap and ill-fitting, and several had slipped to show the torn edges of the sketchbook from which the drawings had been taken.

Gaskin saw Harriet looking at them and commented, 'The works of one of our former guests, the daughter of a churchman whose habits of piety became rather hysteric when she reached thirty and found herself still unmarried. Such things can twist the delicate constitution of a female.' He shook his head very sadly. 'She is returned to her family now, however. Her father was widowed and she keeps house for him. One of our successes.'

'Have you many?' Crowther asked, peering at a rather fantastical landscape of ruined towers and distant mountains.

Gaskin lifted his eyebrows and nodded sagely with a satisfied smile. 'Indeed, indeed. Mostly we offer care to those not fit for the wider world, and give what comfort we can before their enfeebled constitutions fail, but oftentimes people leave us ready to rejoin their families in safety and health. Though I do not know what prospects I hold out for poor Theophilius. He is sustained here by a legacy of his father's.

That wise gentleman arranged for the interest to be paid directly to this house quarterly after his death, which melancholy event occurred soon after his son's removal here. It is nearly sufficient to cover dear Theo's care. The rest of our usual fees I waive.' He turned and forced his smile on Harriet and Susan. 'I am a fool to myself perhaps, but one must be charitable.'

Crowther sighed rather audibly and said, 'What is the state of Mr Leacroft?'

Gaskin stroked his chin and drew his brows together. 'He is melancholic, sir. With some hysteric symptoms. At times he will laugh and sing, and try to teach his nurses and fellow patients to do the same and remain without sleep for a week, playing at his harpsichord and scribbling notes on any piece of paper he can find. Then he will spend a month barely able to raise his head. It is all we can do at such times to persuade him to take nourishment.'

'What do you do with the music he writes, sir?' Susan asked softly.

'We use it to light the fires, Lady Thornleigh.' Harriet felt Susan stiffen at her side, but she made no further comment. 'But how interesting that you ask. The young gentleman in the picture asked the very same thing.'

'Indeed?' Harriet said. 'And what did the other gentleman who visited ask you, sir?'

Mr Gaskin put his nose in the air. 'Hmph. That gentleman . . . I did not take to him, madam. I confess I did not. He asked nothing, and told me no more than his name.' He tilted again towards Susan. 'I sensed no breeding in him,' he added, and winked.

Both Harriet and Crowther were drawing breath to ask something further when they heard a long keening wail from the upper storey. Lady Susan started and reached for Harriet's hand. Mr Gaskin merely looked annoyed.

'Mrs Lightfoot!' He looked between the ladies with a wet smile. 'A tragic case. Confined here only a fortnight ago by her husband. Her behaviour had become so troubling he had no other choice, poor

240

man. She resents it – but she will learn in time. However, you must excuse me. Mr Leacroft's room is at the end of the corridor. You may go in. I fear I am required elsewhere.' He bundled back the way they had come.

Harriet looked with speaking rage at Crowther. He found he could do nothing but drop his eyes.

Jocasta left Ripley and the chophouse satisfied, and found Sam and Boyo waiting for her opposite the door. When she emerged she couldn't help seeing how Sam's eyes were darting about the street. While she was standing and guessing a way through the carts and horses that mired the road, she noticed a tall thin man pass by Sam, and though he gave him no look or word, the boy cowered to the wall. Again Jocasta wished she'd shut Sam up in the cobbler's cellar and fetched him when all was done and laid down, but the one thing the lad hated more than being out and about was being anywhere without her, and remembering the loss she had let fall on him, she couldn't deny him. He beamed when he saw her, and even more when she put a pie into his hand. It was still hot from the oven and he had to pull his raggy sleeves forward to hold it.

'What's the word, Mrs Bligh?' he said, as he blew on it.

'Fred will be in there tonight, and Ripley will find a way to hold him a while. Now be ready to eat that and trot too. We're up to Seven Dials now. Time for you to meet a very old friend.'

Sam took a great bite of his pie and wiped the gravy off his chin.

# VI.3

CROWTHER KNOCKED LIGHTLY on the door of the room Gaskin had indicated, then opened it as Harriet and Susan waited in the shadows beyond. He looked into the room for a second, then gesturing at them to follow him, he stepped inside.

The apartment in which they found themselves was large, but shabby. It was lit by a high bay window, and a number of books and papers were scattered around the surfaces and floors. Some servant of the place had a care of Mr Leacroft, however. The furniture might be worn or fraying, but it was cleaner than the hallway from which they had come. Someone had made an effort to wipe the lower panes of the window to provide a view; a metronome and tuning fork were arranged like ornaments on the top of the mantelpiece, and above it hung a watercolour of a man at a keyboard. Harriet recognised the hand of the artist whose works filled the hallway. She showed herself a better artist in this study than in her landscapes.

The room depicted was recognisably the one in which they now stood, but in the picture it was lit with summer sunshine and there were fresh flowers on the desk in the window. The figure at the keyboard was touchingly caught as if in mid-flourish with one hand raised from the instrument. The whole figure leaned forward into his playing; energy flew from him. It seemed Theophilius Leacroft still had the power to inspire at times.

The contrast between the image and the present gloom of the chamber was distressing. The keys of the harpsichord were covered and the stool tucked firmly away. It took Harriet a few moments to see the model of the player in the room itself, but as they reached the centre of the chamber Mr Leacroft moved in his seat, and her eyes found him in the gloom. He was lost in the folds of a great armchair that looked through the streaked window into the ill-kept garden beyond. He turned towards them, and Harriet was surprised to see a much younger man than she had expected. He could be no more than forty, and his face was unlined. His head had been shaved, but though he wore no wig, he was decently dressed. An auburn stubble marked out the edge of a high forehead and his eyes were as green as Harriet's own. He looked very tired, and having blinked once at the company who had intruded on him, turned back towards the garden.

'Angel, demon or fool? Who visits today?' he said. His voice had the weariness of all time about it, but was still clear and cool. Its habits of musicality could not, it seemed, be hidden even in this air of fatigue. Harriet approached.

'We are none of these, Mr Leacroft, I believe, and we are sorry to trouble you but there are some things we must ask you.'

He continued to stare into the garden and sighed but did not speak. Lady Susan moved towards the harpsichord. Her fundamental nature as a musician best showed itself in that whenever she entered a room where there was an instrument, she could not rest until she had tried it. Crowther, meanwhile, pulled the portrait of Bywater from his pocket again and placed it in front of Leacroft's eyes.

'Do you know this gentleman, sir? We believe he came to see you twice some little time ago.'

Mr Leacroft neither responded, nor looked at the paper in front of him.

Harriet caught Crowther's eye. He removed the paper and put it into his pocket again.

'We are sorry to trouble you, sir, but it is a matter of the greatest importance,' Harriet said.

Susan had lifted the lid, adjusted the stool, and was beginning to try the keys. Her hands found their way into a piece of music Harriet had heard her play many times before in Berkeley Square. She had never really listened to it, nor did she pay much mind now, as she was too preoccupied with keeping the irritation and frustration out of her voice.

'Do you know the name Fitzraven, sir?'

A gentle animation spread over Mr Leacroft's features, and Harriet began to hope for an answer, but rather than speak to her, he stood, and ignoring Harriet and Crowther entirely, crossed over to the harpsichord. Susan stopped suddenly, rather frightened by his approach, but he smiled at her with genuine warmth.

'No, no. Play on.' He took a seat beside her, and Susan began again, a little hesitantly at first, then with greater confidence. After listening a while with an air of great pleasure, he said, 'You like Mr Mozart very much, don't you, my dear?'

Harriet leaned towards Crowther and whispered, 'Who is Mozart?'

Crowther shrugged. 'There were a couple of children brought to London in the sixties. Their name was Mozart. I thought them a curiosity, like dancing bears. Performing monkeys.'

Susan nodded very hard at Mr Leacroft, enthusiasm lighting up her face.

'My father saw him when he played as a little boy in London, sir. Then a friend of his brought this home with him from a trip to Paris. Father made me learn it at once. It was a great favourite of his.'

Mr Leacroft's eyes widened and he suddenly laughed out loud. 'Why! You are Susan Adams – Alexander's daughter! I heard you play this before – when could it have been? In early seventy-nine, yes, yes . . . and thought you a prodigy, though you did not play it so well then as you do now.' He put his arm round the girl and kissed the top of her head. Susan grinned up at him as he went on, 'Alexander had only a manuscript copy, is that not right? Did not Herr Mozart write it out himself for their friend?'

Susan laughed. 'He did. Though Herr Mozart was rather drunk when he did so and wrote something rather rude about the old organist of Versailles at the end. Father copied it out again before he would give it to me to learn. Even though I didn't speak French then.'

Mr Leacroft rocked forward with laughter. 'I remember! I borrowed the original and made my own copy. It was one of the last things I remember before coming here. I still have it, and sometimes when I am well I play it again. One can be lost and reborn in such music . . .'

He became suddenly serious again. Harriet made to move forward, but found Crowther's hand on her arm.

Susan began to play again. 'I think this is my favourite part,' she said. Leacroft tilted his head to one side and listened.

'From the Presto. Yes. You have taste as well as talent, Miss Adams.

It has a dark sort of pressing forwards to it, does it not? The melancholy of A minor, it is like a hand across the sun of the major key. But how is your father, my dear? And you have a little brother, do you not?'

Susan's hands became still on the keys. 'Papa is dead, sir. But my brother is well.'

Leacroft covered her fingers briefly with his hand. 'I am sorry to hear it, dear. He was a good man.'

Susan did not lift her eyes. 'He was. Mrs Westerman and Mr Crowther here found who killed him and saved Jonathan and me.'

Leacroft looked up rather wonderingly at Harriet and Crowther; it was clear he had forgotten they were in the room.

Susan removed her hands from the keys and Leacroft began to play himself. It was a mournful, empty sort of sound. 'Why are you here, sir?' Susan said quietly. 'You do not seem mad to me.'

He continued to play. 'I am not always as I am today, Susan. You have woken me a little, you and Mr Mozart. But there has been such coming and going in the last little while. An old friend came to see me yesterday. She sang to me. It is strange, I had thought seeing her would make me very happy, but I felt as if she had brought all of London into the room. All the hurry and finery of it. I felt she was dragging something out of me. It made me very tired. Though I am glad she is well, I hope she does not come again.' His hands paused. 'Do you understand? I know it is difficult . . .'

'I think so, sir,' Susan replied. 'I went to the opera on Saturday. It was wonderful, but it is exhausting to be so bright all the time.'

He nodded and smiled slightly, and his hands began to move on the keys again. Susan suddenly frowned and began to pick out a tune over the chords which he played. Harriet concentrated. She was sure Susan was playing the theme from the 'Yellow Rose Duet'. Leacroft continued to play as he asked, 'You know this piece of mine? The young man in their picture stole it then.' He indicated Harriet and Crowther with his chin. 'Strange. I wrote it thinking of Isabella.

Then she came yesterday and sang it to me. She was amazed when I played alongside her. She asked too about that young man. Everyone does. It made her unhappy. I do not care that he took it.' He gave Susan a slightly twisted smile. 'He came when I was in one of my shining moods. At such times I play and write day and night and think myself a King. He listened like a thirsty man drinks.'

Susan suddenly paused in her playing. 'That part is different. In the opera house the harmony is this.' Leacroft raised his hands from the keyboard and Susan repeated the passage they had just played.

Leacroft shook his head. 'No, no. The bass collects what has been, and hopes for what is to come.' He played the phrase again. Harriet could only tell it was different from the way Susan had played it, though it seemed more mournful, a deeper colour somehow in the air.

Lady Thornleigh seemed to hold her breath, then nodded very slowly. 'That is a great deal better.'

Leacroft kept his eyes on the keyboard. 'Yes.'

'Do you really not mind, sir, Mr Bywater saying he wrote this piece when it is yours?'

'Miss Adams, I cannot feel it. I do not want the world to come and look at me. I was unhappy in the world. Here I am content. Perhaps that is enough to show I am mad.'

Susan looked down at her hands. 'May *I* come and see you again, sir?'

He stopped for a second and looked into her face with calm consideration before he said, 'Yes, my dear. I think I should like that. Who takes care of you now?'

'Mr Graves. And Mrs Service who lived opposite the shop.'

Leacroft looked up into the air to his right. 'I remember Graves a little. He wrote for newspapers. And Mrs Service. A quiet lady. How far away it seems. Yes. You may come, and bring Mrs Service to watch you, but no one else, and not too often.'

'Thank you, sir.' She watched him for a little while, the way his hands moved over the keys. 'I think perhaps you are weary, sir. We should go now.'

'Thank you, Miss Adams. Yes. I think so.'

Susan stood and gave him her hand; he bowed over it from his seat without standing, then returned to the keyboard. Susan walked towards the door. Harriet and Crowther simply followed in her wake, unnoticed.

Mr Gaskin met them on the porch as they put on their cloaks. Susan fastened hers at her throat and, cutting across Mr Gaskin's compliments, turned and said to him, 'Mr Gaskin, I am Lady Susan Thornleigh. My brother is the Earl of Sussex. Theophilius Leacroft is my friend. We shall send manuscript paper for him to write on when the mood takes him.'

Mr Gaskin's greasy smile froze on his face and his eyes darted about in confusion.

'But, my Lady, they are mere scraps! All in confusion! He writes on what he likes and leaves them fit for nothing but the fire.'

Susan was very still and spoke quietly. 'We shall send paper. If he does not wish to keep his work by him, you must send it to us in Berkeley Square, and you will be paid for doing so. But if you put one more note of that gentleman's music in the fire, I shall burn your house down.'

With that she turned and her footman handed her into the carriage. Harriet and Crowther having nothing to add, followed her in silence, leaving Mr Gaskin gasping and bowing on the gravel.

Harriet felt Susan trembling a little beside her. After a while, the girl turned towards her, and Harriet found herself looking down into her clear blue eyes. They had a thin rim of gold that matched her hair: it reminded her of Rachel.

'I did not want to be a Lady, or rich, Mrs Westerman,' she said. 'But there are times when it is very useful, I think.'

Harriet put her arm around her and Lady Thornleigh settled into her shoulder with a sigh.

'Indeed it is, my love. Indeed it is.'

# VI.4

THE MAN JOCASTA was looking for did not have any fixed place of business. He kept his wife and two boys in a first-floor room and saw that they ate well enough, but one was not likely to find him there after dark. His nature was not settled, nor did he hunger for domestic comfort, and he had made enemies enough in his time to make him wary of fixed sleeping places. His business made it needful though that he could be found by those who wanted him, so he had his public haunts. She knew he'd be in one of half a dozen places, so was ready to visit them in turn. The season had started, so the Quality were beginning to run back to Town and get through their allowances. That meant the start of his hunting season, and as long as there was blood in the water he'd be in one of his haunts, though where he laid his head on any night remained a secret even from his woman.

Jocasta had taken a slow walk round Seven Dials, went first to the Peacock and then to the George's Head before she found him hunched over a pint pot and with a clay pipe of cheap tobacco in his dirty hand. His face was hidden by the pointed brim of his hat and his figure shrouded by the shadows of the dark corner in which he sat curled, but she knew him well enough. Jocasta set herself down on the opposite side of the table. Sam stood behind her like a scrubby footman with Boyo in his arms.

'How do, Molloy?' she said.

The hat tipped slowly back to reveal a face so lined and cracked it looked like a milk jug smashed and restuck a dozen times. His cheeks were caved. He let the smoke drift out of his mouth softly softly, like fog rising off the river.

'Mrs Bligh. And a young friend. There's nice.'

'I need a little tutoring from you, Molloy.'

'Them cards gathered you a bit of capital, have they? Want to learn how to send it to work in rich men's pockets?'

Jocasta sniffed and folded her strong arms. 'I'll leave that business to you and the long beards in Whitechapel,' she retorted, then let her words come out slow after that. 'I want tutoring in the ways of your former trade.'

Molloy leaned back, putting one arm along the back of the settle, his mouth twisting round his pipe.

'And what might that be, Mrs Bligh? I don't rightly know what you mean.'

Jocasta pulled out the pack from her pocket.

'You forget, I've been round here a time. And people who are proper and tight-mouthed in their day-to-day get chatty about all sorts of things when they look at the pictures. I know where you got that first guinea you lent to some fool and made into two. Take a card.'

Molloy reached warily into the pack, looked at the image on the card in his hand and slapped it down on the table. Jocasta spoke over her shoulder to Sam. 'Remember this one, boy?'

The lad concentrated hard, then his face suddenly brightened. 'Thief!' He caught the look on Molloy's face and dropped his eyes, mumbling into Boyo's fur, 'that is, can say a few things, like pulling apart, but mostly that's thief, thieving and that.'

Molloy watched him go red then he reached forward and slid the card suddenly back to Jocasta, following it with his thin body till his cracked face was up close to hers. She didn't flinch.

'Ha! A pretty trick, lady! Say what you like. Old stories and I know how to keep quiet.'

Jocasta looked into his eyes, all reddened with the smoke, his blue irises swimming about in them like devils in hell. 'Me too, Molloy.'

He pulled away from her again, took the pipe from his mouth and blew a smoke ring into the dusty air, watching her cautiously. 'I suppose I can hear you out. What's the matter of it then, Mrs Bligh?'

She spoke low. 'I need to get in somewhere quick and quiet, then out. And I don't want to leave any sign of my coming or going.'

Molloy considered the ceiling for a while.

'You after something of your own, or something of theirs?'

'Something that belongs to another, I reckon. And I reckon they should have it back.'

His eyes narrowed. 'That smacks of philanthropy to me.'

'It's known you've done a favour before where there was no need.'

'I don't like that put about. Doesn't do any good for a man in my business to get a reputation for charity.' He spat on the floor, thick and yellow it came from him, and sank into the wood. 'When?'

'Tonight.'

'You'll never learn the trick of it in a day,' he said angrily, 'even if I were willing to share. Locks are like your fancy cards. They take learning and a little love.'

Jocasta remained still. 'It needs doing, Molloy.'

Behind them, a man rolled up to the bar and set down a coin. The barmaid gave him a measure of gin without a word, and without a word back he drank it and turned to go. Molloy didn't move, but Jocasta could see the blue devils swimming the way the man went out of the room.

'Give me the hour and place and I'll open up,' he grunted. 'Then I'm gone. You see trouble, it's all yours. Coin, and you share – and don't think I won't find out if you don't. Good enough for you?' He put the pipe back into his mouth.

'Good enough. Nine o'clock,' Jocasta replied evenly. 'Top of Salisbury Street.'

She stood and walked out of the room, feeling him watching her all the way.

## VI.5

KNOWING THAT HARRIET and Crowther were to attend the second performance of *Julius Rex* that night, Mrs Service had arranged for dinner to be brought forward, and so the company sat down at the rather country hour of four o'clock. The interim had been consumed with an intense debate between Harriet and Crowther as to the wisdom of going immediately to see Mr Tompkins's acquaintance, Gladys, with only Mr Bywater's picture in their hands, or whether they should wait till Mr Crumley's artistry had provided them with a full set of the leading figures at the opera house. Harriet wished to go at once. Crowther urged caution and was in the end successful, if only because the time had become impossibly short. Susan they had delivered back into the bosom of the household as soon as the carriage had drawn up. Beyond hearing Graves's general greeting as he returned from the shop and various footsteps throughout their discussion, the rest of the household did not enter the library.

'Fitzraven *must* have been attempting to blackmail Bywater,' Harriet stated with great determination. 'He went to visit Leacroft as soon as he saw the parts for the duet. He wished any romance between Bywater and Isabella to end, and no doubt thought he could put some of Bywater's wages in his pocket too. He would never have been able to resist. No doubt he told Bywater what he knew and arranged for him to visit and discuss terms on Thursday afternoon, then they fought.'

Crowther leaned against the library desk, watching her stride back and forth in front of the fire like a General.

'But what of the French, Mrs Westerman? What of the spies and Mr Palmer?'

Harriet threw up her hands. 'Whatever else they are guilty of, perhaps they are innocent of this. Mr Palmer himself thought it odd that Fitzraven was killed.'

Harriet was surprised to find a certain uneasiness in the air when they sat down at table. Graves remained polite, but was distinctly reserved. Rachel looked serious and quiet, and Susan looked rather unhappy and confused. When Graves begged for a moment of her time before she went to dress for the evening therefore, Harriet followed him into the library with a feeling of distinct dread.

Graves stood in front of the fireplace and put his hands behind his back, rocking forward off his heels. He looked steadfastly at the floor in front of him. Harriet began to attempt some light remark but was cut off.

'Really, Mrs Westerman, I must ask you what you are about.'

Harriet took in a breath, but Graves continued at once.

'Lady Susan is eleven years old, yet you bundled her out of this house and took her to an asylum. Took her to visit a madman of whose temperament you knew little, and that little only by report. Took her to a place, a situation, that sounds unpleasant at best and involved her – intimately involved her – in the investigation of a murder. All this without a word to her guardian or friends. I must ask you again, what are you about, madam?' Now he looked up. His face was flushed and he repeated slowly with bell-like clarity: 'She is eleven years old.'

Harriet said in a rush, with a smiling placatory tone, 'Graves! You were not to be found, and I believe Susan enjoyed the visit. She got along with Leacroft quite famously, you know.' She found as she finished that her pulse was running rather fast.

'Indeed, Mrs Westerman. Such is the nature of Susan's open, good heart I find my ward has promised to watch over this gentleman's interests. Lady Thornleigh will be noticed as a regular visitor to this dreadful place, thanks to you. And I returned from the lawyers to the shop within an hour of your departure. You knew perfectly well if you had only a little patience, you would find me there during the day.'

'But Mr Leacroft, it seems, is a family friend. You are possibly acquainted with him yourself!'

'So Susan informs me. But you did not *know* that, Mrs Westerman, did you? The man could have been raving! Even if Trevelyan had told you he was not dangerous, can you tell me you had assurances from him, or from anyone, that he was suitable company for an eleven-year-old girl?'

'I did not think—'

'That much is clear, madam. You *must* think more about the consequences of your actions. You trust again and again to luck and your own forward momentum. At some point you will seriously harm those near to you, who can do nothing to defend themselves against the damage you bring.'

Harriet had been listening angrily, feeling her face growing hot, but at this last a vicious little bud blossomed in her mind and she said with a quick shake of her head, 'My sister has made you her confidante, I see, in the matter of her concerns as to my behaviour.'

Graves looked a little disgusted. Harriet could tell he was clasping his hands together hard behind his back. She felt her own nails beginning to dig into her palms.

'She has done no such thing. But if she has made mention to you of such concerns already, I wish to God, madam, you had listened to her! Miss Trench is a model of good behaviour without ever losing her naturalness. And *she* is possessed of remarkable good sense.'

Harriet felt a jealous flame in her throat. The world seemed suddenly unjust in the extreme. Her words came spitting out, hot and angry as grapeshot. 'Yes, and she can make up a dozen foul-smelling recipes from the household, Doctor!' She held onto the back of one of the armchairs hard enough to whiten her knuckles and showed her teeth in an unnatural smile. 'She is a paragon of all virtues. I admit it. The community round Caveley declare it, just as they used to in my father's parish, and now she is lauded here! Perhaps her virtues even exceed those of Miss Chase. Poor Verity, and just when she has persuaded her father to spend her marriage portion on buying the shop for you from the estate, but instead it seems so overwhelming are my sister's attractions, you will be too busy cutting out Daniel Clode to make use of it. And as to Susan and Jonathan, where would they be now if it were not for my *headstrong* ways and Crowther's knives you all shrink from so!'

She came to a sudden stop, looking at the pain flickering in his young, kind face, and in the silence that followed began to realise with a cold sort of horror what she had just said.

Graves spoke softly. 'The children had other friends.' His hand travelled unconsciously to the right side of his waistcoat, as if the scar there he had received from a blade the previous year had woken and needed calming. He had defended the children. He had put his own flesh between them and danger. Harriet found herself dumb with sudden shame. She could admit she liked to think herself rather above her fellow creatures at times, but when Rachel was praised above her, when her own actions were condemned, she found herself behaving like a jealous child. If Stephen had spoken as she just had, she would have been ashamed of him.

Graves moved away from the fireplace and sat down heavily in one of the armchairs.

'*I* do not care what you do, Mrs Westerman. I am well aware of the debt we owe you. But Susan and Jonathan both look up to you so much. You are a model to them. They must live in the world and learn to do so soberly and decently, despite their wealth, the history of their blood. I am trying to guide them. Yet you do these things . . . Remember they look to you, that is all I ask.'

Harriet took a step towards him. 'Graves, I am so very sorry!' He did not look at her. 'And what I said about Rachel and Verity – it is such nonsense.' He twisted painfully in his chair. 'I am weary, yet this business has lit up my brain and carries me forward.' Harriet sat down in the armchair alongside his own and put her head in her hands.

Graves looked at her with alarm. 'Oh good Lord, Mrs Westerman! You won't cry, will you?' he said, sounding much younger again.

'You can't behave so abominably then take such a feminine way out. Unfair!'

Harriet gave a rather damp snort. 'No, Graves, I promise you I shall not.' She looked up at him. 'I am sorry though. It was wrong to take Susan, and I knew it the moment we arrived, but by then . . . though I'm glad I did.' Graves opened his mouth to protest again. 'No, truly! She was so wonderful with him, Graves. We would never have managed without her. And when she told that horrid Gaskin she would burn down his house if he destroyed any more of Leacroft's music . . .'

Graves shook his head with a reluctant laugh. 'Oh, she did, did she? I was only told she'd asked the man to send Leacroft's music here. Of course, she told me about "*C'è una rosa*".' He turned his head away and fell into a study of the fire. 'She is a remarkable girl. I wish I had met her mother. In fact, it seems as if I am surrounded with remarkable women. Verity is planning on buying me out, is she? Giving me the chance to work for my living?'

'You work very hard for your living and your wards. No one thinks otherwise but you. Yes, I believe that is her plan. But I understand she doubts if you still hold her in the same regard.'

Graves smiled gently into the fire. 'She is the only person in the world that could do so. Though I cannot ask her to be my wife under the circumstances, I think of her every moment.' Then he added, looking at Harriet with an eyebrow raised, 'At least, when I am not trying to save the children from your pernicious influence.'

Harriet let herself smile and placed a hand on his sleeve. Graves nodded to the clock on the mantelpiece. 'You should go and dress, Mrs Westerman. And Stephen made me promise to ask you to come and kiss him goodnight before you leave. I think he wishes to see his mama in her finery. And he has something to ask you. He has thought about it quite carefully, so I would ask that you listen.'

Harriet rose. 'Thank you, Graves. You are a better friend than I deserve.'

'No, Mrs Westerman. Rather the world does not deserve *you*. But here you are, you and your dashings, and Mr Crowther and his knives, and we must learn how to make best use of you. Enjoy the performance. You will not see a better opera in London for five years.'

She left and made her way slowly up to her own chamber.

## VI.6

HARRIET, RACHEL AND Crowther were to have the use of Mrs Service's box at the opera that night, and Mr Crumley was provided with papers for the pit. Harriet was a little surprised to find that the coach did not make its way directly to Hay Market, but matters became clear when she realised they were turning into Sutton Street. The carriage paused and Miss Verity Chase was handed into it by one of her father's servants. Harriet was very pleased to see her. The strained nature of the understanding between this lady and Owen Graves meant that her visits to Berkeley Square to see the children were fleeting, hurried and only to be undertaken when Graves was sure to be away from the house. Mrs Service took the children to Sutton Street whenever their entreaties reached a fever pitch, but she was unsure if she should be encouraging the bond between the children and Verity to continue to flower, and the visits made her uncomfortable.

Rachel patted Miss Chase's hand and smiled reassuringly at her. Verity seemed more comfortable at once and began to ask them about Fitzraven and their investigations to date. Harriet and Crowther were happy to tell her what they could without repeating Mr Palmer's concerns. Miss Chase was a practical and intelligent woman and her remarks were always to the point, and worth attending to. She was quite as beautiful as Rachel, but had a little less of her yielding femininity. Her nature and humour was rather more dry and exact. For all that she had been raised as a gentlewoman, Harriet could see something of her father, the man of business in her, and admired her for it.

'So Miss Marin discovered yesterday what you did this morning. Do you know if she has spoken to Mr Bywater? Surely that would be her first thought if she felt for him as Carmichael and Manzerotti suggested. Her distress must have been extreme.'

Harriet was a little shocked. 'I had not thought of it till now, Miss Chase. She was certainly distressed by something when I spoke to her last evening.'

Crowther frowned. 'Did not Carmichael say she left the party as soon as her portion of his little entertainment was complete?'

Harriet nodded and looked at the elegant reticule she held on her lap. It was a pretty thing, but not practical. 'He did. We must speak to Bywater ourselves tonight, Crowther, and challenge him. Do you think if he murdered Mr Fitzraven he will confess it now?'

Out of the corner of her eye Harriet noticed Rachel shiver a little at the word 'murder'. Miss Chase merely watched their discussion with calm interest.

'Possibly. I've already told you his behaviour seemed to betray guilt of some sort. Though it is just as likely that he was nervous his plagiarism was about to be exposed. He had no great difficulty finding Leacroft. We must assume he realised we would not find it impossible ourselves.'

Harriet nibbled the tip of one of her gloved fingers in thought. 'I am very glad you are here, Miss Chase. It may be a night of unpleasant scenes. We shall have our conversations in private, and you and Rachel may remain in the box together.' She flashed her eyes up at the two young women. 'I hope you will find more pleasant topics of conversation.' Miss Chase lost her calm demeanour for a moment and blushed. Rachel gave a little gurgling laugh, and patted her knee.

'I am sure we will, Harry,' she said. 'After all, we just have to find a way to persuade a proud man to allow himself to be made happy.'

Miss Chase kept her eyes low, but smiled.

Rachel looked past her out of the carriage window. 'Dear heavens. It is even more crowded than Saturday evening.'

The Hay Market was jammed with carriages. It seemed that not only Graves would profit from the popularity of '*C'è una rosa*'. A pair of women in white caps were trying to sell rather tired-looking yellow roses in through the carriage windows from great baskets on their hips, and for those who could not afford fresh blooms, a few young boys were handing out flowers cut from paper for pennies.

Crowther noticed a tall, thin-faced woman in brown emerge from the rear of the theatre with a sack over her shoulder. She called a boy over to her, cuffed his ear and gave him from her bag a fresh stack of librettos to sell. He put some coins in her hand and she counted them over carefully, her lips a hard line, while Crowther watched her.

'What an enterprise this is,' he said, turning away from the window again.

Harriet sent a note to Mademoiselle Marin via one of the servants of the place as her party settled into the box. Before the opera commenced she had received a courteous response from Isabella saying indeed there were many things she wished to discuss with Mrs Westerman, but she did not think she would be equal to such interviews until the performance was complete. Harriet handed the note over to Crowther without comment and he nodded.

'Perhaps it would be best to meet with Mr Bywater after the performance as well,' he said. 'We may send Miss Chase and your sister home in a respectable manner, then confine the unpleasantness to Mr Harwood's office.'

'Should we tell Mr Harwood what we know?' Harriet asked as the musicians began to take their places in the pit. She leaned awkwardly over the edge of the box to try and spot Mr Bywater. The seat at the harpsichord remained empty.

'Let us find him between Acts and speak with him then.'

Harriet was content and settled back in her chair to derive what pleasure she could from the entertainment. The theatre was bursting. The chandeliers were brilliant enough for the company to read their librettos and wave at their friends with ease. Everything was in movement. The Quality moved between their boxes and those of their friends, whispering scandal or politics to make the women laugh and the jewels in their hair sparkle. Some breach of etiquette in the pit had led to a man's wig being plucked off his head and tossed back and forth among the crowd while he tried to struggle towards it. As the overture began, it seemed the pit felt he had been punished enough and a young man handed it back to him with a slap across his shoulders and an order to mind his manners better. There was a smattering of applause as he took his seat again, pulling the bruised horsehair firmly over his ears. The galleries were clamorous, and all through the pit, people were shouting greetings and comments to one another.

Harriet scanned the boxes around her. The Royal Box was taken by a group of women and men, beautifully dressed, but not anyone she could recognise. Friends of the Prince of Wales perhaps. She caught sight of Sandwich opposite and responded to his polite bow with a gracious nod. She was aware that after she had done so, various other pairs of eyes sought her out from the pit and boxes, and so kept her gaze on the stage and did not risk peering over to see Mr Bywater again.

There was movement, and to a stately march a large chorus of singers in an approximation of Roman costume gathered on stage. According to the little book in Harriet's hand that gave both the Italian, and a rather free, she suspected, English translation of it, they were now launching into a rousing musical debate on the politics of their day. The audience turned away from their various discussions and conversations and began to pay attention to the performance. A minor God descended in clouds of fury to a call from the horn section and flew to a position at the front of the stage. The device earned some gasps and some applause of its own. The God seemed pleased.

Harriet let her attention wander to Rachel and Verity, sitting with their own libretto open between them. They made a charming study of young womanhood, and Harriet felt fond of them. They had both found men whom they could love and admire, and as far as it was possible to judge such things, Harriet thought they had as much chance of happiness as any pair of young couples. She remembered the pleasure and excitement of the time of her engagement to James and looked at her hands. She had the promissory ring on her finger again. Stephen had handed it over very gravely to her that evening, saying he thought it best she should have it back. She had forgotten she had left it with him, and felt guilty, so when Stephen asked, after taking a deep breath that seemed to lift his little body up like a balloon, if he might visit his father, she had agreed at once and told him they would go the following morning. A week had passed since her last visit – surely Trevelyan would be satisfied she had waited long enough?

Harriet watched Rachel's pale cheek as she followed the action on stage. She wished her happiness; she wished her comfort and patience and love. She wished she were a better and more generous elder sister to her. If anyone were formed to create domestic harmony, it was her Rachel. All that she could wish for herself was that she might not do too much damage, and from time to time manage to do some good.

The music had lost her. She leaned forward again to look down into the pit, then frowned and touched Crowther's sleeve. He turned towards her and lifted his eyebrow. 'Where is Bywater?' she breathed.

He followed her gaze. The figure directing from the keyboard, though he had his back to them, was certainly not Bywater. This man's girth was considerable and the little part they could see of his face was red and fleshy.

Crowther nodded, but not being one of those who thought the opera house a place for general conversation, did not reply.

On stage the panels of the Forum pulled back, and in time to the footfall of the music, others replaced them. The scene became pastoral, with a great mountain at the back rearing suddenly over the audience. At its summit, a slender figure dressed all in gold and crowned with great plumes appeared and opened its arms. Manzerotti. The orchestra ceased and he sang a single, simple phrase. The last note began strongly, then faded to a whisper that had each head in the audience craning forward, hardly breathing, then it swelled again to a power that could set the lamps fluttering, and pulling down his hand in a fist, Manzerotti brought the orchestra in again in a thundering restatement of the theme. He made his way down the mountainside to the hysterical approval of the crowd and the ringing of trumpets.

## VI.7

'YOU SAW IT in a dream, Mrs Bligh?'
Jocasta and Sam were back in the shoemaker's cellar. Her work for the night prepared for, Jocasta was more comfortable off the streets and quiet till the time came to meet Molloy. Sam and she spent their leisure looking over the cards and playing with Boyo in a corner while their host cursed and sweated at his leather and moulds and his wife cut shapes out of silk and hemmed them narrow and sweet. 'I thought you must have asked the cards while I was sleeping.'

Jocasta bent forward to rest her chin in her hands. 'Way I see it, boy, the stories and stuff the cards show us are only half the skill of it. Lots depends on opening up and hearing what people are telling you without them knowing they are telling, or even knowing that they've got something to tell. Sometimes a fat truth will jump up clear as day without them even twitching. Like Kate's cards. They had an evil snap to them, but that's not the usual way. Other times it's more like the cards are a set of keys and they open up stuff you thought was all dusty and locked in your head, and show you it in a new light.'

Sam looked serious and put his own chin in his hands. 'But the dream? Did God send you it?'

'Ha! Don't recall God ever sending me telling other than through the priest, lad.'

'So how do you know where those writings are?'

'I'm saying the dreams are like the cards. They shuffle stuff about. Reckon I must have seen something when I went to try and warn Kate. Something odd about that ugly furniture when I looked through the window, or maybe she looked at it funny as she went in, or touched it somehow. Then I had the dream.'

Sam looked confused and opened his mouth, but Jocasta cut him off. 'Sam, I think there are things the mind knows loud, and things the mind knows quiet. Times I think dreams are you working out what's important or what's not. Something in my blood wants me to go and look at that table and guess what's in it. I've gotta listen to that. Maybe my blood's wrong. But we'll know.'

She was quiet a space, then put her hand on his shoulder.

'You ain't coming tonight, Sam.'

He started to speak, but she held his shoulder tight and lifted her other hand. 'You ain't coming.'

He was all white and his eyes looked wet. She could see him searching for words and finding nothing but fear. She narrowed her eyes. 'Think, lad. I need you to look after Boyo.' Fear began to change into confusion in his face. She pushed home. 'You're going to be here. Martha will feed you, then shut the lid on you. You've got the lock and you don't open to anyone but me in the night. If in the morning I ain't back, let Martha in and do as she says.'

Jocasta could tell the cobbler and his wife were paused in their work. 'Sam,' she added, 'there's no use fighting me. I'll bind you to the chair all night, if needs be. You stay here and look after Boyo. Head down. I ain't risking either of you on the streets.'

Sam pulled away from her and threw himself into the heap of blankets in the corner, face to the wall. Boyo looked up at Jocasta and sneezed. She shrugged at him, and he trotted over to Sam's side and lay down next to him, crawling under his arm on his belly.

The roars of approval that kept Manzerotti and Marin on stage after the duet were enough to leave Harriet feeling rather deaf and stupid. She was eager to go and find Harwood at once to escape the noise, but as she began to move from her seat, the door to their box was opened and he entered.

He greeted them, then glanced at Verity and Rachel. Miss Chase got to her feet.

'I would like some refreshment, I think. Rachel, will you come with me to the coffee room?'

Rachel was willing, and so with no more loss of time the ladies removed themselves and gave the others the privacy of the box. Mr Harwood did not waste words on unnecessary preamble.

'Mrs Westerman, sir. I must ask you if you believe this business with Fitzraven might put anyone else in harm's way?'

Crowther looked at him with a frown. 'It is possible. Once a man has become desperate enough to take one life, he may be willing to try and hide the deed by killing others. Such was the case in Sussex last year.'

Harwood looked very serious. 'Then I must tell you I am concerned for Richard Bywater.'

'*For* Richard Bywater!' Harriet repeated in surprise.

Harwood nodded. 'You mean . . . ? No matter. Yes, I am concerned for him. I have not seen him here all day. I sent to his house an hour before the performance to ask him what he was about, but my servant returned empty-handed. He had been seen in the morning in apparent health, and his landlady had thought he had returned to his room, but had had no view of him since then. His door was locked and there was no reply to my servant's knocks.'

'You think this is cause for concern?' Crowther asked, and tented his fingers together.

Harwood put his hands to his eyes. 'I fear so. Bywater may not be the most talented of men but I never doubted his commitment to this place. He has attended every performance of his own work, or that of others since I first employed him. He has never been late for a rehearsal, nor late delivering the material we have required of him. This is most unlike.'

Crowther continued to consider his fingernails. 'I see.'

Harwood turned to Harriet. 'But madam, am I to understand that Bywater is under some sort of suspicion himself? I cannot see the man as a murderer.'

Harriet replied seriously, 'We have as yet no proof that he is. But we do know he is a plagiarist. The "Yellow Rose Duet" was composed by a gentleman called Leacroft who is confined in a madhouse in Kennington.'

Harwood looked genuinely shocked, then stood up angrily. 'The fool! I thought it more than a touch beyond his talent, but to take such a risk! His reputation is destroyed. He will not find further employment here or in any other place in London.'

Crowther looked up at him. 'Are not such accusations common? Would it destroy him so completely?'

Harwood's voice was utterly cold. 'Completely. Accusations *are* common, since it is only natural to borrow from your betters, but direct borrowings are acknowledged. It may be that if it were only some minor matter . . . but "*C'è una rosa*" is the shining star in this work. Graves has sold two hundred copies already, and the street singers are warbling it after a single public performance. Are you certain?'

Crowther continued to observe him and simply nodded.

'Fool! Damned fool! The scandal will taint his name for ever, and he has not talent enough to redeem himself. If that is *all* he is guilty of, he is nevertheless condemned. He may eke out a life teaching piano to provincial gentry, but he'll never be spoke to here again. If Marin continues in her affection for him now, she will condemn herself utterly as well. Fitzraven knew?'

'Yes,' Harriet said quietly.

'Yet he told me nothing! What is afoot here? Fitzraven knew he could ask me for a loan of twenty pounds for information such as that.'

Crowther spoke. 'We suspect he wished to use the information to warn Bywater away from Miss Marin.'

Harriet noticed that while they had been talking, a ballet had begun on stage. She thought she could recognise the individual Susan had thought less competent than the rest.

Harwood spoke again, more calmly. 'But perhaps then, there is no cause for great concern for his personal safety. If Bywater is guilty of what you accuse him of, even if he had no role in Fitzraven's death, it is likely he may have fled the town.' Then, frowning, he asked Harriet, 'Might Bywater have known you had found out about this gentleman?'

'He cannot know *we* have discovered his plagiarism,' she replied, 'but Mademoiselle Marin visited Leacroft yesterday.'

The ballet was finishing, but it seemed the opera enthusiasts far outnumbered the lovers of dance that evening, and the applause was lukewarm. Harwood grimaced. 'That reception will put Master Navarre and his troop in a rage. No matter. He must realise the crowd will have its favourites every season.' He leaned against the wall of the box. 'Mademoiselle Marin has visited this gentleman you say?' Harriet drew breath to explain, but Harwood put up a hand to stop her. 'No, Mrs Westerman. Say nothing more. I have heard revelations enough this evening.'

Crowther stood. 'Give me Bywater's address if you please, Mr Harwood. And the services of one of your men. If Bywater will not answer his door, I am afraid we must knock it down. If he is fled, he might have left some trace of the direction he has taken. If he is there, we shall speak to him.'

Harwood nodded. 'Of course. He has a room in Charles Street, a moment away. He would have taken up residence in the theatre itself, if I had allowed it.'

Harriet looked up at Crowther's thin, frowning face. 'You wish me to remain here and speak to Isabella after the Third Act, sir?'

'If that is acceptable, madam.'

Harriet managed to resist the temptation to roll her eyes. 'Naturally. I will send the girls home, and you must come and collect me when you are done turning over Bywater's rooms.'

Harwood opened the door to the box and bowed Crowther out, then bowed Miss Trench and Miss Chase back in, each with an orange in their hand and sparkling with good humour. They found Harriet hunched over, too busy with her thoughts to speak to them and her fingers rapping on her skirts.

Jocasta was almost spitting with impatience when Molloy reached her. He swaggered up and grinned at her mirthlessly.

'Not got your familiars with you tonight, Mrs Bligh?'

'Never mind that, Molloy. You got no mind to the hour? I've been waiting for you for longer than I like.'

He winked. 'I've got a good mind for the time, never you worry. It's just my little test like. If you ain't willing to wait, you ain't got a serious eye to the business, and if you ain't got a serious eye, then I'm not about to risk sticking my head in a noose for you.'

'You could have found some other way, you dog.'

'Watch your mouth,' he said, though his voice was still mild enough, just rough with pipe-smoke and old beer. 'Now where are these doors you need to ghost through?'

Harriet could not have said at what moment the atmosphere in the auditorium began to change. The crowd had chattered or applauded its way through some piece or other from the pit and spat out sunflower-seed shells onto the sawdust on the pit floor for a period, till softly the whispering began to change its tone. Harriet looked up, seeing what was around her for the first time in some minutes. The occupants of the boxes looked irritable and a number of the ladies were hiding yawns behind their fans. The musicians were exchanging shrugs and shaking their heads. Those on the upper part of the gallery began to clap, slow and regular, a few at first, then more and more joined till the walls seemed to shake with the regular rhythm of it. One or two ladies began to follow the beat with their closed fans rapping on the velvet lips of their boxes. Harriet was confused; Rachel leaned over to her to explain.

'The Third Act should have begun some time ago.'

The pace of the handclap began to accelerate. Harriet found herself beginning to stand, a confused wonder and fear crawling up her spine. The thud of the clapping reached a frenzied climax and collapsed. Cat calls, whistles and shouted complaints began to echo around the walls in its place.

'Rachel, Miss Chase . . .' Harriet said slowly. 'I think you should go home at once. Send the carriage back for us when you are safe at Berkeley Square.'

It was Rachel's turn to look confused. 'But Harriet—'

Before she could say any more, there was a scream. A woman's voice, full of rage and grief, poured into the air and scorched it silent. The voice came from somewhere in the wings. For a moment everything was still, then as if the touch of the sound had burned the skin of the audience, everyone began to shout at once. Other feminine cries of distress around the theatre echoed the first. Harriet found herself unable to move. On the stage below them, arranged as for a temple with a sea glittering blue in the back, Mr Harwood staggered out and approached the footlights. His arms raised for quiet.

The flames threw strange shadows up his face and over his arms, and made his shape huge and crowlike on the canvas seascape behind him.

'Ladies and gentlemen – please!' The noise level ebbed away and the audience leaned forward. Harriet found her hands were trembling. 'Tonight's performance of *Julius Rex* cannot, I am afraid, continue . . . One of our performers is no longer able—'

The scream came again, vicious and angry. Harwood paused, his arms still raised, and looked off stage. He seemed terrified, like a man who finds himself fallen suddenly into hell. From the wings a figure in grey crawled forward.

'Morgan,' Harriet whispered through dry lips.

The figure screamed again and lifted her hands; her voice when she spoke was hardly human. 'Who has murdered my songbird?' It asked raging and blind. 'Who has killed my Issy?' Her hands were caught in the lights. They were red with blood.

Pandemonium. Harwood unfroze and dropped to his knees and put his arms round the stricken woman, trying to help her off stage again. The musicians all stood and craned their necks to look up. The entire theatre was full of cries and weeping, every man and woman on their feet and hurrying to be somewhere but knowing not where or how to flee the horror of it. Harriet spun round to the white faces of her sister and friend.

'Lock the door behind me. Stay here until the theatre has emptied – the crush could be deadly – then go. Do not wait for me.' Rachel had started to sob. Harriet hesitated, but met Miss Chase's cool grey eyes.

Verity took Rachel's hands firmly in her own, and said in a voice steadier than Harriet's, 'Go, Mrs Westerman. I'll look after Rachel.' And when Harriet still wavered, Verity stood up and opened the door of the box.

'For the love of God, Harriet, go!' Harriet ran out and, gathering her skirts, dashed down the corridor and towards the artists' apartments as if the devil himself were at her heels.

# VI.8

HARRIET PUSHED OPEN the doors at the end of the corridor, and escaping the pandemonium of the auditorium, found herself in the chaos of the backstage. She fought her way past the Roman women of the chorus weeping and fainting and holding each up in small groups. The God she had watched descend from the clouds at the opening of the scene sat on a plaster boulder in his costume, his

Olympian wreath bent out of shape and his heavy make-up running. He rocked from side-to-side. Manzerotti suddenly appeared beside her and took her arm. He still wore gold, though his magnificent plumes he held now in his hand.

'Mrs Westerman. God be praised.' His black eyes had a glitter to them, and there was sweat on his upper lip. 'Come with me.' He took her arm and dragged her through the crowds and across the stage. The auditorium was still breaking under waves of noise. He dragged her just behind the side panel stage right and released her.

Harwood was on his knees, his head in his hands. In front of him, like a mockery of the *Pietà*, Morgan knelt, Isabella's body hauled up across her thighs and chest. There was blood everywhere, blackening the blue satin of her bodice and skirts. Only her face and neck were clean of it, though they were heavy with her stage make-up: the skin dead white, her open eyes heavily lined, her mouth wide with red paint. Her natural hair had escaped its pins and fell in black about her temples. Harriet noticed the diamonds in her ears.

Getting down on her knees, Harriet crept towards them, as if approaching a holy and dreadful thing.

'Morgan?'

The old woman's head flicked up and stared at her. Harriet crept closer and put her hand round Isabella's wrist. Still warm. 'Morgan? It's Harriet Westerman. What happened?'

Morgan shifted her grip on the girl's body, holding it still closer to her with a keening whine, and continued to rock her. Her face was flushed and so flooded with tears her skin seemed honey-glazed. She touched Isabella's cheek with a fingertip, then seeing that she had dirtied the skin with blood, tried to wipe the mark off with her sleeve, smearing Isabella's rouge.

'Morgan? Can you tell me what happened?' Harriet found herself becoming oddly calm. The other clamour of the place dropped away. There was just her in the world and these two women, one dead, one grieving for the dead. She looked swiftly along the length of the body.

Two wounds. One in her belly which had bled hard and fast. The other was a neat straight line above her heart. It had hardly bled at all.

The wood around the lock splintered at the second attempt. Crowther nodded his thanks to Harwood's man, and stepped into the room. He became still at once. The fire behind them was burning with a fierce light; in front of it, at right angles to the door, was a tin bathtub. Bywater was in it, eyes closed, naked and very white. He had slumped down far enough so that his shoulders were underwater. The firelight swum over it. It was the same colour as Graves's Madeira. One arm hanging over the lip of the tub had prevented the dead man from slipping entirely under the water. The wrist was an angry red mouth. Crowther had time to note that the cut had been made along the artery rather than across it before he was distracted by the sound of Harwood's servant vomiting in the corridor behind him.

'Molloy? How long will you be at this?'

'Hush, woman. Street door you could open with a fish bone. This one into the family rooms is a little more fancy ... little bit more sophisticated, you might say. Needs more than a tickle and a slap to get this lady to open up.'

Jocasta folded her arms. He felt her look even in the darkness of the lobby and laughed softly. 'Patience, Mrs Bligh. I'm nearly there.'

Crowther waited till the sounds of sickness had passed, drew a handkerchief from his pocket and threw it over his shoulder without pausing in his careful scrutiny of the room.

'Go back to His Majesty's,' he told the other man. 'Tell Harwood and Mrs Westerman that Bywater is dead. Tell them to send to Bow Street and inform them of what has passed, and to Justice Pither on Great Suffolk Street and tell him Mr Crowther would be happy to meet him here tomorrow morning early and inform him of developments. Then send two men here to guard the place. I will pay them. Make sure they have stronger stomachs than you yourself.'

He hardly heard the mumbled thanks and apology. The man's footsteps retreated down the stairs at a pace. Crowther set his cane in front of him and leaned on it. But made no further move.

'There, Mrs Bligh! You're in. Just pull it to sharp as you come out, and no one will know different. I'm away and good luck to you.'

Harwood uncovered his face and looked at Harriet. 'I must help get the people out.'

Harriet did not take her eyes away from Morgan. 'Do. I will stay with them.' She heard him stand and move off. 'Morgan? What happened?'

Morgan looked at Harriet again, but this time Harriet thought she did so with some understanding.

'He killed my little bird, Mrs Westerman.'

Harriet came forward till she could slip her arm around the old lady's shoulders. The woman leaned into her and wept. Harriet almost slipped under the weight of her.

'Who killed her, Morgan?'

'Bywater! That fool, Bywater! She'd asked to meet him in the scene room after the Second Act when it would be a little quieter. He's been strange, the last day or two.'

Harriet put her other arm across them, holding Morgan and the dead Isabella in a loose embrace. 'Did she see he was not in the pit?'

'Of course, of course. Though it didn't seem to surprise her, and she still swore he'd be there to meet her. Said he'd *have* to be there.'

'Do you know why she was to meet him, Morgan?'

She felt rather than saw the old woman shake her head. 'No, no. I thought perhaps he was angry with her. Her all followed and courted, and invited places he ain't. She smiles at the rich men, but it's her work. She means nothing by it. Do you, little bird?'

Harriet became aware that she was not alone in listening to Morgan. A couple of the *corps de ballet* were standing behind them, their heads hanging. Two or three of the chorus singers, the leader of the opera band sitting on the bare stage, his violin dead in his hands. There was a stir in the crowd. One of the servants of the place approached, pale, shaking, out of breath, with Crowther's soiled handkerchief still in his hand. He knelt beside her, whispering in her ear.

Harriet nodded and said to him, 'Let Crowther know what has happened here and say that I shall wait for him.'

Jocasta slid into the room like a cat sneaking into a dairy, and pulled the door to just behind her. Then she made for the grey shadow of the side-table. The lip was certainly thicker than it needed to be. She slipped her fingers below it, began to feel along the length hoping her heart would calm enough not to leap out of her chest where she stood. It was not as easy as in the dream. There seemed to be no magic spot to make a secret jump free like a jack-in-the-box. For a second Jocasta thought of turning and running and calling the dreams traitor. But there was something wrong in the make of this. She began to feel along the way a little lower down. Fingering for weakness, for an unhappy joint.

The servant retreated and earnest whispers began to rustle among the groups around them.

Morgan looked drunk, bemused with grief. 'What has happened?' she said.

'Bywater is dead,' Harriet said simply.

'Good. By his own hand?'

'It seems that way.'

Morgan held Isabella up in her arms again and kissed her forehead. Harriet looked around them. There was a face that looked familiar, young and tear-streaked in the corner. She recognised the assistant from the scene room.

'Boyle! We are in need of your help. Fetch something to use as a stretcher and two men to carry it.' He nodded and turned to go. Harriet said more softly to Morgan: 'Let us take her back to her room, Morgan, where she may be more private.'

Morgan gave no sign of having heard, but kissing Issy's forehead again said softly to the cooling corpse, 'We shall make you comfortable now, my sweetheart. Did you hear all the shouting and Bravos? Did you hear them calling for you even when the ballet was begun? While you hurried off to see that silly man. But we must rest now, my love. Come to your room and we will make you cosy.'

Crowther waited till he was sure that he could draw the plan of the room from memory, then stepped into it. He walked the edges of the space. The arrangement of the place was not unlike Fitzraven's, though the house had none of the pretensions to civility of Mrs Girdle's establishment. A clavichord and desk. The latter was covered in manuscript paper. There were many beginnings, many scratched out or torn. On top of them all lay a sheet which Crowther carefully picked up, read and folded into his pocket.

Jocasta's fingers almost missed it. Then she paused and set her hands either side of the circular top. She breathed deep, then gave it a sharp twist. With a little judder of protest the top turned, making the bowl sat in its centre rattle in its place. The sides of the table opened up like a flower, revealing four neat drawers, shaped like petals. Two were empty. Two had rolls of paper in them, done up with string. She pulled one out and unrolled it. Writing, and plenty of it. For a moment she was still, then taking two sheets and laying them on top of the table, she curled up the others again and laid them back in the drawer. With a start she noticed the little brooch that Kate had been so pleased with. She was just reaching for it as if she was in a dream again when she went very still. Footsteps. A woman's and the front door creaking open. She looked about her. The room seemed suddenly bare and small. Her eyes caught on the door. There was a rattle of a key, a pause. The handle began to turn.

Mr Harwood himself and the leader of the band carried Isabella back to her room. Harriet followed behind, trying to support Morgan. She could hear words whispering around her.

'So much in love . . .'

'Jealousy . . . it's killed many a man . . .'

Harriet kept her head down and tried to keep the woman at her side moving forward.

When Harwood's men found Crowther he was stooped over the body in the bathtub. He lifted his head to look at them. One stepped forward and opened and closed his mouth a few times. The lad found himself transfixed. Mr Crowther removed his hand from the bathwater, and wiped it on the underside of his coat.

'Tell me,' he said.

The man struggled to find his voice, and on discovering it somewhere in the chill of his bones, did so.

The door was beginning to open when Jocasta heard a male shout in the corridor. The voice sounded thick and drunk, but she knew it as Molloy's.

'Hey, lady! Give a man a drink and a dance! They've thrown me out upstairs!'

Now a woman's voice. 'Who are you? Who let you visit here?'

'Come on, sharp-eyes! I'll sing you a waltz . . .'

Jocasta looked about her. There was a room with a bed in it just beyond. She twisted the table-top again, so the drawers disappeared inside, and tumbled towards the open door. The bowl rattled. With a silent curse, she turned again to grab the papers off the surface and dived back into the bedchamber, starting to wedge herself under the frame and trailing blankets as she heard a sharp slap connecting outside, followed by a laugh and the sound of a man stumbling. The front door slammed, and she heard the door to the main room opening, then closing.

'Freddy! You here? That whore upstairs has had another drunk in the place.' The door to the bedchamber opened wider, and Jocasta felt a body cross the bare light then go again.

'I'll throw the bitch out on the street,' the voice mumbled. Jocasta tried to breathe easy. There was the sound of the flint striking and a candle flared.

When Crowther entered Isabella's dressing-room, he found the general gloom lit by twin candles set in silver, placed either side of the soprano's head. Some manner of trestle had been set up in the middle of the room, and she lay there as if in state. Her face had been cleaned of its stage make-up, and she looked shockingly lovely in the soft white light of the flames. A sheet was drawn up to her neck. Morgan sat by her head, but did not look up from the corpse when Crowther opened the door. He saw a shift in the shadows and caught sight of Mrs Westerman sitting in a deep armchair in the corner of the room. He inclined his head and she stood slowly, and having looked a moment at Morgan, followed him out of the room and into the corridor.

'Has everyone gone?' she said, as the door shut softly behind them.

'Harwood and some of the servants will remain tonight. And there is a Constable from Bow Street at each of the entrances to the place. I understand your sister and Miss Chase left over an hour ago.'

'Morgan carried her from the scene room. The blood trail runs all the way to the wings.'

'What was her intention?' Crowther asked.

'I cannot say. I think she was become a little mad. She knew Isabella had to be on stage and took her there. I am not sure she even knew she was dead until she set her down and saw how she was covered in blood.' Harriet paused and bit her lip, then added, 'Did he kill himself?'

'We shall talk of that later, Mrs Westerman. But first there is something I must show you. Something rather strange is happening.'

He led her in silence through the darkened lobby and past Mr Harwood's office to the deserted coffee rooms that overlooked Hay Market. Mr Harwood was at the window. On seeing them come in he moved to one side without comment, and Crowther guided Harriet to his former place. She looked out. There was a crowd outside, largely silent, and any that spoke did so in hushed voices.

It seemed every class of Londoner was represented in the mass of people. There were boys in ragged coats and rag-bound feet, neat-looking servant women, standing with their arms linked. The local Watch, leathery and decrepit, rested his weight on his stick. Women in silk and men in evening dress stood in small groups, and as Harriet watched, two sedan chairs stopped and a prosperous-looking gentleman stepped out of one, and handed his respectable-looking wife out of the other. But it was not this that drew a sigh from Harriet and made her lift her hand to her mouth. The flower women stood with their baskets empty, the boys were curled up across the road cutting paper as fast as they could and putting them into the hands of the men and women who approached them. The pavement was covered in roses; all along the front of His Majesty's and ankle-deep in places, the pavement was covered in yellow roses.

# PART VII

## VII.1

*Thursday, 22 November 1781*

'MR PITHER! IF you will only look about you one moment and consider!' It was rare that Crowther found himself to be the most heated person in the room, but his patience had snapped like kindling this morning. It was Harriet, pale and leaning against the broken door of Richard Bywater's room, who managed to remain calm. Crowther was forced to consider that a night of marginal rest had managed to create some strange exchange in their characters. He was all impatience and movement; she still and speaking little. Yet she did speak now, shaking her head as Mr Pither once again, under the guise of congratulation, insisted that the investigation was complete.

'Dear sir,' she said, 'it may well be that Bywater killed Fitzraven to hide his plagiarism, or more likely in a rage on finding himself blackmailed——'

'Undoubtedly!' Pither interrupted with great glee. 'Then on hearing that Mademoiselle also knew of his treachery, and perhaps suspecting this heinous crime, he killed her at the opera house, and then himself in a fit of remorse! Mr Crowther found his confession in this very room.'

Harriet could not help noticing that Mr Pither had gained a certain fluency now he believed his case was made. She did her utmost to remember that Pither was one of the better Justices of London, but his pleasure, undisguised, with Bywater's corpse still lying before them was difficult for her to forgive. She suspected him of imagining the newspaper paragraphs dancing before him.

'Please, sir,' she tried again, 'the note Crowther found was only three words long. "I killed *him*." Not *them*, Mr Pither. My dear sir, do you not think if he had just run back in haste from the murder of Miss Marin in order to bleed to death before Crowther could get here and gain entry, he would have said, "I killed *her*"? or "I killed *them both*"?'

Mr Pither opened his mouth, but before he could restate his case, Crowther had begun to speak again.

'And the valise, Mr Pither. What man packs his belongings before slicing his wrists? Bywater's intention was to leave London yesterday, not to die.'

Pither folded his arms and stuck out his lip, reminding Harriet of nothing so much as her little boy when he was told the orchard could not be converted into a boating lake. 'He may have at first thought to flee, then decided death was an easier exit,' he said very firmly.

Crowther stepped forward to the body and lifted the chin. Harriet watched calmly, but Pither flinched. 'What of these bruises round the face? What of the empty gin bottle on the mantelpiece? I will swear to it I shall find most of this bottle in his belly.'

Pither's voice became a little keening. 'Well you might, sir. What could be more natural than to take a drink before committing such a desperate act. And the bruises may arise from any chance encounter in the street. I think your theory much more far-fetched than mine, Mr Crowther.' He attempted a dismissive laugh. It was not a great success, but he continued undaunted: 'You really think he arrived here, was forced to drink gin enough to render him insensible, was stripped, placed in the bathtub and had his wrists slashed all in the thirty minutes between the beginning of the second interval and your arrival here?'

The growl in Crowther's voice grew almost to a roar. '*Mr Pither, I suggest no such thing!*'

The Justice gave a little instinctive skip away from him.

'What Crowther is suggesting, Mr Pither, is that Bywater was killed some time before the performance, and therefore could not have been the murderer of Miss Marin.'

'But her maid Morgan says—'

Harriet continued, 'Her maid says only that she intended to meet Mr Bywater. Her note to that effect is also on the table. Perhaps he was composing a note to her to be delivered rather than keep his appointment. Morgan found Isabella dying in the scene room. She did not see who attacked her.'

'And more than that, look!' Crowther's voice was another angry shout. He rocked the body over in the tub, splashing the pink waters on his shirtsleeves. Pither lifted his chin as if attempting to see what was indicated without approaching any nearer. 'No, in all damnation come closer.' Pither gave a look of appeal to Harriet, who simply shrugged, then inched towards the tub trying to avoid the suspicious pools on the floorboards. 'His femoral artery has been severed. That was done with a knife. I'd swear his wrists were cut with the same blade. Not with . . .' he let the body fall back into the water then picked up a handkerchief from the mantel, shaking it open to reveal a bloody razor '. . . this cheap shaving kit.'

Mr Pither gave a little shiver at the sight of the blade. 'It is all bloody!'

'Yes – but in the wrong way! All smeared and pasted on, though Bywater's hand is clean. This is a performance – a trick.'

Pither peered at them. 'But can you swear, either of you, that he absolutely could *not* have died after Miss Marin?'

Crowther slammed the razor back down on the mantelpiece. 'The room was warm; the body in warm water . . .'

Harriet raised her head again. 'No one, not a single person, Mr Pither, saw Bywater at His Majesty's at *any* point yesterday.'

Mr Pither became prim, trembling a little with a glorious sense that he was regaining some control of the situation. '*That* was not my question.'

Crowther said quietly, 'I know of no way to ascertain precisely the time of death. With the wound to his leg he would certainly have died in minutes. That could have been at any time between five o'clock and my arrival here. The fire was low, but healthy.'

Mr Pither almost smiled. 'So he could have arranged to have the bath prepared. Popped out to the theatre to murder the lovely Miss Marin then back to kill himself in despair. And you cannot prove otherwise. As to the knife, perhaps he stabbed his leg then . . . then . . . threw the knife into the street, where any vagabond passing might have picked it up!' He looked pleased with his inspiration.

As Harriet's shoulders slumped and Crowther turned away in disgust, Pither continued, 'As to these strange theories of yours, you can provide neither myself nor the Magistrates at Bow Street with any suspect to interrogate, so I see no reason to regard them seriously.'

'But the *evidence*,' Crowther growled again.

'The evidence is quite clear to any reasonable human being,' Mr Pither said, his mouth pursed together like a rosebud. 'Indeed, I am sorry you could not capture Mr Bywater before he killed poor Miss Marin, but there it is. Your assistance has been invaluable. I shall instruct the Coroner and am very happy to inform the newspapers of the debt we all owe you.'

'The papers be damned,' Harriet said in the same weary voice she had used all morning.

Pither sniffed. 'Whatever you say, Mrs Westerman. Mr Leacroft's authorship of the duet will be acknowledged in due course. Or rather we will keep his name out of it if the gentleman wishes to be left alone. Miss Marin's unfortunate origins need not be exposed. She will be honoured as a martyr to truth, sacrificing love and her life so that Leacroft's work would not be stolen. I understand a number of *notable* ladies are already in the process of arranging a subscription for a monument to that effect – one has already been in contact with my wife. Now I wish you good day.'

He turned and scurried out of the place, with nothing but Crowther's black looks to follow him.

# VII.2

JOCASTA CALLED SOFTLY at the cellar entrance, half-expecting she'd have to knock loud before the boy woke up, but the bolt flew back in a hurry and before she could step back, she had Sam throwing himself against her, and Boyo yapping round her feet.

Sam released her almost at once and ran back into the dark of the workshop, hiding himself under the blankets with his face to the wall.

Jocasta came and sat by him, then pulled a fold of newspaper full of fried bits of meat from her pocket. His swift hug had made the grease run, but she divided what was there and put his share by his side, chucked Boyo some scraps and began to eat her portion.

'I thought you were dead.'

Jocasta sniffed. 'Well, I'm not. Got stuck is all.'

There was a long pause then Sam turned in his bed and began to pick away at his food. 'I was up all night.' His voice was sulky and sore.

'What are you, mother to me now, whelp?'

Sam turned his back on her again, through he took his share with him. Jocasta finished eating, balled the newsprint in her hand and said, less fiercely, 'Got it though. And Molloy came good. Got me in and saved my arse ten minutes later.'

'How so?' Sam asked, muffled and damp-sounding.

'Gave me a moment to hide when I needed it.' She looked down at the thin bones of his shoulders. 'Sorry you were scared, Sam. I was scared enough for us both, but I had to wait till Missus and him were sleeping before I could slip out, and they talked half the night. That is, Milky Boy was shouting and slurping his words. Ripley got him good and drunk at the chophouse.'

Sam shifted and looked at her with his strange, serious eyes. 'What were they talking on, Mrs Bligh?'

'I'll tell you. Reckon I met your Tonton Macoute an' all.'

Sam's eyes got wide. 'You saw him?'

'Not saw him exactly, just a little bit. Heard. Or sort of heard. Get us something to drink now, I've been breathing slut's wool all night and my mouth's too dry to tell.'

He was up and grabbing the pitcher so fast, Boyo spun a circle and barked.

Harriet pushed herself away from the wall while Crowther tried to speak a little more like himself.

'We must examine the body here, I believe. If you would care to send Harwood's men into the room, we may arrange the corpse and I can begin.'

Harriet took her cloak from the chair behind her and began to set it round her shoulders.

'I shall certainly send them in. But for myself, I have to go, Crowther. I am taking Stephen to visit James this morning. It is already a little past the hour I promised him we should depart.'

Crowther looked round at her in surprise. 'Surely, Mrs Westerman, you can have no intention of travelling all the way out to Highgate this morning?'

She paused in the fastening of the cloak and said evenly, 'I have every intention of doing so. I made a promise to my son.'

'A promise made before these people were murdered! This is nonsense.'

Harriet stiffened. 'You call it nonsense? I have a duty to my husband and son, and what could I do here? You know Bywater bled to death. You do not need me to examine his stomach contents. I have seen the room and we agree. We shall meet later in the day.'

'As you wish, madam.' His voice was very cold.

Harriet's hands fumbled at her fastenings and she said fiercely; 'Oh, don't talk to me in that tone, Crowther! Lord, I am bullied and harried at every side. Rachel, Graves, Mrs Service's concerned looks! Now you begin. You told me yourself to take Stephen. It is not his fault this blood has been spilled, and my husband is ill, and I must care for him.'

Crowther spoke with a faint drawl. 'Care for him, or *be seen* to care for him, Mrs Westerman?'

She spun towards him, her finger raised and accusing, red spots of colour rising in her pale cheeks. Crowther had the startling impression that if she had been within reach, she would have struck him.

'Do not *dare*, sir! Never for a moment . . . never *dare* question my love for my husband! Not you! There is not another man in England of half his worth, not another man better loved by his family or more valued. I would gladly give my life . . .' It seemed the air went out of her lungs. She turned away with her head down. 'Do not dare, sir.'

Crowther shut his eyes briefly before opening them again and saying, 'My apologies, madam. I spoke in haste.'

She would not look at him. 'I hope to see you this afternoon at Berkeley Square,' she said very quietly, and left the room.

Crowther turned and slammed the wall above Bywater's mantelpiece with the flat of his hand.

In his keenness to hear her, Sam seemed to have forgotten he was angry with Mrs Bligh. Jocasta wiped the small beer off her mouth, took her papers from her pocket and dropped them in front of him. He touched them gently, as if they might sting.

'What do they say?' he asked.

'Can't tell. Looks like a list of some sort, and there are numbers too. We'll go and ask Ripley and thank him for getting Fred so messy at the chophouse.'

Sam sniggered. 'Was he horrid out of it?'

'Heard him meet sharp with every stick of furnishing in the place, and all the time whining and grieving till the old bitch slapped some quiet into him.' Jocasta smiled, then went more serious again. 'He went still as the grave when the other fella came in though.'

Sam shivered. 'Tonton Macoute?'

'Maybe. I couldn't hear him. His side of it was all whispered. Mother Mitchell's voice could cut rock, though. Heard *her*.'

Sam had wrapped his arms round his knees. 'Did they say anything on Finn and Clayton, Mrs Bligh?'

Jocasta leaned forward to pick up Boyo by his scruff and set him on her knees. 'Reckon they did. From her words, it sounded like they'd decided I'd taken warning and was gone. She praised the fella for it.' She pulled at Boyo's ears, and the terrier twisted round to lick her hand. 'She sounded fat and happy. Something happened last night that made her light – as if all their troubles were neatened. Then I heard her open the table and give him the papers.'

Sam's eyes went wide. 'Did they notice you'd filched some, Mrs Bligh?'

She shook her head. 'There were bundles. I just took a few pages from the middle, is all. Then I heard *him* speak.'

'What did he say?'

'If you gave a fox or a crow a voice and told it to speak quiet, I reckon it would sound like that. He said his master thought there was a sailor might give trouble. Something about a bloke picked up on a boat what might have said something he shouldn't, so this sailor needed finding and sorting.'

'Did you hear a name?'

'Maybe. It was said lower than the rest, my mind's still trying to get its tongue round it, and my old heart was banging about so. Then Fred was promising him more papers and the crow voice was out of the place.'

Sam's face was so serious and thoughtful, Jocasta almost laughed. 'Come on then, lad, if your breakfast's finished. We got to go and see Ripley, then Molloy. Make our thanks and make our way.'

'What about the sailor?'

'We'll ask about, and them as we ask will ask too, soon as I can wring a name from my head.'

## VII.3

HARRIET HAD BEEN aware of Isabella's letters to Fitzraven in her possession and the necessity of reading them, but in the rush of the last days she had found it relatively simple to avoid the task. They had not been mentioned at the conclusion of their first interview with Miss Marin, and Harriet had assumed that a tacit agreement had been reached between all those present that they would be read and then returned without comment, unless comment was particularly called for. She had not liked to do so, however; it was a gross intrusion, and her own liking for the soprano had made the issue uncomfortable. Now she opened the package on her lap without any feeling other than a profound sympathy. Crowther had been right. The dead had no privacy at all.

The first letter was written from Milan and was a cautious note saying that she was glad Mr Fitzraven had written and she would be pleased to know more of him. Harriet smiled. She could imagine that Isabella would have wished to say a great deal more, but that Morgan had been authoritative and insisted on knowing something of Fitzraven's intentions before allowing Isabella to admit he was her father.

Harriet glanced up. Her son, Stephen, sat opposite her in the carriage in his best Sunday clothes and cradling on his lap a large model of the *Splendour*, James's last and most loved command. The model had been made for him by two of Harriet's servants at Caveley while the family were in London; both were former naval men as devoted to the boy as they had been to the father. Her housekeeper's husband, James's particular servant on all his commands, had recruited those of the crew he thought sufficiently trustworthy to people the vessel with little figures, and the little painted carvings had been sent back with letters and despatches of the Navy. The result was magnificent and had been sent up from the country some days previously with an enormous quantity of cheese, butter and eggs. These last had been welcomed with delight by the housekeeper at Berkeley Square and applauded as paradigms.

Harriet herself had sat at Stephen's side while he composed his thank-you letter to the boat-builders. He had done so with painful concentration in his own hand, and she helped a little with phrasing and mended his pen. Harriet could imagine his literary style being praised in the high stone kitchen at Caveley for days, and the little boy's pleasure being spoken about even now on the open seas. Stephen had asked if he might bring the ship to show his Papa, and after a moment she had agreed. Now he balanced it on his lap, guarding it from every jerk and dip of the road that the Earl of Sussex's suspension could not iron out, and when he was not lost in contemplation of the rigging, he peered out of the window. He looked, she realised, resolute. Harriet smiled and opened the next letter.

It must have been this note that had led to Fitzraven's commission to go abroad for His Majesty's. In it, Miss Marin said that if circumstances allowed, she would be very glad to spend some time in London. She said further that it would be a great pleasure to meet in person with Mr Fitzraven; she would meet him and listen 'with an open heart' to all he had to say, and do so in hopes of developing a fuller friendship.

Harriet could easily imagine Fitzraven coming to see Harwood with this letter in his hand — how he would have boasted of his cleverness in securing such a positive beginning to negotiations with Miss Marin. To Harwood it would look as if the prize of having the celebrated Isabella Marin singing on his stage was within his reach; to Fitzraven it would seem his luck had finally rewarded his merits and that his bastard daughter would open up a world of new influence, money and connections. And Isabella? Harriet looked out of the window, where the new buildings along Gray's Inn Road were giving way to fields and hedgerow still dewy with the early hour. Smoke reared and bent from the chimneystacks, and Harriet's fingers tapped on the paper in her lap. Isabella was a romantic. She had seen the possibility of redemption for her own fouled childhood; for her mother knocked down in the mud of the street. She had wished to save Fitzraven and call him Father, and now she lay, lost herself, in His Majesty's Theatre while the street outside silted up with the tribute of yellow roses. A touching image, but not what she had had in mind.

How had their meeting been? Isabella, trying not to be disappointed in her father. Fitzraven, finding himself on short commons from Harwood's bankers, and his daughter defended by the indomitable Morgan. It would have been indeed the moment for some enterprising agent of the French to notice him, and see a man with connections and ambition; to whom loyalty was nothing when it could be parlayed into money or influence; who wanted nothing more than to ferret out information from those who liked to have their business concealed.

To be an agent of the French would act like an aphrodisiac on Fitzraven: secrecy, knowledge, money, power – revenge perhaps on all those such as Sandwich who would not be his friend. Harriet could imagine that, if she had been in the position of an agent of the French, she would have thought him an excellent character to put to work. He would also be able to carry instructions and money from France to those already in place in London without arousing suspicion.

She looked again at Isabella's handwriting. It was graceful and flowing and used a great quantity of very fine paper. Then back in London, Fitzraven perhaps could not resist still spying for old reasons, his personal strategies, and, already having to step round Morgan, found in the affection between Isabella and Bywater another frustration. It would have been another opportunity to feel himself at first hard done by, then superior, controlling.

Stephen sat up a little straighter and Harriet realised the carriage had turned into Trevelyan's driveway. The little boy looked at her with an air of slight nervousness. She put her hand on his knee and, meeting his blue eyes with her own emerald gaze, said, 'Stephen, remember, if Papa still seems strange it is only because of his illness. He loves us. Be brave, as he would be.'

The carriage door opened and one of the footmen let down the step. Harriet was handed down first, then Stephen was lifted out, still clutching his model. The footman ruffled Stephen's hair and winked at him. The boy smiled. Harriet thought it best not to see the exchange, but was grateful then stepped smartly forward as Dr Trevelyan emerged from the portico to greet them.

Ripley was quiet for a space. Jocasta sat opposite him in the back of the chophouse and Sam was frisking with Boyo under the table.

'It's a list.'

'That, Ripley, I can see, even with no reading – *but of what?*'

Ripley put his hand up to his chin as if to try and find the bit of fluff that was starting to sprout, and twisted the paper round so it sat between them.

'These are names of boats, I think. I recognise one or two from reports of battles with the Frenchies. They're some of them written out full, some of them noted quick, like. This here at the top . . . and here . . .' his finger drifted further down the page and jabbed at another word on its ownsome '. . . these are places. Spithead and Portsmouth. Then under each are the boats and each name has a note or two. Like here – says *Pegasus*, six months provisioned, ready for sea, and here says *Repulse 64* will be ready in fourteen days.'

Jocasta frowned. 'What's the sixty-four?'

'Number of guns on the boat, I think, Mrs Bligh. And on it goes – both these pages are covered with names like that. Here's one arrived from Ireland, here's another they say on a cruise.'

'What's that then?'

Ripley shrugged and turned the paper back to her. 'When they go out and find another fella's boat and take the stuff on it. Or so I think. Naval types all go to Maisie's chophouse further up the Strand when they're about. Her husband was in the Service till he died of it, see. So I don't hear a lot of naval talk.'

'Fred comes here, mind,' Jocasta said, as she folded up the paper and put it back in her pocket.

Ripley sat back and stretched his arms. 'That's clerks not sailors. We get a fair few of them, all inky and thin and gnawing on the bones past where your dog'd leave them.'

'You did us a good turn with that Fred last night, Ripley.'

'Always glad to do you a favour, Mrs Bligh. Not that it was much of a trial. He was in here with two others and they were glowing before they sat down.' He curled his lip. 'All mighty pleased with themselves and trying to grab Sally's arse, though his wife's only been in her grave a day. I'd call him a dog but that would be an insult to your Boyo.'

'He turned mournful by time he got home.'

'Sally got sick of it and gave him a slap and an earful. He was so pissed by then he turned from up to down like a hoop.'

They paused, both examining the grain on the rough table between them. Ripley spoke up again first.

'Were there lots of papers like that, Mrs Bligh?'

'Aye. Plenty.'

Ripley scratched slowly at the back of his neck. 'It's treason, isn't it? They don't just hang you for that. If that list was meant for the French or Americans, that's cause to cut a man's guts out while he's still breathing. Legal. Have an eye to it. I heard about Finn and Clayton.'

Jocasta stood heavily and beckoned Sam over. 'You're getting awful wise as you grow, Ripley, ain't you?'

He folded his arms. 'Don't have no choice in the matter, Mrs Bligh. Anyways, I'm saying you need a sailor, one you can trust, and a high-up.'

'I know. And higher than I can reach so we'd better find a way to climb.'

# VII.4

CAPTAIN JAMES WESTERMAN got up very quickly when they entered the room. He had been reading in his armchair in the large room that was currently his home. For a moment he seemed confused about what to do with the book that he now held in his hands, then, having laid it very carefully on the side-table, he came towards them with a swift, awkward stride.

Harriet moved forward and said his name. His face brightened as she did so. She held her face to one side to be kissed but found herself instead folded hard in his arms. The strength of the embrace drove the air out of her lungs. 'Harry, Harry, Harry . . .' he said. His stubble was rough against her skin. 'You are my wife.'

She made her body as soft as possible, her voice steady, closing her hands behind his back as best as she could. 'I am, James.' His hand swam down her spine and pulled her firmly against him, pressing his mouth against her throat. Then he suddenly released her, and stepping back, took her shoulders in his hands and studied her. He was smiling widely, his eyes glittering like the water on a fair day.

'My beautiful wife.'

He then turned towards his son. Stephen had set down his model by the door and now approached slowly with his hand extended in front of him. '. . . And my boy!' Ignoring the hand, James picked Stephen up under his arms and swung him round. Harriet saw a moment of fear in the child's eyes and began to step forward, but before the thought could catch into form, she heard her son's fierce high laugh. James gathered the boy to his chest and bent over till the lad was almost upside down, giggling and struggling. James tipped him back up and threw him in the air again before setting him down on his heels and crouching down so they were eye to eye.

'And what will you be when you grow up, Stephen?'

'A sailor, sir.'

James roared with laughter. 'That's my lad! That's my good boy!' Stephen flung his arms around his father's neck and James patted his back. 'That's my good boy! And you shall have fair winds and fine battles and a pretty wife and a clever son just like me.'

Harriet lowered herself carefully into the chair James had vacated and glanced at the book he had been puzzling over. It was a child's book of simple rhymes and stories. On one of the blank pages she saw that someone had tried to write a word, then, troubled by it, had fiercely scrubbed it out and filled the page instead with angry black lines. It took her a moment to recognise the hand as James's.

He and Stephen were now examining the model of the *Splendour*. Stephen was explaining how part of the side planking came away to expose the gun decks. Each battery was in position with its crew. Stephen introduced each of the tiny figures and James nodded slowly over them.

'There is one missing,' he said suddenly, with a frown.

Stephen sat back on his heels. 'Who, Papa?'

'The Frenchman,' said James slowly.

Stephen put his head on one side and bit his fingertip. 'I have no other figures, Papa.' Then, with sudden cheerfulness: 'Might we use the cook?' He pushed his fingers into the boat and pulled out a tiny being hardly bigger than his fingernail. He looked up at his father's frowning face. 'Will it do, sir?' James nodded slowly. 'Where does he go, Papa?'

James reached in a finger through the planking and tapped a spot Harriet could not see.

'In the sick-bay, sir?' His father nodded and Stephen placed the little figure on its back. James picked up the figures on the quarter-deck one by one, examining each till he found the one with epaulettes. He lifted it level with his eyes and looked into its tiny features.

'Ha!' he said, with apparent joy, and placed his model self next to the Frenchman. Stephen watched him.

'What are you talking about with the Frenchman, Papa?'

James bit his thumb. 'He was crying. I made him cry more.' He began to sing some tune Harriet did not recognise. Stephen looked confused, but curious. James suddenly turned towards his son.

'Are you a spy?'

'No, sir!' Stephen said smartly, and lifted his chin. 'Death to traitors, Sir!' James laughed very heartily and clapped him on the back, then leaning close to the little boy and looking up at Harriet, he whispered: 'Is *she* a spy?'

Stephen laughed. 'No, sir! That is Mama. She is very clever.'

James met Harriet's eye for a moment. 'Pretty, too!' Harriet looked away.

Stephen pushed one of the gun carriages to and fro on its tiny wheels.

'I do not think baby Anne is a spy either, sir. I can't answer for her character, but she is very little.'

A slow delighted smile spread over James's face.

'I have a daughter too.' He turned to Stephen and took his shoulders. 'You must look after them, Stephen. Do not let the spies get them!' Stephen looked a little afraid, but nodded bravely. 'Good lad, good lad,' James said, rather distracted, then turned away, singing the same tune again. He brought his palm suddenly to his forehead with a slap that made Harriet jump. 'I cannot get that song out of my head. Hate it. Smells bad.'

Stephen took the tiny figure of his father from the sick-bay and placed it on the quarter-deck with the other officers and fitted the side planking back in place. James turned to watch him and put out a hand to touch the rigging. His fingers drifted down the main topgallant, and skimmed the mizzen staysail.

Stephen looked up at him and said quietly, 'What are your orders, Captain?'

'Are we provisioned and watered, Lieutenant?'

'Yes, sir.'

'Where stands the wind?'

'North-by-north-west, sir.'

'Very good.' James traced the stern with a fingertip. When he spoke again, his voice was so soft Harriet had to strain to hear it. 'You may set topsails, Mr Westerman.'


# VII.5


MOLLOY THEY FOUND in the Pear and Oats wreathed in his usual pipe-smoke — though this time when he looked up at them he gave them a leering smile that made it look as if his face would split and fall then and there.

'Come to make your thanks, Mrs Bligh?'

'I have.'

'Any profit yet?'

'Nothing but extra trouble and questions.'

Molloy pulled his pipe out from between his teeth, spat on the floor and lost his good humour.

'I should never have let you bounce me about with your cards, Mrs Bligh. Now I suppose I am to get my share of those troubles instead of coin.'

Jocasta met his eye steadily enough. 'If you'll take it.'

'Bah! Woman!' He looked about the place. A couple of men in worn coats nursed their beer at the far end of the long bar, and a young woman with nothing but a holed and dirty shawl over her stays pushed a filthy rag across one of the table-tops in the middle of the room. She was ghostly pale, and nothing in her figure or movement suggested she was much taken with the world around her. Molloy selected his places of business with care. There would be some warmth and some liquor to sit over, and not too far from the more populated places; but he needed rooms with corners enough for private conversation and where the few regulars would crawl in quiet and mind their own business, and the bright, noisy, curious or prosperous would stick their noses in only to hurry by again quick. 'Still too early in the day for my usual trade. Send that lad out for food so at least I won't starve listening to you, and listen I will.'

Jocasta took a handful of coins from her pocket and laid them on the table by her side. Sam hesitated a moment then snatched them up.

Jocasta spoke without looking at him. 'Two doors down. Samson's pie shop.' He nodded and was gone without a word. Molloy leaned back against the settle and drew a little circle in the air with the bitten end of his pipe.

'Begin, Mrs Bligh.'

Jocasta hissed between her teeth, and Molloy smiled at it. Then she looked down at the table, wet her lips and opened them. 'This girl came to see me on Friday gone, name of Kate Mitchell . . .'

Stephen was quiet when they climbed back into the coach, but seemed content.

After they had gone a little way Harriet asked: 'Are you glad to have seen your Papa, my pet?'

He nodded and touched the rigging of his model with one hand. 'He is still very strong, isn't he, Mama?'

'Yes. He is.'

'And he liked the ship?'

'Very much, I think.'

'Then I shall bring it again, next time we come.' With that he looked out of the window at the passing hedgerow, and seemed to have no further need for conversation.

Harriet thought of her discussion with Trevelyan in the hallway and tried to will patience and quiet into her blood, then picked up the last of the letters from Isabella to Fitzraven. It was only now she noticed that this one had been franked in London, and the date was only some two weeks ago. What, she wondered, would Isabella need to communicate in a letter, given she must at this time have been seeing Fitzraven almost everyday at His Majesty's? It was short and its tone was so unlike the last that Harriet's heart squeezed a little with the echo of Isabella's disappointment in the man who had sired her. Then her pulse skipped forward, and she found she was holding the paper hard enough to crease it.

'Oh, Isabella! Why did you not think to tell us, child?'

'What is it, Mama?'

Harriet looked up a little guiltily. 'Sorry, Stephen. I did not intend to speak aloud. Something in this letter has upset me.'

He frowned. 'It is not about spies, is it, Mama?'

'I fear it might be, Stephen. It might be a little bit about spies . . .'

*Fitzraven,*

*I had hoped that we might become friends, but I see no natural affection for me in your manner or actions. I hold Mr Bywater in great esteem, but I feel no necessity on commenting further on my friendship with that gentleman to you. I do not believe you have earned any right to be consulted as you suggest about who I should consider as a husband. I would not trifle with his affections by encouraging other men. And even if my heart were completely free I would not use my 'charms', as you refer to them to extract gossip or rumour military or civilian. You mistake my profession.*

*I see the people you are with and I urge you with my last duty as a daughter to cease any contact with them. Until you can assure me the activities you hinted at have ceased entirely, or were no more than figments of your imagination, your strange need to demand respect through pretended or surreptitiously gathered knowledge, rather than earn it by the manners and behaviour of a gentleman, I would ask we meet as mere acquaintances. Morgan has orders not to admit you to my presence.*

*Isabella*

'Why did she not say?' Harriet murmured.

Stephen was looking at his mother with concern. 'Mama! Are there spies coming? I am to protect you from spies!'

She smiled at him and folded the letter. 'And you do a very fine job of it, sir. Continue to patrol Berkeley Square Gardens with Lord Thornleigh and I think we shall all do very well.' Then she added, as she looked out of the window, 'My mind is playing tricks on me. I noticed some smell as we left Dr Trevelyan's . . .'

Her son sat up looking very pleased. 'Paint, Mama. The nice maid Clara was telling me about it while you were talking so *long* to the doctor. There was a man in painting and plastering, and now Clara must keep the windows open even though the weather is cold to drive off the smell. Even though it has been two weeks since he came.'

Harriet thought back some weeks to a visit to James. Dr Trevelyan had been apologising about the works in his house, though Harriet herself had been hardly fit to notice.

'You are a very fine young man, Stephen.'

The little boy shrugged and turned to look out of the window, but Harriet could see the happy flush in his cheeks. She thought about the strange tang in the air her mind had gathered and puzzled on even before she had consciously noticed it. It was not just paint, it was the fresh plaster and wood varnish too. She thought for a long moment before the picture of a room, recently seen and sharing some fragment of that odd combination of odours appeared before her eyes. The picture was of the study of Lord Carmichael. The window open in November she had noticed was to release the hanging taint in the air.

# VII.6

JOCASTA CAME TO a stop and Molloy continued chewing down on his scrag end of boiled meat for so long, she thought he was never going to come to speaking at all. Sam sat close to Jocasta.

'You know there was murder done at His Majesty's last night?' Molloy said at last, gave a loud belch and fitted his pipe back into his mouth.

She nodded. 'A lass, and her lover slashed his wrists is what I've heard.'

Molloy folded his arms together and looked mean at her.

'So it is said – and Christ, how London loves it! I saw three women out on their morning ride with yellow roses in their hair, and two fellas all lace and lavender with red ribbons on their wrists. Stupid fuckers. If they knew how a body felt they'd be less likely to make a romance of it.'

Jocasta shrugged. 'Let them do as they will. You're just fractious you aren't the man selling flowers this morning. You say it's all bound up?'

'This little troop of loveliness you've thrown a rock at, Mrs Bligh, have killed two lads and a woman. Why should killing more trouble them?'

'Maybe.'

Molloy paid some attention to his pipe till he was hidden in billows and dances of smoke. 'You are a singular woman, Mrs Bligh, and noted for walking alone. Given I know that, and you know that, will you be guided by me?'

She put her elbows on the table. 'That's dependent which way you are shoving, Molloy.'

'Good enough. Ripley's right. You need a Navy man, but one that's worth trusting. There's a few on the river that used to serve. We'll go and have a chat. And we're going to let news of the killings spread. No one takes a liking to men that pick off kiddies for sport. Maybe it'll all come apart easy. But it's good to have some angry friends at hand if the knot tightens the other way.' He switched his attention to Sam and pointed his pipe at him. 'And you, fella, are going up to those kilns.'

Sam found reason to pick up Boyo and hold him. The dog licked his face. 'Why so, Mr Molloy?' He threw a nervous glance Jocasta's way, and she caught and held it.

'Because, boy,' Molloy continued, 'I reckon if you spend some time up there you're going to find someone that saw something on Sunday when Blondie got herself killed. If your mistress weren't so used to looking to cards or her own wise self for answers, she'd have thought of that before now.'

Sam opened his mouth, then shut it up.

'The lad can come with us, Molloy,' Jocasta said.

'You scared?' Molloy kept his eyes on Sam.

''Course he's afraid. He had two of his mates picked off.'

Molloy ignored Jocasta and leaned towards Sam across the table. 'When does Tonton Macoute hunt, boy?'

'Night, sir.'

'And what is it now, boy?'

'Day, sir.'

Molloy looked impressed and gave a slow nod, then reached into his waistcoat. There was a flick of his wrist and Sam found himself looking at a folded blade that spun across the table towards him. It had a bone handle, yellow with age and handling. He set down Boyo, but made no move to pick it up.

'You can take that from me, and the dog from Mrs Bligh. Go. Come back before it gets dark and meet me or her here. Tell Sarah at the bar, you've got Molloy's word to pay with, and then stay and wait if you must.'

'Shall I, Mrs Bligh?'

'If you're willing, lad.' Sam nodded and took up the knife. He tucked it in his waistband, whistled to Boyo and left the room. Jocasta watched them go. 'Ten years I've fed that dog. He never even looks back.'

'Ha! He goes where he's needed.'

'What you give him the knife for? He's no notion of the use of it.'

'Bit of steel in the pocket, bit of steel in his spine.'

Jocasta turned back to Molloy and watched his dry, cracked face.

'What's this to you, Molloy? Why you being so helpful when there's no profit in it?'

He let the smoke slip out of the side of his mouth, till it wavered thin like a last breath. 'Maybe there will be. I've learned to take a long view in these days. But as much . . . I've got two boys and a little girl. Eldest wants to get on a boat, younger one is fool enough to fancy a red coat. The girl I'll marry to a shopkeeper and get her to tend me in my glorious age. As for the lads, bombs and bullets they'll have to deal with themselves for their foolishness in choosing so unprofitable a career. But I'll not have their throats cut by an ink-stained murderous clerk and his bitch mother, nor any fucker who goes round slicing up little kids to feed the Frenchies our news.'

He stood and pulled his cloak round him. Jocasta sat where she was and looked at him with her head on one side.

'Molloy, you tight thieving squeezing crack-faced dog. You're a patriot!'

'I used to mark you as a woman of few words, and liked you for it. Now you're running on like a wife. You going to sit there yapping or follow me to where there's business to be done?'

Jocasta heaved herself upright.

As soon as Harriet reached Berkeley Square she summoned Mrs Martin to her room.

'Yes, madam?'

'Mrs Martin, I wanted to thank you for your tact and help when I returned here last night.'

The housekeeper folded her hands in front of her and gave a quiet nod.

Harriet had wanted nothing more on returning home than to kiss her children and her sister at once, when this woman, waiting half the night in the hallway to do her any service she required, had gently drawn her attention to the blood all over her gown and hands. She had guided Mrs Westerman to her room, undressed her and wiped the last traces of it from her palms while Mrs Westerman stared into the candlelight and wept. Then, red-eyed but calm, Harriet had visited her sister and children and seen them safe more like a woman than some devil escaping hell.

'It must have been horrid, madam.'

Harriet thought of Isabella's body lying across Morgan's knees. 'Yes. It was. The stomach wound had bled a great deal.'

After a short silence Mrs Martin spoke again. 'May I ask how the Captain is, madam?'

Harriet put her hand to her neck, and pushed some thread of hair away from her cheek. She had spoken at length to Dr Trevelyan about the little scene with James and the model boat. The doctor had been encouraging, and thought it interesting that the model boat seemed to have shaken loose some memory, but was cautious as always about James's prospects of recovery. Telling Trevelyan the history of Mr Leacroft, Bywater and Isabella had been more difficult. The horror and cost of it had reared up again before her in the shock written on Trevelyan's usually calm face. She allowed herself to remember the pressure of her husband's embrace for a moment, the warmth of the breath on her neck as he said her name, and she touched her throat with her fingertips.

'Much the same, Mrs Martin. Now I have a favour to ask you.'

'Anything, madam.' The housekeeper straightened up and smiled willingly at her. She seemed to be one of those people with the good sense to put down an unpleasant thought and move away from it, treating it as one would a dog of suspicious temper. 'Since you came it's been made clear to us that a word from you is as good as one from Mrs Service or Mr Graves.'

'Thank you. But this is not something I can *order* you to do.' Harriet turned to her and spoke with a slightly brittle brightness. 'I wish to borrow some clothes from you, then have you come with me to Lord Carmichael's house.'

The woman lost her smile, looked a little stunned and gave a mumbling assent, then turned to leave the room. Her hand on the doorknob, however, she seemed to reconsider and turned back towards Harriet.

'May I speak my mind, madam?'

Harriet kept the bright tone as if she might win her point by sheer good humour. 'Do, Mrs Martin.'

'I mean no disrespect, madam, but I think you have in mind to pass for a servant and get into conversation with Lord Carmichael's household. I need to tell you, I don't think you'll pass, madam. Not even if you dress in rags.'

Harriet frowned. 'You think I cannot adopt the proper tone?'

'I think you have no notion of the manner of it, madam. How could you? And if you wish to talk to the people there, I know a better way. The beau of Susanna, maid at the house on the opposite side of the Square, he's a footman at Lord Carmichael's, and there would be nothing strange about me popping in to give him some message or other on my way to elsewhere.'

Harriet thought at first to protest, but something in the calm certainty of the young woman made her falter. Instead she said: 'What is your suggestion?'

'You and I can go in the carriage together. Drop me a little out of the way and I'll swear if it can be done, I'll come back with what you need. Now how's that, Mrs Westerman? And no need for you to be seen playing at being a servant as if it's a holiday.'

'It is a better idea, Mrs Martin.' Harriet hesitated. 'I hope I did not insult you with my request'

The woman paused. 'I am not in a position to take offence, madam. You are as good a mistress as many and better than most, I think. But your feet don't touch the ground in London much between carriage, chair and porch, do they? That restricts your knowing.' She folded her hands in front of her again, and became once more the model of an efficient servant to her house, as if the hand of some

301

deity had passed across her face and masked her from the world. 'You'll wish to be leaving now, madam? I'll have Slater fetch the carriage round.'

Harriet nodded and looked down at the hem of her dress. It was perfectly clean and coloured pale. In the country she could never manage more than half a day without kicking up mud and dust and tearing the thin fabrics on brambles as she went about her estate. How much easier it was to keep decent in Town, for all the blood she walked through.

The river was as crazed with noise and traffic as the Strand. Dozens of wherries with an oarsman or two and little nests of passengers in the stern rowed back and forth across the water. The men held their hats in place and tried to look at ease, while the women pulled their skirts tight around their ankles to keep them out of the wet. Along the river, great merchant ships waited to unload their goods or see to their provisioning, making the Thames a winter forest of masts and ropes.

Jocasta and Molloy went along the banks as best they could, each stopping and talking with whomever they could hold on to by the arm for enough time to get a word and a story out. The faces of those they spoke to looked grim and angry, then like as not they shook their heads and carried on. It took hours, and Jocasta was ready to curse Molloy for a fool and wring the neck of the next fella who pointed to the ships — as if a merchant seaman would do her any good — till a youngish man who wore, with a swagger, a neater coat than most, said, when his headshaking and teeth-sucking was done: 'Try that way, if that's your liking, mate. If I hear Proctor tell me one more time about the great heroes of the sea he's served with, I'll break my oar over his back. You'll find him down along by the by the Black Lyon Stairs — works there with his nephew, Jackson.'

Jocasta twitched Molloy over with her finger. In turning, he slipped a little in the mud and snapped at the man who steadied his arm.

'We have a beginning,' she said.

'At last,' Molloy grumbled, with a bitter and bitten look. 'Though they would point us back all the way we've come and a step more. I don't like water. Never have. I was built to travel on land.'

'I'm of your mind. And the bank stinks worse than the Shambles. Our way lies along it though, so watch your step or the River Gods will grab you and drag you down to drown you.'

Harriet was feeling rather content with herself by the time she and Mrs Martin had returned to Berkeley Square. Mrs Martin had been greeted as a celebrity in Lord Carmichael's kitchen, bringing as she did selected gossip of Crowther and Mrs Westerman's investigations. She had been there a good while and was a little apologetic on returning to her seat in the carriage.

After relating what she had learned, she added quietly; 'I am sorry, ma'am, but I did speak of you coming home last night with Miss Marin's blood on your dress. It is the sort of picture the cook there reads all the true confessions of Newgate for, and it turned her most confiding.'

Harriet immediately reassured her. 'Mrs Martin, you have been wonderful, and I have no argument with you.'

They carried on together to the workshop of a Mr Prothero as a result of the information Mrs Martin had won from the household, and the little shock of Mrs Martin's earlier reprimand was salved by Harriet's own performance as a rich and chatty wife. When the carriage steps were let down in Berkeley Square again therefore, Harriet was most satisfied.

She was keen to share what she had learned, and it was not until she was opening the door to the library that she remembered she was very angry with Crowther. He was standing in front of the fire when she came in, leaning more heavily than usual on his cane. He turned towards her, his expression uncertain. She paused on the threshold.

'Mr Crowther, do you admit that you are at times a cruel and vicious-tempered cur?'

He bowed towards her. 'I cannot do otherwise. Mrs Westerman, I have been trying at various points throughout this long morning to think how I can apologise for my words.'

'Have you indeed? That must have been very unsettling for you.'

'It was.'

Harriet entered the room and closed the door behind her. There was a silence.

'It would appear nothing appropriate occurred to you,' she said finally.

'I fear not.'

Harriet opened her mouth to protest, then, seeing Crowther looking up at her hopefully, found herself surprised into laughter.

'You are beyond hope, Crowther! Though Lord knows, your manners have never given much cause for optimism.'

He nodded his agreement and shifted his weight off his cane. Those intimately acquainted with him might have noticed a look of relief and satisfaction cross his face in a breeze, but Harriet was too eager to share her findings of the day to take particular note, and not another being in London would have seen it.

'Lord Carmichael had a fair amount of work done on his study a little under a month ago, Crowther.'

'Indeed? That *is* of interest.' Crowther took a seat in the armchair that had by custom become regarded as his own. 'How did you discover this, Mrs Westerman?'

Harriet looked uncomfortable and began to walk her usual route back and forth in front of the fireplace. 'I have to admit my first plan was to dress rather more simply and go and present myself at the kitchen door and ask for work and generally get into conversation. However, Mrs Martin convinced me that any London servant would know me as a fraud at once. So I left that end of the business with her.'

Crowther raised his eyebrows. 'Remarkable. After what you told me this morning, I believe that means you have listened to that young woman's advice now twice in the space of a few hours. It seems she is unique in the household.'

Harriet frowned at him and he looked innocently up into the air. She continued: 'I then visited Mr Prothero, who co-ordinated the works for Carmichael, under the guise of possibly employing him myself. I laid emphasis on the fact that my dear husband has fears of security in London, and he informed me that he had recently built a number of secret compartments into the study of "a certain gentleman of rank" to conceal particular items from casual thieves or safe-breakers. He spent a long time admiring my husband's foresight, which was a little wearing. But I believe Mr Palmer would be very interested to hear of his work, do you not think?'

'I do,' Crowther replied. 'The study, you say?'

'Indeed. Mrs Martin learned that the household were not allowed in the room until the works were complete. Mr Prothero, however, spoke of how his workers created two concealed spaces "convenient for the storage of papers or jewels", behind some Latin texts, and behind a false front of a marbled fireplace.'

'Mr Palmer will, no doubt, be grateful for the specifics.'

'Yes. I feel Mrs Martin and I have done the work of a squadron against the French today.' Crowther noticed a certain degree of self-satisfaction in Harriet's face, but as her mind moved on, it slipped away and her expression became serious again. 'Also, I think Isabella knew rather more of her father's involvement with some unsavoury business than she was willing to tell us at first.' Drawing Isabella's last letter from her pocket, Harriet handed it to him before seating herself opposite. Crowther rested his cane against his thigh to take it and read for a few moments in silence.

'I come to you having examined her body,' he said. 'I wish she had thought to share this with us before.'

Harriet's mood darkened a little further. 'I must take my portion of blame for that, I fear. Perhaps she expected me to read these letters in a more timely fashion, and unpack her concerns on my prompting. Did you learn anything more from her poor self?'

Crowther shook his head. 'Nothing but that she died far too young and in the full bloom of health. Though I had some thoughts as to the shape and form of the knife used. It is consistent with that used on Bywater's thigh. Speaking of his body, I believe the damage to the femoral artery was given when he was already in the water. A sort of *coup de grâce*.'

'And the wounds on his wrists?'

'They could easily have been made with the same instrument. But the wound on the thigh gives a better indication of the size and shape of the blade; it matches the wound over Miss Marin's heart quite precisely.' He set the letter down on the table beside him. 'To complete my report, I note there were no marks of attempt on the wrists, and the cut was made along, not across the radial arteries.' He glanced up and caught her look. 'Most suicides who use a knife, at least those I have examined, make lighter cuts at first before learning what proper pressure is needful, and while they summon their courage. It is also more common in my experience that they cut across the wrists. The blows that killed Bywater were unhesitating and accurate.'

They were both quiet a little while, before Harriet said softly, 'We are convinced that Bywater killed Fitzraven.'

'I am sure of it. I do not think that line he wrote could have any other meaning. But I remember what he said to me that afternoon in the British Museum – that he did not put him in the river.'

Harriet sat down and put her chin in her hand, the better to listen. 'Tell me a story, Crowther. What could have happened here?'

He picked up the cane again and began to turn it between his palms. 'Firstly, I believe that Fitzraven hinted to Bywater that he knew the secret of his inspiration. That meant Bywater went to Fitzraven's room to find the extent of his knowledge and his intentions. Fitzraven named a price for his silence that was too high, or else used his knowledge to vaunt himself over the young man. Passions ran high.

I would be surprised if Bywater went there with the intention to kill. The room told the story of an argument. There were some bruises just fading round Bywater's wrists.'

Without standing, Harriet crossed her thumbs, trying a stranglehold in the air. Crowther set his cane aside long enough to lift his own hands, curled, in front of his throat as if to resist a throttling ghost. Harriet nodded and sighed and touched the hair at the nape of her neck.

Crowther continued: 'I believe that later that day, one of Fitzraven's associates in the pay of the French came to see him and, finding him dead and fearing Fitzraven's death might expose him to more scrutiny than he wished, he cleared the place of anything that might implicate him, and disposed of his body – hoping for the case of a disappearance rather than a murder.'

'Very well,' said Harriet, returning her chin to her palm and beginning to rap at her skirts with her free hand. 'So why not just be still thereafter? Why the murders of Bywater and Marin?'

He looked at her silently, and watched as a light of comprehension crossed her face, and, crashing after it like wind behind the rain, a sort of horror that dulled her green eyes. She sat up straight.

'Oh, Crowther! Did *we* cause this by our involvement?'

'I do not know, Mrs Westerman. But suppose you are the man who disposed of Fitzraven and you see that the investigation into his death is pointing towards Mr Bywater. Further suppose that you suspect that Miss Marin knows something more than she should of your activities. I would not be at all surprised if Miss Marin, in her rather distracted state after her visit to Mr Leacroft, betrayed both facts, unwittingly or not, to those who might have been watching her . . .'

Harriet spoke slowly, letting the thoughts unfurl even as they moved across her lips into the receiving air between them. 'You decide it is safer for your enterprise that Bywater should kill himself rather than be subject to arrest and trial, and arrange it so. An admission of guilt, and no living man to say that he neither disposed of the body nor took anything from Fitzraven's room.'

Crowther began to spin the cane again; it gave a soft regular *thrupp* across the fibres. He carried on her thought as if it had been his own. 'In the process, you learn that Miss Marin has arranged to meet him in the scene room.'

'The second bird flies into your hand.'

'Indeed, Mrs Westerman. And we see how readily the law, at least in the figure of Mr Justice Pither, is convinced everything is neatly tied.'

Harriet stood and walked over to the window, where the daylight was already beginning to weaken. She wrapped her arms around herself and swung from side to side. A neat little curricle went barrelling past, containing a party of young people laughing and urging the flush-faced young man driving to increase his speed.

'Crowther, this is a bold and bloody mind! Is Carmichael man enough to do such a thing?'

'Perhaps, but I have always thought him a sneaking sort of beast – one well-versed in secrecy and covert business – but this smacks of a decisive forward stepping intelligence I do not see in him. Am I right in assuming you think Harwood guilty of no more than a sharp nose for business?'

'That is so. His distress last night was palpable. I believe he loves his opera house. Beyond his human sympathy for Miss Marin and Bywater, I think the scandal washing over his place of business was horrible to him.'

'I would agree, so I must look around the place for another figure of authority, a man ready with his knife . . .'

The door swung suddenly open and Stephen stumbled into the room, followed by Lady Thornleigh, who was laughing and telling him to wait. Harriet turned round with a frown.

'What is it, young man?'

'Sorry, Mama. I just had to say, I sang Papa's tune to Susan and she knows what it is.'

Harriet sighed and smiling, turned to Crowther. 'Forgive me, Crowther. James was troubled by a returning melody this morning during our visit. Perhaps knowing the name of it will give him some relief.' Then, getting up from her seat and crouching to be on a level with Stephen, she prompted, 'Tell me then, my dear.'

It was Susan who answered. 'It's just funny, Mrs Westerman, because it is the same tune that Mr Crowther sent over *very* early this morning on the scrap of paper. It is "*Sia fatta la pace*", Manzerotti's favourite aria.'

Crowther's cane came to a sudden stop. 'I sent some of the manuscript from Lord Carmichael's study, but it was untitled. Is that what it is, Lady Thornleigh?'

'Yes, sir. But Mrs Westerman, I am surprised you did not know it yourself when the Captain sang it to you. Did you not hear it last night? It is his last aria.'

Harriet swallowed and answered calmly, 'There was no Third Act last night, Susan.'

The young girl blushed and looked down. 'Of course – Miss Marin. I am stupid – I forgot. She was so lovely.'

Crowther stood and walked over to her, setting his cane very firmly in the space between them. 'Lady Thornleigh, can you explain to me exactly to what degree are the aria and the man interlinked.'

Susan considered carefully. 'As near as they can be, sir. I do not think anyone who knows any music thinks of Manzerotti without hearing that tune, and no one hears that tune without thinking of Manzerotti. It has been popular here some time, and always with the notation that it is as sung by him.'

She looked nervous. 'Did we do right to come and tell you?'

Harriet put out her arms and hugged both the children to her, briefly and fiercely.

'Very right,' she said. 'Very right.'

They had neither of them noticed that Susan was carrying a neat roll of papers in her hand.

'Oh, and here,' she said, holding them out with a slight blush of pleasure. 'Mr Crumley and I have finished the pictures.'

As soon as the children had been sent back out of the library, Harriet stumbled through a more detailed account of that morning's visit with James and his play with the boat.

'The song came to him as he spoke about the Frenchman in the sick-bay. He said . . . he said . . . Oh, Crowther, I think my husband may have tortured that man to get that song from him!'

Crowther did not look at her. 'It was a hard engagement, I think, was it not?'

When Crowther looked up he saw there were tears in her eyes and she was biting her lip. 'Indeed, the French Captain struck their colours, then fired again. Only when he was killed did they surrender. When James's First Lieutenant spoke to me, he was still so enraged by it he shook.' She was looking at him with a desperate sort of appeal in her eyes. Crowther would have been glad to tell her he thought it impossible that James would have resorted to abusing a prisoner in his care, that whatever the battle or the stakes involved he would have behaved righteously, but though he hardly knew Captain Westerman at all, he knew something of men. He offered her the only comfort he could.

'I am sure Captain Westerman thought only to serve his country.'

Harriet choked slightly and put her hand over her mouth.

'Mrs Westerman, we must make use of these pictures.'

# VII.7

JOCASTA LIKED THE look of Proctor as soon as she laid eyes on him. He was taking shelter from the weather in a lean-to close to the Stairs, smoking his pipe with concentration and knocking the ashes out on his stool from time to time as they approached.

He saw them coming and kept them under steady observation, then, having heard all they were ready to say, called out to a much younger man who was still jostling for trade across the river further down the Stairs.

He asked them to repeat what they had just said in the younger man's hearing. They did so. Then he stroked at his massive beard a while, ending by giving it a good hard tug as if his hand was trying to pull his mouth open and get the words out by main force.

'Man I'd want to see in your shoes is an old Captain of mine. Not that he's old himself, and he's in London now, which few of the good ones are, what with the Frenchies and the Americans getting all roused.'

He went quiet again. Jocasta was content to wait him out, but Molloy was getting pulled out of shape with the stopping and retelling.

'Why don't you name him then?' he said, with a narrowing of his eyes.

Proctor knocked out his ash again. 'Poor bloke got hit on the head, and he's gone kind of simple now, it's said. So I hesitate to trouble him with you.' He cast an eye towards the younger man at his side. 'Jackson, I called you here to answer a question, and the question you must answer is this: what do you reckon to handing out his wife's name? She's a smart woman and her husband was known and liked enough, so she'll know a face or two at the Admiralty.'

Jackson lifted his hand to stroke where someday his own beard might grow. 'Pither had her in to look at the body, didn't he? And she didn't look a fool to me. Her, or that bloke she had with her.'

'What body?' said Molloy with quick interest.

'We found a man.' Proctor pointed into the middle of the river with his pipe. 'He was drowned but tethered. Heard him named as Fitzraven, someone from His Majesty's, is the talk.'

'And this lady came to look at the body? Nice entertainment,' Jocasta said.

'Not sure as it was for a pleasure. She seemed to have some concerns with the business.'

Jocasta folded her arms across her chest. 'The opera house? Seems to me this is the lady we need to have words with.'

Proctor and Jackson looked at each other for a long moment, till Proctor turned back towards them and, like a barrelled mirror of Jocasta, crossed his arms as well.

'I can't tell you where she stays at,' Proctor said, 'but her name is Westerman, and the fella she had with her was called Crowther. That help you?'

Molloy looked a little confused and wondering for a second, then began to laugh. He let out a 'Ha!' Then another one. Proctor frowned deeply, and Jackson crossed his arms as well, looking dark.

'I do not take it kindly, sir,' Proctor said in a low rumble, 'that you see that name as an occasion for mirth.'

Molloy wiped his eyes and held up his hands as if to protest. 'No lack of respect, Mr Proctor. None at all.' Then he straightened up, slapping his hand on his thigh. 'Never met her, but know her. Know Mr Crowther too! Never met him neither, but I know him. Know where her friends are!' He turned round to Mrs Bligh, his grin showing off his three remaining teeth like tombstones set in front of a cave. 'What you say to that, Mrs Bligh?' He shut his mouth and his laughter dropped away like a lock emptying. 'What's up, lady? Seeing ghosts again?'

Jocasta's mouth was dry as slate in summer. 'That's it. That's the name.'

'What name?'

'The sailor they had their eye on to do harm. Westerman.'

Molloy grew serious. 'It all bundles up together now, don't it? When you said a sailor was in trouble I thought you meant some bow-legged fool who had staggered in the wrong direction searching out his grog. This is a matter of a different stripe.' He rubbed his nose. 'For one thing, they are rich and inclined to be grateful. We need to find our way to Tichfield Street, and smartly so.'

Proctor had stood; his face was red and his beard seemed to stand out from his chin.

'What can be done?'

'Clode! Lord, as I live, Daniel Clode! What – has Sussex run dry of lawyerly business for you?'

Graves had burst out of the back of the shop with long strides as soon as he heard his friend's voice enquire for him, and now destroyed the space between them in a moment, throwing his arms around Daniel's shoulders and slapping him so hard on the back, it would have wounded a lesser man.

'Graves! I thought I'd find you here. Let me go, man, I'm stinking with the road. I'm just this moment out of the stage-coach and seeing the hour, thought it better to call here rather than at Berkeley Square.'

Graves stood back and looked at his friend as if he were a miracle walking. Clode was a remarkably handsome man with large brown eyes and a face that seemed sculpted more than grown. If he knew what advantages nature had given him in this way, he never showed any sign of it though. Graves had never seen him respond to any of the soft feminine looks cast openly upon him, unless they came from the eyes of Miss Rachel Trench. A look from her was worth the compliments and favours of all other women, it seemed.

'But why are you here? Why no notice of your coming? Is there some problem at Thornleigh Hall?'

Clode looked a little shy. 'No, everything is in order in Sussex, and the rebuilding progresses. I was summoned here by Miss Trench and by young Lady Thornleigh. They seemed to believe you might wish to negotiate the purchase of this shop from Lord Thornleigh's estate. And I am here to see you do not rob yourself or your future father-in-law too far for the children's sake.'

Graves looked sorry for a moment, then laughed. 'Lord, I am plotted against on every side. Everyone insists I should be happy. But I am very glad to see you, co-conspirator that you are.'

313

'Miss Trench said something in her note about her sister and a murder?'

Graves shrugged and turned to a pile of scores on the counter. They were the latest edition of the 'Yellow Rose Duet'. On the title page of each, the name Bywater had been crossed out by hand, and replaced with *Composition of a certain Gentleman*.

Giving up on ever getting the corners square, Graves spoke over his shoulder. 'Yes, Mrs Westerman and Crowther surround us with bodies and horrors again. I can see why Miss Trench might have some need of your support, as well as wishing to see Miss Chase and I properly bound up and established. I do not see what drives them . . . There must be something more to the case, as I cannot think with the Captain so ill, Mrs Westerman would involve herself in such a business for mere amusement.'

Clode smiled, showing an almost unnatural number of good teeth. 'Be comforted, Graves. Mrs Westerman would not do such things without an excellent reason.'

Graves turned back to him and folded his arms. 'You are too trusting a person to be a solicitor, Clode. I fear for the children's fortunes in your hands. But perhaps you are right. You will be a breeze of good sense and clean air among us.'

Clode made a sharp bow, clicking the heels of his boots together as he did, then said more gently, 'But what of the Captain, Owen? Has he improved?'

Graves sighed and wiped his hand across his brow. 'The improvement is slight, but steady. I understand from Stephen that he was both calm and affectionate in his manner this morning, if still rather erratic or childlike in his speech.'

His friend stepped forward and put a hand on Graves's elbow. 'Then I'd say the improvement was considerable.'

Graves looked into his friend's open face above him, saying, 'Was it very bad when he first came home, Daniel?'

Clode nodded and turned away a little before replying. 'Past endurance. He was vicious, hardly rational, horribly demanding and dangerous when thwarted. Mrs Westerman and Miss Trench had so longed for him to return, but when he did it was dreadful. Lord, Owen! If Crowther had not found Trevelyan, it might have become necessary to intervene to keep the children and ladies safe. Did you know their footman and groom at Caveley had twice to forcibly lock their master in his chamber to save Mrs Westerman's neck? These are men who had served with him, who had entrusted their lives to him, now forced to confine him in his own home. Equally I saw him at moments when he was no more than a little strange, but still friendly, affectionate to his children. Stephen, however, I think he must have struck at some point. No boy should flinch in that way when his father approaches. No mother should look so fearful when her son and husband come together.'

Graves was quiet a long while. 'I had no idea it had been so serious.'

'Yes,' Clode said. 'And of course, if during any of his more apparently lucid moments he had sold the estate for less than you keep in your pocketbook, it would have been very hard to retrieve it. There – you see? I do speak like a lawyer from time to time.'

'Was that likely?'

Clode nodded. 'One afternoon he attempted it. He tried to sell the estate, his wife and his children for enough money to buy a horse and cover his expenses to regain Plymouth and the *Splendour*. He even had some of the necessary documents about him. It seems he had sense enough to gather them up when his servants and family refused to have his horse saddled and concealed the cashbox.'

'What happened?'

'He made the offer to Michaels at the Bear and Crown who is a better man than most, and smarter.'

'Yes, I remember him. He refused the offer, I assume?'

'No. I would have done, and I'd have been a fool to do so. Michaels knew that the next man the Captain had the ear of might not be so

315

scrupulous. He gave Westerman money and a horse, took the papers and shook hands with him, then sent word straight back to Caveley. Mrs Westerman's servants restored her husband to her the following day. He did not resist. Indeed David, the coachman, was convinced he had already forgot his purpose and was merely happy to see faces with which he was familiar. Michaels said he had been desperate when he had seen him to warn the crew of the *Splendour* that they had a spy on board and England was teeming with more of the same.'

Graves shook his head. 'Good God. To have the person you love best re-delivered to you, but in such a changed manner. I had no idea . . .'

Clode clapped him on the shoulder. 'Enough! This is too serious a welcome. Come – smuggle me into your home so I may make myself respectable and greet the ladies of your household looking like a gentleman.'

Mr Tompkins was delighted to see Harriet and Crowther, and spent the time it took to walk from Mrs Girdle's to Gladys's house telling them so, when he was not remarking on the terror of an audience with Gladys's mother, Mrs Spitter. The lady was a tyrant, according to his report: fierce in her opinions, final in her judgements and occasionally crushing in their delivery.

'She loves Gladys, though,' Tompkins admitted. 'She'd kill anyone who ever troubled that girl. Funny thing that she is.' Bearing this in mind, they sent up their cards and were swiftly shown into a pleasant parlour on the first floor. The room had generous windows overlooking the main street and by the fire was a low circular table with neat striped settees on either side. The whole gave the impression of modest prosperity, sensibly enjoyed.

Two ladies rose to greet them. Mrs Spitter was a woman of generous proportions with a firm jaw and shoulders that would have made her a Grenadier if she had been born a man. The lines of her dress were certainly severe, bodice and skirt striped purple and black, but what made her appearance a little eccentric was the quantity of jet with which her person was adorned. Three great ropes of glimmering stones hung around her neck, her fingers were hidden to the knuckles with black lozenges, her wrists bristled with beads, bangles and bracelets all pitch polished. They gave her a sort of dark glow. Harriet was sure that in many of the less frequented places she had visited on the globe, Mrs Spitter would, on first sight, have been acknowledged as some Goddess of Revenge or Queen of the Underworld, and Harriet for one would not have thought the natives unwise in their choice.

Next to her stooped a girl whom Harriet guessed to be twenty-five at the most. She was all milk to Mrs Spitter's tar. Her face was not unpleasant, but rather blank, and her mouth never seemed quite shut, while her eyes looked and blinked at the company with an air of mildly curious surprise. She was so pale her complexion seemed tinged blue, and her hair was blonde but very thin and weak. Her gaze picked out Mr Tompkins and she gave him such an open-hearted smile of welcome that Harriet found herself oddly touched.

It seemed Mr Tompkins was a little at a loss as to who to introduce to whom, so simply opened his mouth once or twice and shut it again. Mrs Spitter started to raise her eyebrows, which Harriet guessed to be an unhappy sign, so she took a step forward towards the lady with her hand held out. Something about this matron suggested to her it would be best to state her business with the minimum of flummery.

'Good afternoon, Mrs Spitter. Thank you for receiving us. We would like very much to talk to Gladys about her angel.'

Mrs Spitter's eyebrows descended and she smiled. Harriet thought of a dragon folding its wings.

'You are Mrs Westerman, and that man next to whom Mr Tompkins is bobbing about like a cork is Mr Crowther, I suppose.'

'Quite so.'

Mrs Spitter looked Harriet up and down with great care, then took her hand and shook it firmly. She indicated the unoccupied sofa and, as her visitors seated themselves, said, 'You could wear jet with your colouring, Mrs Westerman. Gladys, of course, could not. But I have seen redheads carry it off to great effect.'

Harriet sensed that this remark was a sign of approval and gave her thanks, and promise to consider it with great seriousness.

'Mr Tompkins,' said Mrs Spitter in a tone that suggested he had *not* been recommended to wear jet, 'tells us you have been looking into the business in that house out back.'

'We have. And we have some pictures to show Gladys, if she is willing to see them. We wish to know if we have caught a likeness of her angel,' Harriet replied, and looked at Crowther.

He produced the sheets Susan had given him from his pocket and passed them to Harriet without comment, sensing that this conversation was to take place exclusively between the women. Harriet passed them to Mrs Spitter. The lady turned to her daughter.

'Gladys dear, attend to me.' Gladys's attention seemed to wander a second then with a slight wobble she turned her face towards her mother and blinked at her. Mrs Spitter patted the girl's knee. 'Now I wish you to look at these pictures and tell me if you know the people here.'

She held the papers in front of Gladys, showing her each one in turn. Gladys appeared to be delighted to look at pictures, and examined them with interest but no apparent sign of recognition in her expression. Mrs Spitter lowered the pages and asked, 'Do you know any of these people here? I mean, have you seen any of them before? Think now, child. Answer as best you can for your mama.'

Gladys picked through the papers in her mother's hands and pulled one out with great care, her tongue caught between her teeth as she did so.

'This one?' her mother asked. She was answered with a swift nod. Harriet tried to decide who was most likely to be on the page as it turned. Despite Manzerotti's tune, she was so convinced the picture would be that of Lord Carmichael that when Mrs Spitter turned the paper and she saw the familiar picture of Bywater, she was more disappointed than she thought she had capacity for. After a moment she looked at Gladys.

'Gladys, may I ask you a question?'

The young woman bobbed her head happily. Perhaps more importantly, Harriet caught Mrs Spitter's almost imperceptible nod from the corner of her eye. 'Thank you. Now can you tell me when you saw this gentleman? Was it the same day that the angel took Mr Fitzraven away?'

Gladys bobbed her head again and then said in a perfectly fluent voice, but rather high-pitched and rushed, 'It was a walk day. When I have seen both of the cats from Mrs Pewter's on the roof, but not together, and three birds have sat on each of the chimneypots of Mrs Girdle's house, that means *God* wishes me to walk down to the corner and back three times and pay very close attention to everything I see. Sometimes He tells me to go in the morning. Sometimes I have to wait until afternoon. *God* made me wait that day till it was afternoon. Five minutes past three o'clock by the big clock in the upper parlour which *was* my nursery but is still *my* room where I listen to *God*, and He instructs me.'

Crowther was looking with fascination at the young woman. Mrs Spitter was perhaps used to seeing her daughter's eccentricities mocked. While Gladys spoke she was looking very hard at Crowther – indeed, such was the force of her gaze that the jet about her throat seemed to quiver. When her daughter paused she addressed him very fiercely.

'Mr Crowther, perhaps you find my daughter's communications with the deity amusing?'

Crowther shifted his attention to the mother, looked at her for a long moment, and blinked.

'I rarely find anything amusing, Mrs Spitter. I am not a religious man, but I am convinced we are all unique. If the deity wishes to communicate with us, I see no reason to suspect He would not communicate with us all in unique ways.'

Mrs Spitter stared a moment longer while she considered this comment, then her face and form relaxed a little and she went so far as to bestow on Mr Crowther a faint smile. She motioned for her daughter to continue. The girl did so, plucking at the folds of her dress a little with small unconscious, regular movements.

'As I was coming back the second time from the corner, two hack carriages and a wagon passed me by and after the wagon, that gentleman crossed over the road and I saw his face for he was looking out for further passing vehicles and he walked up ahead of me and turned to the left at the top of the road just as the butcher's boy was coming down towards the house. I saw twenty-three horses in total without turning my head, fourteen coming towards me and nine going away, so more coming than going – so that meant *God* was pleased with me and I had understood *His* meaning, and on entering the house I might sit at the window with the picturebook and turn a page every time a bird landed on Mrs Pewter's chimneypot until I could count fourteen candles in the windows then I might go to bed. And I did that well too, even though I had to wait a long time after my supper was taken away because I saw *His* angel come and take *His* servant away – and that is a very special gift from *God*.'

Harriet tried to stop herself from looking at Gladys's little hand plucking away at her dress. She noticed the fabric there looked a little worn. Mrs Spitter gently laid her fingers on her daughter's wrist. The hand was stilled at once, and the girl looked up at her mother with a grateful smile.

'Indeed it is, Gladys,' Harriet said. 'Tell me, when you went to the window with the picturebook, did you see Mr Fitzraven in his room? We think this gentleman in the drawing you have shown us was going to visit him.'

The girl shook her head rather violently. 'I did not see Mr Fitzraven until *His* angel came to fetch him. He was sitting at his desk making his own picturebook when *God* told me to go for my walk. But he was not there when *God* told me to come back.'

320

Crowther frowned. 'The corner is not far away. If you saw Mr Bywater arriving, walked your path one more time then returned here, his visit must have been very brief.'

Gladys looked at her hands. 'If the man in the picture is Mr Bywater then his visit lasted not more than twenty-three minutes. It does not take that time to do the walk, but I had to wait, and Mr Bywater, if that is his picture, was one of the persons who released me.'

Harriet leaned towards her a little. 'I'm sorry, my dear?'

'When I have finished my walk I must wait very quietly with my eyes down until three pairs of shoes have gone by in front of me. Sometimes I have to wait a long time, particularly if the weather is dirty, and sometimes when people see me waiting they walk a ways away, then I cannot see the shoes, even if I hear them, and that does not count. I was released by a lady who I did not see the face of, by Mrs Little who is not little but very nice and always makes sure she walks where I can see her too, for I have told her about what *God* wishes and she always wears black shoes and white stockings not very much muddy, and by him.'

'Are you sure it was him?' Harriet asked. 'Only seeing the shoes?'

'Yes. I had already seen his shoes and his buckles so I knew them again. Then I looked at my pocket-watch and it was seventeen minutes from the moment I had to wait, to the moment he crossed past me, and that was six minutes from when I saw him first. When were you born?'

'I was born on the eighteenth of April, Gladys.'

'What year?'

'Seventeen forty-eight, my dear.'

'Thursday. A blue day. I like Thursdays.'

Gladys turned and looked very directly at Crowther. It took him a moment to realise what was being asked of him before he said, 'The twenty-seventh of July, Miss Spitter, in seventeen twenty-nine.'

'Oh, a Sunday which is green, and the best day! Mr Tompkins

was born on a Monday which is the colour of,' she pointed very carefully at the stripe on the settee on which she sat, 'this.'

'I see,' Harriet said, somewhat amazed. She kept her voice soft. 'But you do not see the angel in the pictures?'

Again she gave a violent shake of her head. 'No. None of these are *His* angel. But this one . . .' she merrily plucked the picture of Manzerotti from the pile and pushed it towards them '. . . he *looks* a little like *His* angel. And he came in earlier, before I had my supper.'

Everyone was very still. Mrs Spitter said to her daughter, 'Dear, will you tell us what you saw of this gentleman.' She tapped Manzerotti's picture, and the jet on her fingers clicked.

'Yes, Mama. It was between the seventh picture and the eighth. I saw that man in Mr Fitzraven's window. He waited by the window a second and looked down. Then he went past, then two minutes later he walked back. Then a long time after supper there was a candle lit in the room and I saw *His* angel pick up Mr Fitzraven to carry him to heaven. Perhaps *this* gentleman was a lesser angel come to see where the *great* angel should come to later, for there are many sorts of angel in heaven all ready to do *His* will. But even if he was an angel he was not Fitzraven's angel. *God* let me see Fitzraven's angel only after the fourteenth candle was lit.'

Crowther swallowed and said carefully, 'Gladys, what do great angels wear? Do they wear bright colours? I think I would expect to see an angel in gold or silver . . .'

Gladys leaned forward very eagerly. 'No, not at all. I thought *His* angels would be dressed in gold too, but no! *His* angel dresses all in brown. This colour,' she added helpfully, tapping the knee of the astonished Mr Tompkins's breeches. 'Which is also Saturday, but only the mornings.'

Harriet turned to Crowther in astonishment. He gave a twisted smile in return. 'We did not ask Mr Crumley to draw Johannes, Mrs Westerman.'

Harriet was a little angry to find Crowther's interest was as much awakened by the strange condition of Gladys Spitter, rather than by the revelation of her angel.

'We must have Mr Crumley draw Johannes too, if one of us has a moment to give the description, do you not think so?' she said, as they mounted the steps towards the door of Berkeley Square. 'Then I think we must ask Mr Palmer's advice. Surely he must have the power to employ the King's Messengers and press the Bow Street Constables to service. We have done all we can. Bywater murdered Fitzraven, Manzerotti is the spy-master, and Carmichael most likely the channel through which information flows. Probably he is making use of his poor stepson to carry information to France even now.'

'Yes,' Crowther replied with a slight drawl, 'I suppose there was no "mutual acquaintance" in Milan. Manzerotti realised Fitzraven would be of use placing him at the heart of society in England, and sent him to France, then England to warn Carmichael of his coming and prepare for it.'

'I would like to see in what hand he writes music. That fragment of "*Sia fatta la pace*" you found in Carmichael's study was likely his signature and seal. Well, now we may return to the usual pattern of life, though we have very little we can say against Manzerotti. His activity in this, all we can lay at his door at this point, is caught in two rather lost and searching minds and that scrap of music.'

'I would pay a fair proportion of my fortune to have that young woman's brain under my knife,' Crowther replied.

He was spared the commentary of Mrs Westerman by the flinging open of the street door and a great number of voices telling them all at once that Daniel Clode had arrived and they were all very pleased to see him. The principal descended the stairs with a smile and a blush at all the fuss his arrival seemed to be causing, and Harriet gave him her hand with great pleasure. She glanced at her sister and saw a bloom on her that made her both happy for Rachel, and perhaps a little jealous. Crowther's retreat was prevented by Mr Graves none too subtly closing the front door before he could escape.

'Excellent! Let us dine. You too, Mr Crowther – you will be part of the party if you like it or no. And Mrs Westerman, a man left a message for you during the afternoon. It is that Mrs Wheeler's friend will call during the course of the evening – if that means anything to you.'

Harriet acknowledged the message and made her way upstairs to dress. The light had almost faded from the day.

Molloy put all his weight behind it and released a thunderous knocking on the door of Adams Music Shop.

'Open up! Open the door, damn your eyes! I see a light in there and I will not stir from here till I have speech with you! Now open the door!'

Jocasta had made her way to Tichfield Street via the Pear and Oats and came up to join him now at a brisk pace, with Sam and Boyo at her heels. As she reached his shoulder there was a stir of movement in the shop and a young woman's face appeared at the window.

'Jane! It's Molloy here. Open up, girl!'

She did quick enough and held the door open with her foot, her hands being occupied with holding and guarding a candleflame. At the doorway to the parlour behind, Mr Crumley appeared patting his mouth with a napkin.

'Molloy! What do you want here?' Jane said. 'I know for a fact there isn't a person here owes you a penny.'

'I need to know where Graves is. And better yet, Mrs Westerman's address in Town, if you know it.'

Jane scowled at him. 'Of course I know it, but why should I tell you? What you got to say to either of them?'

Molloy breathed hard. 'I hate to make it habitual but I've a warning and it touches on Westerman. You know me as a serious type, Jane. Do I look like I'm playing the fool to you?'

The girl made her decision quickly and stepped back into the parlour, leaving the door ajar.

'Wait there.' She returned with a handful of coins and thrust them into Molloy's hands. 'Berkeley Square – number twenty-four – and use this for a hack. Mrs Westerman's in the same place.'

Harriet heard the knock at the door as she was finishing dressing, and expected her sister to come in when she issued the invitation, but was surprised to find it was Daniel Clode who had entered the room.

'Mr Clode!' she said, and dropped the comb she had been fastening her hair with in surprise.

The young man hesitated a second, then stepped into the room, shutting the door behind him.

'Mrs Westerman, forgive the intrusion, but I wished to have some private conversation with you. I have been speaking to your sister.'

Harriet turned back carefully to her mirror and made another attempt with the comb. 'If it is regarding an engagement with Rachel, you know you have my hearty approval, but I had hoped you might wait, given the state of my husband's health, before speaking about that.'

He took a step further into the room. 'No, it is not that. But I suppose it touches upon it.'

Harriet finished with her comb and turned towards him. The candlelight made the red of her hair glint as if it had its own fire. She never powdered it when they dined at home. 'If you come to bring further weight to bear on me regarding my behaviour, I wish you would not trouble yourself. The business, it seems, is successfully concluded. We have, we think, found who is responsible and will inform those who need to be informed this evening. There our involvement in the matter will end.'

'No, not that either. Really, Mrs Westerman, if you wish to know what I have to say, it would be as well to let me speak!'

Harriet was silent.

'Thank you. It is simply this. Miss Trench has, I feel, placed far

325

too much weight on what damage any totally unreasonable remarks may be made from the steps you have taken in this, and in previous matters.' He blushed and looked at his boots. 'Madam, I have the honour, in relative youth, to be one of the men trusted with the affairs of one of the great estates of the country. I handle many legal and financial matters for the estate of Thornleigh.' He lifted his hands and said with a sigh like a man abandoning a prepared speech, 'Really, Harriet, you could dress as a heathen and ride a donkey from St James's to the Pulborough Hotel and you will do *me* not one ounce of damage. As long as my association with Thornleigh continues, I shall have to spend my best efforts avoiding the kindnesses of every person of quality in the neighbourhood, rather than searching them out. Rachel underestimates the force of the Thornleigh name, seeing it embodied in Jonathan and Susan rather than in the estates and investments held in their names, and I have just told her as much.'

The image of herself dressed as a heathen and the loving exasperation in Clode's voice drew a laugh from Harriet. 'Oh Daniel, I thank you. But I fear I may be an awkward sister to have. Graves would probably agree with Rachel. He was angry with me yesterday.'

'Nonsense. Well, perhaps. But know this: Owen would defend you and your actions to the bitter end. To you he will voice his concerns, but if anyone else spoke of you in terms of less than respectful admiration, he would horsewhip them. As would I.'

Harriet felt a warmth creeping through her body. 'And what of the damage I do my daughter?'

Clode grinned at her, and Harriet almost wished herself young again. 'I understand Lady Thornleigh herself has given you her own assurance on that point.'

Harriet stood and placed her wrap around her shoulders, then crossed the room to take his arm. 'You are perfectly correct. Clode, I am glad you are here.'

'I hear the Captain improves.'

'It changes from day to day. This morning he was well, but last week he called me a whore and a spy and drove me from his room.'

'I am very sorry to hear that, madam.'

She sighed then patted his hand. 'But in general, I believe he improves. Now take me down to dinner. In a few hours all this shall pass away from us and we may concentrate on more suitable occupations. Crowther suggested at one point that if I couldn't sit still, perhaps I could devote my energies to writing religious tracts.'

'Dear God!' said Clode. 'I presume he was trying to read his paper at the time?'

Harriet laughed again.

'I've never ridden in a carriage before, Mrs Bligh.' Sam knew the urgency of their journey, but the novelty of watching the streets pass at such a pace was too bright a thing not to be loved and held tight.

'Do not . . .' said Molloy from his corner, and briefly removing a toothpick from his mouth '. . . get used to it.'

Jocasta allowed herself a half-smile in the darkness. 'Tell Molloy what you found today, Sam.'

'Yes, do. And give me my knife back.'

Sam passed it across with some reluctance. Molloy looked at the blade and tucked it into his waistband.

'Not stuck any malefactors with it then, I see?'

Sam lifted up his chin. 'Maybe I just wiped it after, Mr Molloy.'

'Ha! You improve upon acquaintance, young one. Now tell me who you found.'

Sam settled into the corner of the coach. 'There's a boy spends time round the kilns. Gets pennies off them for bits of work, and sleeps there most nights for the warmth. He'd seen it. Said it was the woman what did it. Raised the rock and brought it down hard.'

'And the rest.'

Sam rubbed his nose hard on his sleeve. 'He said he started peering because he heard them arguing like. When he looked, he said the girl was pulling away and shaking her head, but Fred was holding on to her hand and being all pleading and that's when Mrs Mitchell picked a brick up and struck her.'

'Did he not think to tell anyone?' Jocasta asked.

Sam wrapped his thin arms around himself. 'He was scared. Ran away for a few days, but it's cold, so in the end he went back. He's littler than me.'

Jocasta felt a pang of memory tickling her throat and thought of the rainy fell all those years ago, her trembling and confusion. She hunched her shoulders in the shadows.

'You got a name for him? A promise to bide where he is?' Molloy said.

'Yes, sir. He is called Evan. And I gave him the rest of the sugar cane the cobbler's wife bought for me, and a promise of another if he waits till I come again. He'll bide for that'

# VII.8

THOUGH THEY DID not as yet know the particulars, the household realised that Harriet and Crowther's investigation into the affairs of His Majesty's Opera House had reached some sort of conclusion. That, and the arrival among them of Mr Daniel Clode made for something of a holiday atmosphere as they went in to dinner. It was one of those rare moments when it seemed everyone in the company was looking at each other with satisfaction and affection. The women, from little Lady Thornleigh to Mrs Service, looked beautiful, the men handsome and wise.

'We received cards from Mr Harwood, Mrs Westerman,' said Graves, pushing the game pie towards her over the tablecloth, and spilling gravy onto it in the process. 'Manzerotti is to give a benefit tomorrow night, and all profits of the occasion are to go to the Foundling Hospital in Mademoiselle Marin's name.' Harriet helped herself to the food, but made no immediate comment. 'I suppose,' Graves continued, 'that it is a civilised gesture. But it seems terribly quick.' He examined the air in front of him, full of candlelight. 'Perhaps they were afraid the town's supply of yellow roses and paper would have become completely exhausted, were they to delay any longer.'

'Perhaps,' Harriet said mildly, and allowed herself to watch Clode and Rachel for a moment. Clode was talking to Crowther, or rather listening with furrowed brow as he encouraged Crowther to talk, and Rachel was making some remark to Mrs Service about the egg dishes, made with the latest consignment from Caveley, but their delicious consciousness of each other was touchingly clear. Harriet had a slight pang for Lady Thornleigh. The little girl loved Rachel dearly, but was likely to become rather quiet when Clode was in the room.

There was a sudden knocking at the street door, so loud it could not be ignored and conversation around the room fluttered to a halt. A door in the hall opened and closed and a voice, cracked and raised, bounced its way along the corridor and into the room.

'I don't give a damn if he's at dinner. I need him now and I'll have him!'

Lady Susan leaped excitedly to her feet. 'It's Molloy!' she said, and ran to the double doors at the bottom of the table and threw them open. The party turned to see the man himself in the doorway, tall and slightly stooped in his greasy hat, occupied in knocking the hand of one of the footmen off his sleeve. Beside him stood a woman of middle age and comfortable stature. She wore a skirt made from a patchwork of many pieces of coloured material; blues and green mostly. There was something of the gypsy about her, though her colouring indicated an Englishwoman. As they stared, from behind her emerged a little boy of about Susan's age, holding a grizzled terrier in his arms.

'Mr Molloy! How do you do?' said Susan happily. 'And you have brought friends with you.'

Molloy touched the brim of his hat to her and, letting his eyes trace the faces in the room, said to Susan, out of the corner of his mouth, 'How do, Your Ladyness.' Susan giggled. 'Now can you tell me, sunbeam, which of these gentlewomen is a Mrs Westerman. I have some business touching on her.'

Harriet stood up, her wrap settled in the crook of her arms. 'I am Mrs Westerman.'

Molloy nodded to her. 'I am Molloy, and though Graves there will tell you gladly I'm not normally allied with respectable company, he'll also tell you I have a useful bone or two in my frame.'

Harriet looked over at Graves. He folded his napkin and gave her a slight nod, saying, 'It was Molloy here who gave us a warning when it was most needful last year. He has made no attempt to capitalise on the help he gave as yet.'

Molloy's face crumpled with a frown. 'Don't think I won't yet, son. I save my favours and maybe add to them, is all.' He turned his attention back to Harriet and, perhaps a little belatedly, took off his hat. 'This Mrs Bligh here,' he jerked his thumb behind him at the woman in the patchwork skirt, 'has heard a man wish danger on a sailor called Westerman. Might that be your husband, ma'am? Some matter of treachery and information. Mention of the French with whom we are all at odds.'

Harriet felt very cold; she sensed the eyes of her friends on her. Crowther looked shocked and the muscles in his jaws clenched. Graves and Clode were intelligent men; she could almost feel them shaking up the incidents of the last days and weeks and seeing them settle into some pattern that chilled them. 'It might.'

Jocasta stepped forward and the patchwork on her skirt rippled as if the individual fragments of cloth remembered when they had been in elegant rooms like this by wax candlelight, and were inclined to dance again. 'I was where I shouldn't have been, ma'am, for reasons there's no need to waste air on the telling of. He's a serious fella, this man – he said his boss wanted Westerman quieting, had heard he might know something he shouldn't. Thin. Was wearing brown each time we've seen him, and I think he's done for two little friends of this boy in my care and through my fault. Voice like a dove being throttled. Works by night. It's dark now, and he don't seem a man who delays. Is your man here?' She was looking into the faces of the men round the table. None of them looked simple, or like a sailor to her eyes. 'Can you guard him?'

Harriet steadied herself on the table. 'Johannes. James. Highgate.'

There was a moment of silence, then Graves was suddenly on his feet and hallooing the household together.

'Don't bother with the carriage! Mounts for four! At once.' The footman stood back from Molloy and hurried off. 'Mrs Westerman, go and change your dress. Miss Trench, help her. Clode! There are a pair of pistols in the study. Susan, go look to the children. Mrs Martin?' The housekeeper appeared swiftly in the doorway. 'Would you take Mr Molloy and his friends to the kitchen, please, and see they are fed.' Graves then turned to Crowther. 'Sir. I presume you will ride with us?' Crowther nodded, then as the party dispersed, calling for cloaks, boots and horses, Crowther turned to Mrs Service.

'Might I trouble you to spend a few moments with me in the library, madam? I have some information I should like you to pass on to a friend.'

Harriet had flung herself into her riding clothes and was coming back down the stairs before a very few minutes were over. The street door was open, and already the horses were saddled and waiting. They seemed to have caught the urgency in the air and were stamping on the ground and shaking their great heads. Graves and Clode stood in the entrance hall, checking their pistols and then sheathing them under their coats. Crowther emerged from the library and took the riding cloak that was offered to him without comment. Harriet's last image of the house, fleetingly caught as she was lifted up into the saddle and took the reins, was of the dinner-table still laid. The candles and crystal, the food, and silverware all fine and shining.

# VII.9

Mr PALMER HESITATED as the library door closed behind him some little time later. Instead of Mrs Westerman or Mr Crowther he saw sitting in front of the fire a thin, elderly woman with steel-rimmed spectacles and a workbasket on her knee.

'My apologies, madam. I believe I have been shown into the wrong chamber,' he said, and began to retreat.

The lady put down her work. 'No, Mr Palmer. I have news from Mrs Westerman and Mr Crowther. Manzerotti, the castrato at His Majesty's, seems to be the lead of the French intelligence activities in London. Lord Carmichael is the conduit through which the information travels to France, and Johannes is his pet killer and fixer. Oh, and I am Mrs Service.'

Mr Palmer was at a loss for words.

'Perhaps you should sit down, sir, and I shall elaborate,' Mrs Service said with an encouraging smile, and touched a bell at her side. Mrs Martin appeared in the doorway. 'Port for myself and Mr Palmer, if you please, Mrs Martin. The gentleman has had a shock. And if our friends downstairs have finished eating, perhaps you might invite them to join us.'

Some months later, Rachel asked her sister what her thoughts had been during the ride to Highgate. Harriet lied, saying that she remembered little of it beyond her growing physical exhaustion and her continual calculations of how many hours of darkness would have elapsed before they could reach Dr Trevelyan's house and James. In truth, though she had awareness of both of these, it seemed that during her ride through the darkness she had seen a steady progression of images, a storybook of her husband since their first meeting. She felt that each view was being held up before her eyes like the pictures Mrs Spitter had shown Gladys. She would have said it seemed like the pages of her life being turned in front of her. She could not stay with the images she loved, or avoid those she did not. Their progress was inevitable: with each thundering phrase of her horse's hooves they changed and demanded she see and acknowledge.

There was his face, the first time they had met, her impressions of the line of his throat, the light in his eyes when he talked of the sea, then strange, but exciting, later a trick of movement on his face that would become so familiar; the sight of him in shirtsleeves at the chart-table in his cabin, dividers in hand, his smile when he saw her enter. His grey pallor, the stubble on his chin and throat as he supported her by the grave of their first child who lived but a few days under a foreign sun, the expression of hope and belief when he put the key to Caveley in her gloved hand. Even as her fingers gripped the leather of the reins, she felt its weight. She thought of him with Stephen in his arms, looking at the baby as if he were some miracle. You would have thought to see him smile that no man had ever had a healthy son before. Some images were soaked in sea air, some drenched in some taste, sensation. His first kiss came back to her, joyous, clumsy and full of a new and unnameable longing; she bit her lip.

The hooves thudded beneath her, the cold November air drenched her. Then, as they reached the open road, she saw his face altered almost beyond knowing by bitter confusion and frustration; felt the crack of the back of his hand across her face a week after he had returned to Caveley. The pain had been such that for a moment the world shattered into fragments, her vision run over with hot white filigree, but worse than that was looking up from the ground where the force of the blow had thrown her to her knees to see him impassive, empty of any feeling, watching her and waiting for her to rise. Such had been her shock, she had simply stood and left the room, and could have been found only a few minutes later at her desk reading over some of the estate correspondence and apparently her usual self, while black panic and horror washed back and forth in the craters of her mind.

Mr Palmer turned the pages Jocasta had just given him over in his hands. It was as serious as it possibly could be.

'And there were more like this?'

Jocasta was seated on the settee dealing and redealing her cards with a soft steady slap onto the upholstery beside her.

'Two bundles – like that, as far as I could tell. Reckon there will be more tomorrow. Fred seemed eager to please the thin fella, the one with the voice like a crow.'

'Tonton Macoute,' said Sam. He was lying curled on the hearthrug with the dog beside him, watching the flames. Mr Palmer looked up with a slight frown.

Molloy would not sit, regarding the fine furnishings with suspicion as if he thought they might tip him out again if he took the chance of denting them with his narrow behind. Instead, he had leaned his thin frame into the corner on the far side of the mantelpiece with his cloak wrapped round him despite the fire. He had his pipe on the go, permission to light it having been politely asked of Mrs Service, and whole-heartedly given. 'It's the name the street children have given him, him having picked off two of theirs,' he said. 'Creole name for the Bogey-man. Mrs Westerman named him as Johannes.'

Mr Palmer nodded slowly, reading the papers again. The information was accurate and current. The force of His Majesty's Navy with detailed notes on the location, armament and provisioning of each ship of the Channel fleet. If the bundles were more of the same, it could be all the ships available to His Majesty would be described in this way. There were notes here too about the current problems some ships were having with their new copper sheathing. As yet, the French knew only that the coppering of the hulls made the ships faster. If they discovered the weaknesses they also brought with them, especially in the Indies . . . Mr Palmer shuddered. These were not musket shots, but heavy guns. If Manzerotti had the reputation for delivering matter of this sort, no wonder the French Intelligence Officers had been rubbing their hands and toasting themselves in Paris. Then he frowned and looked again at the drowsing boy.

'Do I not know you, Sam?'

The lad stretched and looked up, the light warming his thin face. 'You gave me a shilling once, sir. For bringing a message.'

Jocasta's cards slapped softly on the table-top. The pictures were almost hypnotic: Cups, Swords, Coins. Mr Palmer thought of the papers that would pass through a clerk like Fred Mitchell's hands. He could gather the lists of the ships, but these notes on the copper sheeting were something else. 'Do you think, Mrs Bligh, that Fred has been working alone at the Navy Board?'

There was no pause in the rhythm of the cards. If they were telling her anything, she did not share it. 'Maybe. Though Sam and I have seen him leaning in close with a couple of others. And they were all free-spending and over-bright at St Martin's chophouse last night. One has a face like a freckled fish. The other is a fleshy pudding of a man. Lips always wet and his wig stood up as if it's leaping off his head. Wouldn't shock me to hear he gathered from them too, by their looks and manner.'

'I know them. One is another of the clerks. The other is my personal secretary. You have good eyes, Mrs Bligh.'

'I've grown practised at seeing,' she replied, without looking up from the cards.

Sam settled himself again and pulled at Boyo's wiry mane, saying, 'Maybe you should have given them more of your shillings, Mr Palmer, rather than me.'

Before Crowther could dismount, Clode was already at the top of the steps of Trevelyan's porch and hammering at the door. The doctor himself opened it, looking at first angry, then amazed. He saw the party racing towards him.

'Mrs Westerman . . . ?'

'My husband.'

'In his rooms and quiet, I think.' But she had already pushed past him and made for the stairs. On the first step, she stumbled. Crowther stepped forward to catch her elbow before she fell. He glanced over his shoulder. Clode and Graves had taken up positions at the foot of the stairs and were pulling out their pistols. As he did so, Graves was speaking to Trevelyan.

Harriet threw herself up the stairs and Crowther followed her. Ahead of her he could see the door to James's room. A slight breeze stirred the drapery around an open window on the landing. She fought forward, lifting her skirts to move faster along the corridor.

As her hand touched the wood of the door, Crowther heard a fierce grunt from within; the door swung open and he saw James bent double in Johannes's arms. The latter's right arm was over James's back, his left under his stomach. Harriet screamed.

Johannes looked up at them, his face as white and smooth and expressionless as the first time they had seen him. Giving a cry, James yanked the knife from his own belly and drove it into Johannes's thigh. The assassin twisted and swore, rolling James onto the floor. He heaved the blade from his leg and limped towards the window. Harriet fled to her husband with a groan. Crowther fell towards Johannes, wrapping his arms around the ankle of the dragging, injured leg. Johannes turned and hissed, then brought his right leg back and kicked hard at Crowther's throat and jaw.

There were footsteps and a shout outside; Crowther felt his world dissolve into a red mist. His grip slackened. There was an explosion and the taste of gunsmoke in the air. Then the world left him.

The first face he saw on waking was Clode's, looking down pale and breathing hard.

'Thank God, Crowther! I feared he'd killed you.'

Crowther managed to turn his head a little. 'The Captain?'

Clode moved slightly to one side. Crowther could see James's body lying a few feet from his own. His torso was hidden by the figure of the doctor. Crowther could hear the sound of fabric being ripped and folded. Harriet was kneeling on the far side of her husband, holding his hand between her own, looking down at him and whispering. Graves was at his feet holding his legs as they jerked spasmodically. Crowther could see the pool of blood inching towards him. The world went dark again.

When next the room swum towards him he was being helped into a chair. A brandy glass was held to his lips. The first sip he took, the next he pushed away. The Captain had been lifted onto his bed. Harriet was seated at his head with her hands on his arm. She looked as if she had been carved from ivory like the figures the Westermans had brought back with them from their stations abroad. On the other side of the bed Trevelyan sat with his head in his hands. Graves was leaning against the door. It was Clode who was still holding the brandy glass to Crowther's lips. He turned his head to look at him and a spasm of pain tore through the surface of his brain like a knife through wet cloth.

'Did you kill him?' he said in a whisper. Clode shook his head.

'I think I may have winged him as he went through the window,' he said softly. 'And Graves loosed another as he fled, but his aim is appalling. I made a quick survey of the grounds while you were unconscious and found his horse, but no sign of him.'

Crowther struggled to his feet, pushing away the arm that tried to support him. He hobbled towards Harriet and stood behind her, looking down at the Captain. His eyes were open, and fixed on his wife. His breathing ragged and terrible. Crowther put his hand on Harriet's shoulder. She lifted her own hand and let it rest on his for a moment, without taking her gaze from her husband's face.

Crowther crossed to Trevelyan with a firmer step, leaned in close and spoke to him a moment, then, trying to fight down the nausea and bitterness which rose in his throat as he straightened, approached Graves.

'Clode can stay here. We must return to Berkeley Square. You need to bring the Captain's children to him, and I have business to attend to.' Graves nodded, and Crowther looked again at Harriet. She had turned towards him. Her face was calm, and her voice distinct and clear.

'Gabriel, do not let him live.'

'You have my promise, madam.'

She nodded, turned back to her husband, and Graves opened the door.

As he mounted his horse, the pain made him gasp. Graves looked at him in concern.

'Can you ride, sir?'

'Yes.'

'There was a rope. I think he intended to make it seem a suicide, but our arrival surprised him into action, or the Captain was too strong.'

'What is the hour, Mr Graves?'

The younger man removed his pocket-watch and consulted it. 'A little after midnight, sir.'

Crowther urged his mount into a trot and they began to ride at a pace into the city and the cold dark morning.

# PART VIII

*Friday, 23 November 1781*

ONLY THE YOUNGEST children slept. Graves found Susan and Rachel in the latter's chamber drinking chocolate and saying little to each other. Rachel, after Graves had told them what had passed, went calmly to wake Stephen, and Graves for a moment took her place by his ward.

'Susan, my dear. This will be another heavy day. And you have had too many in your life.' The girl did not answer but curled her hand around his own. 'How would it be, my dear, if, as soon as it is light, you send a note to our friend Miss Chase and ask her to come and sit with you today? Miss Trench should be with Stephen and her sister.'

Susan looked up, searching his face for signs of awkwardness or distress. 'I should like that very much, Graves, if it does not trouble you. She and I may look after my brother and Eustache.'

He returned the pressure of her hand, fear and love for her drenching him like a hopeless tide. 'It does not trouble me. I think I must learn to swallow my pride a little and accept the care I am given.'

'That would be much more sensible of you. You ask Jonathan and me to accept all you do for us without thanks. It is unfair of you not to do the same.'

He lifted her small hand to his lips and kissed it. She shuffled into his side and laid her head on his shoulder.

'You are growing, little woman.'

Rachel returned. She carried baby Anne sleeping on her shoulder, and led Stephen, white-faced and confused, by the hand.

'Graves, Stephen wishes to bring his model of the *Splendour* with him. I said we should enquire if there is room enough.'

'Papa likes it.'

Graves got to his feet. 'Yes, of course you must bring it then.' He crossed to the little boy and picked him up in his arms. 'Susan, will you fetch it and bring it down?' She nodded and scudded out towards the nursery. Graves felt Stephen's arms link behind his neck and he began to carry him down to the waiting carriage.

'Did the spies attack Father, Mr Graves?'

'They did, Stephen. Now Mr Crowther and his friends will hunt them down.'

'Tell Jonathan I am sorry not to be there when he wakes. Sometimes he has bad dreams.'

'I did not know that, Stephen. Thank you. I will see he does not wake alone.'

Once Rachel and the children were comfortable and the model safe he stood back and looked at his coachman.

'Are you armed, Slater?'

'Yes, sir.' He shifted his seat to show the pistol at his side. 'As is Gregory.' The footman on the carriage with him touched his hat as he was named.

'Good,' said Graves. 'If any footpad tries to delay you, shoot him.'

Mrs Service met him in the hallway. 'Do go in, Mr Graves. Mr Palmer, who seems to be the man behind it all, is in the library with the rest. Mr Crowther has told us what has passed, and now I feel my duties must return to the domestic. It seems there will be a quantity of people coming and going today, and very few of them through the front door. I must speak to Mrs Martin and the servants. How is Susan?'

Graves leaned against the wooden panelling of the hall as he replied, his hand shielding his eyes from the lamplight. 'I have told her to send for Verity Chase as soon as she may.'

'Good,' said the little woman and began to move away.

'Mrs Service?' She turned back towards him. 'You are very calm.'

She let a smile hover over her lips. 'I save my vapours up, like Molloy saves his favours. Go in, sir. We all of us have work to do this day.'

Harriet knew quickly that there was no hope that Trevelyan could offer. Having seen her husband made more comfortable with laudanum and cold presses, she dismissed the doctor to see to his other guests, disturbed by the noise and hurrying. Clode did not leave the room, but retired to a chair by the fire and angled his face away.

James's eyes fluttered open. 'Harry?'

'Here, my darling.'

'I fear I am leaving you again.'

She could not reply to this, only wrap her warm fingers round his palm. It seemed colder to her now than a few minutes before. 'Harriet, I know I am not what I was . . .'

'That is not important, James.'

He breathed a little raggedly, then closed his fingers tightly around her own. 'But Harriet, tell me . . . before . . . It was a good marriage, was it not? I always thought of it so. I remember loving you . . .'

Harriet's voice struggled up through the darkness in her throat. 'It was a good marriage, James. Very. You made me happy.'

'I am so glad.' His eyes fluttered closed again, and Harriet watched his chest rise and fall, listening for a carriage on the gravel.

'Then we are decided?' said Mr Palmer. There were nods around the room. 'I thank you for your hospitality, Graves. I must, however, appear at the office if we are not to frighten away our birds, and I must meet quietly with Lord Sandwich. Mr Crowther will coordinate our activities during the day. I shall take control in the evening. There are four messengers I trust to be discreet. Graves, how far can you trust your people?'

'I recommend them without question.'

'Very well. I shall summon my people.'

He stood up and there was a general stir in the room. Palmer put his hand to Crowther's shoulder and leaned into him. 'Sir, it would be a great boon to the Crown, and the prosecution of these traitors, if Johannes was brought into my custody alive. I believe Molloy and Mrs Bligh have certain . . . forces to draw on. I wish to question the man myself.'

Crowther looked at him down his long nose. 'I am aware of that.'

Palmer chewed his lip. 'I am glad. Johannes will not move from whatever hiding-place he has found in daylight. No doubt his fear and need will drive him back into Town this evening as we close on Lord Carmichael and these creatures of Mrs Bligh's discovering.'

Crowther looked over his shoulder at Jocasta, Molloy and the little boy. 'That is the consensus.'

Palmer turned towards the door, saying, 'But I note you make me no promise.'

Crowther did not reply, and Palmer met the fate of any man who had tried to stare him down and left the room, shaking his head.

Rachel knocked lightly on the door, and on hearing Harriet's quiet, 'Come in', ushered Stephen in, in front of her. Clode came immediately towards them, and Daniel had just enough time to take the model from the little boy before he charged across the room and into the arms of his mother. She held him for a second, then seeing that James's eyes were opening again, addressed her boy.

'Stephen! Stephen, my love, look at your papa.'

The boy struggled to hold his head against his mother, his eyes tightly shut.

James managed to open his lips. 'Stephen,' he coughed fiercely.

The boy flinched but feeling the gentle pressure of his mother's hand managed to turn his body a little and open his eyes. James smiled at him, and without apparently knowing he did so, Stephen loosed his grip on his mother's waist and smiled shyly back.

Harriet could not quite bear to look at her husband. She knew how great his pain must be, she could see it in the fine lines around his eyes, the furrows of his forehead. She wondered what part of his mind was serving him now, causing him to try and shield their son from that pain. It spoke a finer understanding than any he had shown since the accident.

'Thank you for coming to see me, my boy.'

Stephen forgot his fear enough to move away from Harriet entirely, and put his small hand on his father's massive wrist.

'I brought the model for you, Papa.'

'Thank you.' James's eyes travelled the young boy's face with a sort of curious wonder. 'Let it be put where I can see it.' Clode dragged one of the side-tables to the opposite side of the bed and set the *Splendour* on it. If James noticed or recognised Clode himself, he gave no sign. Only, when the boat came close enough for him to see, he gave a great sigh. Stephen seemed to feel the lack of his attention.

'I found out the name of the song, Papa,' he said, and sang a line or two in a quavering falsetto. 'It is called "*Sia fatta la pace*". Manzerotti sings it.'

James kept his eyes on the ship, but opened his fingers to take his son's hand in his own. 'Manzerotti. Yes, of course. Thank you, Stephen. It does not seem as important now.'

Jocasta was back on the sofa dealing the cards by the time the first of the King's Messengers returned. 'It seems you were right, sir,' he said, shifting his weight from one shoe to the other as he spoke to Crowther. 'Fred Mitchell came out to take the air at lunch, and I saw him meet with Mr Palmer's secretary at Whitehall. Then he high-tailed it back to his place in Salisbury Street. I'd swear his jacket pocket sat smoother when he came out again.'

'Very good,' Crowther replied, without looking up from his writing. 'But your information came from that lady,' his quill pointed out to Jocasta, 'not myself.' The Messenger cleared his throat and looked uncomfortable.

'Yes, sir.'

'What further?'

'There was a boat taken from a pitch at the bottom of One Tun Alley on Thursday night. Or at least, something queer went on. Fella who owns it came to it in the morning and found the ropes done up wrong and a hearthrug shoved under the bench.'

Crowther lifted his eyes. 'What became of the rug?'

'The man took it home to his woman, and she weren't too pleased to let it go again.'

'And now?'

'The thin lady in the kitchen, Mrs Service, took it from me, sir. Before she showed me up.'

'Excellent.' The man did not leave. Crowther waited.

'Thing is, sir, seems like there's a funny mood abroad – down by the river and over the streets. Can't put my finger on it, but people are on edge. As if they're watching and waiting. There's something going on. I haven't seen so many people with that look on them . . . I've never seen it, sir.'

Crowther looked at him impassively. 'I understand you, sir. You have done very well. What are your further duties?'

'I am to wait near Lord Carmichael's, sir. Discreet like, till I am called for.'

'Then do so.'

The man backed out of the room. As the door shut behind him, Jocasta stopped laying her cards and studied Crowther from under her brows. The ceasing of the regular beat of her cards disturbed him and he glanced towards her.

'Wasn't sure of it last night, but now the daylight's on you, I know you.'

'Do you, madam?'

'Ask me where I was born and when.'

Crowther laid down his pen and sat back in his chair. 'Where were you born and when, Mrs Bligh?'

'Keswick. Seventeen thirty-seven.'

'I see.'

'I don't hold as a rule with waking up what's been left resting a long while, my Lord. But should you ever wonder about the days of my youth, and what I remember of it, you may find me and ask me.'

Crowther felt his throat tighten. 'I would prefer you called me simply Mr Crowther. Or as we are acquaintances from childhood, you may call me Crowther.'

Jocasta did not reply and the cards began to slap down again. Some moments passed before she said, 'Sam has returned with the lad that saw my Kate done for.'

'Where are they now?'

Jocasta nodded upwards. 'Making friends with Lady Susan and her little uncle and that grey-eyed beauty, Miss Chase. That young girl's a smart one. You could throw her on a dung-hill or into a palace and she'd prosper. If they feed my boy macaroons he'll be sick on their carpet. He's not used to it.' Crowther was unsure if she meant the dog or Sam. 'It's a queer household this, Mr Crowther. I turn my cards here, I see blood and harmony all woven together. Strange rope to swing from.'

Crowther's pen made small scratching movements on the paper. 'As good as any. Did you make your arrangements?'

'I did. And Molloy continues with his own.'

Crowther looked across at her. 'I will be there?'

'Don't fash yersel'. You'll be there, and you'll be fetched when needed. I wouldn't walk the rookeries as a general habit, gentleman like you. But tonight you'll pass in and out again.'

'Thank you.'
Jocasta said nothing but continued at the cards.

The world was becoming simpler again. The strange aching fog that
had been battering at his mind, the whistling headaches . . . his
stumbling senses were beginning to clear. He opened his eyes a little.
The ship, his other darling, was there waiting for him, trim and
thirsting to be away. He saw old comrades on the deck; men he'd
thought drowned or shattered were there whole and urging him towards
them. And on the quarter-deck, with the baby in her arms and Stephen
at her side, was Harriet. She was wearing the green riding-habit she
had been dressed in the first time they met. It matched her eyes. And
she was laughing, trying to stop the wind driving her red curls across
her face and waving to him, telling him to hurry because all was ready
and the ship was straining for the off. The smell of the sea flooded
his nostrils, the wind stung his cheeks and he began to run down the
slope to the bay where the jolly-boat was waiting to take him onboard;
he could already hear the bosun's whistle, feel the shift of the timbers
on the deck as the wind caught her sails, feel his wife's hand cool and
loving in his own as they made their way out into open water.

She held on to his hands as if she could pull him back from the
flood, as if by fastening her fingers where his pulse now threaded
away to nothingness, she could hold him back from the wastes beyond.

'James?' she said in a whisper, as his breath emptied from him.
'James? No, please stay, James! Stay! Stay, my love!' He was gone.
She fell forward over his body and promised any God who might
listen her breath and bones, offered every sacrifice, every love, she
tried to offer them her life, her children, and taking him by the shoulders,
buried her mouth in his neck.

Her sister fell on her knees beside her and wrapped her arms around
Harriet's waist and called out to her through her own weeping.
Harriet drew her husband's lifeless arm across her shoulders and
swore to die herself, go with him rather than carry on a moment alone.

346

Taking Stephen by the hand, Clode led him out of the door and called for Trevelyan in a breaking voice. The boy at his side began to cry and the man lifted him in his arms and held him so hard he feared the little bones might break under his hands.

Night began its slow belly-slide up over the streets as if it were escaping the Thames. No man or woman with anything worth stealing on their person should be abroad at such a time, but tonight they might walk unharmed. The rookeries swung open and from the hovels of St Giles, the doss-houses of Clerkenwell, the dens and pits of Southwark, the lost people of London began to move. Men and boys set down their drinks and shrugged into whatever clothing they had, the whores let down their skirts and walked with their eyes clear. So many people on the street, and so serious. They moved out like a fog across the city, nodding each to each, putting aside their other business for an evening. Death sat on their shoulder, pinching their cheeks and pulling their hair every day with his long greasy fingers, but some things should not be done, and some action could be taken.

At the opera house Mr Harwood sat in his office, his hands clasped on the desk in front of him as he listened to Graves speak. The noise of the arriving hordes danced in through the windows, fought at the padding of his office door, kicked up with the laugh of some diamond-studded female. Winter Harwood, however, heard nothing but Owen's voice. After a few minutes he nodded, and Graves left the room. Harwood looked down at his hands and swallowed. He thought of the wreckage of his season and even while his mind was white with surprise, some part of him was already thinking of singers and composers who might be available, might be recalled to favour, might come scrabbling to him for another chance at glory in front of his silk-strangled crowd.

The carriage, over-decorated with footmen powdered and liveried, left from outside Carmichael's porch. Mr Palmer stepped out of the gardens of the Square and whistled. At once there were men at every entrance to the house. As Mr Palmer crossed the road he continued to whistle, forming his lips around the aria of Manzerotti. When he reached the door it was opened and flung wide by his men. Others forced the servants to the walls and held them there to allow Mr Palmer clear passage through; still with the song on his lips, he made his way to the study, the brilliants on his evening shoes dancing with Carmichael's candlelight. Finding the door locked, he turned and beckoned to one of his men. The man adjusted his cape – he carried a hammer in his arms like a child.

Johannes had managed to bind the leg as he lay in the muck of an overgrown ditch not far from Highgate. He had then set out as soon as he dared, knowing that the way between his hiding-place in the hedgerow and the security of his friends in Town was long. He leaned on a length of ash torn green from the tree and thought of his lost knife with a pang, as a man remembers the lover he has just deserted and wonders if the new fields are greener, after all. Then he shuffled forward again along the road.

Despite the fact that the benefit had only been announced the previous afternoon, and the tickets engraved and printed with a haste not compatible with fine workmanship, His Majesty's was brim full. Most of the women wore or carried a yellow rose, or a paper one, some of these so lush and elaborate in design they shamed nature. Lady Sybil had done something cunning with the family citrines, arranging them in her hair into the shape of the same flower. Many of the men wore red ribbons on their wrists. The applause when Manzerotti appeared on stage was immense. He stepped forward into the footlights and lifted his arms.

'My friends,' he said in that light and delicate voice, letting his eyes travel over the rows and boxes so it seemed to each person present he had called them by name, 'for whoever shares this night with me, is my friend.' He placed his hand over his breast, and the auditorium was filled with the breeze of a hundred feminine sighs. 'We are brought here together by tragedy and love. This concert tonight is for the memory of my beautiful colleague, the singer who has thrilled kings, courts and emperors with her voice, her talent, her artistry. *Miss Isabella Marin*.'

The theatre flooded with cheers. 'Bravo, Marin! Brava, Isabella!' At the back of the gallery a little woman in black felt the noise break over her. It seemed she could gather it all in her aching heart like a cup, and it being filled, offer it up to Isabella.

Manzerotti waited, head bowed, till the waves of sound had ebbed a little way, then nodded to the florid-looking leader of the orchestra who began to play, and into the honey-coloured air, he unleashed his voice and let it lift.

Outside the chophouse three men embraced and hit each other across their backs, drawing a belch from the fish-faced man and laughter from all. They turned to go their separate ways, but before any of them had lost sight of the others, three King's messengers, their shapes hidden by long dark capes and tricorn hats worn low over their eyes, had stepped free of the shadows. Each man felt a firm hand on his elbow, a murmur in his ear, a pressure pushing him towards the three separate carriages that were even now drawing out of the darkened side street. Two men turned to water and went like lambs. The third, a handsome blond man, began to wriggle and cry, protesting he knew not what through snot and misery. The man at his arm did not even trouble to pause. His grip was secure.

Johannes began to sense there was something wrong in the air as he hugged the shadows in Red Lyon Street. He stopped and lifted his chin. There was a sudden movement in the darkness behind him and a whistle. He heard it to his right, then its echo down the street in front of him. He stood still a moment and swung his gaze like a lighthouse beam around him. Nothing but dark windows. The streets were oddly quiet. A slight frown passed over his brow like the water stirred in a millpond. He hobbled forward his leg pulsing and aching.

Johannes was sure the wound was beginning to open again. Something curled and uncurled below his ribs. Again that whistle. It seemed to haunt him, guide him – but no one approached. He sensed eyes in the darkness. The hairs on the back of his neck prickled and stung, and he realised with a detached surprise that he was afraid. He had seen fear on the faces of others, but had had no experience of it himself till now. He remembered seeing fear on Manzerotti's face – but only once, when they were children and one of the young students in the musical academy who had not had the operation had struck Manzerotti down and called him a freak, an affront to God. Johannes had knocked the offender on his back and offered the little boy in front of him his hand. At that time Johannes had been the jewel in the school's crown; his voice was of a clarity declared miraculous, his artistry exceptional. Since coming from Germany he had been treated like a little God. Now a boy brushed past him in the dark street, a fleeing shadow. He put his hand to his pocket and cursed. His money taken. He hissed into the thick gloom where the boy had disappeared. There was a laugh. A soft female voice called from some dark corner: 'All fleeced, uncle?' He took a couple of painful steps towards it, but heard the light step of feet running from him. The laugh again. More distant. The whistle, closer and from the other side of the road.

Johannes had begged for the operation; gone down on his knees to his father, a woodturner in Leipzig, with the priest standing behind him. The priest had told them he was a gift from God, that his voice could serve the Church in all its beauty for ever. The boy had begged to give himself to his Saviour's glory. Reluctantly his father had agreed, and Johannes had thanked the Lord, though through his ecstasy he could still hear the softened clink of money being placed in his father's hand. He had left his home that day; travelled with the priest to the local court where a doctor from Italy happened to be staying and seeing to several boys. He heard the soft exchange of currency again and travelled to Bologna at the doctor's side, overjoyed that God was bringing him to His bosom. Manzerotti, by contrast, had *not* wished it. Had tried to run. Had failed. Had arrived at the school for a life of daily vocal and musical practice as a possible, a potential – his voice still all thin and empty. Then Johannes had helped him to his feet and looked into those black eyes for the first time.

'You speak strangely,' Manzerotti had said as he stood upright again.

'I was born in Germany,' Johannes replied in his clear bell-like voice. 'I have studied here two years. Every language I speak now, I speak with a foreigner's tongue.'

Molloy twisted the top of the table and moved away. The King's Messenger with him stepped forward and pulled out a neat roll of papers.

'There we have it then,' he said. Molloy nodded and began to feel about in the hidden drawers a little more, but the Messenger put a hand to his sleeve. 'Why don't we have the witch woman with us, or that boy?'

Molloy pulled his hat down over his ears and wrapped his cloak around him.

'Mrs Bligh has other business.' He found and picked up the brooch of flowers. The Messenger watched him with narrowed eyes, but Molloy put the brooch in his pocket anyhow. The man would make nothing of it, and he had been asked to fetch it. He heard a whistle on the street outside and was satisfied.

Johannes thought of the river. If he could get to the far shore, then

to the anonymity of Southwark, he could send to Manzerotti for help
from there. He limped towards the crowd of men at the Black Lyon
Stairs. The whistle came from behind him. The watermen turned
and looked at him a moment, then without speech to him or to one
another, each retired to his boat and cast off. Johannes lifted his
pocket-watch so it caught the light of the oil-lamp guttering greasily
by the steps to show he had money, but the skiffs and wherries drew
away. Johannes swallowed and put the watch back in his pocket. Fear
flowered into a sweat on his brow. He turned up the hill again,
making for the rookeries of Chandos Street, where he had tracked
one of the witch's spies. There a man could hide. The significance
of the watermen pulling away from him so silent and of one mind,
he would not think of.

Mr Palmer stood in the centre of Carmichael's study, a still moment
in the activity of the room, and looked through the papers that had
been found behind the Latin texts and in the false front of the
fireplace. There was a considerable amount of money in banknotes
and gold, and a letter in French confirming 'the recommendation of
the man that carries it, who can be recognised in the usual way'.
Fitzraven, Palmer supposed. There were four charts showing details
of Portsmouth and Spithead and the arrangement of vessels within
them, and a model of a gun he had himself given into the hands of
his secretary to be placed in one of the vaults. There was also a dense
page of notes full of fresh gossip from the Admiralty and the competing
political factions within it. He paused in his reading to push the little
model to and fro across Lord Carmichael's desk.

'Field?' he said.

One of the men shaking out the neat volumes in the rear bookcase
paused in his work and turned round.

'Yes, sir?'

'Go and tell Lord Sandwich we are ready for him.'

Johannes did not know at what moment he realised his voice was leaving him. During a practice, a strange hum had begun at the back of his throat. When he spoke, the edges of his words started sounding a little shrill. He thought he was merely tired, as he had sung for the school several times in the evenings, and still had to be awake at dawn for the morning service. It was about a week after he had helped Manzerotti to his feet. He saved the little Italian boy and suddenly the boy's voice was beginning to flower and grow. A few days later, Johannes had opened his lips to sail across the surface of Scarlatti's *Stabat Mater* like a swan on water, and as the first phrase lifted into the second, the ice of his voice had cracked and a strange yelping croak leaped from his mouth like a toad. He had stopped. Horrified. The boys next to him began to look afraid. He gazed across to the singers on the opposite side of the choir, terrified, and had met Manzerotti's black eyes. They were calm, loving; he gave Johannes the faintest ghost of a smile, then turned his attention back towards the priest.

Johannes bowed his head and submitted; his great grief seemed to rise from the centre of the earth, poured up his body through his throat and out into the world. It was a wave of silence, taking whatever was left of his voice with it. He never opened his lips to sing again.

Mrs Service rapped lightly at the door and went in.

'Mrs Bligh, a young man called Ripley just called. He said you and Crowther should attend at the place thought of. Do I have the message right?'

Jocasta swept up her cards and pocketed them. Crowther shrugged on his frock-coat and smoothed the sleeves.

'Aye, Mrs Service. You have it right.'

When the audience heard the introduction to the 'Yellow Rose Duet' they called and wept afresh. The leader of the band stood and put his violin to his chin, and as Manzerotti gracefully stepped aside and offered him up to the audience, he began to play Isabella's part. From the back of the stalls Mr Harwood observed his theatre. It was a world of light; the oil-lamps blazed above him and cast down across the gilt mouldings on the boxes, across the jewels and dresses of the women and threw their shimmerings to and fro like fireworks, blest by the colours around them.

It was a woman in one of the boxes closest to the stage who began it. With trembling fingers she undid the yellow rose from her bodice and threw it down onto the stage at Manzerotti's feet. Then, from the box opposite, another woman in red silk did the same. Soon the theatre was alive with the rustle of foliage and paper, and the roses began to flow forward. Those who could not reach the stage dropped their flowers into the stalls, and they were passed forward and overhead till those nearest the footlights could gather them in armfuls and, passing them over the heads of the musicians in the pit, lay them with the other tribute.

Manzerotti began to sing his line, stepping forward so the petals made a carpet for the jewelled heels of his shoes to rest on. That clarion call of his voice . . . it seemed to Harwood that the song of duty and loyalty was not simply the voice of a single man, but the spirit of all he loved about the opera sculpted into sound. He knew he was an illusionist and a businessman, knew better than any the petty betrayals and rivalries, the viciousness of ambition and ambition thwarted that lay behind the music and the golden stage; knew too his house was full because his audience came to see where blood had been shed, and try and imagine they could see the stains, but for a moment he let his spirit rest on the glories of Manzerotti's voice and forgot that anything else had ever existed in time but music and light.

Lord Sandwich watched Carmichael across the auditorium. He was observing the stage with such profound satisfaction one could believe Manzerotti was his man, not his master. Lord Sandwich was not a man easily shocked, but the story Mr Palmer had laid out for him that morning in his office at the Admiralty had shaken him. Worst was the note he had received telling him that Carmichael's stepson Longley had been killed attempting to flee the King's Messenger sent to stop him at Harwich. He had panicked and been trampled to death by a startled horse on the main thoroughfare of that town. They had hoped to turn him. Give him a chance to redeem himself in their service, but on being approached, the child had only thought of the executioner's noose and knife, and was dead before Palmer's letter could be put into his hand.

And there sat Carmichael in his box as assured and comfortable as a cat on silk. Sandwich crushed the note in his hand received from Mr Palmer's man. It was a singular pleasure to be about this business himself. The First Lord then bent over the delicate white palm of the lady with whom he was seated and with a smile left her to flirt with her fan alone for a little while. He closed the door to the box behind him and began to walk the corridor round to the other side of the auditorium, nodding to a man waiting there as he went.

Johannes was becoming dizzy from the pain in his leg. A black-skinned boy appeared from the shadows behind him. Johannes looked about him. The braziers were lit, but the filth-floored roadway was deserted. There had been people here before.

The boy, when he spoke, did so with the soft-water French accent of a Creole. 'All alone, Tonton? Do you need a place? I'll show you somewhere warm.' Johannes gritted his teeth and nodded. The boy took him by the hand and began to lead him forward through the leaping shadows, the flames thrown up on either side. The whistle again. Another laugh.

The door to Carmichael's box opened, and he twisted round in his chair. Seeing the First Lord of the Admiralty enter he started to stand, but Sandwich placed one hand on his shoulder.

'No, no, Carmichael. Do not get up.' He took a seat next to him and whispered to Carmichael's heavily rouged companion, 'My dear, I have confidential business with this man. Would you be so kind?' She gave him a bold look, then smiled and cocked her head so the jewels about her handsome throat glimmered. She made her way out into the corridor. Sandwich watched her go with an appreciative eye.

'Carmichael, I congratulate you. I had no idea you could afford a whore that fine.' Then Sandwich leaned into him, murmuring, 'Tell me, does she fuck your friends for titbits useful to the French, or is she pure recreation?'

Carmichael's arm spasmed and he tried to stand but Sandwich had him firmly pressed to his chair. He continued in his pleasant whisper.

'No, no, my dear. Do not attempt to leave. Do you not wish to answer? No matter, we shall ask her ourselves.' Again Carmichael made an effort to stand, again he was forced down. 'Really, Carmichael, be still. There is a gentleman outside the door to whom I have paid a large sum of money for his assurance that he will shoot you if you try to leave. And I think Harwood has had enough blood spilled in his theatre in the past few days. Shortly we shall return to your house to discuss matters more fully, but for now, stay still. Enjoy the end of the aria. It will be the last music you ever hear, you know. He sings prettily, does he not?'

'Yes.'

'How it must have burned, to have him sent here to take control of your activities. A half-man like that, a performer. Yet he would never have tried to use your stepson to carry messages. I am sure that was your plan, and not approved. Longley was too young, too honourable; even given his debt to you and fear of you, he was bound to be too open in his ways. Manzerotti did far better with the woman who sells coffee and oranges here, and that runt Fitzraven. Did you even notice that Longley told Mrs Westerman he was going to Harwich?

You were too busy flaunting your power. Your wish to see others dance to your tune has made you a bad spy, Carmichael, and the boy is dead with some of your papers still on him. All that chatter about corruption in the Admiralty, and who in London supports the rebel cause. You did well there, I admit.'

He watched Lord Carmichael's face for any reaction. The man did not move, but he looked as if some light had disappeared from under his skin.

'What will happen to my collection, Sandwich?' he said finally as on stage Manzerotti extended his arms to the painted skies.

'We could arrange for it to be donated to the British Museum. Anonymously, of course. In a month, Lord Carmichael, it will be as if you never existed at all.'

'This way, Tonton,' the boy said, and led him up the last few steps to the attic. 'You shall be taken care of here.'

Johannes could barely see, but if it was the pain or the gloom of the place, he could not tell. He guided himself up the stairs leaning his palm on the plaster walls. The love he had given to Manzerotti was the greatest glory of his life. His own talents with the trickeries and artistry of the scene room were insignificant to him, their only merit being that they allowed him to travel at Manzerotti's side and do his bidding. Manzerotti traded government to government across Europe, charmed them into thinking him their own creature, but never loyal to anything other than his music and himself.

There had been a hard time in Paris three years ago, when Johannes had found himself cornered and alone. He had managed to get a message to Manzerotti, but no help had come. Three days later, having freed himself and left a cellar gory by his escape, he had made his way to Manzerotti's rooms and fallen at his feet, asking to know why he had been forsaken. Manzerotti had paused in his practice only long enough to look at him, but had made no response and recommended his work. After an hour Johannes had crawled away and presented himself at the proper time the following day. Manzerotti had greeted him as usual and the matter was never spoken of again. His belief was that he had been tested and succeeded.

Johannes thought of the moment when he had looked up at the Christ hanging above him in the church, sad and sorry. He had realised that he had been punished for his pride, that his role in loving God was not to sing His praises but to serve His true instrument – the boy with the black eyes. The sense of complete submission filled his heart and seemed to burst it open. His love poured from the cracked vessel of his soul in a flood. It was joy, freedom, a certainty that had never left him again.

The Creole boy pushed the door open in front of him. Johannes saw a shadowy attic; at a stove in its centre an obscenely fat women was staring at something in a pan. Johannes's fear suddenly screamed through him as she turned his way. He spun round to flee but found his passage blocked. Two boys and two men had followed them silently up the stairs. One raised a rough wooden truncheon and brought it down behind his ear. He fell to the ground.

The bravos were hysterical. As Sandwich helped Carmichael to his feet, feeling the man trembling under his coat, he looked down onto the stage. Manzerotti was bowing deeply, but lifted his head and looked directly into Sandwich's eyes. The Earl did not acknowledge the look but pushed Carmichael angrily out of the box and through the empty corridor and lobby while the ecstatic yells of the crowd still echoed behind them. He paused by the man outside.

'The woman?'

'We have Mrs Mitchell, my Lord.'

'And Manzerotti?'

'It is all arranged as you requested, sir.'

'Good. I am taking Lord Carmichael home.'

Johannes awoke to find himself bound to a greasy chair. The room was full of people. He hissed at them, and one or two of the ragged boys stepped back. He picked out the witch woman and the last of her little rats. By her side stood a tall man, dressed like a gentleman. He recognised him as the one who had caught hold of his leg the previous night. He was pleased to see an ugly bruise gilding his throat.

'*Let me go.*' The voice was between a hiss and a croak. '*Let me go, and I will not hunt each and every one of you down. You do not know with what you meddle, you filth.*'

Crowther stepped forward and slapped the man across his face with enough force to swing his head round.

'Oh yes, we do, Johannes. Carmichael, Mitchell, his friends, Manzerotti – all are taken.'

Johannes laughed and shook his head. '*You will never touch my master. He is beyond you.*' His eyes were bright, exultant.

Crowther said calmly, 'If he escapes tonight, he will be taken tomorrow. He has nowhere to hide.'

Johannes's eye was beginning to swell. '*He does not need to hide!*'

Crowther hit him again, and drew a gasp. The fat woman nodded her head in approval.

'Where are the two boys buried, Johannes?'

Johannes tasted the blood in his mouth. '*In the tenter grounds where they stretch cloth off Holborn, unless the rats have eaten them already.*'

Crowther struck him again. Then began to pull on his gloves. A voice or two in the crowd murmured; they began to creep forward. A woman in rags spat at the seated figure. Her yellow bile crawled down his face. A man balled his fists. Johannes looked around.

'*You leave me here?*'

Crowther felt the comfortable stretch of leather over his knuckles. 'Yes, I do.' He turned to the fat woman. 'You know where to take the body. Make sure it is before dawn.' She nodded and Crowther looked towards the prisoner again.

'Why, Johannes? You have renown, money of your own. Why do you serve as Manzerotti's knife-man?'

A look of bliss crossed Johannes's bloody and bruised face. He looked up at the ceiling as if transfixed by some vision of ecstasy, some untouchable joy.

'*I had to serve him. He is my voice.*'

Crowther did not look round again, though he sensed Jocasta and Sam following him down the stairs. As they paused on the road, from the top of the house they heard the sound of blows, and a muffled sobbing scream.

They hastened in silence to the outer limits of the rookery, where the carriage of the Earl of Sussex stood waiting for them. Jocasta sniffed, recognising The Chariot again, and nodded to herself, seeing the right and the pattern of it.

'We'll walk from here, Mr Crowther. My sorrows and blessings to Mrs Westerman.'

The footman leaped down from his perch and opened the door. Crowther began to climb into the carriage, then stopped and turned towards her.

'I shall come and ask you of your childhood memories, Mrs Bligh, when this is done and the grieving passed. I thank you for offering them to me.'

'They'll do you as much hurt as good. But such is the way of the world.' She let her hand rest on Sam's shoulder and Crowther took his seat. The footman closed the door on him and fitted the latch. 'You know where to find me, Mr Crowther. Me and Sam.'

He tipped his hat to her and struck his cane on the roof. The coachman stirred his horses into movement and the carriage rattled off into the deserted streets.

'What's that, Mrs Bligh?' Sam asked.

'Old wounds that still bleed, lad. But that is for another time. Let us to our own sleepings now.'

Lord Sandwich and Mr Palmer put the matter very clearly to their reluctant host. Once Carmichael had understood, he was frank with them and explained every part of the business quite thoroughly. He had indeed communicated with the French from time to time and been rewarded for it. At first it was simply for the pleasure of seeing great and influential men listen to him with care and praise, then the habits of subterfuge had become part of him, and he thirsted for the risk of it. He had met Manzerotti in the distant past, but knew of him only as a talented singer until Fitzraven had arrived and presented himself with the letter from Paris and instructions to take Manzerotti into his home and confidence. Fitzraven had been all but drooling when he told Carmichael that Manzerotti had suggested the construction of some hiding-places in his home. He had resented the intrusion, but realising he had little choice, acquiesced.

From the moment Manzerotti arrived, Carmichael was forced to admit he was a master spy and recognise that he himself had only been a dilettante till now. Manzerotti had seen something in the hard features of the woman who ran the coffee-room in His Majesty's and found out her son was an Admiralty clerk. He had then made Johannes his go-between, and soon Carmichael's hiding-places were overflowing with material for France. His public snubbing of Fitzraven went hand-in-hand with private confidence. He had encouraged the man to try and whore his own daughter for information, and sympathised with his annoyance over their estrangement and her partiality for Bywater. When he found Fitzraven dead he had emptied the room of anything he thought incriminating and summoned Johannes.

Manzerotti's reasons for ordering the murders of Bywater and then Marin were much as Crowther and Harriet had speculated. He saw the chance to put an end to their investigations before Bywater confessed and the question of how the body ended up in the river grew pressing, then when he heard of Miss Marin's note he saw the chance to neaten matters still further. Carmichael told them that he only heard of Harriet's connection to the *Marquis de La Fayette* at his party, from Sandwich's own mouth. He was aware of who had been on the ship, but not the name of the Captain who had taken the prize, and when he heard Harriet speak shortly afterwards of her husband's returning memory and his talk of spies, he had decided to take action.

Carmichael's words were written out for him by a trembling clerk, and his signature was made and witnessed while Palmer wondered if it was possible to conceal this last from Harriet. The clerk then left the room and a few moments later so did Sandwich and Mr Palmer. The latter turned the key in the lock and they made their way down the stairs in silence, pausing only briefly when the report of a pistol shot rang out from behind the closed door.

'I know you would wish a trial, Palmer. You are young enough to look for justice. But it is better so,' Sandwich said.

'My Lord,' was all Palmer had by way of answer.


Crowther spoke briefly to Graves in the hallway when he returned to Trevelyan's house, and to Rachel and Clode in the parlour where they rocked Baby Anne in the firelight, before letting himself quietly into the room where Harriet sat vigil by the body of her husband. She looked up as he entered. She held her sleeping son on her lap. Her face was calm, tearstained, still. He came into the centre of the room and placed his cane on the ground before him, resting his weight on it with sudden realisation of his own exhaustion.

'It is done, Harriet.'

'He is dead?'

'Yes. They beat him to death, and the surgeons will have use of his body. Manzerotti, I am grieved to tell you, escaped.'

She stroked the head of her sleeping child and kissed his white brow. 'I know. Graves has told me.' Crowther watched her for a second longer then with a sigh turned back towards the door. His fingers were on the handle, still wrapped in black leather, when he heard her speak again.

'Thank you, Gabriel.'

He turned and bowed deeply to her, then left the room.

# Epilogue

*14 December 1781*

JOCASTA HAD SEEN hangings enough in her twenty years in London, so felt no need to go and watch Mrs Mitchell swing for her daughter-in-law's death. It was on that day though that she went to St Anne's burying ground with the brooch Molloy had found, leading Sam by the hand. He was looking better for some weeks' feeding, and a lot cleaner than when they had first met. At the grave, he stood back a way with Boyo in his arms. The ground was hard and Jocasta had a job to scrape into the dirt more than a few inches. Still, the brooch was small and there was space enough for it before many minutes had passed. She laid it down very carefully, brushed the dirt back over it, then stood up, her knees complaining.

Sam stepped up next to her. 'I thought you'd be saying something to her, Mrs Bligh.'

Jocasta ruffled his hair.

Mr Palmer came to meet Mrs Westerman in Adams Music Shop as arranged. She smiled when she saw him and beckoned him into the private parlour away from the business of music, into the quiet, and took a seat at the worn table there. Mourning became her, and the fierce grief of the first days after her husband's murder seemed to have mellowed into a relative calm.

'You return to Sussex tomorrow, Mrs Westerman?' Mr Palmer said when the door to the main body of the shop was closed.

'I do. Now the trials are done with, there is nothing to hold me here and I find I miss the country air.'

'I am very sorry.'

'Lord Sandwich had the decency to come and tell me himself why Manzerotti was allowed to leave the country.'

'Yes, it appears he transmitted vital information to us in 'seventy-five. It would have been too great an embarrassment for the government to have him come to trial.' Mr Palmer shifted in his seat.

'He wrote to me, you know,' she said.

'Good God! The man is a devil.'

'Yes, I rather think he is. He sent me his condolences and said he understood my grief, having lost a dear companion himself, and was sorry circumstances prevented him from offering his sympathies in person.'

'By "dear companion" I assume he means Johannes.'

'Indeed. Clode and Graves had to be physically restrained from making for the coast at once with their knives between their teeth. All the women in the household had to cry their eyes out at them before they would relent.'

'That does not surprise me, Mrs Westerman.'

Harriet sighed and looked out of the window at the back of the parlour. Mr Crumley could just be made out in the workshop beyond, bent over his punches hammering music onto metal sheets as if it could be trapped there, pinned down, made absolute.

'Mr Crowther returned to the country yesterday,' she said. 'I believe he did so to answer all the curiosity of my household and neighbours before I face them myself. For such an impossible man he can be sensitive at times.' She turned to look at him. 'Did you attend the executions of those three men, Mr Palmer?'

'I did. They did not die well. The crowd will cheer a thief, but show them a traitor and their mood is darker.' He paused. 'Yet, I feel some guilt at their deaths and their manner of dying. Manzerotti we all but escorted from the country, it appears, and we allowed Carmichael to shoot himself in the comfort of his own home.'

'They were not important enough to deserve such niceties.'

'I fear that is so.'

She waited a moment, then said, 'The young gentleman is outside?'

'Yes, Mrs Westerman. He waits in the street. Though you do not need to see him.'

'I wish it.'

Palmer stood and returned a few moments later with a young boy dressed in the uniform of a Midshipman. Harriet smiled at him. He was as pale as Stephen was dark, and looked far too slight a being to be cast about on the open oceans. 'You are Mr Meredith?' she asked.

The boy nodded. 'Mrs Westerman, I felt I couldn't go back to the ship without seeing you, if you were willing.'

'Say what you need to say, Mr Meredith,' said Palmer. 'This interview is not easy for Mrs Westerman.'

The boy dropped to one knee in front of her, as if before a queen, and lowered his head. 'Ma'am, it was the day after the engagement with *Le Marquis de La Fayette*, and the rigging was half shot away. So we were making the repairs, and I was up top of the mizzen mast helping to sort out which blocks were sound still.'

Harriet felt her heart contracting in her chest.

The boy continued. 'I had one in my hand and was just saying to Picard I thought it cracked, and leaned over to show him the spot . . . and it slipped from my hand.' He began to cry; the words came out wet and broken. 'It just slipped . . . The rope it was hung on had been torn up worse than I'd realised, and it ripped through like a cotton. I couldn't even understand it, and Picard shouted, "Look out below!" and the Captain was there on the quarter-deck and he looked up as the shout came and we saw it strike him.' His voice shuddered. Harriet reached forward and put her hand on his bent head. 'And he went down, ma'am. So heavy and quick, and by the time I got on to the deck they were lifting him and carrying him away and they shoved me back. Oh God, I am so sorry, ma'am! I am so sorry. He was the best Captain in the Service and he had been so kind to me and helped me and the other young gentlemen. I'd have died rather than do him harm.' He hung his head low. 'It just slipped.'

Harriet put her arms around the boy's shaking shoulders and drew him towards her. Her own tears were falling now, and they dropped from her face onto the boy's yellow hair. She held his head against her knees and bent over him, then spoke into his ear with her throat tight and raw.

'He mentioned you, Meredith.' The boy squirmed. 'Listen to me now, my boy. He mentioned you in a letter to me. He said he was proud with the progress you had made under his command.' She leaned back, lifted his face and looked into his eyes. 'He said he thought you'd make a fine Captain yourself one day.' Meredith bit his lip and met her gaze. Harriet sighed. 'That is what you must do now, Meredith, for my husband and for me. Be the best officer you can be. Care for your men and your ship and be faithful to them, and I will be proud of you, and I'll know James would be proud of you too.'

The boy got unsteadily to his feet. 'Thank you, madam.'

She took a great breath and wiped her eyes. Then stood and, opening the door, stepped forward into the shop, leading Mr Meredith with her.

'Stephen! Come here!'

Her son looked up from where he was throwing jacks in the corner with Lord Thornleigh and came obediently to her side. 'Stephen, I want you to meet Mr Meredith. He was one of your father's young gentlemen on the *Splendour*.'

Stephen put out his hand and shook Mr Meredith's with great vigour. 'French spies killed my father.'

'I know, Stephen. I was very sorry to hear it,' Meredith replied.

Stephen looked up at him, narrowed his eyes and said cautiously, 'When I am older I shall be a sailor too, like you. May I come and sail on your ship?'

Meredith glanced up at Harriet and saw her nod her head.

'You may, and I shall take very good care of you, young Westerman. I promise you.'

Mr Palmer appeared from the doorway, exchanged bows with the company then left, guiding Meredith before him.

Mrs Westerman retreated into the parlour and did not emerge for some time.

Morgan neatened a stack of songbooks on the counter. 'I shall miss her when she goes, that Mrs Westerman. As fine a lady as ever I've met.'

Graves looked up from his figures. 'What, ready to desert me already, Morgan? Do you wish to go and buy a place in the country and live like a lady?'

'Humph. Not likely. I'll be your manager here, and then I can visit Issy's grave whenever I take a notion to do so. And Mr Leacroft too from time to time, when Lady Susan wants company.'

'Thank you.'

'I should think so too. You'll waste away all Miss Chase's wedding portion, the deals you and Crumley have been making on paper. Then all your children will go hungry.'

Stephen laughed, and they looked up to see Lady Thornleigh making faces for him, and her brother giggling. Graves swallowed and Morgan put her hand on his sleeve.

'It goes on, Mr Graves; whether we will it or no, life tumbles forward.'

# Historical Note

Cornwallis had already surrendered at Yorktown on 19 October 1781 before the main narrative of *Anatomy of Murder* opens, but the news did not reach London until 25 November. It marked the end of the campaign on land during the American War of Independence, though the combat at sea continued. The Treaty of Paris was signed on 3 September 1783 and the last British troops left New York that same November.

John Montagu, Fourth Earl of Sandwich (1718-92), was First Lord of the Admiralty three times, lastly as part of Lord North's government between 1771 and 1783. His wife's deteriorating mental health led to the couple separating. She was declared *De Lunatico Inquirendo* in May 1767. Sandwich's much-loved mistress, opera singer Martha Ray, was shot in the foyer of the Royal Opera House, Covent Garden in 1779 by a rival for her affections. Lord Sandwich was a great and influential lover of music. The quality of his stewardship of the Admiralty, however, is still under debate.

For an account of insanity and its treatment in the period, I recommend *Madmen: A Social History of Madhouses, Mad Doctors and Lunatics (Revealing History)* by Roy Porter.

Mozart visited London as part of his tour of Europe with his sister and brother in 1764 and 1765, and received lessons from J.C. Bach. His *Piano Sonata No. 8* in A minor K310, which is the piece Susan

371

and Leacroft play together, was composed in Paris in 1778 while he was campaigning for employment and patronage.

The fictional opera house, His Majesty's Theatre, is based on the King's Theatre London of this period. For details of how an opera house was managed, from the music to the performers to the refreshments, I owe a great debt to *Italian Opera in Late Eighteenth-Century London* Volume 1, *The King's Theatre Haymarket 1778-1791* by Curtis Price, Judith Milhous and Robert D. Hume.

The castrato who took the *primo umo* roles in the 1781-2 season at the King's Theatre was the mezzo-soprano Gaspare Pacchierotti (1740-1821). He was renowned as a great singer and also loved for his modesty and excellent manners.

For an account of the lives and training of the castrati, I would recommend Patrick Barbier, translated by Margaret Crosland: *The World of the Castrati: The History of an Extraordinary Operatic Phenomenon.*

The 1781-2 season *was* marked by a plagiarism scandal involving the castrato and composer Venanzio Rauzzini (1747-1810), and one of the house composers Antonio Sacchini (1730-86). This was a case of disputed authorship between former collaborators, however, not comparable to the outright theft of Leacroft's music by Bywater.

The arias mentioned, and the opera *Julius Rex* are, to the best of my knowledge, fictions of the author.

On 20 June 1781 the *Public Advertiser* reported that the *Endymion* had captured a French ship called the *Marquis de La Fayette* on the banks of Newfoundland 'loaded for congress with arms, clothing and bale good's bound to Philidelphia', and valued her at 'not less than 300,000 l'. The *Endymion* was under the command of Captain Philip Carteret. In a letter to Carteret's wife in Southampton dated 19 June 1781 from his friend Noah Lebras, the date of the engagement is given as 3 May. The *Endymion* lost five men, and four wounded.

All further details are invented.

*London Life in the Eighteenth Century* by M. Dorothy George gives an excellent account of the capital at the time.

For a layman's guide to the effects of brain injury on both the patient and their families, please see *Head Injury: A Practical Guide* by Trevor Powell, published by Headway, the brain injury association. *www.headway.org.uk*

All errors and anachronisms are my own.